Entwined

Entwined

Lynda La Plante

WILLIAM MORROW AND COMPANY, INC.   NEW YORK

Library of Congress Cataloging-in-Publication Data
La Plante, Lynda.
    Entwined / Lynda La Plante.
        p.   cm.
    ISBN 0-688-09243-8
    I. Title.
PR6062.A65E57   1993
823'.914—dc20   92-7961
                            CIP

Printed in the United States of America

First Edition

1 2 3 4 5 6 7 8 9 10

BOOK DESIGN BY CLAIRE VACCARO

I dedicate this book to Jeanne F. Bernkopf.
Not just my editor, but my wise, my trusted
and beloved mentor.

ACKNOWLEDGMENTS

Thank you to all the people who gave me so much of their time, especially to those who opened their past and painful memories with such heartfelt frankness and honesty.

I also wish to thank Rose Marie Morse.

Three hundred and fifty thousand
to four hundred thousand children
were admitted to Birkenau and Auschwitz
and only eight hundred survived.

1

HILDA DEIKMANN moved silently across the sitting room of the suite and paused to check her appearance in one of the floor-to-ceiling gilt mirrors. Her dress had seen better times—but then so had the hotel. It had not been restored yet to its original splendor, but already it reflected the changing times. East Berlin was now free; the wall had come down.

Standing by the sashed windows, she could see the porters in their new red and gold uniforms, way below in the street. From her post Hilda watched the Mercedes limousine glide to the entrance, and a tall man in a fur-collared coat step from the front passenger seat. He gestured to the porters to remove the luggage from the trunk as a car drew up behind them. A blond woman in a bright red coat was helped out of the backseat. She turned to speak to the tall gentleman as another woman, wearing a dark coat and hat, hurried from the second car. The threesome conferred before bending to the remaining passenger seated in the rear of the Mercedes.

Before Hilda could see who was about to come out of the car, the doors to her suite opened.

A set of matching leather cases and trunks was wheeled in on a porter's cart. Hilda directed the luggage toward the master bedroom, then turned to deal with the second cartful. The room was suddenly alive with movement as the porters removed the cases and placed them on racks. Champagne was brought by a waiter; he was followed by another carrying a crystal scalloped dish arranged with caviar, finely chopped onions and egg whites.

From the corridor Hilda could hear voices speaking in French. The manager's stilted, heavy-accented reply was in English.

"You will be assured of the utmost privacy . . . please, this way."

Baron Louis Maréchal, his coat now loosely on his shoulders, entered the suite. He was a handsome man, gray-white wings at the side of his temples, his thick hair combed back from a high forehead. He wore a gray pinstriped suit, and an oyster-gray tie. A signet ring on his left hand gleamed as he gestured.

The baron turned around as the woman in the red coat, carrying a square leather jewelry box, appeared at the doorway, where she was soon joined by a rather plain, drab young woman. The young woman also carried a square leather vanity case. She looked back to the corridor.

"Madame . . . please."

Baroness Maréchal appeared in the door; everyone fell silent waiting for her approval. She was very tall, exceptionally thin; a black mink cape seemed to weigh her down. She wore dark glasses that hid most of her face. Her black hair was short, almost boyish. She gave the impression of fragility, as if at any moment she would faint, or fall, or float. She moved as lightly as a dancer as she walked into the suite.

Suddenly, she was everywhere—touching and admiring, running to the bedroom suite, throwing wide the doors. As if by magic she brought the sun into the room.

The manager quickly introduced Hilda to the baroness, who laughed gaily as she repeated: "Lady's maid, lady's maid! My lady's maid . . . how divine! I love this hotel— Close your eyes, Louis, we have traveled back in time!"

Hilda saw the exchange of glances between the baroness's own maid and the woman in the red coat. Suddenly the room, as if by unspoken command from the baron, had emptied. The baroness didn't seem to notice.

Hilda asked the baron if she should unpack.

"Yes, immediately." The baron responded in German. He introduced Hilda to Anne Marie, the maid, and to Dr. Helen Masters, a family friend who was to use the adjoining suite.

Hilda was startled as the baroness cupped her chin in her hands. The tall lady looked down into Hilda's face.

"Do you speak English? You do? Good. I don't speak German, I apologize."

The baroness jumped as the baron wrapped the mink around her shoulders. He then gripped her elbow, whispered something in her ear, than guided her out of the suite. Anne Marie followed them out.

Hilda opened the first of the baroness's standing trunks.

One trunk contained delicate silk lingerie. Not one item appeared to have been worn; even the shoes looked new. Each pair had a small handwritten note tucked inside, indicating which handbag and scarf would complete the outfit.

The large leather vanity case which the young woman had carried was placed at the side of the bed. Hilda carried it into Anne Marie's room, and could not resist peeking inside. It was not filled with jewels, as she had expected, but with countless bottles of pills.

Just then the door flew open, and the baroness burst in.

"Hilda!" The baroness looked momentarily startled. "I can't remember if I carried my jewel box in with me. It's a square dark blue leather box."

Hilda followed the baroness back to her room; she did not recall seeing it. The baroness rushed to the dressing table. The vanity case, smaller than the one Hilda had placed in Anne Marie's room, was stashed on a shelf beneath the mirrored top. She hugged it tightly. Hilda watched her take out small silver-framed photographs and arrange them on the bedside table.

"My children, my two daughters, Sasha, Sophia, and my sons . . ."

Hilda studied the photographs of the smiling children.

The baroness began to rifle through the unpacked clothes, throwing them on the floor.

"My makeup box, where is my makeup box?"

Anne Marie walked in.

"The photographs . . . you've unpacked the box, Baroness!" she said.

The baroness retorted that she had found her children, now she could not find the other case. She was on her hands and knees, looking under the bed, when the baron walked into the room carrying yet another square case.

"Darling, do you want your jewels put into the hotel safe?"

"*No!* I want them with me!"

She held tightly to the jewelry box. He shrugged.

"All right, all right, but take care of them!" He then turned to Hilda, impatiently.

"Run her bath—the baroness needs to rest!"

◆ ◆ ◆

The bathwater was laced with oils and perfumes. Hilda tested the temperature, and then warmed the towels on the heated rails. The baroness, wrapped in a white terrycloth robe and still wearing her glasses, sang at the top of her voice as she dropped her robe. Skeleton-thin, white-skinned, she had the body of a young girl. She handed Hilda her dark glasses, and then sprang into the bath.

"Hilda, will you order some hot chocolate, and biscuits?"

The baroness was not as young as Hilda had first thought. There were telltale signs under her chin: The skin was a little loose, she had fine lines around her eyes and mouth.

She immersed herself in the soapy water, blowing at the soap bubbles, then lay back and let the water cover her face, her dark hair fanning out behind her.

Hilda stood transfixed as she watched the baroness's hands break the surface of the water like a ballet dancer's. Her back arched and the nipples of her small breasts lifted. Finally her face emerged, cheeks puffed out. Like a child she spurted a stream of water from her mouth.

Hilda laughed nervously, and left the bathroom.

◆ ◆ ◆

Hilda saw the baroness emerge from the tub, go to the closet, then to the dressing table. She did not look at herself in the mirror. Quickening her pace, the baroness arched her back, her hands in front of her as if pushing something away. She caught Hilda's reflection in the mirror, and saw that she was being watched. She bared her teeth and her body arched again, like a cat's. Hilda was agape.

The moment was broken as the baron entered. He took one look at his wife, ordered Hilda from the room, and called out for Anne Marie, while gripping his wife's wrists.

Anne Marie walked into the bedroom with the case of pills and slammed the door behind her. Hilda heard screams of terror mixed with a stream of abuse in French and English. Then silence.

When the baron left the bedroom, he found Hilda still waiting "My wife is very sick. She is in Berlin for treatment. I would be grateful were you not to repeat what you saw tonight."

Hilda nodded. "I will be here in the morning," she murmured.

"That won't be necessary, Anne Marie will take care of my wife's needs."

✦   ✦   ✦

Helen Masters hurried into the suite and found him looking at the teeth marks on his hand.

He shook his head. "I've seen this coming all day. She gets excited, and then explodes with this terrible rage."

"I know, Louis."

"It's as if she hated me, hated the children. She attacked Sasha. I think she will kill someone!"

Helen stood by the mantel, running her fingers along the cold marble. She felt uneasy, she had never spent time alone with the baron before, except for brief meetings when he came to collect Vebekka from her office. It was she who had suggested that they consult Dr. Franks, her mentor and former teacher in Berlin, because Vebekka was clearly beyond her help. She had offered to travel with them, taking a two-week holiday to do so, never suspecting how deeply involved she would become.

"I have not seen her this bad; all the more reason to consult Dr. Franks."

She looked at the baron; his face was taut with anger. She chose her words carefully.

"Dr. Franks will ask you many questions. He'll need to probe into the background of her illness; this includes your own history and your marriage."

Louis sprang to his feet. "Illness! Every doctor she has been to insists on calling her madness 'illness'! Well? What do you think, now that you've seen her in one of her rages?"

Helen coughed. "She is obviously very distressed tonight."

"Distressed? You tell me she has been like this with you?" he snapped.

"No, but I expected the journey to upset her, and her behavior is not surprising. Now, if you'll excuse me, I think I'll turn in."

"I'm sorry, you must be tired, forgive me. Good night, Doctor."

As she left, he noticed that she had very shapely legs.

◆　◆　◆

Vebekka didn't know whether it was day or night but she knew it had happened again. She couldn't recall what she had done, what she had said or who she had hurt this time. How many strange rooms had she been brought to over the years? She stared at the ornate chandelier above the bed, and hoped it would fall and crush her. Why had she agreed to come to this place, why had she insisted they stay in East Berlin? *Had* she insisted? She could not remember. She could not even remember why Louis had brought her here.

The tranquilizers made her thirsty; she slipped out of bed and stood by the partly open door. Louis was sleeping in the bedroom suite, one arm crooked over his face, the other spread across the empty space next to him. She'd often watched him sleeping, sometimes for hours, fascinated by the contours of his handsome face. Vebekka moved silently around the bed.

She was close enough to touch him. She wanted to lie next to him, wanted to slip her hand into his, but she saw the dark red bruises, the teeth marks, and she crept out, knowing now what she had done. She wanted to cry, but she had wept too many times, for too many years. She knew she had alienated him and the children. It was a terrible thing to see the fear in their eyes if she laughed too loudly, called out too sharply; no matter what assurance she gave them, their fear hung in the air. And lately she could no longer fight it. Vebekka knew it was just a matter of time before the darkness swallowed her.

The streets were empty. As she stared from the window, a disembodied voice in the distance overwhelmed her with panic. It was coming, it was beginning.

"Oh please, dear God, no . . ."

She tried to draw the dark green curtain, but her hand pulled back. Something was crawling inside the curtain; she didn't want to see it. Her heart began to beat rapidly and she couldn't catch her breath, she was suffocating. She whispered, for someone, anyone, to help her, she didn't want the curtain to open.

Anne Marie had heard the muffled sounds; she quickly checked the baroness's room, and saw the empty bed; she ran into the adjoining bathroom in a panic. The tiles and floor were covered with blood. She found Vebekka, naked, curled up by the toilet. She had slashed her arms with a razor. She was weeping, saying over and over she wanted to leave Berlin. As Anne Marie touched her, she struggled and kicked out viciously. She wanted to be taken home, she wanted to die. Her voice rose to a screech as she cried out that it was here, it had come for her, it was here, it was taking over, and they should let her die.

Anne Marie woke Helen Masters, and the two women sedated and bandaged Vebekka and together carried her back to her room. The struggle had exhausted her, and at last she was calm. They waited until she fell into a deep sleep.

It was a sleep of nightmares. As the darkness overtook her, she could no longer ask them to stop the demons, the devils in white coats who worked on her brain when she slept. She fought against them, but she was helpless.

Helen sat by Vebekka's bedside, her head throbbing; she was startled when the baron looked in.

"What happened?"

She drew her dressing gown closer. "Rather a lot, but she's quiet now; I'll stay with her."

He leaned over his wife, gently brushed her hair from her brow, and stroked her cheek. "My poor baby."

He saw her wrist was bandaged, lifted her hand, kissing the palm, and then tucked it beneath the duvet. As he returned to his bedroom, he said to Helen, "I am glad you are here."

The door closed silently behind him. Helen concentrated on her patient, sleeping deeply, her face in repose like an innocent child's.

◆　◆　◆

At ten-thirty Hilda was ushered into the suite. The baron was having a late breakfast in the restaurant with Dr. Masters. Anne Marie whispered to Hilda that the baroness had specifically asked for her to assist in her dressing, but that Hilda must make no mention of what had occurred the previous evening. The baroness had been taken ill during the night, but she was calm now.

"Don't worry, she's sedated, she may not even remember she asked for you!"

Hilda entered the bedroom. The baroness's hair and makeup were immaculate, and she had painted her nails a dark crimson. Her eyes were expressionless, her voice low and husky.

"I apologize if I caused you any embarrassment yesterday."

She pushed away her breakfast tray. The glass of fresh orange juice was untouched, there was almost a full cup of black coffee. The bread, however, had been carefully rolled into balls; small gray pellets surrounded her plate.

Hilda helped the baroness to dress in silence. Vebekka spent a long time deciding what to wear, picking up various outfits and holding them up against herself. She chain-smoked, taking no more than two or three puffs of the gold-tipped cigarettes before she stubbed them out. She carefully placed a gold cigarette case, a lighter, a handkerchief, and a gold compact into a small black purse. Nothing else, no wallet or cards.

She tried on three hats before she was satisfied. She flipped open the jewelry case with a trembling hand, removed an ornate brooch of a tiger's head, and then, shaking her head, let it fall back into the suede-lined box. Next she took out an exquisite sapphire-and-diamond bluebird clip. She held it to the light, whispering to herself, oblivious of Hilda.

The baroness sat patiently by the drawing room window for half an hour, chain-smoking while she waited for the baron. She had pinned the bluebird to the side of her hat; the bird's wings glittered as if about to take flight.

Both Hilda and Anne Marie saw the baron come in and take Vebekka's arm. They saw her withdraw from him. Eventually she gave way to his quiet persistence.

Before leaving the apartment, the baroness gave the sweetest of smiles to Hilda, then put on her dark glasses and bowed her head. But Hilda saw the fear in her eyes.

After they left, Hilda looked over the breakfast table.

"The baroness did not eat," she commented, pointing to the small balls of bread.

"She always does that, or hides food in her pocket," retorted Anne Marie.

"She seemed very frightened."

"She's always frightened, frightened of doctors, frightened of anyone in a white coat. They are going to hypnotize her, this time!" Anne Marie added.

Hilda placed the bloodstained towels into a laundry bag.

"Have you worked for them long?" she asked Anne Marie.

"Five years. I think I'm number thirteen . . . unlucky! Not many stay long: When she's nice, she's very very nice, but when she's bad . . . she can be very dangerous. . . . I was told not to tell you, but you should know, especially since she has taken a liking to you. Don't trust her, these violent moods of hers come on without warning; she simply goes crazy, and she'll go for you like an animal. So be prepared."

Hilda pursed her lips and continued to tidy the room. Anne Marie drew the curtains. "I used to like her; she was the kindest, sweetest woman I had ever met. I also felt deeply sorry for her." She turned to Hilda. "She was exceptionally kind to me and my little daughter."

Anne Marie let the drapes fall back. "But she can be so hurtful, say such terrible things, things you cannot forget, or forgive. She can be evil, and she is very strong. So be warned, when she turns, get out—just run away from her. All the others did, but I need the money."

Anne Marie sipped the orange juice, looking at the small pellets of bread.

✦ ✦ ✦

The Mercedes moved slowly through a group of cheering students. It was almost time for the celebrations to begin, marking the one-year anniversary since the wall had been torn down. Vebekka sat between Helen and the baron, clasping and unclasping her gloved hands. Her husband took her hand and held it tightly. "It'll be all right . . . no one is going to hurt you."

When she replied, her voice was almost inaudible. "It's close Louis, it feels so close, I can feel it. You should take me away from this place, please, I've never felt it so close to me before, I'm so scared."

Helen glanced at the baron, and then turned to look out of the window. Vebekka's small gloved hand reaching for hers took her by surprise. They each held one hand, as if she were a child, and they both felt her tremble.

2

DR. FRANKS'S WAITING room was comfortable, with deep sofas and thick pile carpeting. The friendly receptionist offered coffee and tea, trying to put the visitors at ease.

Dr. Franks walked into the reception room in a sweater and shirt, his hands stuffed into a pair of corduroy trousers. He had been told that the baroness had a deep distrust of anyone wearing a white coat. He was sixty-nine years old. His craggy face and gnarled hands belied his sharpness; he had a warm smile and a penetrating gaze.

The baron shook Dr. Franks's hand, while Helen embraced her mentor. Dr. Franks sat beside Vebekka, and took her hand and kissed it.

"Your mustn't be afraid. Today I will spend most of my time with your husband. You will chat with my nurse and my assistant. Maybe tomorrow you and I will spend some time together. Would you like coffee? or tea?"

Vebekka kept her head down and withdrew her hand; she said nothing.

"Helen, do you want to join us?" asked Franks.

Helen bent her head to try to meet Vebekka's eyes. "Would you like me to stay with you? Vebekka?"

The baroness looked up, and her wide amber eyes met Doctor Franks's.

"I am quite capable of being left on my own, thank you."

Dr. Franks noticed the way she recoiled from Helen, as if she did not want her to touch her. He gestured to Maja, his assistant, to stay with the patient, but Vebekka did not notice. Nor did she see Maja switch on a tape machine; she was watching Dr. Franks, the baron, and Helen leave the room. Their conversation would be recorded, so that Dr. Franks could listen to it before he began his formal session with Vebekka.

There was a worn storybook on the table for the younger patients; Vebekka leaned over and slipped it under her coat. Maja pretended not to see. She sat opposite Vebekka, as the elegant woman slowly, surreptitiously began to inch the book into her purse.

"Will they be long?" the baroness asked.

Maja smiled. "Knowing Dr. Franks, yes!"

The lovely throaty giggle took Maja by surprise.

"Oh, my husband won't like that, I'm supposed to be the crazy one."

Maja laughed, and Vebekka reached over and tapped her knee. "I've forgotten your name!"

◆　◆　◆

"Everything you can tell me will be of importance."

The baron sat opposite Dr. Franks, asked if he could smoke and lit a cigar without waiting for a reply. Helen Masters had also drawn up a chair.

"Tell me everything you know of your wife's childhood, her relationship to her family, how many brothers and sisters, et cetera . . . I see from the files there is very little information."

The baron shrugged. "I know very little. I met Vebekka in Paris, in 1960, she was twenty years old. We married two years later. The year I met her, her mother died, and then a few years later her father also died. I never knew either of them. They were originally from Canada, then emigrated to Philadelphia when Vebekka was still young. She is an only child, and I have never met any relatives—she has said there is no one. All I know is that her parents were wealthy. On her father's death, Vebekka was left a considerable amount of money. When I have questioned her about her childhood she has always said it was unexceptional, but very happy . . . she speaks fondly of her parents."

Franks seemed to doodle on a notepad. "So your wife is not French by birth?"

"No, Canadian, but she has always spoken fluent French. Over the years I have questioned my wife to determine if any other member of her family suffered from a similar illness. We have four children . . ."

"Has she made *any* mention of mental illness in her family?"

The baron's lips tightened. "No . . . she is adamant about that. She cannot recall any of her immediate family ever being ill."

"Does she speak about her family?"

The baron hesitated, then shook his head. "No, she has never really discussed her family with me. In fact when I offered to accompany her to her father's funeral, she refused. Perhaps I should mention that my own family was very much against this marriage. I was the sole heir; my family felt Vebekka was not a suitable match. I was only twenty-three years old."

"Do you know if there is any way we can contact anyone who knew your wife in America?"

The baron flicked his cigar ash. "I know of no one, but if you think it is important, I can try and trace someone."

"It is of the utmost importance. I would appreciate your trying to find any medical or scholastic documents—schools, friends, anyone who knew your wife in her early childhood."

The doctor leaned back in his chair. "So you met your wife in Paris . . ."

"She was an in-house model for Dior. I was at a reception with my mother when we met. I asked her to dine with me, and she accepted. We were married two years later. My first son was born ten months later, in 1963. He is twenty-eight, my second son was born eighteen months after that, and my first daughter after another eighteen months. My fourth child, Sasha, is only twelve years old."

The doctor swiveled in his chair. "Is your wife a good mother?"

The baron nodded. "Excellent, very loving, but firm—they adored her. They are normal children . . . however of late, her behavior has greatly disturbed them."

The baron stared into space and then looked down at his hands. "My younger daughter has suffered the most. Perhaps it was unwise for us to have her. Vebekka's breakdowns had begun before Sasha was born."

The baron paused.

"After the birth of each of my sons she became depressed and unstable—twice spending some time in a clinic."

"So you think her illness is connected in some way to the children?" asked Dr. Franks.

The baron twisted his signet ring around his finger. "She was always afraid that the babies would be born deformed; this became an obsession with her. She insisted on visiting doctors sometimes five times a week, demanding X rays, et cetera. She even considered abortions, although her doctors insisted her pregnancies were normal. After giving birth, she would sink into a depression. She did not want to hold the baby, or touch it. She seemed almost afraid of the child, but then the depression would lift, and she would be exhilarated."

"When did you first detect a breakdown, as you call it, not connected to her pregnancies?"

"There have been so many, but the worst came after a lengthy period when I believed our problems were all in the past. Then she became as obsessive about having another child as she had been about the fear of them being born deformed. She wanted a daughter and, when she recovered, I gave way."

Dr. Franks frowned, and tapped his desk with his forefinger. "But you have two daughters, so the pattern continued when your second daughter, Sasha, was born?"

The baron nodded. "Sasha was—how do you say? . . . not expected, and my wife's gynecologist did suggest terminating the pregnancy." He paused, crossing his legs, and shrugged. "This was unacceptable, on two counts. I am Catholic, and . . ."

Franks waited, but the baron seemed disinclined to continue.

"So, when did the problems not directly linked to the births of your children actually begin?"

The baron sighed. "The birth of Sasha was not as traumatic, for in fact Vebekka recovered quite quickly. Sasha was doted upon, spoiled I suppose. She is the most delightful child, and the one most physically like her. I thought the problems were over, but they began again. This time my wife said she felt that someone was taking over her body."

"Did that culminate in another breakdown?"

The baron stubbed out his cigar and clenched his hands.

"Yes. We were in Monaco for the polo season. Vebekka took Sasha to a circus. During one of the acts, my wife began to behave strangely, she kept on getting out of her seat, she seemed to want to get into the circus ring. She became abusive when she was restrained by one of the ushers—she was screaming about the clown, it was a midget or a dwarf. She became totally hysterical. Somehow she got into the ring and attacked the clown. By the time I was called she had been taken, incoherent, to a hospital. To my knowledge that was the first time she had actually been violent. Since then, her violence and irrational behavior has spiraled. She has attacked every member of the family, including me. Sasha is very much afraid of her."

"Are you saying she has attacked her own daughter?"

"No, no, but she has destroyed Sasha's possessions."

"What do you mean?"

The baron looked to Helen, and then back to Franks. "The child's toys, her dolls. She breaks them, burns them."

"Has she ever been self-abusive?"

"She has tried to kill herself countless times, in fact she attempted to do so in the hotel last night. But surely you have her medical history?"

Dr. Franks raised his bushy eyebrows. "Of course, but I want to hear firsthand. Please continue."

Franks observed how the baron looked to Helen Masters, as if for approval or reassurance.

"In my estimation, this present attack has been coming on for weeks. Helen suggested this would be the best time for you to see her. Vebekka agreed because of Sasha."

"If I can help your wife, would you agree to let her stay in my clinic for as long as is needed?"

"If you can help her, I will agree to anything you suggest. I cannot subject my children and myself to any more torment. I have had enough."

The doctor could see a muscle twitching at the side of the baron's mouth.

"Do you regret marrying your wife?"

"That is an impossible question. I have four beautiful children; of course I do not regret marrying her. But my sons, my daughters must know if this illness is hereditary. If my wife is to be institutionalized it will affect each and every one of us. You are my last hope."

"Would you please descibe the very first time you noticed your wife behave in an irrational manner."

The baron remained silent for at least half a minute, then sighed. "She was four months pregnant with my first son, she was very beautiful, and being pregnant made her even more so. She took great care of herself, and seemed content. We both were. We were very much in love, exceptionally close, idyllically happy. One night I woke up, and she was not beside me. I went to look for her. I found her in the kitchen; there was food everywhere, she was stuffing her mouth. She must have been doing it for quite some time because there was vomit on the floor. Her face was rigid, she was like a stranger. It was awful."

Franks held up his hand. They could hear laughter from the next room. Helen stood up, as if to go into the reception area, but Franks waved her back to her seat.

"Maja is with her. She is very adept at relaxing patients. It seems she has succeeded!"

✦   ✦   ✦

Vebekka was telling Maja about her days as a model: the gossip and backbiting. She was very entertaining, and the more she relaxed the more animated she became. She stood up to demonstrate how she had first been taught to cat-walk. She arched her back, pushed her hips forward, and paraded up and down.

"You know how many models have back trouble? I mean can you imagine any sane person walking in this way?"

She swiveled on her heels, then glided to the sofa and sat down.

"The gowns were spectacular, and it was amusing to see which celebrity bought which design. Can you imagine the fun, seeing those superb creations on frumpy, rotund women!"

Maja was entertained, it was difficult not to be, but she also detected a strange wariness in Vebekka. Her eyes frequently strayed to the closed door, then she would fall silent, sometimes in mid-sentence, before quickly recovering and launching into a different story. Maja did not attempt to steer Vebekka into discussing how she felt, knowing it would either happen naturally or not at all. But as experienced as she was, she was still taken by surprise when Vebekka suddenly gripped her wrist.

"What are they doing in there? Why are they taking so long?"

Maja made no move to withdraw her hand.

"He's talking about me, isn't he? Of course, stupid question, stupid question . . ."

She released her hold.

"Dr. Franks needs to know so much about you," Maja said kindly.

"Why doesn't he ask me?"

"He will, but your husband will probably speak more freely without you there."

Vebekka nodded. "Yes, yes, that's true, poor Louis. I am all right now. This is a waste of time, you know. . . ."

Maja looked at her watch. She got up and went toward a glass panel between the rooms. She was going to pull the blind up to see if one of the kitchen helpers was there to make some coffee, but, as her hand reached for the string, she froze.

"*Don't* . . . please don't. I don't want to see through the glass."

Maja turned to Vebekka. The baroness was hunched in her seat, staring straight ahead. Before Maja could say anything, the baron came in alone, gray with fatigue.

"I'm to take you home, darling."

Maja watched Vebekka closely, and saw the relief when she learned she would not have to see the doctor. She kissed Maja warmly as she left.

Dr. Franks walked into the reception area.

"Well, Maja, what do you think?"

"I think she is a very disturbed woman. She is very entertaining, very sharp and witty, but I think she is also . . ."

"Dangerous?" he inquired. Maja touched her wrist, remembering Vebekka's strong grip. She nodded. "Yes . . . very!"

Dr. Franks returned to his study, where Helen was still waiting. He shut the door, and stuffed his hands into his pockets. "Maja agrees with you."

He poured Helen a glass of sherry.

"Tell me about the violence, have you witnessed it?"

"Yes, she becomes very disoriented, very angry, verbally and physically. She is quite frightening. Although she loses control, and claims to have no recall, I believe she has. She knows what she did to Sasha, but denies it."

Franks asked Helen to elaborate on the destruction of the dolls, and listened intently as she described what the baron had told her.

"He said he had run in response to Sasha's screams. To his horror he had found that his wife had taken every doll belonging to the child, smashed their faces, and torn off their arms. Then she had stacked them, and set fire to them. The house could have caught fire, but she just stood, watching the toys burning, forcing her daughter to watch with her. Sasha was terrified; Vebekka held her by her hair, forcing her to watch the dolls melt. The baron heard her saying 'Watch the babies, Sasha, watch the baby dolls!' He had to release his daughter from Vebekka's grip."

Franks interrupted. "Did she give a reason for her actions?" Helen shook her head. "I spoke with Sasha, and asked her to tell me about the incident. She kept repeating that her mama looked strange. Oh, yes, I remember something else. Sasha said Vebekka screamed for her father, said she called out, 'Papa.' While holding Sasha by the hair, she repeated: 'He is my papa, not yours, my papa. Papa loves me.' I asked the baron about this, and he said that the baroness did not allow any of the children to call him Papa. When I asked her about it, she said only that she didn't like them using 'Papa,' and when I pressed her, she had no answer."

"The baron said she attempted to take her own life last night, is this true?"

Helen shrugged. "She cut herself. I don't think she would have killed herself. She wants attention, screams for attention all the time . . . she is a great attention seeker."

"What about the violence to her husband? I noticed he had a nasty bite mark on his right hand."

Helen drained her sherry glass.

"When she is irrational, she will attack anyone who is close to her. He happened to be there. I guess she mistrusts everyone during these episodes, including her children. But I find it interesting that she did not attack her daughter, just her toys. Yet her daughter was close by . . ."

"What about the other children?"

Helen referred to her notes. "Some of these attacks have occurred in their presence. When she is in her so-called irrational state, she bites, kicks, punches . . . but she has not to my knowledge taken a weapon, a knife, or anything like that!"

"What does she say when she is in this condition?"

Helen flicked through her notes. "Back in 1982 she was to be given sodium pentothal, the truth drug, but she refused it. I sent you the transcript."

Franks opened his file and leafed through.

Helen continued. "She believes someone is taking over her mind, just as she believes that anyone in a white coat, doctor or nurse, is going to hurt her. She has a terror of injections. She has refused shock treatment and, until now, objected to any form of hypnotherapy."

"What do you think has made her change her mind?"

"She knows she is becoming more dangerous, has even told me she fears she will kill someone . . . I have gone as far as I can. I hope you can help her."

"I never give up hope. But first things first, my dear Helen, we must eat. I am starving and there's a nice little restaurant close by. We can continue our discussion over lunch."

❖ ❖ ❖

Hilda had helped Vebekka dress for dinner, and was delighted by her exuberance. Louis, however, was tired and not in good spirits. He could hear his wife on the telephone to Sasha; Vebekka's resilience was astonishing, unnerving. She was telling Sasha about their plane journey, about Berlin, as if they were on a vacation. The call completed, she danced over to the dinner table and began lifting with relish the silver lids from the tureens. She ate little, just sat with her chin cupped in her hands, watching his every mouthful. She reached over and stroked his hand gently.

"I'm sorry for all the trouble I cause you, my darling."

He smiled, as she poured a glass of wine for him. She was forbidden any alcohol. He took his glass and raised it to her. In the candlelight her amber eyes were as bright as a cat's. Looking at her now made him feel deeply, horribly sad. . . . This was the Vebekka he had fallen in love with, the young girl he had showered with gifts and flowers until she had succumbed to his charms. She had been crazy, fun-loving, madcap, and willful. She was still all those things, but now, the craziness, the madness, was a hideous constant torment.

"What are you thinking about, Louis?"

"How beautiful you look! You remind me of when we first met."

The next moment she was on his knee, kissing him frantically.

"I'm still your favorite baby, I haven't changed. Please, please take me to bed, carry me into the bedroom, the way you used to, please Louis, let's pretend this is a honeymoon."

He lifted her from his knee. "Eat, finish your dinner."

Pouting, she returned to her side of the table. She picked at her food, nibbling on the green beans as she watched him. She slurped some lemonade, trying to amuse him with coy, sweet smiles, smiles that had won him over so many times. Louis wondered how long it would be before she turned on him. He could no longer tell how long the bad spells lasted; all he knew was that this sweet creature would turn, if not tonight, a month, a week, or a year from now into a vicious, violent monster.

Her eyes narrowed, but she smiled. "Take me home, Louis, please, I'm all right now, it's over. I know I have said this to you before, but this time I know it's over. The darkness is gone. I felt it lift in the waiting room at Dr. Franks's. And Sasha misses me, she needs me to be with her."

He drained his wineglass, patted his lips with his napkin. She brought him a cigar, clipped the end for him, and struck the match. "Please, Louis, take me home, we can be together, a family. I really am fine now. . . ."

He grabbed her wrist and held it tightly. "No, no we stay here, we stay until Dr. Franks has seen you, that's what we came for."

She made no attempt to free herself and he released his hold.

"Bekka, please don't do this to me, please don't . . . Maybe you feel fine now, but it could change, in the car, on the plane. Please give it a try, if not for yourself, if not for me, do it for Sasha!"

Vebekka wrapped him in her arms. "I would never hurt my baby, please believe me. Just say you will take me home, I don't want to stay here."

Louis pushed her away. "Sasha is afraid of you!"

Vebekka recoiled as if he had slapped her. "She is not, I just talked to her on the phone; she is not afraid of me."

Louis spun around. "You don't even know what you do to her! You will stay here, you will go to Dr. Franks. I'll make you see this through."

She cocked her head to one side and smirked.

"Then you will leave me? That's why I'm here, you want to get rid of me. I will never divorce you, Louis, not for any of your women, I will never release you. You are mine."

The baron ignored her, turning toward Anne Marie's room. "I'm going to bed, I suggest you do the same . . . *Anne!* . . . Anne!"

Anne Marie appeared.

"The baroness is retiring—will you see to her needs?"

Vebekka swiped at the dishes on the table. "I don't want any pills, I don't want that ugly little bitch near me! I won't be locked in my room."

The baron looked hard at his wife. Her act was coming apart already. He walked into his room and slammed the door.

Vebekka turned on Anne Marie. "I don't need anything, especially from you. Go to your room, you plain, ugly bitch . . . go on, get out of my sight—get those short squat legs moving . . . you smell! In fact you *stink* . . . your body is putrid!"

Anne Marie paused at the door to look back to the baroness.

"At least *my* daughter isn't terrified of me." She shut the door quietly.

◆　◆　◆

The baroness's bedroom was lit by a bedside light. Vebekka threw herself onto the bed, then sat up panic-stricken. Where was her jewelry box? her makeup box? . . . Finding the boxes comforted her. She carried them to the bed. Then, she gleefully began to make up her face.

◆　◆　◆

Louis's eyes were closed, but he was not asleep; he knew she was in the room. He felt the covers on his right side lift. He sighed, raised his arm, and she nestled against him. Slowly he turned to look at her.

It took all his willpower not to push her away. Her face was hideously streaked, like a clown's. He tried to keep his voice steady. "What's that over your face, Bekka? What are you doing?"

"Your clown, don't you remember? When we were in New York that time? How we laughed at the little midget, the little clown. . . ."

She slid off the bed and fell to her knees, bouncing up and down, pulling at her face grotesquely. He sat up, looked at the clock, then back at his wife. She jumped up on the bed, rolled on top of him, giggling and tickling him until he held her tightly.

"It's one o'clock in the morning, I'm exhausted, this is crazy."

She looked downcast. "Under the circumstances, I don't think this is a very funny thing to say!"

He sighed. It was as if she were balanced on a high wire; if he said the wrong word, made the wrong move, she would fall. He could contain himself no longer; his body shook as he wept.

Vebekka held him as though he were a child, soothed him, quieted him.

Louis had taken a mistress within months of the birth of his first son, and he had continued this pattern throughout the marriage. He told himself that he needed it because of the anguish Vebekka caused him, and yet she could still make him want her like no other woman he had ever known.

She whispered for him to forgive her, then asked again if he loved her. He could feel himself giving in, too tired to protest. She rested her head against his shoulder, her lips inching upward toward his.

Her feather-light touches to his cheeks, his ears, his temples, began to arouse him.

"Don't do this, Bekka, please don't."

"Let me make love to you, please, Louis, I know you want me."

Her hands unbuttoned his pajama top, then pulled it from his body. She began to kiss his nipples.

"Bekka, listen to me, it's over between us. I will always take care of you, I promise you, but . . ."

She untied the cord of his pajama bottoms, easing them over his buttocks, caressing, never stopping her sucking, kissing, licking until she eased herself to her knees. He moaned.

"You see, Louis, you do want me!"

Suddenly she sprang off the bed, and smiled at him. He drew up his pants to hide his erection—and she laughed a soft, low, vicious laugh. "You'll never get rid of me."

She twisted the handle on his door, and she was gone.

He felt wretched, sick to his stomach. He didn't follow her, not this time.

✦ ✦ ✦

Helen Masters had covered her head with a pillow so as not to hear them, and yet hours later, even though she knew Vebekka had left Louis, she was still unable to sleep. She got up and went into the main suite to get a brandy. As she began pouring from the decanter, her heart almost stopped. There was Vebekka, hideous makeup smudged over her face, curled up by the window—like a broken doll. Her eyes were staring into the darkness beyond the windowpane.

Helen touched her shoulder gently. "Come to bed, you'll catch cold, come on . . . Vebekka!"

Helen tucked the quilt around her. "Do you want a hot drink?"

Slowly Vebekka turned her head, tears streaming down her face. She whispered, "No, nothing, thank you, Helen." She was gazing straight ahead, as if listening for something. "There's something here, can you feel it?"

"Feel what?" Helen asked.

"I don't know . . . I don't know, but it's here, it's taking me, Helen. It's taking me over."

Helen felt Vebekka's brow; she was sweating. "Do you need Anne Marie to give you something to help you sleep?"

"No. Please, take me away from this place."

"I can't, this is for your own good. It will all be all right, you'll see."

Vebekka clung tightly to Helen. "Something takes over me, Helen, I have to leave, please talk to Louis, tell him I must go home."

Helen embraced her. "There's nothing here, try and sleep."

Vebekka whispered: "We have done something terrible."

Helen went rigid, dear God—had the woman hurt Louis? She eased Vebekka from her arms, tucked her in, sat with her until she was quiet, and then ran to his room. Louis was sleeping deeply. Makeup covered his pillows, his face. She shut the door and leaned against it.

◆   ◆   ◆

Vebekka could not sleep. It was almost two-thirty. Dread slowly began to envelop her, a dread she was incapable of describing. Her feet felt leaden, and a terrible weight slowly began overwhelming her body—a deadly white substance that left only her brain to fight the terror of the whiteness inching toward it, only her willpower to keep the creeping mass at bay. She could not call out, could not move; it trapped her arms, constricted her throat. It took all the energy she could conjure to replace the whiteness with brilliant colors and force the colors to cut across her brain: bright primal reds, greens and sky blues. Each color was like an electric shock, shaking her, swamping her with such intense violence she became exhausted, had to give in, had to let the mass consume her. While sinking she caught a glimpse of a girl in a white frilly dress, little white socks and black patent leather shoes, a little girl holding a doll in her arms. She was so far away. A white gloved hand pulled a dark curtain, hiding the child, and darkness descended. She heard a soft, persuasive, voice whispering for her to remember, remember the colors. The gloved white hand began to draw the heavy curtain back again, inch by inch, but what lay hidden behind it filled her with such terror that she gave in to the darkness.

✦ ✦ ✦

Hilda was the first person in the suite that morning to see Vebekka. She was lying on the floor, catatonic, staring into space.

Hilda called frantically for Anne Marie, the baron, and Dr. Masters. Dr. Masters was the first to appear and told Hilda she would not be needed that day. It was not until she was on the bus heading for home that what had occurred that morning began to have an impact on her. Distracted, she got off the bus a stop early.

As she waited for the next bus, she decided she would walk instead, and prepared to cross the street. It was then that she saw the brightly colored poster: Schmidt's Circus was appearing in West Berlin.

Hilda moved closer, and stared in disbelief. The poster showed a massive lion's head. Below it was the defiant face of a woman with wild hair; a woman with wide, daring, amber eyes. THE WORLD'S MOST FAMOUS FEMALE WILD ANIMAL TRAINER, RUDA KELL-ERMAN—*award-winning act straight from Monte Carlo!*

For a moment Hilda could have sworn that the woman in the ad was Baroness Vebekka Maréchal.

3

RUDA KELLERMAN STEPPED down from her trailer. The sky was overcast, with rain falling lightly. Ruda drew up her raincoat collar and tightened her belt. Her black boots barely showed beneath the long trench coat. She wore a man's old cloth cap and her long hair was braided. She carried a small riding crop and was tapping it against her leg as she strode toward the Grimaldi cages.

There were sixteen tigers, four lionesses, five lions, and one black panther. The animals were three or four to a cage, except for one lion, Mamon, and the panther, Wanton, who each had his own. Ruda had, as always, supervised their unloading from the circus train. Now she was making her second inspection of the morning, her eyes noting each animal with a piercing stare of her wide amber-colored eyes.

The tigers were very vocal now; occasionally, she stopped as one or the other called to her. She pressed her face to the bars, blowing a kiss.

The purring sound was so loud it was like a rumble, but there was no sound from the smallest cage in the semicircle, the cage that housed Wanton, her young panther. Ruda called out to him, but kept at arm's length as he sliced his paw through the bars, his sharp claws always ready to lash out against anyone passing close. Wanton was the smallest cat, but one of the most dangerous, and Ruda glanced upward to check that the tarpaulin over the top of his cage was well battened down. She checked to make sure that there was no loose rope for Wanton to leap at, and possibly hurt himself.

Ruda moved on to her babies, her lionesses. The rain was heavier, and she snapped orders for her helpers to keep the tarpaulins on all the cages until it was time to move the cats into their sheltered quarters. Hearing her voice, the lionesses pressed their massive bodies to the bars, and each one received a rub on the nose. Ruda spoke softly, knowing they would be restless for some time. They always were when they arrived at a new site.

Ruda ran her crop along the bars of the next to last cage, and three of her prize babies, the fully grown male lions, loped toward her, their massive heads bent low, their paws too large to reach through. These lions with their full manes never ceased to touch a chord inside her; they were kings, magnificent killers, and she admired the sheer force and power of their muscular bodies. Their straw needed changing. She turned angrily to one of her helpers, snapping out the order to prepare the clean straw.

A young man, who had been with Ruda for only six months, muttered for her to give him a break, he had just arrived himself. In two quick strides Ruda was at his side.

"Do it now! No back talk!"

The boy hurried toward the trailer, where four helpers were pitchforking the new hay and sawdust. Ruda made sure every bale was checked out for dampness, and every sack of sawdust was checked for poison, often laid by farmers to get rid of rats. Ruda insisted that the sawdust be sifted by hand.

Turning to the last cage, she quickened her step. She gave a soft whistle, and then leaned by the side of the cage. Mamon was in solitary confinement, a state he seemed to prefer. Ruda often wondered if he acted up to ensure he was solo; and could do so like none of the others, but then, even his name was unique. He had it when Ruda purchased him. Mamon was moody, uncooperative, a bully, but he could also be playful and sweet-natured. Lions on the whole are family oriented, they like each other's company, but Mamon was a loner, and he constantly tested her. She liked that.

As soon as he heard her soft whistle, Mamon swung his head toward Ruda; then he loped slowly to the side of the cage. When she whistled for the second time, he bent down onto his haunches, his nose pressed to the bars, his massive black mane protruding through the rails. As Ruda peered around to him, his jaws opened and snapped shut.

"How you doing, eh? Want to say hello to your mama? . . . Eh?"

Mamon rolled onto his back, and Ruda reached in and tickled his underbelly, but she never stopped talking to him, soothing him, always aware that even in play he could bite her arm off.

The high-pitched voice that interrupted this scene was like that of a pubescent boy, slightly hoarse, half low, half falsetto.

"So you got what you wanted after all. . . ."

Mamon sprang to his feet, all four hundred and ten pounds of him ready to attack. The cage rattled as he lunged at the bars.

Ruda gripped the riding crop tighter. The voice was unmistakable.

"You got even taller, Ruda."

Ruda turned and snapped. "I wish I could say the same for you, Tommy. What rock have you crawled from under?"

Tommy Kellerman gave a mirthless, twisted smile. "You're doing all right for yourself. That's some trailer parked up front! How much does a trailer that size set you back?"

Ruda relaxed her grip on the riding crop, forced a smile. This was something that she had expected after all. Ruda had to look down to waist level to meet his eyes. Tommy Kellerman looked very spruce; his gray suit and red shirt had to have been custom made, as was his red and gray striped tie. She was familiar with the white trench coat, he wore it as he had always done, slung round his shoulders; he also sported a leather trilby, a hat being the only normal garment Tommy could buy outside of a children's wear department. Kellerman was a dwarf.

"That raincoat's seen some wear!" She tried to sound casual, but her heart was hammering, and she glanced around furtively to see if there was anyone she knew close by.

"We got to talk, Ruda."

"I've got nothing to say to you, Tommy, and I'm busy right now."

Kellerman inched his leather hat up a fraction. "You didn't change your name. How come?"

"I paid enough to use it; beside, I like it."

Ruda walked a few steps to the side of the cage, out of sight of passersby. She leaned against the cage, gestured for him to come to her. After a moment, Kellerman joined her. His sweet-smelling cologne wafted up, mixing with the smell of the cats' urine.

"Like I said, Ruda, we need to talk. I just got in from Paris, I got a room in the Hotel Berlin."

Kellerman had a small leather bag; he dropped it by his tiny feet. Then he leaned against the wheel of the cage, his square hands stuffed into the small pockets, his polished child's shoes and red socks scuffed with mud.

"Have you been to my trailer? . . . asked for me there?"

He laughed his high-pitched laugh, and shook his head. "No, I came straight from the station. I've been following you, I keep on seeing your posters, your face. You are the star attraction. You got what you wanted, eh?"

"What do *you* want, Tommy?" Her voice was flat and emotionless.

He looked up at her, and inched his hat further up his domed forehead, scratching his head. Then he removed the hat and ran his stubby fingers through thick curly hair flecked with gray. The last time Ruda had seen him, it had been coal black. It was the nicest thing about him, his curly hair. She noticed it was dirty now, sweaty from the hat.

"I said, what do you want, Tommy? You're not here for a job are you? Not after what happened—they wouldn't touch you. I'm surprised you can still find circuses that'll employ you."

Kellerman spat into the mud.

"Isn't there someplace we can discuss this comfortably? It's raining, and I could do with a bite to eat. . . ."

"I'm real busy, Tommy, it's feeding time, maybe we can meet someplace later."

He stared up at her, and his eyes searched hers before he spoke.

"You owe me, Ruda: All I want is my fair share. I can't get work, good work. I'm broke, I've had to sell most of my props and, well, I reckon you can give me a cut."

"Cut of what?"

"Well, there's a few ways to look at it. I'm still your legal husband, and I bet any dough your old man doesn't know that!

Now you are rollin' in it, and you're on the number one circuit, this must be one hell of a contract . . . and all I want is a part of it, you either get me in on the act . . ."

"They'd fucking eat you, Tommy . . . no way!"

One of the helpers passed the small alleyway between the cages. He paused. "Excuse me, Mrs. Grimaldi, but the freezers are open. You want to come over and sign for the meat?"

Ruda nodded. "Be right with you, Mike."

Ruda hid Tommy by standing in front of him, and she remained there until Mike had left.

"Ruda, I need money, I'm broke."

She turned on him, snapping angrily. "When have you not needed money, Tommy? If it moves, you'll slap a bet on it. You owed me, remember? I paid you off years ago, I owe you nothing."

Kellerman's face twisted with anger. "You had nothin', not even a fucking passport, I got you out of Berlin. Me! I put food in your mouth, clothes on your back. Don't give me this bullshit, you owe me a lot, Ruda, and if Grimaldi were to know you are still married, he'd hit the fuckin' roof . . . I keep my ears to the ground, bitch, I know you took over his act, and I know he's relegated to watchin' outside the ring like a prick! And I hear he hates it, he's still screwing everythin' in a skirt, so how do you think he'd feel if he knew you never got divorced? I reckon he'd be a happy man, Ruda. Now you tell me how much you owe me? I am your husband, and I got the marriage license to prove it. You got the divorce papers? Huh? . . . Well?"

Ruda pawed at the ground with the toe of her boot.

"Don't mess me around, Tommy, how much do you want?"

"Well, you got two options, sweetheart. Make me a part of the act, cut me in, or—I know what they pay top acts, so I don't think it's too much—just give me one hundred thousand dollars."

"Are you crazy? I don't have that kind of money, everything I earn goes into the act. I swear I don't have . . ."

Kellerman ran to the front of Mamon's cage. He pointed with his stubby finger. "Well, sell this bastard, they're worth a lot of dough, aren't they? Or sell your trailer, I know how much that's worth, and I know Grimaldi must be set up. I need dough, I got to pay some heavy guys off, and I got no one else. What you want from me, want me to beg? Fuck you! *You owe me!*"

Ruda remained in the narrow alley between the cages. It took all her willpower to contain her anger. "Tommy, don't stand in front of the cages, they don't like it. I'll get you as much as I can, but not dollars, not here."

Kellerman leered at her. "That's not good enough, Ruda. You want me to go over and have a chat with Grimaldi? You can get the cash from the head cashier. You think I dunno how much dough you're getting paid per show? It was the talk of Paris, so don't give me any bullshit."

"I'll see what I can do, and I'll come to your hotel tonight after I fix the night feed. But only on condition you don't work here. I also want our marriage license. Is it a deal?"

Kellerman looked at his watch. "Okay, I'll go grab a bite. You get me the dough, I'll give you the license. We got a deal, my love."

"Then leave now, I don't want you yapping to anyone!"

Kellerman grinned. "Eh! There's guys here that'd cut my throat if they saw me, so I'm gone . . . but you'd better turn up, you got until midnight." He scrawled on a card the hotel and phone number, tucking it into her pocket, smiling. Then he perched his hat at a jaunty angle and departed.

Mike was already sorting out the meat for the midday feed. He used a hatchet to slice the meat from the bone, and a carpenter's sledgehammer with a short handle to crack open the carcass. Ruda collected the large trays, carefully tagged for each cat. They weighed the feeds, placing the trays in readiness for the cages. She wore a rubber apron; blood covered her hands and arms. Like Mike, she wielded the knives and hatchets like a professional.

After they washed off the blood, Ruda said, "You can grab a coffee, Mike, I'll do the next feed. What time have they allocated the arena for us?"

Mike handed her a carefully worked-out schedule showing when the main rings would be available for her to rehearse the act.

Ruda looked over the sheet, frowning. "Have the new plinths I ordered arrived yet?"

"I think so, but until everyone's settled, I can't get to the delivery trucks. They're all parked out at the rear."

She swore under her breath and snapped, "Go and check, I'll need them tonight, we've no time to mess around!"

Ruda fed the cats herself, as she always did. That way she could monitor their diet and see if they had any problems. After the feed, she helped the boys sweep and wash down the boards.

It had been a long journey. Ruda's helpers retired to their trailers exhausted. None of them had ever been able to keep up with her; she seemed to have unending energy and stamina; she was stronger than most men, and had high expectations. Anyone not prepared to give one hundred percent was fired on the spot.

Until now she had not allowed herself to concentrate on the Kellerman problem. She was so engrossed in her thoughts, desperately trying to think what she should do about her first husband, that she virtually moved on automatic pilot. She had been so anxious to leave Kellerman that she had never considered divorce, but she had always consoled herself that no one would ever know because when she married Grimaldi, Kellerman was in jail. He wouldn't know, and Luis would have had no reason to suspect she wasn't divorced. Now she knew what a stupid mistake she had made. For Luis Grimaldi to find out now that they were not legally married would be very dangerous, especially since Ruda was poised to make her move and take over the act. Ruda and Grimaldi were partners, everything split fifty-fifty, but they were at loggerheads. Only the act tied Ruda to Grimaldi; the act that she had built up. Ruda was planning to draw up new contracts to increase her share to 70 percent of the proceeds. After months of bitter quarrels, she felt Grimaldi was ready to sign. But what if he were to discover she wasn't legally married to him and had no legal hold over him at all? The act was still in Grimaldi's name; every contract she signed was in his name, it didn't matter that everyone knew she had taken over. The act was still his.

Ruda dragged her boots over the iron grill outside the trailer steps, inched them off and stepped onto the portable steps in her stocking feet, and opened the door. She carefully placed her boots just inside, and then hung up her raincoat.

The trailer was spacious. Her large bedroom was off the central sitting room, while her husband's was off the far end by the kitchen. Ruda showered and washed her hair. Wrapped in a robe with a towel around her head she went into the kitchen. The coffee pot was still warm, and she poured herself a cup of the thick black liquid, then sat down with the mug in her hands.

The walls of the trailer were hung with framed photographs of herself, of Grimaldi, and of the various animals and circuits. Her eyes rested on the large picture of herself. It was the new poster, the first time Ruda was the main attraction of a circus. The fame of Schmidt's was worldwide; she was at the pinnacle of her career.

The coffee tasted good, bitter, and she clicked her tongue against her teeth. Her big, mannish hands were red raw, the skin rough, the nails cut square. She wore no wedding ring, no jewelry. Slowly she removed the damp towel, and her hair uncoiled in a wet dark twist. When it was combed back from her strong, raw-boned face, strange deep red scars were evident on her temples. They looked like burn scars, as if someone had held a red-hot poker to either side of her head.

Ruda often aggravated the scars, because she had a habit, when she was thinking, of rubbing her forefinger over them, as if the feel of the smooth scarred skin comforted her. She began to do that now, worrying about Kellerman, wondering what she should do—what she could do—all the while staring at the picture of herself. In the photograph, surrounded by her lions, she looked powerful, invincible. At stake were not only her career and her partnership, but also her life. And no one was going to take it from her. No one had a right to take it away.

Ruda rinsed out her mug and placed it on the draining board by the small sink, and she suddenly realized she was not alone in the trailer. She moved silently toward Luis's bedroom; a low or- gasmic moan make her step back. Then she heard her husband gasping, his moan louder, louder until he sighed deeply.

Ruda remained standing by the bedroom door, wondering which of the young girls was being serviced—it was more often than not one of the eager starstruck grooms. Grimaldi earmarked these young girls virtually on arrival at the site. In his heyday he wouldn't have looked in their direction, but now he fucked what he could still dazzle.

Ruda sat down on one of the comfortable cushioned benches and lit a cigarette. She inhaled deeply, letting the smoke drift into rings above her head. She heard a soft girlish laugh, and looked in the direction of the bedroom, wondering if they were about to start over again, but then the clink of glasses and the low voice of her husband asking for a refill made her think she should remove herself since they could both be coming out. She half rose to her feet.

"I love you."

Ruda raised her eyebrows; poor little whore.

"When will you tell her?"

Ruda sighed; the stupid little girl didn't know that she was more than aware of these affairs. She thought to herself, "Well? Answer her!"

"I'll discuss it tonight, after the show, she'll be too busy beforehand." Ruda could tell by the slight slur in Luis's voice that he had been drinking.

The girl's voice rose to a whine: "You said that days ago, you promised me . . . if she doesn't care about you, why wait? You promised me, Luis, you promised."

"I'll discuss it tonight, sweetheart, I give you my word. . . ."

Ruda decided she had heard enough. She was about to open the main door of the trailer and slam it hard, so they would know she was there, when she was stopped in her tracks.

"The baby won't wait—I want you to promise me you'll tell her tonight, ask for a divorce tonight, promise me?"

"Shit!" Ruda pursed her lips. The bloody tart was pregnant!

Grimaldi's voice grew a little louder. "Come here, look at me, Tina, I promise you we'll talk tonight, okay? But it's feeding time now, I can't talk it over until tonight, she's gonna have to rehearse, it's not the right time."

Ruda walked out of the trailer, stuffing her feet into her old boots. What was another bloody Grimaldi brat? But could this one turn his head? He was over sixty. Could this one make his warped, drink-befuddled mind take some kind of responsible action? The timing could not have been worse. If Grimaldi was to discover he was not legally married, maybe he would, out of sheer perverseness, think about marrying this tart.

Ruda's mind began to spin. Grimaldi was old, he was feeling bitter and jealous of her success, he had been relegated to nothing more than an observer of the act. A child coming now could give Grimaldi a sense of power. Would this bitch give her husband the strength to confront her?

Shoulders hunched, Ruda sloshed through the mud, her hands clenched into fists at her sides. Rage made her whole body stiffen, and the cats picked up on it. As soon as she reached the perimeter of their cages, they began to growl, pacing up and down, heads low.

The cages had to be driven undercover. The rain was pelting down, and the big animal tent had been erected; all the animal trailers were being moved into the covered arena, each having a delineated site within the tent. Ruda climbed on board the tractor with the first caged wagon ready and Mike gave her the signal to drive it in.

Ruda wheeled the tractor around, hitching and unhitching each cage, her arms straining.

Not until all the cages were secured and positioned in their allocated space did she relax. The large heaters were on full blast to ensure that the tent and grounds were kept dry and warm. All the tarpaulins from the tops of the cages were removed, laid out flat, and rolled up in readiness for the next journey.

When she at last returned the tractor to the parking lot, she started checking the equipment trucks to make sure that all her props had arrived. Then she had to check out the show cages: Each one weighed a ton, but they had to be carried and stacked. She lifted and stacked along with her boys until the sweat ran down her face.

Time was now short. She had to be ready for her rehearsal period; each act had its specific rehearsal time, and if she was not ready she would lose hers. The new plinths and pedestals were still in their wrappers. Ruda helped the workers heave them down from the truck and roll them into the practice ring. They were reinforced steel-framed leather-based seats and stools for the cats, ranging in height with reinforced interlocking frames; some were barrel shaped, some used under the ends of the planks. Each section had to be stacked for easy access and quick setup. They ranged from three feet to forty feet high, and they were very heavy.

Ruda was stripped down to a T-shirt. Sweat glistened on her face and under her armpits as she drove herself to work harder than any man. Her boots were caked in mud, her big hands covered in old leather gloves as she used wire clippers to uncover the first plinth. Standing back to view it, she swore loudly, then ripped off the second and third covers. The plinths were correct in measurement, and exceptionally well made, but she swore and cursed louder than any of the men as she pointed to the leather seat base. She had given the specific colors to be used: red, green, and blue. They were as she had instructed—but they were too bright, too primal, and the gold braid too yellow.

Ruda had just completed unwrapping the last plinth—stacking them side by side, all the covers and wires removed—and was standing hands on hips in a fury, when Grimaldi made his appearance.

He stood over six feet tall, and had thick black curly hair, very black since he dyed it regularly. His once exceptionally handsome face was bloated now from age and excessive drinking, his dark eyes red-rimmed, but he could still turn heads. He was wearing high black polished boots over cords, and a Russian-style shirt, belted at the waist. He reeked of eau de cologne; Ruda could smell him before she saw him.

"We got a problem?"

Ruda snapped that indeed they had, and it was all his fault.

"All you had to do, Luis, was give the colors for the plinths and you fouled that up—look at them, they're far too bright, I'm

gonna have to use the old ones when I link up the pyramid formation. Look at the fucking colors, too bright. I want our old
ones."

Grimaldi shrugged. "You can't have them. I sold them in Paris.
These are okay, they'll get used to them. What's the panic? A few
rehearsals, they'll get used to them."

Ruda turned on him. "It's not you in the ring with them, Luis,
it's me—and I'm telling you, those colors are too fucking bright!"

Ruda's face was flushed with fury. Luis knew, probably better
than anyone else, the danger new equipment always presented. Even
a different-colored shirt worn in the show could disturb the cats;
they hated change of any kind. Although they accepted Ruda's old
rehearsal clothes, they seemed to know instinctively when she wore
a different stage costume and they could act up. They had to be
given time to accept the changes, and two days, Ruda knew, was
not long enough.

Ruda glared at her husband.

"Get the old ones back, Luis, and get them by tonight!"

His eyes became shifty; he hated to be spoken to in that way in
front of the workers. "I said I sold them. Just work through the
act, they'll get used to them. I can't get them back from Paris in
time for the opening."

Ruda kicked one of the plinths in fury. "Just do what I ask, Jesus
Christ! It was the only thing you had to do and you fouled it up!"

Luis began to pick his teeth with a matchstick. "I'll call around.
What time do you rehearse?"

Ruda was walking out of the tent. Over her shoulder she shouted
for him to check the board. Luis noted they were not on until later
that afternoon, so he joined a group of men going off to the canteen.

Alone in the trailer, Ruda paced up and down. She opened the
safe, counted the money kept for emergencies, and noted that Luis
must have been dipping into it. She slammed the safe closed. There
were about fifteen thousand dollars left. She then checked her own
bank balance. In her private account she had fifty-two thousand
dollars. She rubbed her scar until it pained her, then began to open
drawers in her dressing table, feeling under her clothes for the small

bundles of dollars she kept for minor emergencies. Like a squirrel she hid small stacks of notes in various currencies and denominations, but no matter how she searched and calculated, she did not have one hundred thousand. The more she mentally added up the amount, the more her fury built. This was hers, every single hard-earned cent was hers, and that little bastard felt he had a right to it.

The cashiers said they could give Ruda an advance on her salary, but not until after lunch when they would go to the bank. Grimaldi would have to sign the release form, but if she came back at three they would have the money in dollars as she had requested. Ruda smiled, and shrugged, then said she'd changed her mind. She was smarting with the thought that she needed Grimaldi's signature for an advance on her own wages.

Ruda fixed herself a salad in the trailer, and then changed into her practice clothes. She was just about to leave when Luis returned. He shook his head, his hair soaked. "It's really coming down, maybe going to be a storm. The forecast isn't good."

"Did you try and sort out the pedestals?"

Luis had totally forgotten. He nodded, and then lied, saying he expected a return call at the main box office. She watched him in moody silence as he unlocked the wooden bench seat and checked over his guns; he rarely had a gun when watching out for her, but it was a habit from the past when his watchers had always been armed. Out of habit he checked his rifles, but never took them out of the box.

"I'll need you in the arena. Can you get the boys ready? We're due to start in an hour."

Luis sat on the bench, picked up the towel Ruda had used to dry her hair and rubbed his head. "Ruda, we need to talk, maybe after rehearsal."

Ruda was already at the trailer door.

"Which tart was it today?"

Luis laughed, tossing the towel aside. "It's been the same one for months and you know it—it's Tina, she's one of the bareback riders."

"You'll be screwing them in their diapers soon, you old goat."

Luis laughed again; he had a lovely rumbling laugh, and it relieved her: Maybe it wasn't as serious as she had thought.

"See you in the ring then! After, we can go out for dinner someplace."

Ruda paused by the door. "Maybe, but I've got a lot to do, we'll see."

He gave a rueful smile. "I'm sorry about the mixup with the plinths, I'll get onto them and see you in the ring."

The door clicked shut after her, and Luis lifted his feet up onto the bench, his elbows behind his head, and stared at the photographs along the top of the wall. Some of them were brown with age. They were of him in his prime, standing with his lions, smiling to the camera; there was such a powerful look to him, such youthfulness. . . . Slowly his eyes drifted down, he watched himself age from one poster to the next; it was as if his entire life was pasted up in front of him. He stared at the central poster, Ruda's face where his had always been. The side wall was filled with Ruda. He eased his feet down and stood, slowly moving toward the pictures that showed he was a has-been.

He opened a bottle of scotch, drank from the bottle, and looked at a photograph brown and curling with age. The Grimaldi family. There was the old man, the grandfather, his own father, with Luis beside him no more than ten years old. Luis's father had taught him everything he knew, just as his father had done before him. Three generations of big game trainers.

Luis downed more scotch as he stripped to shower. He bent to look at himself in the bathroom mirror, staring at the scars across his arms—warrior scars his papa used to call them—scars from breaking up the tiger fights. But there was one, deeper than the others, a jagged line from the nape of his neck to his groin. His fingers traced it, and he started to sweat, as his mouth dried up. He could never go back into the ring. She had done that to him. Ruda had made him feel inadequate, but it had been Mamon, her favorite baby, that had almost killed him.

The cold shower eased the feverish sweats, and he soaped his chest. He had been mauled so many times; how often had he stepped between two massive tigers, more afraid they would hurt themselves than him? Only the terrible scar on his chest made the fear rise up from his belly.

Mamon had lunged at him, dragged him like a rag doll around the practice ring, and Luis had been overcome with a terror he had not believed himself capable of. It had frozen him. He had no memory of how he had been dragged from the arena, no memory of anything until he woke in the hospital, with the wound already filling with poison, a nightmare wound that opened with pus every time he moved. The anguish and the pain had kept him feverish for weeks. In his dreams the scar opened and oozed and suffocated him.

Luis Grimaldi had almost died. To be incapacitated physically was hard enough for him to deal with, but harder still was the relentless fear. A fear that he could tell to no one. At first he had tried hiding it, making excuses, so many excuses, why months after he was healed, he had still not been near his cats. It was during those months that Ruda had begun working solo. He had said that he wasn't fit enough, that he needed more time to regain his strength. But Ruda knew he was afraid. Ruda had encouraged him—half-heartedly, he realized now—because she didn't want him back in the ring, she wanted the act for herself.

The bottle was almost empty, and the drunker he became, the more embittered he felt. He did not consider to what lengths Ruda had gone to salvage the act, how she had worked herself to exhaustion, keeping him and his cats at their winter quarters. Luis had forgotten that he never lifted a hand to help her, never asked how she had managed to finance them. All he could recall was her humiliation of him.

It was all Mamon's fault, he had decided. He could not get back into training with a cat that had mauled him, a cat that no longer showed him respect. Luis had entered the arena, and a cold sweat had drenched his body. He felt it as if it were yesterday, the terrible fear as Mamon's cage was drawn closer to the gate. A number of people at the winter quarters had gathered to watch. They came to see the famous man face his attempted killer, and they stood in silence as the cage drew closer and closer.

Mamon was motionless, his head lowered, staring at Grimaldi. Ruda had spoken calmly, softly, asking Grimaldi when she should release the cat. Grimaldi took another gulp of scotch as the heat of his humiliation made him shake.

Alone in the arena, he could not stop his legs from trembling, his breath felt tight in his chest. He looked from Mamon to Ruda. He wanted more than anything to give her the signal. But he froze, and she kept on watching him, her eyes like the cat's, and she was smiling. It was her mocking smile that finished him. The great Grimaldi walked out of the arena and back to their quarters. That moment finished his career.

He began to cry as he remembered the way she had held him close, later that night. He recalled every word she had said.

"It's not the scar on your body, Luis, but the ones inside; they are always worse. I understand more than anyone else, I understand."

Luis had pushed her away from him then, shouting that she did not understand, there was nothing wrong with his mind, and he had pulled his shirt open to display the raw, ragged scar. Mamon, he said, was dangerous, should be shot. He had then tried to get his gun, pushing Ruda out of his way. Ruda's physical strength had stunned him, she had almost lifted him off his feet with a back-handed slap that sent him sprawling. Standing over him, her eyes as crazy as a wild cat's, she had virtually spat out the words.

You touch Mamon, and I swear to God I'll kill you!"

Luis had dragged himself to his feet. "You shoot him then, it's him or me, Ruda."

Ruda had taken his whip, the whip Luis's grandfather had used, and, for a second, he thought she was going to use it on him. Instead, she laughed in his face.

"Watch me! Just watch me, Luis."

From the trailer window, he had seen her stride to the practice arena. Luis heard her shrill voice instruct the old hand who had been with Grimaldi for thirty years, heard her give the order for Mamon to be released into the arena.

Ruda had wheeled the old, well-worn plinths into the center of the ring, and then stood waiting, hands on her hips. The massive lion moved slowly and cautiously through the makeshift barrier tunnel from his open cage. Luis inched open the window to hear her. Her voice rang out, a high pitched call: "Mamawwwwwwwwww, Mamawwwww UP . . .YUP YUP . . . Mamon . . . come on, angel . . . good boy mama's angel."

Mamon swung his massive black-maned head from side to side and then, to Luis's astonishment, reared up onto his hind legs and walked toward Ruda, his front paws swung toward her. He kept on walking toward her and then, as she called out to the animal, he turned, as if dancing for her. Her high-pitched voice called out a rolling 'Rr' sound—"REH! rey, REH . . . REH . . . "—and then Mamon jumped onto the red plinth. After steadying himself, he cautiously tested the plank, a thick wooden board balanced between the two plinths. Carefully, cautiously, right front paw patting the plank, he still balanced himself, and she now called: "HUPPPPPPPPPPPP! BLUE . . . BLUE . . . M'angel!"

The animal trod the narrow board toward the blue-based plinth. He eased himself into a sitting position, his thick tail trailing the ground as he perched.

Ruda moved closer and closer to the blue plinth, until she was close enough to be within the lion's territory. Only another trainer would know this was, in actual fact, reasonably safe. The animal sitting on the plinth, needing all four paws to give him balance, is unlikely or unable to attack, his hind quarters overhanging due to the position of his tail. If he attacked from a seated position, he would automatically lose his balance.

Luis couldn't take his eyes off Ruda as she moved in close, and then audaciously turned—leaving her back within a half foot of the animal. She never stopped talking, whispering encouragement, as she then knelt down on one knee, her head beneath the massive cat's.

Ruda gave a high-pitched command: "UP . . . UP . . . GREEeee GREEEE . . . " The green-based plinth was five feet in front of her.

She was encouraging him to leap from one pedestal to another, from the red to the green.

Mamon lifted his front paws and balanced himself on his hind legs on the pedestal. All his muscles strained as he made a flying jump, right over Ruda's head, onto the green pedestal.

She ran to him and gave him a tidbit, rubbing his nose. She then looked to the trailer window with a small, tight smile on her face. Finally she lifted both her arms, giving the final command for Mamon to head out of the arena.

Ruda gave a mocking bow to the small group of onlookers who applauded her, as Luis slunk away from the trailer window.

The word spread fast that the great Luis Grimaldi had lost his nerve. They joked that his wife had taken it from him.

✦ ✦ ✦

Grimaldi staggered slightly as he left the trailer now. The rain had not ceased and the ground was muddy. He made his way toward the rehearsal tent. The cashier who had talked with Ruda earlier that morning called out to him. He turned bleary-eyed toward her large brown umbrella.

"I can give you the advance, Mr. Grimaldi, if you come over and sign for it." Luis had not the slightest idea what she was talking about, and stumbled over to her.

"Your wife wanted an advance on your salary. If you need it, I've come back from the bank, I just require your signature."

Grimaldi mumbled incoherently, and she passed on, turning to see him slither and slide against one of the trailers. The cashier shrugged, disinterested; his drinking problem was well known.

The big man mumbled to himself. Not content with taking over his act, Ruda was trying to steal his money! He was going to face her, and nothing was going to stop him.

✦ ✦ ✦

Ruda had made the boys dismantle the cage arena twice, and reerect it. She timed them to the last second, and even bolted and heaved two of the walls herself; the whole operation was to take less than two minutes. This was tough going, the arena cage was very heavy and unwieldy, the tunnel sections even heavier. As they took it all apart for the third time, they moaned and muttered to one another, out of "Madame Grimaldi's" earshot.

Mike asked if they were to use the new pedestals, stacked outside the ring. Ruda pursed her lips and shook her head. "No, I'll do that first thing in the morning when I'm fresh. Let's just do the easy routine today, give them some exercise, and tomorrow we'll have a real crack at it. So for now, it's the herd, then the leap, followed by the roller roll."

Ruda called up to the electrician. "Can you give me a few spot-lights, in the usual places, just to keep them on their toes, red, green, and blue formation?"

A voice answered that he would rather have it be on her toes than his! A few spots came on and off. Ruda shaded her eyes, calling out to the technician again.

"The most important one is directly after the leap, Joe. Last time it was a fraction late."

Ruda paced up and down, her head shaking from side to side as she relaxed her shoulders. There was to be no music, this was simply a warm-up to get the cats used to the new place. It also kept the animals on their mettle after a long night's traveling; it would calm them.

The cages were now lined up, ready to herd in the animals. Ruda gave a look around the ring and did not see Luis, but two of the boys had already placed their chairs at either side of the arena, to watch over the act. They carried no guns; they could, if needed, break up trouble by creating noise and yelling.

"Okay, Mike, let's go for it!" she ordered at the top of her voice.

Ruda used the small trapdoor at the side and entered the arena, then turned back to head into the animals' entrance tunnel. When the act was live, she always entered from the tunnel itself, straight into the ring, as if she were one of the cats.

As she headed down the tunnel, she double-checked that the

sections were bolted, bending her head slightly where the bars joined at the top. Midway she signaled to Mike to release the cats on the count of ten, to coincide with the opening music bars. She tightened her thick leather gloves, her voice hissed . . . one . . . two . . . three . . . As she reached nine, she spun around, running into the arena, back down the tunnel into the wide caged arena. She carried only her short practice stick. She wore old trousers, a shirt knotted at the waist, and the used black leather boots, caked with mud and excreta. They had not seen a lick of polish since Luis had given them to her.

The cats were now released; any second they'd be heading in. Ruda paced herself; she bowed to the empty auditorium—she practiced every move to be performed in front of the live audience. Arms raised, she could feel the ground shudder as the animals charged down the tunnel. She felt a rush of adrenaline. She loved this moment, when the sixteen tigers hurtled into the main ring, as though frighteningly out of control, because she knew the cats understood who was their leader, which place each was to take. Ruda backed to the wall of the arena and picked up a heavy double-sided weighted ladder. The cats whirled around, forming a wide circle around her, as she stood in apparent nonchalance next to a small ladder plinth. They were loping, moving faster and faster. . . .

The circle tightened as she yelped a command. Her second command, hardly detectable, was a lift of her right hand to the lead tiger; she never took her eyes off him. Roja was the number one cat, and it was Roja who split the circle by breaking to his right. Now the cats gathered into two groups on either side of her. A third command, and the animals began to weave around each other.

The circle became tighter and tighter, closing in around her. Ruda became more vocal, now calling each tiger by name. They were high-pitched calls. Then, on a signal to Roja, the cats touched, pressing their bodies hard against one another. Ruda, her back to the small ladder, slowly eased herself up the steps one by one, as the cats kept circling, like a catherine wheel, turning and turning.

Ruda reached the top rung of the three-foot ladder. There was total silence as off-duty circus performers watched the rehearsal. Luis entered the arena, lifting the flap aside, and stood for a moment before he began to thread his way through the seats.

Ruda bellowed: "Down . . . R-OHja, down . . . Jajaja down!"

Tigers are instinctive fighters; the crossing of each other's body territory was very dangerous, accompanied by snarls and teeth-baring. But one by one they lay down side by side, until all sixteen tigers formed a wondrous carpet. Twice Ruda reprimanded two females for having a go at each other by banging the flat of her hand on the top rung of the ladder.

Those watching were uneasy now, aware of the danger. If a tiger accidentally knocked over the ladder by brushing too close, they could all attack.

More and more performers had slipped into the arena. But Ruda saw nothing, no one, her attention was riveted on the carpet of cats. Satisfied they were in place, she lifted both arms above her head, never stopping talking to them. Then she issued the command: "UPO . . . UPAHHHHHHHH."

Sixteen tigers rose—all in almost perfect formation—then lowered their heads. It was a magnificent sight—as the glorious carpet of gold and black stripes lifted magically into the air.

Ruda called out again, made it onto the top rung of the ladder and then flung herself forward, facedown, to lie spread-eagled across the cats. They began to move, carrying her around in a terrifying wheel. She then dropped to her feet, arms above her head, at the center of the seething mass. She flicked Roja with her stick and he broke the circle and spread wide at a run; the others followed, spreading wider, running around her as she gave a low bow. She held the bow for three long beats, then turned back toward the tigers who formed two lines facing her. Her voice cut through the air, high pitched, and up they reared to sit on their hindquarters. They clawed the air, Helga and Roja in a snarling match; Ruda pushed Helga aside and flicked her hand at Roja, stepping back. Facing them, she spread her arms wide, giving a small signal to Sasha, one of her females, leading the second section of the lineup.

They were ready, and she gave the command. "HUP . . . HUPPPPPPPPPPPPPPPPPPPPPPPP."

From their squatting position they all reared up to stand on their hind legs. Their growls and swiping paws denoted their displeasure. They were perfectly poised to attack—for tigers always attack from the front, never the rear. Shouting, she urged them back into a chorus line . . .

Grimaldi wanted to weep. She was spectacular. Even at the zenith of his career he had never attained such perfection. Her face shone, her eyes were brilliant in the spotlight, as though risking her life was an exhilaration. Her radiance humbled him and, drunk as he was, he bowed his head, trying to steady himself on the seat in front of him. The seats had not been battened down yet; the chair was loose and it fell forward, and Luis came down with it onto the second row of seats. The bang was as loud as a shot.

Ruda turned and saw him, and at the same time Sasha and Roja lost concentration, coming down onto all fours. Ruda gave the command to move out, and signaled for the watchers to get the trapdoor open—fast. One of the boys hurried to Grimaldi's side and helped him to his feet.

Ruda turned all her attention on Roja, dominated him, knowing that if he went into the tunnel the others would follow. As he hesitated she never took her eyes off him, then he wheeled around to head back down the tunnel. After a moment, the others followed him out. Ruda clamped down the trapdoor, shouting for Mike to hold the rest of the act.

She moved like a cat, but she didn't go for Grimaldi; instead she went for the boy who had helped him to his feet and grabbed him by the scruff of his neck.

"What the fuck do you think you're doing? You watch out for *me*. Were this place to go up like an inferno, *you watch out for me!*" She swiped him with the back of her hand, so hard that he fell to his knees.

Still ignoring Grimaldi, Ruda turned to the watcher to her left, and snapped for him to put the rest of the act on hold.

"*Now. Do it right now,* get to Mike, tell him to keep the cages shut!"

The boys ran, leaving the drunken man alone, his face flushed a deep red. Then slowly she removed her thick leather gloves and spoke to her husband, her voice low.

"Get out of here, Luis, get out before I have you thrown out."

Grimaldi held his own. Swaying slightly, he glared at her.

"I'm sorry, I fell, you know I'd never . . ."

Ruda snapped the glove in his face. "Get out of my sight, you drunken bum!"

Luis touched his cheek. "I want a divorce, you hear me, bitch? I want a divorce . . . *I want you out of my life!*"

The show continued for those performers still hanging around. Ruda gripped her husband by his shirt and hauled him to the exit.

She pushed him out, and he fell facedown in the mud. She turned on her heels and strode back into the tent. Seeing a sweeper standing with a wide long-handled broom, she ordered him to get the drunk out of there, and not to let him near the arena until she was through.

By the time she had finished the rehearsal, got the cats back into their cages and fed, it was after six. She hoped Luis had passed out so she wouldn't have to confront him, but when she returned to the trailer he was remarkably sober, and waiting for her.

The windows of the trailer were thick with condensation from the steaming coffee pot. She switched on the air conditioner. Without saying a word, Luis handed her a mug.

"I'm sorry, I should never have done that, I was drunk, I am ashamed, I'm sorry."

Ruda threw her coat over the heater and began to unbutton her shirt. "You know how dangerous it was. You don't need me to tell you that, dangerous and stupid, and from you of all people."

Grimaldi nodded glumly and held out his hand, but Ruda didn't take it. She unzipped her trousers, and kicked them off. He picked them and her shirt from where she tossed them, and took them to the laundry basket. She wore a silk one-piece bodysuit with dark green stains under the armpits. She didn't strip completely; after all the years they had been together, she was still self-conscious about her body. She put on an old robe, and wrapped it around her before she took a sip of the coffee. She uncoiled her hair, the nape of her neck still damp from the workout.

"Did you mean it, Luis? About the divorce?"

Grimaldi looked at her sheepishly and sat down. He held his big hands between his knees.

"I guess so, I've been wanting to talk to you about it for a while now, but . . ."

"But what?"

"Well, why not? We don't have a marriage, we haven't ever really had one, you know that . . . and she's, Tina's, going to have a baby."

"You've got kids all over Europe, what's one more? Anyway, knowing that little tart, how can you be sure it's yours!"

Grimaldi cocked his head. "It's mine, I may be worn out and past it, but my dick works, it's about the only thing that never lets me down."

"What about the act?" She tried to keep her voice casual, but she was shaking. He still wouldn't look at her. "Luis, what about the act? We're partners—if we divorce do you still want me to run the show?"

He turned to her then. "You can do what you like with it, it's not mine anyway, but . . . I'll still retain my fifty percent—half the animals are mine."

Ruda felt drained. "I see . . . so my money, all the money I've earned and poured into it, everything, all the new cats that I've trained, my cats, it's all split fifty-fifty, is that right?"

Luis nodded. "That's only fair, you had nothing when we met, everything you have is from me. I mean, if you want, you can pay me what the act is worth, what the animals are worth, and then, do whatever you want, but you can't use my name."

Ruda snatched the poster off the wall. "Look at it, Luis—it's not your name, it's mine! I've not used your name for the past two years, I don't want your name!"

"Just my act! You think nobody knows? My name is still a crowd-puller, may not be on the fucking headlines, but it's the Grimaldi Cats."

"It's not *your act anymore!*"

Grimaldi shook his head and half smiled. "All I want is my fair share, my cut. Anyone can take over an act. I can work in someone else."

"You can what? *What did you say?*"

"I said, I can train another girl to replace you. If you want to take the act as it stands, then pay me—it's as simple as that."

Grimaldi opened the trailer door. She snapped at him: "Where are you going?"

"I'm going out, okay? And while I'm gone, Ruda, just sit down and remember, remember where you came from, what you were before you met me. Sit on what you made your living on and *tell me how much you fucking owe me . . . !*"

The trailer rocked as he slammed the door. She gripped her head in her hands, wanting to rip her hair out. What did he know about pain? What could he know? She felt a burning sensation in her temples. He couldn't stand pain, but she could. She kicked the trailer wall, punched the doors, the walls, with all her strength until she gasped for breath. It was then that she shouted, "I was tested. He tested me, *I was Papa's favorite!*"

She began to pace the confined space, clenching and unclenching her hands. First Kellerman, now Luis, both wanting to take from her everything she had fought to get. She wouldn't let them, either of them. As she showered and changed, she tried to contain the blinding fury boiling up inside her. She forced herself to think what to do.

Ruda checked the cats one last time, staying a moment longer with Mamon than with the others. He was restless, as though he felt her anxiety, and he pressed himself close to the bars, then lay down, submissive. She reached to touch him. Ruda let his rough tongue lick her hand. She whispered to him. "You know, you know, I won't be kicked, I won't take it, nobody kicks me, yes? *Yes?*" She loved this creature more than any other living thing. It was Mamon, her angel, who had elicited from her a love she had believed herself incapable of feeling.

She clung to the bars. "I'm ready for him, I can deal with him, I am strong, I am strong."

The metal felt cold to her brow as she pressed closer and closer. The voice whispered to her, soft, persuasive, "You can do it, fight through the pain . . . that's my little girl, that's Papa's girl. You can do it, pain is sweet, pain is beautiful, come on Ruda . . . give your Papa what he wants, you love me, prove it!"

She was ready, ready to face Kellerman, ready to go to East Berlin. She pushed herself away from Mamon. "I'll be back!"

Ruda passed by the trailer, and through the window saw Luis take out a fresh bottle of brandy. She walked on. She caught the bus into the city center; first, she had gone to the taxi stand, but then changed her mind. She waited for a bus to take her into East Berlin.

◆ ◆ ◆

It was a strange experience crossing the shabby Kreuzberg district, which in the old days hugged the wall, but now was home to a large Turkish population. She was shocked to see anti-Semitic slogans spray-painted on the walls of the rundown houses: "*Ausländer Raus*" "Foreigners . . . get out!" Bricks were thrown at the bus as it passed through the area. The mostly women and children passengers cowered in their seats. More anti-Semitic slogans were smeared on the sites of former synagogues and on the walls of the Jewish schools. Ruda began to sweat as a group of young skinheads spat at the bus, their hands lifted, their voices screaming "*Sieg Heil!*" Their shouts made Ruda bow her head. She hissed under her breath, "Bastards . . . bastards!"

A woman seated in front of Ruda shook her fist at the skinheads, then turned to her companion, and they began talking to the rest of the occupants of the bus. "If your skin is the wrong color, if it isn't pale enough, if your hair is too dark, too curly, these pigs will attack. Something must be done! Why has this hatred been allowed to continue and fester? Turn the machine guns on them, fascist pigs!"

When Ruda got off she was engulfed in a strange fear. Two yards from the bus stop, she saw a huge poster of herself. The incongruity made her gasp, but the image calmed her, comforted her.

She took out her map, and looked for the direction to Kellerman's hotel. She hesitated, checked the dwarf's scrawled note, and headed down a dimly lit street to a small bed and breakfast establishment that could hardly be described as a hotel.

It was almost ten when Ruda walked into the dingy reception. There was no one around; she then turned to what looked like a guest register, scrawled all over with memos and messages. "T. Kellerman" was listed in Room 40. She waited another minute before heading to the elevator. On the fourth floor, she stood outside Kellerman's room listening to the sound of a television, the volume turned up loud. She tapped and waited, tapped louder, then the door inched open.

"They should have called from reception," he said petulantly as he opened the door wider. He was in his shirt, tie loosened, and he was wearing suspenders, wide, red suspenders. Ruda closed the door and looked around the small room, dominated by the TV set.

"Jesus, Tommy, what made you choose this dump?"

"It's cheap, nobody asks questions, and nobody's likely to come looking for me, that answer enough?"

"Yeah, I suppose so, but I'm surprised you haven't had a brick thrown through the window, or found a turd in your bed!"

"Got scared, did you?"

Ruda shrugged, then after a moment: "More like sickened."

She put her large leather bag on the edge of the bed. As she turned, Kellerman suddenly clasped her tightly around the thighs, and buried his head in her crotch. She didn't resist.

"Still working the same foreplay game, are we?" she asked sarcastically.

He chuckled, and stepped back. "Lemme tell you, that's turned on more women then I can count, they love it, hot breath steaming through their panties. Just a taste of what is to come, because when

I ease the skirt down, really get into it, no woman can resist me, not when I've got my tongue working overtime."

Ruda laughed and unbuttoned her coat, tossing it over her bag.

"You disgusting little parasite, I thought you'd have grown up by now, but then I suppose it's tough—not ever growing, I mean."

Kellerman hitched up his trousers and crossed to the mini bar. "Want a miniature drinkie? From your own miniature lover?"

He peered at the rows of bottles in the fridge and chose a vodka for himself.

"I won't have anything."

"Suit yourself," Kellerman said as he opened some tonic and found a glass. His stubby hands could reach only halfway around the tumbler.

Ruda sat on the bed watching him as he fixed his drink, dragged a chair from the small desk by the fridge, moved it closer to the bed, then waddled back to get his glass, handing it to her as he gripped the chair by the arms to haul himself into it.

Sitting, his feet hung just over the edge of the chair, small child's feet encased in red socks to match his suspenders, his scuffed shoes on the floor.

"Cheers!"

Kellerman drank almost half the contents of the glass, burped, and wrinkled his nose.

"So! You came. I was half expecting you not to turn up."

Ruda opened her bag and took out her cigarettes. Kellerman delved into his pockets for a lighter.

"Did you go to the cashier?" he asked, looking at the large leather bag.

"Yes."

He flashed a cheeky grin. "Good. I'm glad we understand each other. The license, all our papers, are in that drawer over there. They still look good . . . guy was an artist!"

Kellerman eased himself off the chair. "You may not believe this, but I don't like asking for the money."

Ruda laughed. "Asking? Blackmailing is the word I would use."

"You have to do what you have to do. I'm flat broke, and in debt to two guys in the U.S. It's been tough for me ever since you left."

Ruda smiled. "It was tough before I left. I'm surprised they employed you in Paris. Those folks worked hard for their dough. Way I heard it you were blacklisted, you'd steal from a kid's piggy bank, you have never given a shit for anyone but yourself. How long did you get?"

Kellerman shrugged. "Five years. It was okay, I survived, the cons treated me okay . . . the guards were the worst, bastards every one of them, called me monkey or chimpy."

"You must be used to nicknames by now . . ."

"Yeah, haw haw . . . sticks and stones may break my bones but . . ."

He leaned forward, a frown on his face. "I'm shrinking, Ruda, do you notice? Prison doc said it was someting to do with the curvature of my spine. I said to him, Jesus Christ, Doc, I can't get any smaller, can I? I said to him, if this goes on I'll be the incredible shrinking man, and he said . . ."

Kellerman shook his head as he chortled with laughter. "He said, that was done with mirrors! They built giant chairs and tables, then . . . fuck it! How could he know, eh? How could he know!"

Kellerman was referring to his obsession, a fun-house mirror he used to haul everywhere he went. The mirror distorted a normal human being, but it made Kellerman look tall and slender—normal. One night in a fit of rage he had smashed it to pieces, and wept like a child at his broken dream image. He turned now to peer at himself in the dressing table mirror, his head just reaching the top of the table. The effect was comical, even funny, but Kellerman was not a clown. He was a man filled with self-hatred, and convinced of the fact that if he had grown, he could have been recognized as handsome as a movie star, a Robert Redford, a Clint Eastwood.

He cocked his head, grinning. "You know they got drugs now to prevent dwarfism? If they detect it early enough, they pump you with steroids, and you grow. Ain't that something?"

Kellerman loathed his deformity; when drunk he was always ready to attack anyone he caught staring at him. The circus was his only employment, his short body rushing around the ring, being chased and thrown around. He opened another vodka and drank it neat from the small bottle.

"Did you work with the Frazer brothers in Paris?"

Ruda asked the question without really wanting a reply; her heart was hammering inside her chest. She had to get him into a good mood, she didn't have the money.

Kellerman nodded. "Yeah, the Frazers had bought my electric car just before I went to jail. So when I turned up and told them I needed a few dollars they put me in the act. My timing was right— you know little Frankie Godfrey? He had joined the act about four years ago. Well, he's been really sick, water on the brain maybe, I dunno. Some crazy woman a few years back got up from her seat and attacked him, she just hurtled into the ring and began knocking him around. The audience thought it was all part of the show, but she was a nut case. Ever since the poor sod's had these blinding headaches; still they paved the way for me to earn a few bucks. Then the management found out about me—gave me my walking papers, they told the Frazers to get rid of me. Cunts all of them."

"Serves you right, if you steal from the people who employ you, and virtually kill a cashier, what else do you expect? . . . I did that show, Monte Carlo, wasn't it?"

"I borrowed the dough, I was gonna pay it back. Yeah, Monte fuckin' Carlo, I only went there to date Princess Stephanie! . . . haw haw!"

Ruda laughed. "Oh yeah, where were you going to find two hundred thousand dollars? From Prince Rainier?"

Kellerman chortled, and pointed to her handbag. "I'm looking right at half that amount now! You know something, we made a good team, we could do it again, I'm good with animals."

"Fuck off . . . you hate anything with four legs."

He shrugged. "No, I'm serious. You hear what that high-wire act got paid for a stint in Vegas? I mean the real dough is in cabaret. And there's a double act with big cats, you know, mixed with magic—they make their panthers disappear. I dunno how the fuck they do it, but it's got to be a con. You ever thought of trying the Vegas circuit? I got contacts there, I mean maybe to have me in the act might not be a good thing, but I could manage you. I mean Grimaldi's washed up, or filled up with booze, I hear, and you were shit hot with that magic stuff."

"The day I need you to manage me, Tommy, *I'll* be washed up."

Kellerman continued talking about acts he had managed, and she let him carry on, only half listening. There had been a time when Ruda had felt deeply sorry for him, because she had been in the same dark place. In retrospect, she had made herself believe that that was the reason she had married him, it united them. Earlier, he had been the only connection to this past, now he was the reminder.

When they met, Kellerman was not as grotesque as he was now. He seemed boyish, innocent, his full-lipped mouth and exceptionally white even teeth always ready to break into a big smile. But as he aged, the anguish inside him, his self-loathing, not only seemed to have deformed his body, but was etched on his face.

She was so engrossed in her thoughts that Kellerman startled her when he suddenly hopped onto the bed beside her.

"You aren't listening to me!"

"I'm sorry, I was miles away."

Kellerman rested his head back against the pillows; his small feet in their red socks pushed at her back and irritated Ruda, so she got up and sat in the chair he had vacated. She was tense, her hands were clenched, but she told herself to be patient, to be nice to him. She mustn't antagonize him.

"Strange coming back after all these years, isn't it?"

She made no reply. He tucked his short arms behind his head, and closed his eyes. "You think it's all stored away, all hidden and then—back it comes. I've had a long time to think about the past, in prison, but being here, I dunno, it makes me uneasy, it's like a secret drawer keeps inching open."

Ruda was trying to figure out how to tell him that she did not have the money. She racked her brain for a deal she could offer him. She was surprised by the softness, the sadness in his voice; he spoke so quietly she had to lean forward to hear him.

"When my mama handed me over, there were these two women, skeletons, I can remember them, their faces, almost as clearly as my mama's. Maybe even clearer. One woman was wearing a strange green satin top, and a torn brown skirt . . . filthy, she was filthy dirty, her head shaved, her face was like a skull. She hissed at Mama through her toothless gums. 'Tell them he's twelve years old, tell the guards he's twelve.' My mama held on to me tightly. She was so confused and said, 'He's fourteen, he's fourteen but he's small, he's just small.' The woman couldn't hear because one of the guards hit her, then I saw her sprawled on the ground. I still remember her shoes, she had one broken red high-heeled shoe, and a wooden clog on her other foot."

"I've heard all this! Come on, why don't we go someplace for a meal." She had to get him out, stop him drinking, talk to him, reason with him.

Kellerman ignored her. "The next moment Mama and me were pushed and shoved into a long line. Eva, my little sister, was crying, terrified, and then the second woman whispered to Mama: 'Twins . . . say your children are twins.' "

Ruda arched her back. "Shut up!" Her heart began to beat rapidly, as if she were being dragged under water. She felt the damp darkness, smelled the stench, and she clenched her teeth, not wanting to remember.

"Don't, Tommy, stop . . . I don't want to listen!" But she could hear the voice: "Twin . . . *twins* . . . TWINS," and she got to her feet, hugging herself tightly. She moved as far away from the bed as possible, to stand by the window. She could feel the hair on the nape of her neck stand up, her mouth felt dry, and the terror came back. The rats were scurrying across her. In the gloom, the white faces of the frightened, and the gaunt faces of the starving glowered at her. The stinking sewer water rose up, inch by inch, and they held her up by her coat collar so that she wouldn't drown. A blue woolen coat with a dark blue velvet collar. Hers had been blue, her sister's red.

"Don't, Tommy, please don't . . ."

But he wasn't hearing her, he was too wrapped up in his own memories. He gave a soft heart-breaking laugh. Eva was almost as tall as he, with the same curly black hair: She was only ten years old. Eva had always been so protective of him, so caring. How he had adored her!

Ruda moved closer to the bed determined to calm him, but it was as if he were unaware of her presence. He stared at the ceiling and began to cry.

" 'My son is fourteen,' Mama shouted, and all around us was mayhem, but all I did, all I could do, was keep staring at the second woman who had approached us. She was wearing a pink see-through blouse. It was too small, you could see her breasts, her ribs, she was covered in sores. She had on a blue skirt, it had sequins on it, some hanging off by their threads. The skirt must have been part of a ball gown, because it had a weird train. It was gathered up and tied in a knot, a big knot between her legs. Like the other skinny woman, she had one high sling-backed gold evening shoe and what looked like a man's boot. I was so fascinated by these two skeleton women that I couldn't catch what was going on. But the next moment, a guard dragged Eva away; he kicked Mama, kicked her so hard she screamed in agony. She was screaming, screeching like a bird: 'He's fourteen, but he's a dwarf, he's a dwarf, please don't hurt him, he's strong, he can work, but don't hurt him, don't kick him in his back, please . . .' "

He sobbed.

"She said it, my mama said it, for the first time I heard her say what I was. . . ."

Ruda sat on the bed, she reached out to touch Kellerman's foot, to stop him talking, but he withdrew his leg, curling up like a child. His voice was no longer a whimper, but deeply angry. "He took me then, pointed with his white glove, first to me, and then to a lineup of children on the far side of the station yard. That was the first time I saw him, that was the first time. I've never told you, I have never told you that, have I?"

Ruda's nails dug into her own arms. She was pushing shut her own memories with every inch of willpower she possessed. She forced herself to move closer to him. "Stop it, Tommy, I won't hear. I won't listen to you."

"Yes, you will," he snapped. "You will listen, because I want you to know, you more than anyone else. I want you to know."

She wanted to slap him, but she forced herself to contain her mounting, blinding anger. "I know, you've told me all this before, and we made a promise . . ."

He was like a child, his red-socked feet kicking at the bedspread. "Well fuck you! I won't keep the promise—I want you to know!"

He clenched his hands, punching the bed. "I was dragged away from Mama, and still she screamed, first for Eva and then for me, but no one took any notice, everyone was crying and shouting, but I heard her clearly call out to me . . . 'Wait for me at the station, I'll be at the station.' "

Ruda snatched one of the pillows and held it over his face. "Stop it! I know this, I don't want to hear any more!"

She pressed the pillow down hard on his face, and he made no attempt to fend her off or push the pillow aside. After a moment she withdrew it and looked down at his face. His beautiful, haunted, pain-wracked eyes looked up at her.

"No more, Tommy. Please . . ."

He nodded, and turned away, his cheek still red from the pressure of the pillow. "Oh, Ruda . . . she never said which station. She never said which station."

Ruda lay beside him, not touching, simply at his side. He was calmer now, and she heard him sigh, once, twice.

"You know, Ruda, no matter how many years have passed, how long ago it was, I still hear her calling me. Every station, in every town I have ever been to, there is a moment . . . it comes and goes so fast, but no matter where I am, here or in America, in Europe, whatever station, I say to myself: 'Which station, Mama, where did you wait for me? Did Eva find you? Why didn't you tell me which station?' It's strange, I know they're dead, long, long ago, but there is this hope that some day, some time I'll be at a station and my mama will be there, with Eva. Walking the streets, at every corner I think maybe, just maybe I'll see Eva. I never give up hope, I never give up."

Ruda whispered she was sorry, and he turned to face her.

"Is it the same for you?"

He searched her eyes, wanting and needing confirmation that he was not alone in his pitiful hope. The amber light in her cruel eyes startled him. With a bitter half-smile she said: "It is not the same for me. It never was."

With some satisfaction she felt the chains, the locks tighten on her secrets. Kellerman leaned up on his elbow, touching her cheek with his index finger.

"I'll tell you something else my mama said. She said never tell a secret to anyone, a secret is a secret, and if you tell it, it is no longer a secret. You are the only person I have ever told what they made me do, and what I have done since. I mean, I admit I have stolen, I am a thief, I know I did wrong. I stole from the circus, from my people, but they are not me, they don't know who I am."

Ruda sat up, took a sneaking glance at his alarm clock. It was almost ten-thirty, she knew she had to discuss the money, and the fact that she didn't have it.

"I'm not blackmailing you, Ruda. All I want is my fair share."

It was as if he had read her mind. He rubbed the small of her back. "You don't hate me, do you? You know I've no one else but you."

His touch made her cringe inside. He rested his hands on her shoulders and stood up behind her, planting a wet kiss on the nape of her neck.

"If you do that again, I'll throw you off the bed!" She pushed him away. "Get off me!"

Kellerman began to jump up and down as if the bed were a trampoline. "Oh you liked it once. You couldn't get enough of me once!"

He slipped his arms around her neck, she could feel his erect penis pressing into the small of her back.

"Let me have you one last time, please, Ruda, the way you liked it, let me do it!"

Ruda didn't push him away this time. There was no anger in her voice, just revulsion.

"I never liked it. I loathed it so much I used to get physically sick. Now take your hands off me or I'll elbow you in the balls. They are about the only normal-sized thing about you, as I recall— and I will make your voice even higher."

He released his hold, but remained standing behind her. "Did you mean that? Did you mean what you just said?"

She sighed, angry with herself. She had to be nice, she had to be calm. "Oh come on, Tommy, we both know why I married you, so why pretend otherwise. Sit down and have another drink."

"Physically sick, I made you vomit?"

She couldn't stop herself as she snapped back: "Yes, as in puke."

Again, she could have slapped herself; never mind him, why was she getting into this? She could so easily have laughed it off, teased him into a good mood, but it was as if she were caught on a roller coaster, and out came words, her face twisted in a vicious grimace.

"Sick, you made me sick! Have you any idea what it felt like? To have you clasped at my back, shoving your dick up my arse? It was like I had some animal clinging to me. All I did was grit my teeth and pray for you to get it over with. I hated it, hated every second you touched me with those squat square hands, pawing me like a dog, rough hands, hideous rough hands like dog's paws."

Kellerman was stricken. He backed away from her, treading the mattress as if on water. Ruda glared. Her eyes frightened him because he knew what she was going to say next.

"But then you, Tommy, you must really know what it felt like, what it really felt like . . . because you know, don't you, Tommy?"

His small hands clenched into fists. "You fucking bitch. Whatever I have done, for you to throw that in my face . . ."

"I warned you to shut up, but no—you kept on and on. I warned you."

Kellerman slithered off the bed, and punched Ruda hard in the groin, then he reached for her bag, shouting at her.

"Give me my money, and get out, I never want to see you again—you whore, you two-faced bitch!"

Ruda snatched her bag back, hugging it tightly to her chest. He made a grab for the handle, and again she stepped back but he had the handle gripped in his hand, and he tugged. Kellerman was very strong and they struggled. Suddenly he released his hold and Ruda fell backward.

"You haven't got it, have you? You lied, you haven't got my money."

Ruda was shaking, she fumbled with the bag, lying. "Yes, I have, but I want our marriage license before you get it."

Kellerman crossed to the wardrobe and opened a drawer, his back to Ruda. He delved around, and then threw the envelope at her.

"Take it—and you owe me more than one hundred thousand. I saved your skin, I gave you a life, you bitch. If it wasn't for me you'd still be on the streets, you'd still be a whore, a cheap disease-riddled whore . . . taking it up the arse like a dog."

She spat at him, and he spat back, then kicked out at her again. "Whore!"

She swung the bag and it hit him in the face, he dived away from her and picked up the chair. "Come on, lion tamer, try me, try and tame me, *come on.*"

Kellerman pushed at her with the chair, she thrust it away, and he crashed it against her thigh. She stumbled against a coffee table, tripped and fell backward. He came at her, the chair above his head. "You can't fight me, Ruda, I'll fucking beat the living daylights out of you!"

She rolled to one side as the chair crashed down onto the table. The heavy green ashtray slid to the floor. Ruda grabbed it, and as Kellerman came forward to hit her again, she held one chair leg with her left hand, and with her right hit him with the ashtray.

Kellerman seemed stunned for a moment. He touched his temple, saw the blood on his hand. "You asked for it now!"

He started to shriek, jumping up and down like a chimpanzee, then threw the chair aside and grabbed the bedspread, a bright red candlewick bedspread, holding it up and out in front of him like a matador. "Come on . . . come on, Ruda. Try, try and hit me!"

Ruda lunged at him, and he dodged aside, laughing, tossing the bedspread this way and that. The red blurred, like a red-hot fire in her brain. "Stop it, Tommy . . . *just stop it!*"

"Ohhhhhhhhhh, you never used to say that to me, you used to say, 'More, more, I love it.' That's what you used to say. *You loved it from the dog in heat . . . come on, bitch!*"

The swirling bedspread swished this way and that, and the next minute she was on top of him, throwing the bedspread over his head, and the heavy ashtray came down, again and again. The bedspread swamped him, he struggled frantically. She heard him laughing, shrieking that she had missed him and it drove her into a frenzy. Ruda hit him, over and over again. She could feel his head—at one point she held it firmly in her left hand, pressing it down as she struck him. She could feel the blows finding his face, again and again.

She didn't know how many times she had struck him, but at last he was still and she sat back on her heels.

"Tommy? . . . *Tommy?* Get up!"

He lay still, and she pulled at the coverlet, and drew it away from his head. His face was a mass of blood, bloody bubbles frothed at his mouth and nose. She pulled herself away from him.

"Oh God . . . Tommy, get up! . . . *Get up!*"

He was motionless, his body swathed in the coverlet. She felt for his pulse, could find no heartbeat. She backed away, terrified, and sat leaning against the wall, her legs stretched out in front of her. She could feel every muscle tensing, then giving way as she slithered down the wall to sit like a rag doll.

"Oh God, now what do I do . . . tell me what to do?"

The television screen flickered, and she crawled over and turned up the volume, afraid someone could hear. Slowly, she began to think logically, and to calm down.

"Get out fast, save yourself, Ruda . . . get out, be careful, no one must know you came here. You never came here . . ."

Ruda picked up the envelope and looked for the marriage license. She then took all his papers and stuffed them into her bag. His passport, his diary, his address book. She dragged him by his feet to the side of the bed, then attempted to lift him, and it was then that the terrible realization dawned. Cradled in her arms was the only link to her past. Only Kellerman knew, he was the only person she had ever told, and now she had killed him. She sobbed because she remembered what it had meant to be able to tell someone, someone who had shared the same darkness. She hugged him tightly. Hard, dry, tearless sobs shook her body as she recalled how, shortly after they had arrived in the United States, Tommy had tried to purge the past that clung to each of them.

In their small trailer he slammed down two tumblers on the table and opened a bottle of bourbon, hitching himself up onto a chair oposite Ruda. He had filled a glass almost to the rim before he pushed it toward her.

"Right. You and me are gonna get loaded, and we're gonna let the ghosts free, because I think we'll both go crazy if we don't. We got a new life. Now we open and close the old. So, cheers!"

It had been one long, memorable night as they tried to exorcise the terrors that haunted them. The more they had drunk, the more horrors they had whispered. They had cried, they had comforted one another, and they had promised to keep these terrible revelations secret.

Now Ruda rocked him gently. She had broken the pact, she had hurt him more than any living soul could have done. She had thrown back in his face what he had been forced to do in shame. "I'm sorry, Tommy, forgive me. . . ."

His blood stained her face, clung to her hair, but she held him close in a last embrace. Eventually her gentle rocking stopped. Only Tommy knew she had killed before; no one must know she had killed again.

She began to gasp with panic, unable to get her breath. She felt dizzy and filled the glass he had used with water. She gulped it down, her hands shaking uncontrollably.

She saw her reflection in the mirror, the bloodstains, her frightened eyes staring back at her.

"It was different for me, Tommy. For you, every station, every corner. For me, every mirror." She put her hands over her ears as if to block out those words: *"Twins . . . twins . . . twins . . ."*

Ruda shouted, "I know she is alive. . . . *I know, I know!*"

The fury rose up within her, the fury which had kept her alive in the early years, a fury which now gave her the inner strength to survive. With a forced calmness, she began to erase all trace of her presence in the room.

Ruda packed all of Kellerman's belongings in his case; she emptied every drawer, checked the bathroom and collected his shaving equipment. They would find out who he was soon enough, but they would also find out something else. Ruda took Kellerman's toilet bag in her hand and rifled through it, and found the razor. She hurried to his side, rolled up his left sleeve until she found what she was looking for.

The razor slit deep into his arm. . . . She cut a square, and began to slice deep, cutting away the tattoo, but then fell back. As she sliced the artery his blood spurted over her face, her chest. Kellerman was not dead. Her rage went out of control.

She wanted to be sick, could feel the bile rising from her stomach. But she had to stay calm. She picked up the ashtray and hit him again, and again, her teeth clenched as she used all her strength. Then she waited, knew this time he had to be dead, and she carried the heavy marble ashtray into the bathroom, washed it, dried it, left it wrapped in the stained bloody towel, sure it was clean of prints. Then she washed around the sink, the taps. Suddenly she caught sight of her reflection again. Her eyes were crazy, her face white, blood rivulets now running like tears down her face. She backed out of the bathroom, rubbing frantically at her skin.

She had to face Kellerman again. The force of the last blow had made his head jerk sideways. His top set of dentures had fallen out.

As she tried to drag and push his body under the bed, the heel of her boot ground the dentures into the carpet. She was panting now, but she kept on working. She cleaned the room, the door handles, anything she might have touched. Then she found Kellerman's hat, was about to tuck it into his case, but changed her mind. She turned over the blood-soaked rug he had been lying on, tucking the stained area beneath the bed. She then fetched the DO NOT DISTURB sign and hung it on the door. Carrying Kellerman's belongings in his case, wearing his hat, she slipped down the stairs. There was still no one in reception; she grabbed the book, and tore out the pages with Kellerman's name.

✦   ✦   ✦

Ruda was back at her trailer by midnight. She could hear Luis snoring loudly, his door ajar. She slipped out as silently as she had crept in and went over to the freezer trailer. Knowing she wouldn't sleep, Ruda needed to keep herself busy, and she began to prepare the morning's feed for the cats. She was so intent on her work that she didn't hear the door open. When Luis spoke she sprang back in shocked surprise.

"Jesus Christ, what are you doing? Do you know what time it is?"

"I couldn't sleep."

"I saw the lights on, I thought someone was breaking in. What are you doing, it's after midnight . . ."

Ruda continued cutting the meat. "I couldn't sleep because of your snoring! You left your door open, I've told you to keep it shut!"

Luis grinned sheepishly, and offered to give her a hand. She refused, and he came to her side, "I'm sorry, I know what I did this afternoon was unforgivable. . . ."

He backed away from her then, a look of horror on his face. Her blouse was covered with blood.

"Why haven't you got one of the rubber aprons on? Have you seen your shirt?"

Ruda looked at her shirt covered with Kellerman's blood.

"It doesn't matter, it was falling apart. I'll chuck it out in the morning. You go back to bed, I'll be a while yet."

Again Luis offered to help her, but she ignored him, and after a moment he left. Ruda washed down the tables and cleaned the knives, hammer, and hatchets before she scrubbed her own arms with a wooden brush, paying particular attention to her nails.

She stared at her left wrist, and once more the full impact of what she had done that night dawned on her. But she would not give in to it, she pressed it down further and further inside her, locking it out of sight of her mind.

She took off her blouse and stuffed it into Kellerman's case. When she saw that the inside of her raincoat was stained, she knew she would have to destroy it along with the rest of his belongings.

Ruda returned to her trailer and changed into an old sweater, and an old pair of Luis's trousers. She then carried Kellerman's suitcase, her raincoat, shirt, and trousers to the big garbage barrels. She tossed his case into the huge bins which were waiting for the morning collection. She then carried Kellerman's papers and her marriage license to the main incinerators and eased back the burning-hot lid. She stuffed the papers inside, one by one, making sure each caught fire. She watched the flames slowly lick and eat his treasured green passport, watched the black letters disintegrate. The charred black smoke made her so desperate to replace the lid that she forgot to use the holder, but picked up the red-hot lid of the incinerator in her bare hand. Her burning skin hissed, but she didn't even feel the pain.

There was a low rumble of thunder and the rain became heavier. The ground was still muddy underfoot, and she stumbled over the gangplanks in her haste to get inside. In the vast arena, all the animals were sleeping. The heaters were on full blast, and three night lights gave off a soft pink light. Ruda headed toward her cages as there was a second rumble of thunder. The animals loathed thunder, and lightning made it even worse.

Ruda passed the tigers, who were huddled together; a few raised their heads as they recognized her smell, then returned to sleeping. Only Mamon was awake, his amber eyes bright. Ruda pressed close to the cage and called to him; he crawled on his belly toward the bars and rubbed them with his head. She stayed with Mamon for a while, comforted by him.

By the time she got into bed she was exhausted. She drew the sheet to her naked body, tired but relieved it was over. Kellerman's passport, their marriage license, the hotel guest register sheet, all were charred to a cinder, gone. It was over at last, and there was no witness, no one to threaten her newfound security.

Ruda concentrated hard, just as she had done as a child, waited until she felt the leaden weight creep upward from her toes, to her knees, to her arms, to her heart. She breathed deeply, willing her mind to lose consciousness. Gradually she allowed the weight to cover and spread, from her lungs to her mouth. She slept in a deep, dreamless whiteness, protected, peaceful; no one could break through that whiteness.

4

THE NIGHT THAT Tommy Kellerman died was the night Baroness Maréchal tried to kill herself, it was the night she experienced the horror of a living death, the terrible white weight she was powerless to control or stop. The attack had left her so exhausted she remained sedated the next day.

Vebekka had no memory of Dr. Franks's visit, or of how many people monitored her slow recovery to consciousness.

Dr. Franks asked that Anne Marie be allowed to visit him at his office. He also wanted another interview with the baron and Helen Masters, to find more clues to Vebekka's mental disorder.

It was agreed that Hilda be brought in to sit with the baroness during Anne Marie's absence.

When Hilda reached the suite, the baroness was in a deep sleep. Hilda sat down in a chair by the bed. Soon, all that could be heard in the vast silent bedroom was the clicking of her knitting needles.

Vebekka slept peacefully, her hands folded on the starched white linen sheet. She was wearing a white frilly negligee that couldn't disguise the sharp bones of her neck and shoulders, the thinness of her arms. Her face was drawn. There were deep dark circles beneath her closed eyes.

Saline and glucose drips were still hooked to Vebekka's hands. The tubes and needles had left dark black bruises. A thick bandage covered her left wrist. The room was filled with flowers and baskets of fruit, and their scent was very heavy. Hilda would have liked to open the window, but it was raining.

Finally, Vebekka stirred and turned her head to face the maid. "Would you be so kind as to take the drips out of my hand? It hurts me."

"I don't think I can, Baroness, Anne Marie is not here, and the baron and Dr. Masters are also out."

Vebekka sighed and Hilda returned to her knitting. Suddenly Vebekka ripped off the adhesive, pulled out the needles and tossed them aside.

Vebekka smiled coyly at Hilda, and curled up on her side. Hilda could do nothing but pick up the adhesive from the floor, and hang up the drips, switching them off.

"Hilda, will you call room service? I want some vanilla ice cream, with chocolate sauce and nuts, and those chocolate biscuits."

Hilda obliged, and in due course a trolley was sent up with some chocolate biscuits and the ice cream. She helped Vebekka sit up, and watched in amazement as the baroness slowly began to eat. Like a squirrel she nibbled and sucked at the spoon with such childish delight that Hilda felt even more motherly toward her than before; she tried to hint that perhaps eating so much sweet food was not good for her, but her words were ignored. Slowly, Vebekka demolished the entire tray of sweets.

Vebekka snuggled down in bed, dark chocolate stains around her mouth and on her fingertips. The clicking of Hilda's knitting needles was soothing, and she slept again. When a roll of thunder was heard, her hand slipped from the warmth of the covers to hold Hilda's, and the knitting was quietly put aside.

Anne Marie inched open the door, and crept into the room; she put her fingers to her lips and looked at the dressing table. She began to take all the bottles of medicine and pills and then she rifled the vanity cases. Her arms full of bottles, she came to Hilda's side and whispered. "The doctor said she is to have no more medication, no more sedation, unless from him!"

Anne Marie hurried from the room and returned with a large packet, unwrapped it, and held it out to show Hilda.

"You know what this is?"

Hilda shook her head, and put her fingers to her lips for Anne Marie to lower her voice.

"It's a straitjacket! I don't know about this great doctor, if you ask me he's yet another quack . . . so I got this just in case."

Anne Marie put the jacket down, was about to leave when she saw that the drips were not attached. "Who took those out?"

Hilda gripped Vebekka's hand and whispered, "I did, they were causing her pain; let her sleep."

Anne Marie pursed her lips. "She needs glucose, she's got to keep up her strength. I'll have to redo them."

Hilda felt the baroness's fingers tighten, her grip was so tight it hurt her. Hilda knew she was awake, but she didn't give her away.

"When she wakes, I'll call you, but she has just eaten, and I think it is better she sleep."

Anne Marie hesitated and then walked to the door. "But I have not seen them, and I will not take any responsibility. . . ."

The grip relaxed, and Hilda gently patted Vebekka's hand. She straightened the bedcovers, and was touched when the sick woman slipped her arms around Hilda's neck and kissed her in gratitude.

"I have a terrible fear of needles—of things in my body—she knows, but she hates me. Thank you."

Hilda smiled, returned to her chair. She picked up her knitting, and Vebekka laughed softly. "Not knitting needles, though!"

✦　✦　✦

Dr. Franks swiveled in his chair. "Your nurse, Anne Marie, says your wife has some kind of, well, not exactly an obsession, but boxes, vanity boxes . . . she always travels with three, sometimes four, yes?"

The baron looked puzzled. "Yes, they are part of her luggage, one is for her jewelry, one for makeup, one for medical and . . . I suppose it seems excessive, but not out of the ordinary. I can't understand why on earth the girl would even discuss my wife's traveling accessories with you!"

Franks leaned on his elbows. "Because I asked. You and your wife travel extensively? And these boxes always accompany her?"

"Yes, so do our cases, and trunks. Perhaps you will find some ulterior motive in the fact I always have more . . ."

Franks interrupted. "I am interested only in your wife at the moment, Baron, and the fact she always travels with an extensive wardrobe, but rarely if ever wears three quarters of the contents. According to Anne Marie many items your wife insists on traveling with have *never* been worn, yes? What I am trying to determine is, does your wife appear, in your personal opinion, to have items of clothing in very different styles? Does she, perhaps, appear to you as different characters, or seem different to you at times?"

"That is the entire reason I am here. My wife has periods of sanity and insanity."

Franks wandered around the room. "Has anyone ever suggested to you that your wife may have a personality disorder? Could she possibly be a multiple personality?"

The baron shook his head and glared at Helen Masters.

Franks turned his attention to her. "What do you think?"

"No, I don't think she is, or I didn't, but she said something that'll interest you. I wrote it down actually."

Helen opened her bag and took out a small notebook. "When I found her last night, she said, 'We have done something terrible.' Not I, but we."

The telephone rang. Franks snatched it up, but spoke only a second before he handed it to the baron.

"It's for you, long distance. If you need privacy, I am sure Dr. Masters and I can . . ."

The baron gestured with his hand for them to stay, as he listened to the caller. He then covered the mouthpiece. "It's all right, it's Françoise, my secretary, from Paris."

The call went on for some time, the baron saying little but making notes. Helen whispered to Franks. "She is very particular about her clothes, but I have never noticed a marked difference in styles—say, little girl to tart. I would simply say that the baroness has a wardrobe any woman would be envious of. However, she does seem to be very obsessive about the vanity cases."

Helen was interrupted as the baron dropped the phone back on the hook and sighed. "Gerard, my man in New York, has been having great difficulty tracing my wife's family. He started at her old modeling agency. They had no record of Vebekka ever having signed with them. They then passed him on to someone who had run the agency before them. He said that he never had anyone by the name of Vebekka, but later that evening he called back to say he had made a mistake, that in fact he had represented a girl called Rebecca Lynsey; he recalled she later changed her name to Vebekka, using just her Christian name for work. He had no records on hand but would see if he could find his ex-wife, who ran the business with him. But one thing he was sure about, or as sure as he could be."

The baron seemed very disturbed as he continued: "He said that my wife's maiden name, Lynsey, was not her real name, but one used for modeling. He could not recall ever having heard her real last name. Why would she have lied to me? I don't understand it!"

Franks rubbed his head. "But when her father died, didn't you see a name, something to indicate Lynsey wasn't her family name?"

The baron shook his head. "Gerard'll call again as soon as he has anything else. He's going to Philadelphia tonight. I don't understand. Lynsey was the name on her passport, I'm sure of it. I've asked him to fax any new information to the hotel."

Franks raised an eyebrow to Helen. "She has never referred to herself as Rebecca?"

The baron shook his head. "No, never. I have always known her as Vebekka Lynsey."

"When she was in New York, did she meet anyone there, have friends there?"

"No, we have mutual friends, or family friends, but I have never seen anyone walk up to her and call her Rebecca, if that is what you mean. I have never seen her birth certificate. There never seemed to be a reason before now, that is, if there *is* a valid reason now!"

Franks's eyes turned flinty as he said, "I am simply trying to find clues to your wife's mental problems because I want to begin my treatment as soon as she is physically capable of walking into this place unaided."

The baron's antagonism irritated Franks, but he didn't show it. Pleasantly he asked:

"Yesterday—Baron? are you listening to me?—you recalled the first time you witnessed your wife's mental instability, yes?"

The baron nodded. Franks asked if he could recall any other instances. The baron sighed, crossing his legs, staring at his highly polished shoes.

"I mentioned the circus. To be quite honest there have been so many, over so many years and . . ."

He paused, and Franks knew the baron had just remembered something; he could see it in the way the baron frowned, then hesitated, as if recalling the moment and then dismissing it. Franks leaned forward. "Yes? What is it?"

The baron shrugged. "It was in the late seventies; this episode had no connection to any of the children. We were in New York. We were at my apartment, reading *The New York Times*. She was reading the real estate section, while I had the rest of it. Suddenly she snatched the paper from my hands; as she did, it fell onto the table and the coffee pot tipped over me. I don't think she intended to spill the coffee, though I believed she had taken my paper for some perverse reason—perhaps because I wasn't paying enough attention to her. I don't know. Sometimes she is incredibly childish. I suppose I was silly too, because I insisted she give me back the paper. She refused. We had an argument, not a very pleasant one, and . . ."

The baron shrugged his shoulders, as if he suddenly felt the episode not worth pursuing. Franks pressed him. "Go on . . . she took the rest of the paper, and then what?"

"Well, as I recall, I went into my bathroom, showered, and was dressing when the maid said there seemed to be some fracas in the foyer. Next door to the building is a small newsstand. My wife, still in her dressing gown, was, so I was told, in the foyer, her arms full of newspapers. When I went down I found her sitting on the foyer floor, ripping the newspapers apart, throwing pages aside. She was on her hands and knees, scouring each page, but to this day, I have no idea what she was looking for. All I know is it was very embarrassing, and it took a great deal of cajoling to get her to return to the apartment."

Franks waited, expecting more, but the baron gestured with his hands. "That's it, really."

"Did you ever ask her why she wanted the papers?"

"Of course."

"Did she give you an explanation?"

"No, she actually didn't speak for over a week. She seemed very elated, slightly hysterical at that time, but I couldn't get a word out of her as to why she was behaving in such a way, or what on earth had sparked the breakdown."

"Breakdown?"

"Well, that is what the therapist called it. Vebekka calmed down eventually, and even seemed to forget the entire incident."

"Did you ever check through the papers, find anything that provided a reason for her behavior?"

The baron shook his head. "I took it to be just another of her—problems."

Franks remained silent for a moment before asking if the baron could get his contact in the United States to obtain copies of the newspapers from that day. The baron looked to Helen Masters with an exasperated shrug of his shoulders, but he agreed to try.

Franks fell silent, closing his eyes in concentration, and then asked, softly, when the baron said his wife behaved childishly, whether this meant she also spoke like a child.

"I meant it in a manner of speaking. Her act was childish. She didn't, as far as I recall, speak in a childlike voice."

Franks noted again a fleeting look of guilt, or recall, passing over the baron's face. "Yes? . . . You've remembered something else?"

The baron stared at the wall. "Last night I was wakened by her crying. I was confused because it sounded—dear God I've never thought of it before—like a child . . . so much so that for a moment, in my half-sleep, I thought it was one of the children, before I remembered they were in Paris."

Franks waited. After a long pause the baron continued.

"I went into her room and she was sitting up in bed. There was a shadow on the wall from the drapes. She was sobbing, pointing to the wall. She said, oh yes, she said the drapes were a . . . no, they were a 'Black Angel.' Then she said over and over, 'It wasn't true! It wasn't true.' I have no idea what she meant, but when I closed the drapes tightly and there was no more shadow she went back to sleep. But her voice . . ."

The baron looked to Helen, helpless.

"It was like a little girl, the way she shook her shoulders, and . . . that hiccup, you know, the way children do? It was as if she were a child having a nightmare."

Franks clapped his hands. "Now we are getting somewhere, and I think some tea would go down well. For you Baron? And you, Helen?"

Before either had time to reply Franks had scuttled out, but he did not close the door. He returned in a moment, after barking to some unseen assistant that he wanted tea, and produced a children's picture book. He held it like a piece of evidence, as if in a court of law.

"Your wife slipped into her handbag a similar book yesterday while she was waiting in reception. Interesting?"

"When did she do that?" asked Helen Masters.

"When she was here, sitting with Maja. Maja saw her. Odd, don't you think? Especially since it's in German. Do you know whether this book exists also in French, or in English?"

The baron was standing with his back to the room, staring out the window, his hands deep in his trouser pockets. "How would I know?"

"Has your wife ever been involved in shoplifting?"

"No, never, my wife is not a thief!" the baron snapped.

Helen took the tea tray from Maja at the door and carried it to the desk. Franks joked that kleptomania was about the only thing the baroness had not been diagnosed for! His attempt at humor failed, and Helen quickly passed the teacups around, then sat on a hard-backed chair.

Franks seemed unware of the atmosphere in the small room. He munched one biscuit after another until the plate was cleared.

"Would you say your wife suffered from agoraphobia?"

The baron replied curtly that his wife was not agoraphobic, or claustrophobic, turning to Helen as if for confirmation. She wouldn't meet his eyes.

Franks brushed the biscuit crumbs from his cardigan. "But she is obsessive, tell me more about her obsessions."

"What woman isn't!" the baron retorted, and then he apologized. "I'm sorry—that was a stupid reply, under the circumstances. Forgive me, but I find this constant barrage of questions disturbing, perhaps because I am searching for the correct answers, and I am afraid that everything I say, when placed under the microscope as it were, makes me appear as if I have not been caring enough, when, I assure you, nothing could be further from the truth."

The room was silent. The baron had cupped his chin in his hands, his elbows resting on his knees. Helen Masters focused on a small flower-shaped stain on the wall directly in front of her. Franks looked from one to the other.

"Maybe we should take a break now!"

Helen picked up the files, as Franks gave her a tiny wink. She went ahead to the waiting car, and was about to step inside when Louis announced he had to return to the doctor's office. "I won't be a moment, wait for me here!"

✦　✦　✦

Dr. Franks looked up in surprise as the baron knocked on his open door and entered, but he did not ask if the baron had forgotten something. He knew the baron wished to speak to him alone. He cleared his throat. "You know if you would prefer to have these sessions with me alone, Helen is a very understanding woman, perhaps more than you realize. She is, after all, a very good doctor herself."

"Yes I know, of course I know, I have tremendous respect for her. I wanted to talk to you privately, though."

The baron could not meet Franks's eyes.

"I'd like to tell you something concerning my wife." He smiled, and Franks was struck anew by the man's handsomeness.

The baron moved to the office window, stood with his back to the room. "I have had many women, I suppose you might call me a promiscuous man, but I did love my wife—I say did, because over the years her illness had gradually made me hate her. I have, may God forgive me, wished her dead more often than I care to admit, and yet, when she attempts to kill herself my remorse, my dread of her dying and leaving me is very genuine, and my relief when she recovers, very real."

The baron rested his head against the glass.

"She was, Doctor, the most beautiful creature, I wanted to possess her the moment I laid eyes on her. She simply took my breath away. She was sweetness itself, she was naïve, she was nervous, like an exquisite exotic bird. Her fragility made me almost afraid of her, as though if I held her too tightly, kissed her too deeply, she would be crushed. The more I got to know her, the more delightful she became, but in those days my fear of . . ."

He hesitated as if searching for the right word, then he turned to face Franks. "I had a fear of breaking her. She soon assured me I could not, and during our courtship she became more vibrant, even more outgoing. She was very amusing, with a wicked sense of humor. She was a great tease. She was, Doctor, everything I had ever dreamed of. I married her against tremendous opposition from my family, especially my mother. Perhaps Mama had some insight into Vebekka, but I would hear none of it. The first few months of marriage, I don't think I have ever known such happiness, such total commitment. I had never loved like that, or felt so loved, or been so satisfied."

The baron took two steps from the window, then turned back. His voice was hardly audible. "I had my first sexual encounter when I was fourteen. I had countless women, from society women to prostitutes. I was a normal, healthy man, obviously eligible, and known to be wealthy. I very rarely, if ever, had to court a woman. Perhaps that was why I wanted Vebekka so much, because she was, to begin with, unobtainable and completely disinterested in me. We did not sleep together until after we were married. I know it may sound laughable but I presumed she was a virgin."

Franks leaned back in his chair, waiting, but eventually he had to ask as the baron's silence continued.

"Was she? A virgin?"

The baron drew out a chair and sat down. "No she was not, she was very experienced. I was a little—no, more than a little—I was shocked. My bride was sexually aggressive, demanding, explicit, and insatiable. As I have said, the first few months with her—I have never known anything so totally consuming, I never experienced such peaks of emotion, such sexual gratification, and then, then she became pregnant."

Franks made a steeple with his fingers, waiting. After a moment the baron continued, but was obviously very uncomfortable, running his index finger around the collar of his shirt, as if it constricted him in some way.

"A few months after she became pregnant, she changed. She would not allow me to touch her, allow me anywhere near her, she was terrified she would lose the baby if we had sex. And then, this illness, whatever we want to call it, began. She broke my heart, Doctor. It was as if I had never known her. She behaved as if she hated me, and even when I was told that it was because she was ill, all I felt was her rejection."

Franks placed his hands flat on the desk.

"But after the birth, she was herself again? Did you resume your old sexual relationship?"

"No, she continued to reject me as a husband for a long time, at least ten months. Then all of a sudden it was as if it had never happened. I returned home one evening and she was my Vebekka again. But I could not be turned on and off like a faucet."

"So you rejected her?"

The baron laughed, a gentle, self-mocking laugh. "My wife was a very persuasive woman. For two months it was like a second honeymoon, and then as quickly as it had begun, it was over—she was pregnant again."

The baron explained that after his second son was born he attempted to persuade his wife to use birth control, but she adamantly refused. So the pattern had repeated itself yet again, but after that third time, when she had been ill for six months, he had no desire to be reunited with her.

"So you stopped loving her, after your third child?"

"I realized she was sick, knew by then that she did not really know what she was doing during these periods. So I simply arranged my life around her."

The baron's face flushed with guilt. He blamed himself. He had not been at home as often as he should have been. Then the guilty expression in the baron's eyes was replaced by an icy coldness. When he spoke, his voice grew quieter, almost vicious.

"My wife had taken to leaving the house late in the evening. She never took the car, always hired a taxi, and on many occasions did not return home until the following morning. I began to have her followed, for her own good, you understand."

"Were you considering a divorce?"

The baron dismissed the question with a shake of his head. He spoke quickly, not disguising his disgust. "She was picking up men, truck drivers, cab drivers, wandering around the red light district. As soon as I discovered this, I confronted her with it. She denied she had ever left the house, but she continued her midnight crawls, even when I was threatened with blackmail, she denied she was— virtually soliciting."

"You mean she was paying for sex?"

"Occasionally, or she was paid. It was a terrible time, and I was at my wits' end. I have never considered a divorce. She is my wife and the mother of my children, we are a Catholic family. It was out of the question."

"Was? Have you changed your mind?"

The baron picked up his coat, gave a distant smile. "Just a slip of the tongue."

His arrogance returned. He was again distant, icy cold.

"If you can't help her, then I am—and I assure you I have never considered this before—but I am prepared to have my wife certified."

The control slipped again. The baron leaned over Franks's desk. "I don't understand myself, you see, I just don't understand, after everything I have been through!"

Franks slowly stubbed out his cigar. "Understand what, exactly?"

"That I can . . . last night, I felt attracted to my wife. I did not believe myself capable of wanting her again. I must not allow her to manipulate me. I am tired, worn out by her. You are my last chance, perhaps hers. I ask you not just to help my wife, but me. Help me!"

Franks nodded. It was time for dinner, his stomach rumbled. He hoped the baron would leave. At that moment, Maja knocked on the door and popped her head in.

"I'm sorry to interrupt, but Miss Masters said to tell you the car's still waiting, but not to worry; she has taken a taxi back to the hotel."

Franks gave a pleading look to Maja.

"And you have another appointment in half an hour, Doctor!" Maja closed the door.

Franks rose to his feet, and the baron was already by the door, his hand on the handle.

"Thank you for your time, I appreciate it."

Franks clasped the baron's hand in a firm handshake. "I thank you for your honesty, and let us hope we will achieve some results."

At last Franks was alone and he slumped into his chair, buzzing the intercom for Maja. She appeared almost immediately, and smiled. "My, that was a long return visit! I hope it was fruitful!"

Franks laughed, and rubbed his belly. "I need food; I am starving to death!"

Maja brought in a tray of sandwiches and coffee, and the evening paper. He settled back, making himself comfortable, his eyes skimming the headlines, and then he flipped the paper open to the second page, glancing over the ads for the circus, paying no attention to the late afternoon news bulletins. One small five-line article stated that the Polizei had discovered a body in a small East Berlin hotel that evening.

5

THE CHAMBERMAID had not changed the bed linen of Room 40, because the DO NOT DISTURB sign was hanging from the door. It was not until later in the afternoon when she was vacuuming the corridor that she tapped on the closed door, and, receiving no reply, entered using her master set of keys. The curtains were drawn and the television set turned on, the sound so low it was hardly audible. The room was neat, except for the unmade bed, its coverlet bunched on the floor.

The maid fetched clean towels, sheets, and pillowcases, and went back into the room. She tossed the clean linen onto the chair, and drew back the curtains. She went into the bathroom, collected the dirty towels, and dropped them onto the floor. Two were blood-stained and she picked them up distastefully between finger and thumb. She then replaced the towels with fresh ones, and was washing down the sink and bath when a friend popped her head around the door to ask if she was nearly through for the day, as it was after three.

Both women got off at two-thirty, they each had other jobs in the evening. Together they began to clean the room, and one pulled the sheets back.

"It's not been slept in. Christ! it's freezing in here, they must have turned off the heat. Some people are weird."

Together they bent down to the rolled bedcover, and tugged it from underneath the bed. And screamed virtually in unison.

Tommy Kellerman's body rolled out of the cover, the section over his head dried hard with dark blood.

Screaming at the top of their lungs, the women ran down the corridor. A waiter carrying a loaded tray of dirty dishes was about to step out of the elevator when they appeared, shouting garbled words as they pointed frantically to the room. The man ran into the room and was in no more than a few seconds. When he came out, his face drained as he whispered: "Dear God, it's a child—somebody's killed a child in there!"

✦ ✦ ✦

By the time the Polizei arrived, the corridor was filling with gaping onlookers and guests. The manager of the hotel tried to keep some semblance of order, shouting for people to stand back. He looked disheveled, having just been dragged out of his quarters. His collarless shirt hung out over his hurriedly pulled-on pants.

Polizei Oberrat Torsen Heinz pushed his way through the throng, holding up his badge. Three uniformed officers followed behind him. Torsen was the first of them to arrive at the open bedroom door. He asked if the doctor or forensic team had been there. He could see the tiny body, the small foot in the red sock, and his stomach turned over. He did not attempt to remove the congealed mess beneath the bed cover as he walked gingerly around the body.

The manager hung in the doorway, demanding to know who had torn pages out of his register.

The doctor arrived and took only a second to certify the body as deceased. The pathologist scuttled in, followed by two lab boys from the forensic department. They began yelling for everyone to clear out of the room.

Oberrat Heinz checked the room quietly, using a pencil to open a couple of drawers. The doctor looked over to him as he departed. "It's not a kid, it's a dwarf or a midget and he's taken one hell of a beating, but that's stating the obvious. G'night."

The pathologist carefully slipped plastic bags around the tiny red socks; he applied a bag to Kellerman's right arm and hand, then reached for his left. He stood up rubbing his knee and, looking down, realized he was kneeling on a set of broken dentures. He gestured to Heinz.

"I'm sorry, I think I may have broken them; my mistake, but someone should have checked this area."

Heinz stared at the broken teeth, and then stepped out of the

way as the pathologist continued his work, about to wrap Kellerman's left arm in a protective plastic bag.

"Jesus, look at his arm, it's been hacked, a big chunk of skin
removed, just above the wrist."

Heinz sent one of the uniformed officers out to check for any
garbage that might have been removed.

The pathologist's team slipped a plastic sheet beside Kellerman,
rolled him on top of it, then tied all four ends and lifted up the
body.

"He booked in early yesterday, according to the chambermaid,"
Torsen Heinz said to no one in particular. He tugged at his blond
hair, watched as two men dusted door handles and the mirror, then
made his way down to the reception area. The manager, now wearing a jacket, insisted he had been on duty and had seen no one come
in other than official guests. Heinz listened, knowing that local
prostitutes used this hotel, but said nothing; he simply asked to see
the guest book. The manager shoved it toward him, pointing with
a dirty fingernail to the torn pages. He scratched his greasy head,
and tried unsuccessfully to recall the dead man's name.

"What about his passport, did you see his passport?"

The manager was sweating. "I saw it and checked it. I know
the rules. He had luggage, a sort of greenish carryall. Did you
find it?"

"But you don't recall his name?"

"No . . . he just signed, and I gave him the key. I was on the
phone when he checked in."

"What nationality?"

"American. Kellerman!" The manager beamed. "I remember,
it was Kellerman!"

No one Heinz questioned had seen anyone entering his room.
Heinz and his sergeant took off for the morgue.

The morgue had closed for the night.

Heinz returned early the following morning. Tommy Kellerman's naked body was even more tragic in death than in life, his
stubby palms turned upward, his legs spread-eagled, his pride ex-
posed. It was a wicked freak of nature to give this small, stunted

body a penis any man would be proud to boast. The penis dangled virtually down to the kneecaps on his twisted legs.

The bed cover had to be cut away from his head, because the blood had congealed like glue. There was hardly a feature left intact; blood clotted in his eyes, his nose, his ears, and his gaping mouth; the bottom row of false teeth had cut into his upper lip, giving him the look of a Neanderthal man, a chimp, even more so as his thick dark curly hair was spiky with his own blood.

The pathologist was able to ascertain that Kellerman had died close to midnight and had eaten some four hours before he was killed. The pathologist had spent considerable time over the open wound on Kellerman's left forearm. He could tell that the skin cut away from Kellerman's arm was probably a tattoo, judging by the faint tinge of blue left along one edge. The pathologist added that whoever murdered Kellerman must have been covered in blood, since the main artery had been severed on the once tattooed wrist.

Kellerman's clothes were spread out on the lab tables; again they gave a tragic impression of the wearer, so small and childlike. His underpants were disgusting, semen stains mingled with the death throes of his bowels.

His pockets were empty, apart from a rubber band and a Zippo lighter. His clothes were labeled and listed, his body washed and tagged, placed in a child's morgue bag, and then laid on a drawer and pushed into the freezer.

Kellerman's terror of being shut in small spaces, his fear of the darkness couldn't hurt him now: It was all over for him.

Heinz hung around for a while, then returned to the hotel to question the janitor.

The toothless man could not recall anyone entering the hotel during his shift, or at least no one who warranted special attention. He did remember seeing a big man outside the hotel, wearing a black hat. In fact the man could possibly have just come out of the main entrance, he couldn't be sure, he had simply passed him on the street as he emptied the trash. He could not describe him in any detail, just that he was tall, wore a black hat, and that it was around eleven or perhaps a bit later.

✦ ✦ ✦

Torsen Heinz sat at his large wooden desk, surrounded by his officers. The station was housed in a baroque-style building in the
Potsdam district of East Germany, and for equipment there were a
half dozen old typewriters and an obsolete telephone system incapable of connecting with West Berlin without interminable delays
and disconnections. The principal piece of modern technology was
a microwave oven, recently installed to heat up the officers' lunches.

Torsen and his men had been unable to keep up with the sharp
increase in criminal activity since the fall of the socialist regime.
Previously East Berlin's criminal incidences had been hushed up by
the Stasi secret police or played down by the state-controlled media.
Now, Polizei Oberrat Heinz and forty-odd uniformed officers had
to learn fast to make their own decisions.

Sitting with his microwave-heated breakfast sausages, Heinz felt
swamped. There was little to report from any of the officers he had
assigned to the Kellerman case, because after their day's work they
had clocked out promptly at six o'clock. No matter how much
Torsen argued that they were no longer working from nine to six
but if necessary around the clock, they were too used to the old
regime to change their working habits. There was not one man on
duty yet, and it was half past eight!

Alone, Torsen sifted through the statements and facts he had
gathered so far about the dwarf. He thought that Kellerman was
probably an American citizen since, according to the hotel manager,
he spoke with an American accent. Without a passport or other
documents to substantiate this, he decided he should first contact
the U.S. embassy to see if they had any record of his arrival in
Berlin. The next call would be to the circus which was being her-
alded as the biggest event of the season. He tried to contact the
embassy, but the station's telephone switchboard was still closed.
He finished his breakfast and looked at the photograph of his father
on the wall behind his desk. Gunter Heinz's picture was brown
with age. Torsen gave the photograph a small nod and determined
that until it was absolutely necessary he would not go hat in hand
to the West Berlin police. They had already assisted him on a number

of cases, and he had taken a lot of ridicule from his "colleagues" with their high tech computers and fax machines. He wondered how well they would cope without so much as one single telephone connected after 6 P.M. or before 9 A.M.! He swiveled in his chair and looked at the memo taped to the wall under his papa's severe face. "Accept no coincidence—only facts." He had put up this admonition after he had been promoted to chief inspector at exactly the same age as his father had before him. The memo had been written when Torsen first made the decision to follow him into the Polizei.

Suffering from senility, Gunter Heinz, Sr., was now residing in a home for the elderly, most of the time happily unaware of his surroundings—or for that matter of who he was. But there were the odd flashes of recall. In these moments Torsen was able to talk with him, even play chess. Torsen had arranged for the nurses to call him whenever his father was lucid. However, the last time he had hurried over for a visit, the old man had glared at him and asked who the hell he was. Torsen had replaced his chessboard in its case.

The nurse had apologized, whispering that she was sorry, but earlier that day his father had asked to speak with his son on an important matter. During Torsen's conversation with the nurse, his father ripped small pieces of tissue paper from a box, carefully licked each tiny scrap, stuck them on his nose, and blew them off like snowflakes. A spectacle that would have been comic were the man not his father.

＋　＋　＋

Torsen called the U.S. embassy. They had no record of a Kellerman in residence in East Berlin, but suggested the border patrols be contacted. The flow of refugees arriving in Germany was causing mayhem, but there was an attempt to record everyone coming in by automobile or train. There was a possibility that Kellerman had landed at the main airport and crossed to the East; the airport authorities, too, should be contacted.

Torsen sent two officers to try and discover Kellerman's origins, and then set off with Sergeant Volker Rieckert for the circus.

✦ ✦ ✦

The patrol car labored through the mud, but the attendant would not let them come close to the private trailers and the performers' parking lot. The long walk to the trailer sections and big tents was hazardous. Their trousers were soaked at the bottom, their hair plastered to their heads as they made their way toward the cashier's trailer.

The cashier had bright red-dyed hair with a pink comb stuck in the top that matched her pink lipstick. She looked at Torsen's ID and blew a large pink bubble with her gum, then pointed toward the manager's building. Torsen swore under his breath as he felt the mud squelch into his hand-knit woolen socks.

✦ ✦ ✦

The circus's administrator welcomed the men into his office. It was tiny and overheated, in a small building at the side of a massive tent. It was filled with filing cabinets, and the walls were covered with large circus posters. Romy Kelm, the administrator, a balding bespectacled gentleman, introduced himself to the detectives and ordered tea.

The two officers were settled on folding chairs, and Mr. Kelm seated himself behind his pristine desk. He told Torsen the dead man could very well be Tommy Kellerman. Kelm hastened to add that Kellerman was not employed by the circus, but had been more than twenty years earlier. He knew also that Kellerman had been in jail in the United States, was prone to fighting and drunken brawls, and was a thief. Kellerman had absconded with the company's wages eight years previously when he was associated with the Kings Circus, a smaller touring company. A circus trade paper had given the details of his theft and subsequent jail sentence. Kelm suggested that there were a number of people who resented Kellerman, because he owed them money.

Torsen was given a list of all the performers who might have known Kellerman. Kelm told him that the dead man's ex-wife, Ruda, a star performer, was still using the name Kellerman, although she had remarried long ago.

Torsen's head was reeling. He and his sergeant spent more than two hours in the little office, and the small room became so overheated that they could feel their socks and shoes drying out, along with the bottom of their trousers.

Finally, Torsen was helped into his raincoat and handed a layout of the trailers. The circus did not want any adverse publicity, because their biggest show of the season was to open in a few days' time. Kelm made it clear that if anyone from his company was involved in the incident he wanted it dealt with as quietly and as quickly as possible.

As he ushered them into the corridor, he said he was sure no one in the company was involved in the murder.

Torsen suggested that surely if many people detested Kellerman, perhaps one could have wanted to kill him. There was no reply, just a cold stare from Kelm, who smiled perfunctorily.

Torsen eased open the exit door and looked at the downpour. He swore, then hunched up his shoulders and stepped out. His sergeant followed, tucking his thick notepad into his pocket, along with the free posters and cards that had been pressed into his hands by Kelm for his children.

"Las Vegas, you see that poster on the high-wire act! How much do you think a setup like this costs?" Rieckert asked. He received no answer from Torsen. "That Kelm was pretty helpful, wasn't he?"

"Yeah, he was, wasn't he! It's called get off our backs, schmuck! We've got our work cut out for us."

A herd of horses was led past them, draped in protective covers, led on a single rein by a young sour-faced boy. Rieckert stared with open curiosity, and then looked at four equally sour-faced men wearing dark blue overalls. They carried pitchforks, and one promtly cleared away some horse dung as the others hurried on toward the practice arena. Rieckert's jaw dropped again as coming up behind him were five massive elephants. He shouted to ask Torsen if he had seen them. Torsen looked at him—it was exceptionally hard to miss five fully grown elephants.

The two men plodded through the mud, heading toward the main trailer park. Torsen had decided he would interview the ex—

Mrs. Kellerman first. By the time he discovered they had been reading the trailer route upside down, his hair was dripping wet. After asking for directions from a number of scurrying figures with umbrellas and waterproof capes, they arrived at the Grimaldi trailer. Torsen dragged his shoes across the grids outside the glistening trailer and tapped on the door. Behind him Rieckert looked at the trailer with admiration, wondering how much it had cost. The door opened, and Torsen looked up.

"My name is Detective Chief Inspector Torsen Heinz, and this is Detective Sergeant Rieckert. May we come in?"

As Grimaldi stared, Torsen asked politely if Grimaldi spoke German, and received a curt nod of confirmation.

"We would like to speak to your wife—she was Mrs. Kellerman, yes?"

Grimaldi nodded, and then stepped aside. Torsen moved up the steps to enter.

Grimaldi gestured for the men to follow him. Torsen observed they were both six feet tall. Grimaldi was big, raw-boned, with very broad shoulders, whereas Torsen bordered on being skinny.

Grimaldi sat down on a thick cushioned bench seat and offered them coffee, but both men declined. The officers sat side by side on the padded bench seat opposite him.

"Ruda's feeding the cats, should be back shortly."

Rieckert took quick glances around the spacious room, while Torsen looked at the posters and photographs. He then turned to Grimaldi.

"I saw you, many years ago. I was just a kid, but I have never forgotten it, you were fabulous."

Grimaldi's dark eyes were suspicious. He hardly acknowledged the compliment, but turned in the direction of the posters. He pointed to Ruda's, and then looked back.

"This is Ruda, you see, Ruda Kellerman. She still uses his name. What's that little piece of shit done now?"

Torsen straightened. "He's been murdered. We are both from the Polizei. He was murdered in East Berlin sometime the night before last."

Grimaldi smiled, showing big even yellowish teeth, then he laughed out loud and slapped his trousers with his huge hand. "Well, you'll have a lot of contenders . . . he was a detestable creature, real vermin, somebody should have smothered him years ago. What was he doing in East Berlin?"

"We don't know, and as yet we have had no formal identification of the body, but we are led to believe it was Tommy Kellerman. Would you mind telling me where you were last night? I mean the night before last."

Grimaldi banged his chest. "Me?"

Torsen nodded. "We will have to ask everyone at the circus if they've seen him. Did you, by any chance?"

"Me?"

Rieckert's jaw dropped slightly; he had never come across anyone as large as Grimaldi. The man appeared to be built like an ox, his hands twice the size of any normal man's.

Grimaldi leaned back and then looked at Torsen Heinz. "You serious? Night before last? Oh, yes. I was here, all night, ask my wife—she couldn't sleep because of my snoring. As to Kellerman, let me think, I've not seen the creep for maybe five, no, more, I thought he was in jail, last saw him—must be eight to ten years ago."

"You have recently been in Paris? Was he working with you then?"

Grimaldi shrugged his massive shoulders. "No one would employ him, he stole an entire week's wages, from . . . can't remember, but no circus would touch him. Besides, he was in jail! I think he got extra time for beating up some inmate, that's what I heard."

The door opened, and Ruda walked in. She leaned against the door frame, looking first to Grimaldi, and then to the two men.

"Kellerman's been murdered," Grimaldi said.

Ruda eased off her boots. "What do we do, throw a party?"

Grimaldi grinned, and introduced Torsen Heinz and Rieckert. Ruda shook the officers' hands as they both stood up to greet her. To Torsen, Ruda's hand felt like a man's—rough, callused. She was almost as tall as he was, but judging by the handshake, a hell of a lot stronger. They made quite a pair, Mr. and Mrs. Grimaldi.

"Is this true?" she asked.

Torsen nodded. He had never seen such a total absence of emotion. Kellerman had, after all, once been this woman's husband.

"Would you mind if I asked you some questions, Mrs. Keller—Grimaldi?"

Ruda placed her boots by the door. "Ask what you need to know! Is there coffee on, Luis?"

Grimaldi eased himself out of his seat, went into the kitchen and poured his wife coffee, again asking if either of the men would care for some. They both replied that they would, and he banged around getting the mugs.

Ruda sat on the seat vacated by her husband, rubbing her hair with a towel. Torsen rested his elbows on his knees. "When did you last see him?"

She closed her eyes and leaned back. "That's a tough one, let me think. . . . Luis? When did he come to the winter quarters, was it six, eight years ago?—I can't think!"

Grimaldi put down the mugs of thick black coffee. He didn't offer any milk, but a large bowl of brown sugar.

As the two policemen spooned in their sugar, Ruda and Grimaldi exchanged a few words about one of the cats. Ruda was worried she was off her food; if it continued she'd change her feed, maybe put her back on meat and stop the meal. They seemed totally unconcerned about Kellerman.

"Do you have a photograph?"

Ruda looked at Torsen and raised her eyebrow. "Of the cats?"

"No, of Kellerman."

"You must be joking. Do you think I would want a reminder that I was ever in any way connected to that piece of shit! No, I do not have a photograph."

Torsen sipped his coffee. It was odd that neither had asked how Kellerman had died. When asked where she had been at the time of the murder, Ruda lit a cigarette and rubbed her nose.

"The night before last, shit, I dunno. Last night I was here working the act until after twelve."

"No, the night before."

Ruda thought for a moment, then frowned. "Guess I was here, worked the routines, then had supper over at the canteen, then came to bed. What time did I come in, Luis?"

Grimaldi took a picture of himself from the wall. He handed it to Torsen. "That was the last time I played Berlin. You said you saw my act, more than fifteen years ago . . ."

Ruda interrupted. "It would be more than fifteen, let me see. . . ."

Ruda looked over the wall of photographs, and Torsen put his mug down. They were both discussing the exact time they were last in Berlin! Ruda suddenly turned to face him. "You're sure it is Tommy Kellerman? I think he's still in prison."

Torsen stood up, straightened his sodden trousers, the creases no longer in existence.

"We would be sure if you would be so helpful as to identify him. May we ask for your cooperation?"

Ruda hesitated. "Don't they have fingerprints for that kind of thing? Contact the prison—I don't want to see him, dead or alive. Get someone else, there's many around the camp that knew him."

"But you were his wife."

Ruda stared hard at Torsen. "Yes, I was his wife, but I am not now, and I haven't been for a very long time."

"For me to cable America, and wait for prints, could take a considerable time."

"If there's no one else . . ." Ruda said, obviously put out.

"Thank you. Thank you for your time, I may have to question you again. Oh yes, one more thing, the tattoo. Kellerman had a tattoo on his left arm, could you tell me what it was like?"

Grimaldi laughed. "Probably gave the size of his prick, he was so proud of it. Don't look at me, I never let the creep within two feet of me. Ask her, she was—as you so rightly say—married to him!"

Ruda looked to the thick carpet, her stocking feet digging into the pile. "A tattoo? He might have had it done in prison, he didn't have one when I knew him."

Torsen shook their hands again, and again felt how strong her grip was. "Maybe he was looking for work, ask at the main administration office," Ruda suggested.

Torsen smiled his thanks, and just as he opened the door, Grimaldi asked how Kellerman had been murdered. Torsen dragged on his raincoat. "Some kind of hammer, multiple blows to his head."

Grimaldi wiped his mouth with the back of his hand. "Ah well! Poor little sod had it coming to him."

Torsen said tersely that no one had to be subjected to such a horrifying death. He then smiled coldly at Ruda, and asked if she would accompany them when he was finished taking statements from the rest of the people he needed to speak to.

Ruda was tight-lipped, asking how long it would take—with the show due to open shortly she had very little time.

Torsen said he would be through as fast as he could, perhaps in two hours, if it was convenient. He did not wait for a reply.

When the officers left, Grimaldi leaned back, then lifted his feet up to rest on the bunk seat. "Maybe he left some dough to you in his will!"

"Yeah, the only thing he's left is a nasty smell and a string of debts. He can get someone else to ID him, I'm not going."

"But you were his wife . . ."

She swiped him with the towel. "You knew him, you identify him. It'll give you something to do."

"Ah, but I didn't know him as well as you, sweetheart, you can't get out of that."

Ruda sat down, pushing his feet aside. "I can't do it, Luis—don't make me, don't let them make me see him."

Grimaldi cocked his head to one side. "Why not, he's dead. You telling me it's affecting you? I thought you detested his guts."

"I do, I did, but I don't want to see him."

Grimaldi pinched her cheek. "You use his name, sweetheart! Serves you right!"

Ruda swung out at him, this time with the flat of her hand. She hit hard, and he gripped her wrist, shoving her roughly aside. "Give me one good reason why I should do anything for you."

"Fuck you!"

Ruda punched him, and Grimaldi swung back, landing a hard, open-handed slap on her face. She kicked him, he slapped her again, and this time she didn't fight back—her face twisted like a child's and he drew her to him. "Okay okay . . . I'll take you, I'll go with you!"

He began to smooth back her hair from her face, massage the throbbing scars at her temples. Her body felt strong as a man's in his arms. For her to be vulnerable like this was rare. He held her closer.

"Ruda, Ruda, why do we torment each other the way we do?"

"Just be with me, Luis, just stay with me, I don't want to go by myself," she whispered.

"Stay with you, huh? Until the next time you want something?"

As soon as he said it he wished he hadn't. Ruda backed away from him, her fists clenched. He threw up his hands in a gesture of impotence.

"We have to get divorced, Ruda, you know it. I can't live like this anymore, we're at each other's throats."

"I don't want to talk about that, not now."

"Because of that shit Kellerman? Jesus Christ, Ruda, who gives a fuck if he's alive or dead? What concerns me is us, we have to settle our future. I'm through Ruda, through standing around waiting to be at your beck and call."

"You can't have the act!"

Grimaldi clenched his hands. Like two fighters they faced each other.

"Fine, you want it, then we arrange a financial settlement. Simple as that, Ruda."

He saw the way her face changed, the way her dark eyes stared at and through him. Her voice was as dark as her eyes.

"Every penny I have earned has been put back into the act. You want out—then you go, take your stupid little whore. Take her and *fuck off.*"

Grimaldi smirked. "Takes one to know one."

She went for him like a man, punching and kicking. Soon they were slugging each other. Crockery smashed, pictures crashed off the walls, and they fought until they both lay sprawled, panting, on the floor. She still punched him, blows that hurt like hell.

"Take your clothes and get out! Without me you'd have nothing, without me you'd be a drunken bum!"

She spat at him, and he staggered to his feet. He began to open the overhead lockers, throwing her belongings at her.

"You take *yours,* you take *your* belongings and get out, go sleep with the animals, sleep with your precious angel! Sleep with any twisted, fucked-up thing that'll have you."

Ruda kicked him so hard in the back of his legs that he slumped forward, hit his head on the side of the cupboard and fell backward. He lay half across the bunk, half on the floor and she was on top of him, spread-eagled across his body. For one second he thought she was going to bite him, she was snarling like a wild cat. He then rolled her and her head cracked against the floor. He bent his head closer to scream at her to stop. Suddenly he felt her body grow limp beneath him, and her arms wound around his neck as she drew him closer.

They looked into each other's faces, and moaned, in unison, chest to chest, breath to breath, their hearts thudding. The kiss was gentle, his lips softly brushing hers. She buried her head in the nape of his neck.

They lay together on the floor of the wrecked trailer—their clothes and crockery around them. They lay together with broken glass and shattered pictures of the Great Grimaldi and the fearless Ruda Kellerman.

When he spoke, his voice was filled with pain.

"Let me go, Ruda. Because this is where it always ends. I want you now, you can feel I want you, but it has to end."

Her voice was muffled, a low half-plea, begging him to take

her, to have her. She eased her hands down his body, began to unhook his belt. He leaned up, gently turning his face, forcing her to look at him.

"Do you want me? Or is this . . . Ruda, look at me, *look at me!*"

His big hand cupped her chin, forced her to face him. Her eyes were expressionless, hard, dangerous eyes. She couldn't fake it. She had never been able to, she couldn't even do it now when she needed him. Slowly she let her hands drop to her sides. She moved as if to turn over, to let him ease down her trousers, since she could not take him naturally, normally. Small slivers of glass cut into her cheeks, the pain excited her, but she felt no juices, nothing to prepare her body for sex, for his erection. She gritted her teeth, waiting.

Grimaldi stood up, carefully avoiding the glass. He stepped over her, tightened his belt as his erection pressed against his pants. The hardness left by the time he walked into his room and quietly closed the door.

Ruda lay in the debris. It had always been this way. They had always fought each other, and that part had always excited her, but she had never felt any sexual desire beyond the fight; sex pained and hurt her too much, hurt her insides like sharpened razors. She felt a tiny drop of blood roll down her cheek and she licked it, tasted it as though it were a tear. She hadn't cried for a long time, too long even to remember.

Ruda went into her room, closing the door as quietly as Grimaldi had shut his. She showered, feeling the hot needles pummel her, then gently began to soap herself. Her fingers massaged her shoulders, her arms, her heavy breasts, and then she began to lather her belly, her strong hands feeling each crude, jagged scar. She massaged and eased the foam down, until she reached between her legs. She ran her hands over the ridges of the scars, her hideous, thick, hard, rough skin—always a dark plum red, like a birthmark. She rinsed the soap with cold water, grabbed a towel, her hair dripping. She hadn't heard him come in, but he was there, holding out the big white bath towel. Gently he wrapped her, as if she were a child, trapping her arms in the softness.

He held her close. Her eyes were frightened, childlike, as if the animal in her had gone into hiding; there was no longer any ferocity. He guided her toward the bed and sat her down.

She sat with her head bowed, her hair dripping, covering her face. Luis reached for a small hand towel and began to dry her hair.

"I'll go to the morgue, no need for you to do it, I'll go if they need someone."

She nodded her head.

"Ruda, look at me. I need someone. I'm not talking about getting my rocks off, I'm talking about needing—I need, you know? As it is now, I feel like half a man, and watching out for you every show isn't enough. It can't go on. This is my last chance. I'm old, maybe Tina can give me a few more good years, give me back my balls. I don't want to fight with you anymore, I can't fight you anymore. I will need to be able to keep Tina and the baby when it comes, so we have to work out an agreement, one we can both live with. I know how much money you've put in, I know how you've kept us going, I know, Ruda, but I can't go on like this."

He rubbed her head gently, knowing the burn scars at her temples should not be irritated by the rough towel. He was careful, showing more tenderness than he had in years.

There was a tap on the trailer door; it was the inspector asking if Mrs. Kellerman could accompany him to the morgue. Ruda could hear Grimaldi asking if he would be acceptable, and she heard the inspector saying that Mrs. Kellerman would be preferable.

Grimaldi's voice grew a little louder as he said he also knew Tommy Kellerman. Then there were whispered voices, and the trailer door shut.

Grimaldi called out that she had better get dressed, they needed her but he would accompany her. She began to dress very carefully, choosing a dress, high-heeled shoes, and for the first time in many years, she applied makeup other than her stage makeup. She took her time, a soft voice inside her whispering to stay calm, take things one at a time, she would deal with Luis when the time was right.

Grimaldi had a quick shave and stared at his reflection, uneasy over the exchange with his wife. He had felt such compassion for her, it confused him, she confused him, but then she always had. He rinsed his face and sat for a moment, remembering Florida, shortly after they were married. Ruda had wanted a child so badly, he knew how she must feel now with the Tina situation. He understood, but what could he do? It was not his fault.

Luis had held her when she told him, he had wrapped her in his arms when she came out of the doctor's, but she had pushed him away. He had so much love for her then that he hadn't been angry, just saddened by her rejection. He knew she was fighting to keep control the way she knew how—head up, jaw out. She didn't cry, he had rarely seen her crying. Somehow, her attempt to speak matter-of-factly, as if she were not affected, was very touching.

"I can't have a child, artificially or any other way, so that is that!"

She had put her coat on and walked out of the doctor's. He had paused a moment, digesting the news, before following her to the car. They had driven back to their winter quarters in silence, Ruda staring ahead, giving him instructions as she always did—Luis was never good at directions, and their quarters were far from the center of the city. But he would never forget that journey, the Florida heat and her quiet calm voice, flatly telling him to go right, then left. . . .

Ruda had become deeply depressed; nothing he said or attempted to do seemed to distract her. It was then that he asked her to participate in the act; until now she had simply helped the boys muck out and clean the cages. He had not contemplated that she work in the ring with him, he had suggested it now only to give her something to think about. He began to train her, and to his relief her depression lifted, the dark sadness dispersed, but their relationship deteriorated. Ever since the visit to the specialist, she shrank from him whenever he touched her. He let it go, hoping that in time she would come back to his bed.

The animals, his cats, had brought out a side of her that at first impressed him: She worked tirelessly, fearlessly. No matter how he reprimanded and warned her, she continued to take foolish risks. She almost dared the cats to attack her, dared them to maul her.

Luis was a good trainer, and a respected performer, a man brought up around big cats. It was he who told her that she must love and nurture the animals. Nothing would be gained from threats or impatience. Everything took time, but above all it was the caring, the loving which would bring results. At first, she refused to heed his advice, and they'd had violent arguments, but he kept on warning her that unless she listened, showed respect for him and for the cats, she would never learn. He told her she was not to tame the animals, but to train them: There was a vast difference.

Patiently, Luis gave her his time. And when she saw results, she began to smile again. Her wonderful laugh returned. But she did not come back to his bed. When he took a mistress, one of the stable girls at the winter quarters, she had said nothing, and so the pattern began then, all those many years ago.

And then Ruda bought Mamon, and their relationship took a terrible turn. They had been looking at cats and they had seen and rejected many. Luis was exceptionally intuitive, he had been taught by his father to be very selective, often turning down ten or twelve before he found an animal he felt would work well. One look and he could tell the young lion was trouble: Mamon had been in too many homes, too many circuses, had moved too many times. His previous history would have given any trainer a clue to his temperament, but Ruda did not want to listen, even when Luis refused to pay for him.

A week later Luis had gone to inspect four Bengal tigers. These were four cats he was quick to buy, because he trusted the owner, and liked the act they had already been worked into. He bought them on a handshake. Then he had returned to discuss the purchase with Ruda.

During Luis's absence Ruda had made the decision to buy Mamon. He had been furious, but she had shouted that Mamon was not Luis's but hers, and she would train him, with or without his help. It had been her money, and Mamon was hers. The argument had grown into a fistfight, but in the end he had given way. When she had said that Mamon was her baby, he had walked away, walked into the arms of . . . As he sat trying to recall her name, he suddenly realized that Ruda was calling him. She banged on his door, shouting that she was ready, and that the Polizei were waiting.

Luis looked for a clean shirt and began to dress. Luis had never told Ruda that he had gone back to the gynecologist. He wanted to hear the diagnosis firsthand, since she had refused to discuss it. He wanted to know if they should seek a second opinion. He had cared that much then.

The doctor had refused to discuss his patient with Grimaldi, even though he was her husband. Ruda had asked him not to. Simply he stated that there was no hope of his wife ever being able to conceive.

Grimaldi had accepted the gynecologist's word, and yet sensed that he had not been told the entire truth. When he tried to push for further details, the doctor, without meeting Grimaldi's eyes, said quietly, "Your wife cannot have normal sexual intercourse, and even if insemination were to take place, she could not carry a child. I am sorry."

Though the gynecologist would not discuss his patient's condition with her husband, he had shared her X rays and tests with two colleagues. He did not identify her by name, he simply showed them the appalling X rays and photographs of her genital area. All her organs had been removed, as if her womb had been torn from her belly. The internal scar tissues were even worse than her external scars. Nothing could be done. The entire genital area had been burnt by what the surgeon felt was possibly an early form of chemotherapy.

The colleagues listened in appalled silence. The clitoris had been severed, and the vagina was closed. The crudeness of the stitches and the scar tissue formation had left no opening. The only possible form of intercourse was anal; her urinary tract had been operated on to enable her to pass liquid, and a plastic tube inserted when the infected tract had festered. The anal area was large, denoting that sexual practice had obviously occurred on a regular basis over a period of years, stretching the colon.

The three men examined the X rays. What they had on their

screen was a shell of a woman. She had been stripped of her female organs. This was all the more horrible because the butchery had been performed when she was a small child.

The three doctors commented on the resilience of the human body, but did not talk about the patient's present state of mind. They couldn't. Ruda Grimaldi had refused to discuss what had led to her condition, and she never returned to the gynecologist.

Grimaldi knew something of Ruda's past, but she would never tell him her full story. Only Kellerman had known more. Ruda had told Grimaldi the first night she had met him that she couldn't have straight sex. She had told him in her stubborn way: head up, jaw stuck out.

Grimaldi combed his hair. It was strange to think of it now. He hadn't cared, he had no thought of marrying her then. That had come many years later.

He slipped his jacket on, brushing the shoulders with his hands. He had married her, but not out of pity. Ruda hated pity. Grimaldi had married her because by the time she had come back into his life, he was in desperate need of someone. He had been slipping, drinking too much, and his act was falling apart.

He sighed, knowing he was lying to himself. For reasons he couldn't understand, he had married her because he had loved her, and he had believed she loved him. Only many years later did he realize that Ruda loved no one, not even herself. No, that was wrong: She loved her angel, she loved Mamon.

By the time he was dressed and ready to leave the trailer, Grimaldi had made a decision. He had to leave Ruda, but to fight her, making ridiculous demands, wouldn't work; he had to make it a fair split. He determined that after the Kellerman business was sorted out, he would discuss it calmly and realistically with her, and this time he would not back down.

"Luis—come on! You've been ages, that inspector is waiting!" Ruda banged on his door again. "What are you doing in there?"

Grimaldi came out. He smiled, made her turn around, admiring and flattering her. He had not seen her so well dressed in years. He had also not had a drink for more than twenty-four hours, another good sign. He felt good, and teased Ruda: "How come you dress up for a corpse?"

Ruda wrinkled her nose, and hooked her arm in his. "Maybe I need to give myself some confidence! I'm scared."

Grimaldi laughed, and helped her down the steps. Then, because of the mud, he held out his arms and carried her to the waiting police car.

By the time Inspector Heinz and his sergeant had returned to their bogged-down patrol car, they were both reeling from all the statements they had heard from all the people who had known Kellerman. Not one had a nice word to say, everyone seemed rather pleased he was dead. None had been helpful, none had seen Kellerman on the day or night of his death, and everyone had a strong alibi. Torsen was grateful the ex–Mrs. Kellerman had agreed to identify the dead man.

Torsen held open the back door, and Grimaldi helped his wife into the car. She looked very different from the woman Torsen had visited in the trailer. She was in a good mood, laughing with her husband, a strange reaction, thought Torsen, considering she was being taken to a morgue to identify her ex-husband's corpse.

Ruda was determined not to be recognized in the event someone had seen her enter Kellerman's hotel. She had dressed carefully in a flowered dress and a pale gray coat. She had left her hair loose, hiding her face, and with her high heels, she seemed exceptionally tall. Torsen looked at her in the rearview mirror. It was hard to tell her exact age, but he guessed she must be close to forty, if not more. He felt the direct unnerving stare of her dark, strange, amber-colored eyes boring into the back of his head as he tried to back out of the mud-bound parking area.

Ruda wasn't looking at the inspector, but past him, about fifty yards in front of him. Mike, one of their boys, was hurrying toward the canteen, a rain cape over his shoulders, but what freaked Ruda was that he was wearing Tommy Kellerman's leather trilby. She remembered she had forgotten it in the meat trailer. The car suddenly jerked backward free of the mud, turned and headed out of the parking lot. Ruda didn't turn back, she couldn't: Her heart was pounding, her face had drained of color. Grimaldi gripped her hand and squeezed it. He murmured that it was all right, he was there, and there was no need for her to be afraid.

The rain continued to pour throughout their journey to East Berlin. The patrol car's windshield wipers made nerve-wracking screeches on the glass.

Grimaldi and his wife talked quietly to each other, as if they were being chauffeured. They spoke in English, so Torsen could only make out the odd sentence. He wondered what the word "plinth" meant. Rieckert sat next to him in the front seat, thumbing through his notebook in a bored manner.

In an attempt to calm down, Ruda was talking about the new plinths, having tried them out that morning. She was telling Luis she had had a lot of trouble, particularly with Mamon; he seemed loath to go near them, and had acted up badly. Grimaldi said the retrieval of the old plinths was out of the question, they simply couldn't get them back in time for the act. They would tone down the colors. Ruda snapped at him, saying that the smell of fresh paint would be just as disturbing, and that to skip the *pièce de résistance* of the act would be insanity. They considered asking for more rehearsal time.

They fell silent for a while as they drove through Kreuzberg, passing refurbished jazz cellars, Turkish shops, bedraggled boutiques, and small art galleries. It was the same route the bus followed the night Ruda had murdered Kellerman. Ruda felt a heavy foreboding.

Torsen looked at them through his rearview mirror.

"It was perhaps naïve of us to expect that the freedom would unleash some exciting new era overnight. People who have lived in cages get used to them, people in the East are afraid. Financial insecurity spreads panic. People here have been denied creative and critical expression for so long, they suffer from a deep inferiority complex. Under the old regime many cultural institutions were supported. We had good opera houses, two in fact, but now the West holds our purse strings and a number of our theaters have been closed for lack of funds."

The inspector felt obliged to talk, as if giving a guided tour.

"We had no unemployment; of course there was much over-staffing, but that was the GDR's way of disguising unemployment. Everything has doubled in price since the deutsche mark took over, but I do believe we are on the threshold of a new era."

Ruda sat tight-lipped, staring from the window, wishing the stupid man would shut up. They crossed into East Berlin. Fear and the thought of seeing Kellerman made Ruda angry. She had to unleash this fury somehow, she was going crazy. As they passed a building with JUDE scrawled over its walls, she found the perfect excuse. Suddenly she snapped, her voice vicious. "Some new beginning! Look what they daub on the walls. He should stop the car and grab those kids by the scruff of their necks, better still, take a machine gun and wipe them out! Those . . . !"

The inspector and the sergeant exchanged hooded looks. The screech of the windshield wipers was giving Torsen a headache.

Grimaldi stared at the anti-Jewish slogans, and touched Torsen's shoulder. "How come this kind of thing is allowed?"

Torsen explained that as soon as they washed down the walls, the kids returned. The sergeant turned to Grimaldi. His pale blue eyes and blond crew cut made him look youthful, but there was a chilling arrogance to him. He spoke with obvious distaste, his pale eyes narrowed.

"The city is swamped with immigrants. Romanian Gypsies are flooding in; women and children sit on every street corner, begging. The Poles are not desirable either. They fight like animals in the shops; they park their cars any old way, they steal, they urinate in the entrances to apartment buildings. This new Germany is in chaos. Eastern Europe is poverty stricken, and they come in droves! There are more illegal immigrants than we know what to do with! We have no time to wash down walls."

They drove on, past peeling buildings, collapsing sewer systems, electricity cables hanging from broken cages on street corners. The car went by acres of grimy nineteenth-century tenements that had withstood the bombing, their occupants staring now from filthy windows. Ruda was tense; she shifted her weight on the seat, crossing and uncrossing her legs. She took out her cigarettes and lit up, her hands shaking. She opened the window. She didn't care if she got soaked. She needed fresh air. She tossed the cigarette out, breathing in through her nose and exhaling, trying to stay calm.

Aware of her nervousness, Torsen began pointing out sights, a few new art galleries and the like. He tried to lighten the atmosphere. Now there was a gale blowing on his back: To add to his headache, no doubt, he'd have a crick in his neck the following morning.

They went past a gray stone hospital, to a low cement building, with parking places freshly painted in white. There were no other vehicles to be seen. The inspector pulled on the handbrake. "We are here, this is the city morgue."

Ruda and Grimaldi were led to a small empty waiting room and were asked to wait. Sergeant Rieckert remained with them, his eyes flicking over Grimaldi's jacket, his shoes, his Russian-style shirt with its high collar. He tried to imagine how he would look in that getup.

Inspector Torsen Heinz walked down a long, dismal corridor into the main refrigerated room. "Can you get Kellerman ready for viewing?" He shut the door again, returned to the waiting room, and gestured for Ruda to follow him down the corridor. Grimaldi asked if he should accompany them, and Torsen said it was entirely up to him.

The three walked in silence, their feet echoing on the tiled floor. They reached a door at the very end, which was opened by a man wearing green overalls. He stood to one side, removing his rubber gloves. They entered the cold room. Three bodies were lying on tables, covered in sheets, and Grimaldi tightened his grip on Ruda's elbow. Her heart was pounding, but she gave no other indication of what she was feeling. Grimaldi looked from one shrouded body to the other, then to the bank of freezers, with their old-fashioned heavy bolted drawers. He wondered how many bodies were kept on ice.

The inspector stood by a fourth table—shrouded like the others, this body seemed tiny in comparison. In a hushed voice he addressed Ruda:

"Be prepared, the dead man had extensive wounds to his face and head."

Grimaldi moved closer to Ruda, asked if she was all right. She withdrew her arm, nodding. Slowly the inspector lifted the sheet from the naked body, revealing just the head. Grimaldi stepped back aghast, but Ruda moved a fraction closer. She stared down at Kellerman's distorted face, or what was left of it.

"Is this Kellerman?"

Ruda felt icy cold, and continued to stare.

The inspector lifted the sheet from the side. "The tattoo was on his left wrist; as you can see, the skin was cut away. It would have been quite large."

Ruda stared at the small hand, the open cleaned wound, but said nothing. Torsen waited, watching her reaction, then saw her turn slowly to Grimaldi.

"Is this Kellerman, Mrs. Grimaldi?" he asked again.

Ruda gave a small, hardly detectable shrug of her shoulders. She showed no emotion. It was difficult for the inspector to guess what she was thinking or feeling. She seemed not to be repelled by the corpse, or disturbed by the grotesque injuries to the dead man's face.

Grimaldi stepped closer, peered down. He cocked his head to the right, then the left. "I think it's him."

Grimaldi returned to Ruda's side, leaned close and whispered something. She moved away from him, closer to the dead man. She looked at Torsen. "I can't be sure, I'm sorry. It has been so long since I saw him."

"It's him, Ruda. I'm sure even if you're not!" Grimaldi seemed impatient. Turning to the three shrouded bodies he asked if they too had been murdered. He received no reply.

Again Grimaldi whispered to Ruda, and this time he smiled. The inspector couldn't believe it, the man was making some kind of joke! Grimaldi caught the look of disapproval on Torsen's face, and gave a sheepish smile.

"The little fella was very well endowed, I suggested my wife perhaps could remember . . ." He shut up, realizing the joke was unsuitable and tasteless.

Ruda touched Kellerman's hair, a light pat with just her fingers to the thick curly gray-and-black hair. She spoke very softly. "He had a mole, on the left shoulder, shaped like a . . ."

The inspector pulled the sheet down, exposing the left shoulder and a dark brown mole. Ruda nodded her head. She whispered that the dead man was Kellerman, then she turned and strode out of the room—had to get out because she could hear Tommy's voice, hear him telling her not to switch out the light. He hated the dark, was always afraid of the dark and of confined spaces. She had teased him, calling him a baby, but she had always left the lights on. He didn't need them now.

◆ ◆ ◆

Back in the waiting room Inspector Heinz thanked Ruda for her identification. Torsen opened his notebook and sat on the edge of the hard bench. He searched his pockets, took out a pencil and looked at Ruda. "We have been unable to find any of Kellerman's documents, how he entered Germany, and if there are relatives we should contact. Was he an American citizen?"

Ruda nodded, told the inspector that Kellerman obtained his American citizenship in the early sixties, that he had no relatives and there was no one to be contacted.

"Where did he come from originally, Mrs. Grimaldi?"

Ruda hesitated, touched the scar at her temple with her forefinger. "Poland I think, I can't recall. . . ."

Grimaldi frowned, almost waiting for her to tell the inspector that she had met Kellerman in Berlin, but then she surprised him. She suddenly asked about Kellerman's burial, suggesting he be buried locally as there would be no relatives to claim the body. Ruda added that she would cover any costs, and asked that a rabbi be called. Although Kellerman had not been a practicing Jew, she felt that he would have wanted a rabbi present.

The inspector wrote down her instructions carefully, and looked up quickly as she said in a low sarcastic tone: "I presume there is a rabbi left in Germany who can perform the funeral rites. He must be buried before sunset.''

Torsen said he would arrange it. He then asked if Kellerman was the deceased's real name. Ruda looked puzzled, said of course it was. He saw that at last she seemed disturbed.

Ruda lit a cigarette, inhaled deeply before she replied once more to his question, apologizing for her rudeness. As far as she knew it was his name, it was the name she had taken when she married him. Torsen snapped his notebook closed, and offered to have the couple driven back to West Berlin. They refused the offer and asked for a taxi.

Grimaldi asked if they had a suspect, and Torsen shook his head. "No one as yet. We have not found his suitcase, the hotel room was stripped.''

"But didn't anyone see the killer? That was some beating the little guy took, I mean, someone must have hated his guts, and surely someone must have seen or heard something?''

The inspector shrugged. They had nothing to go on, but for a number of motives. Kellerman was not a well-liked man.

"Well-liked is one thing, but you don't beat a man's head in because you don't like him, it must be something else.''

Torsen nodded. He said that until he went further into his investigation, there was no further information he could give. He excused himself and left his sergeant to arrange their transport.

Rieckert, annoyed at having to walk back to the station, called two taxi companies but there were no available cars. He suggested that they could get a car from the Grand Hotel: It was not too far, if they wished he could walk with them.

Ruda refused his offer to accompany them, and turned to stare out of the grimy window. Grimaldi came to her side, whispered to her that she should have kept her mouth shut—now she would have to fork out for the little bastard even in death. She glared at him and, keeping her voice as low as his, she hissed that what he was pissed off about was her request for a rabbi. Then she whispered: "That little blond-haired Nazi prick will probably send us in the wrong direction anyway, now he knows I'm Jewish!''

Grimaldi gripped her elbow so tightly it hurt. "Shut up. Just keep it shut! Since when have you been a fuckin' Jew!"

Ruda smirked at him and shook her head. "Scared they may daub us on the way back to the trailer?"

Grimaldi glared back at her; he would never understand her. She was no more Jewish than he was, certainly not a practicing one. She had no religion, and he was a Catholic—not that he'd said a Hail Mary for more than twenty years.

The sergeant handed directions to Grimaldi, and left with a curt nod of his head. He'd heard what she had called him, and he smarted with impotent fury: Foreigners, they were all alike, and Detective Chief Inspector Heinz bowed and scraped like a wimp to that Jewish bitch! What kind of pervert was she to have been married to that animal on the morgue slab? She repelled him.

Ruda and Luis walked together, arm in arm. The walk was a lot longer than the sergeant had suggested. It took them over an hour to arrive at the newly refurbished Grand Hotel, and it was such a sight that Grimaldi decided they should order a taxi and have a martini while they waited. Ruda resisted at first, but then, having been told that the regular taxis were engaged at present and that there would be no taxi for another hour, she relented.

Ruda and Grimaldi walked into the foyer and headed for the comfortable lounge. They made a striking couple. Grimaldi began to enjoy himself. Guiding Ruda by the elbow, he inclined his head.

"Now, this is my style, and I think since we're here, we might as well order some lunch. The restaurant looks good, what do you say?"

Ruda looked at her wristwatch. She had to get back to rehearse and feed the cats, but still they had to wait for a taxi, so she suggested they just have a drink and order a sandwich.

Grimaldi decided this was as good a time as any to have a talk, away from the trailer, away from the circus. In the luxurious surroundings they might have a civilized conversation.

They sat in a small booth with red plush velvet seats and a marble-topped table. Ferns hid them from the rest of the hotel guests, mostly American as far as Grimaldi could tell.

They sipped their martinis in silence, and Ruda ate the entire bowl of peanuts, popping one at a time into her mouth. Grimaldi took an envelope from his pocket and opened it.

"I have been working out our financial situation, how much the act costs, living expenses, and what we will both need to live on. Maybe we should sell the trailer and each buy a smaller one."

She turned on him. "Your priority is to get back the old plinths! I can't work with the new ones."

"We've already discussed that, for chrissakes. Just go through this with me, we have to sort it out sometime."

Ruda snatched the sheet of paper, and looked over his haphazard scrawl. It was quite a shock to her that even after their closeness, he was still intent on leaving her.

"She's pregnant, Ruda, I want to get a divorce and marry her!"

Ruda tore the paper into scraps. "I'll think about it."

Grimaldi signaled for the waiter to bring more drinks. Ruda's foot was tapping against the table leg.

"I don't want to have an argument here, Ruda, okay?"

She stared at him, telling herself to keep calm. She had to deal with things one at a time. She had dealt with Kellerman, Grimaldi would be next, but her priority now was to get the act ready for opening night. One thing at a time—this show was to be her biggest, and if she performed well she knew that with live coverage, there would be no more need for second-circuit dates; she would be an international star. Above all she wanted to get to the United States again, and win a contract at New York's Ringling Bros. and Barnum & Bailey circus.

"Ruda, we have to discuss this, Ruda!"

"I'll think about it, we'll work out something!"

As the waiter came by their table, passing directly behind him was a very handsome man accompanied by an attractive blond woman. They were both in deep conversation, not giving Grimaldi or Ruda a glance. They seated themselves in the next booth, and the waiter, after taking Grimaldi's order, moved quickly to the elegant couple's booth.

"Good afternoon, Baron."

Helen Masters asked for a gin and tonic, and the baron a scotch on the rocks. He spoke German, then turned back to continue his conversation with Helen in French. They paid no attention to the big broad-shouldered man seated in the next booth. They could not see Ruda.

Grimaldi had ordered two more martinis. Ruda said she didn't want another, but he ignored her. He looked around the lounge, then noticed she was playing with the bread. It always used to infuriate him, the way she would pick at it, roll it into tiny little balls, twitch it, and pummel it with her fingers.

"Stop that, you know it gets on my nerves. We'll sort out the plinths when we get back. Now, can we just relax, Ruda?"

She nodded, but under the table her hands began to roll a small piece of bread tighter and tighter, until it became a dense hard ball—because she kept on seeing the boy, Mike, wearing Kellerman's hideous black leather trilby. Mike, Grimaldi and his bloody divorce . . . it was all descending on her like a dark blanket, and suddenly she felt as if her mind would explode. Her fingers pressed and rolled the tiny ball of bread mechanically, as if out of her control. She swallowed, her mouth was dry, her lips felt stiff, her tongue held to the roof of her mouth. It was seeping upward from her toes. . . . She fought against it, refusing to allow it to dominate her—not here, not in public. "No . . . no!"

Grimaldi looked at her, was not sure what she had said. He leaned closer. "Ruda? You okay?"

She repeated the word "No!" like a low growl. He could see her body was rigid, and yet the table shook slightly as her fingers pressed and rolled the tiny ball of bread.

"Ruda! . . . *Ruda!*"

She turned her head very slowly, her eyes seemed unfocused, staring through him. He slipped his hand beneath the table. "What's the matter with you? Are you sick?"

Grimaldi held her hand, crunched in a hard knot. She recoiled from him, pressing her back against the velvet booth.

"I have to go to the toilet." She rose to her feet. "I'll meet you outside, I need some fresh air."

Grimaldi made to stand, but she pushed past him and he slumped back down in the seat, watching as she walked stiffly toward the foyer, hands clenched tight at her side. She brushed past an elaborate display of ferns and then quickened her pace, almost running to the cloakrooms. There was only one other occupant, a tourist applying lipstick, examining her reflection in the mirror. Ruda knocked against her, but made no apology, hurrying into the vacant lavatory. She had no time to shut the door, but fell to her knees, clinging to the wooden toilet seat as she began to vomit. She felt an instant release, and sat back on her heels panting; again she felt the rush of bile, and leaned over the basin, the stench, the white bowl—she pushed away until she was hunched against the partition.

"Are you all right? Do you need me to call someone?" The tourist stood at a distance, but was very concerned.

Ruda heaved again and forced herself once more to be sick into the lavatory bowl.

"Should I call a doctor?"

Ruda wiped her mouth with the back of her hand, and without even looking up snapped: "Get out, just get out and leave me alone. . . ."

Ruda slowly rose to stand, pressing herself against the tiled wall, then crossed unsteadily to the wash basin. She ran the cold water and splashed it over her face, then patted herself dry with the soft hand towels provided. She opened her purse and fumbled for her compact. Her whole body tingled, the hair on the backs of her hands was raised, the same strange, almost animal warning at the nape of her neck. Was it this hotel? Something in this hotel? The white tiled walls, the white marble floor—had she been here before?

She seemed to be outside herself. What was wrong? And then, just as she had always done, she began to work to calm herself, talking softly, whispering that it was just the whiteness, it was the white tiles . . . it was seeing Tommy, it was nothing more. It was a natural reaction, it was just shock, delayed shock at seeing him, seeing Tommy.

• • •

Ruda crossed the large foyer, her composure restored. She paused, wary, as if listening for something, to something, but then she shrugged her shoulders and headed toward the main revolving doors.

As Ruda stepped outside, Hilda was scurrying toward the staff entrance, a small hidden door at the side of the hotel. She stopped in her tracks, seeing the tall woman standing on the steps. For a moment she thought she was seeing the baroness, but then she shook her head at her stupidity; this woman was much bigger, her dark hair long. Still, as she continued through the staff entrance, she wondered where she had seen the woman before. She unpacked her working shoes and slipped them on, carefully placing her other shoes into her locker. As she closed the door and crossed to the mirror to run a comb through her hair, she remembered. The circus poster. It was the woman from the circus poster, she was sure of it and rather pleased with her recall. She wondered if she was staying at the hotel; perhaps, if she was, Hilda could ask for her autograph.

A chambermaid coming off duty called out to Hilda, and scurried over to her. She asked if it was true that the baroness was insane; rumors were rife and she was eager to gossip.

Hilda refused to be drawn into a conversation, and the young girl was forced to change the subject, moving on to other news. A dwarf had been found murdered in the red light district just behind the hotel, his body beaten. They had first thought it was a child, his body was so small. She knew about it because her boyfriend worked with the Polizei. She came close to Hilda and hissed: "He was a Jew!"

6

GRIMALDI LEFT the Grand Hotel, unable to find Ruda. He walked awhile, then caught a bus back to the circus.

Baron Maréchal and Helen remained in the hotel bar. The baron apologized for having left Helen to wait for so long. She said no apology was necessary, because if he needed to speak with Dr. Franks alone, he should be able to do so. He kissed her hand, saying that her understanding never ceased to amaze him.

"She is so much better, Louis, did you notice? Perhaps tomorrow she will be able to see Dr. Franks; sooner than we hoped."

The baron sipped his drink, placing it carefully on the paper napkin. "He knows that the present situation cannot continue."

The manager approached their table, and excused the intrusion. The baron half rose from his seat, his face drained of color. "Is it my wife?"

The manager handed the baron an envelope containing a number of faxes. Helen saw the relief on Louis's face as he tipped the manager lavishly, opening the envelope. He read through the five sheets, passing them on to Helen.

There was no record of a Vebekka Lynsey in Philadelphia. The woman who had once run the modeling agency that had employed Vebekka confirmed that her name was Rebecca. Checks on Rebecca Lynsey in Philadelphia produced no results. Two women who had once modeled for the same agency had been tracked down. They did recall Rebecca, and one thought her last name was Goldberg, but could not be absolutely sure. She had shared a room with Rebecca, and remembered her receiving letters addressed in that name.

A Mr. and Mrs. Ulrich Goldberg had subsequently been traced in Philadelphia, and although they had no direct connection to the baroness, they were able to give further details. Ulrich Goldberg's cousin, Dieter (David) Goldberg, had run a successful fur business until 1967. David and his wife, Rosa, had arrived in Philadelphia from Canada in the late fifties. They had one daughter, Rebecca. Was Rebecca Goldberg Vebekka Lynsey? Ulrich Goldberg, when shown recent photographs of Vebekka, was unable to state that they were definitely of her, but admitted there was a great similarity.

According to Ulrich Goldberg, Rebecca was last seen in January 1972 at her father's funeral. She had been distant and evasive, speaking briefly to only a handful of mourners, and had departed very quickly. No one had heard from her since. A number of photographs taken when she was about ten or twelve years old were being forwarded by Federal Express.

Mr. and Mrs. Goldberg had arrived in the United States from Germany in the late 1930s. They knew that David Goldberg's wife was born in Berlin, and that she was or had been a doctor. When she had married and emigrated to Canada was something of a mystery. Although the two Goldberg families were related, Ulrich admitted that he and his wife had not been on close terms with David Goldberg—and found his wife a very cold, distant woman.

The baron finished reading the last page and handed it to Helen. She read it in silence, then folded the fax sheets and replaced them in their envelope. The baron lit a cigar, and turned to her.

"This could all be inaccurate. These are not from a detective, he's my chauffeur!"

Helen paused, and then chose her words carefully. "The date of the funeral, is that when Vebekka left Paris?"

The baron frowned, but after a moment nodded.

Helen spoke quietly. "First you have to deal with the cover-up or lies. For reasons we don't know, she simply didn't want you to know anything about her family, but if she is Rebecca Goldberg, and her mother was born in Berlin, we can do some detective work of our own. Maybe there are relatives still living here, or someone who knew them. We could try to trace them."

The baron pinched the bridge of his nose; all this was too much for him to take in.

"Perhaps the reason, or a possible reason, was that your family were against your marrying Vebekka," Helen suggested. Would Vebekka's Jewishness have been one of the reasons why the baron's family disapproved of the marriage? She decided not to broach the subject. She sipped her drink. Perhaps, as Louis had said, this was all a misunderstanding. But if Louis was hesitant to check out this Goldberg connection, there was no reason why she shouldn't.

✦ ✦ ✦

Hilda had almost finished a sleeve and was beginning to check the measurements when Vebekka opened her eyes. Slowly she turned to face Hilda and smiled.

"Have I been sleeping long?"

Hilda nodded, said it was after two, but that she needed sleep. Hilda helped her from bed, and wrapped a robe around her thin shoulders. She walked her to the bathroom, where big towels were warming on the rails. She had to help her into the bath, but Vebekka slid into the soap- and perfume-filled water with a sigh of pleasure.

Hilda gently toweled Vebekka dry when she was done, feeling protective and motherly as the thin frame rested against her. Vebekka seemed loath to let her go, clinging to her as they returned to the bedroom. Then the baroness sat in front of her mirror and opened one of her vanity cases.

"I need my hair done, Hilda."

Hilda said that she would try, but was not sure how to go about it. Vebekka giggled while taking out small pots and brushes.

"No no—my roots, I need my roots done. See, the gray hair is showing!"

Hilda watched as Vebekka mixed her color. "It's called Raven. It looks purple, but it comes out black."

While Vebekka parted her hair and clipped sections, Hilda brushed the thick purplish liquid into the hairline. Then Hilda sat and waited: the tint had to be left on for twenty minutes. Meanwhile, Vebekka manicured her hands, put cream on her elbows and neck, then on her legs and on her arms.

Together they returned to the bathroom and Hilda shampooed and washed out the tint. Then she wrapped a towel around the clean, tinted head and they returned to the bedroom. Next Vebekka directed Hilda to hold the dryer while she used the brush.

"I'm young again, Hilda, see? You were very good . . . now I want to look beautiful, a little makeup, rouge. . . ."

Hilda was fascinated at the transformation; then she helped the baroness into a silk and lace robe, so delicate it floated when Vebekka moved, the lace on the sleeves trailing as in medieval costumes.

Hilda ordered a light luncheon, boiled fish, some milk and vegetables, and she was pleased to see that Vebekka ate every morsel. Just as she was ringing for room service to take the table away, the baron entered to find his wife sitting like a princess at the window. His face broke into a smile of delight. "You look wonderful! And you have eaten? Good, good . . . do you feel better?"

Hilda left them alone and went into the main bedroom to tidy the room and make the bed. Louis bent to kiss Vebekka's cheek; she smelled sweet and fresh, her hair gleamed like silk. She smiled, and looked up into his concerned face. "Did you come in to see me earlier?"

"No, I had a drink with Helen. If you need her she is in her room."

Vebekka cocked her head. "Well, don't you two get too cozy!"

He turned away, irritated.

"I was just teasing you, Louis. It was just—well, strange. I was sure someone came in . . . maybe I was dreaming."

With her husband's help she stood up, clinging to his hand. "I think I will rest for a while now. You don't have to stay, I have Hilda. Maybe Helen would like to go sightseeing, she must be very bored."

They walked slowly to the bedroom, and suddenly she leaned against him. "Remember in that old movie with Merle Oberon, when she said: 'Take me . . . take me to the window, I want to see the moors one last time!' "

Vebekka did such a good impersonation of the dying heroine from *Wuthering Heights* that she made Louis laugh; he swept her into his arms and gently carried her to the bed.

The baron stood by watching as Hilda fluffed up her pillows, remained watching as Hilda gently drew the sheet around her, and then let the drapes close, leaving the room in semidarkness.

Hilda asked if she might take a break for an hour. He nodded, dismissing her with an incline of his head, and sat in the chair she had vacated.

Vebekka lay with her eyes closed, as though unaware of his presence. She was so still she could have been laid out at a funeral home, the perfect makeup, the long dark lashes, her hair framing her beautiful face. He took out his gold cigarette case, patted his pockets for his lighter, and kept his eyes on her as he clicked it open. She didn't stir. He inhaled deeply and let the smoke drift from his mouth to form a perfect circle above his head. Had she woven all these lies about herself? Why? He couldn't think of a reason for not telling him—unless she was ashamed, but ashamed of what?

The more he stared at her, the more unanswered questions crossed his mind. Was it his fault? He could hear her now, as if she were saying it to him now.

"My father's dead. I have to go to America to see to the funeral."

She had said it so matter-of-factly, as if suggesting she fly to New York for a fitting. He had asked if she wished him to accompany her and she had smiled, shaking her head, reminding him that he was flying to Brazil for a polo game. He could remember his relief at not having to alter his plans. He was not in Paris when she returned, and so the funeral was not really discussed. She had bought many gifts for the children and for him, and had laughed at her extravagance, saying she was surprised at how much her father had left her. Louis knew it was a considerable amount, because his own lawyers had called to discuss the matter, but she had been disinterested in the money, as he was. She had been happy, she had been well—above all, happy.

These episodes always remained vivid to him, because when Vebekka was happy, the whole family's spirits lifted. When she was energized, she would arrange surprise outings and parties, like a child. Her good spirits would extend beyond the family circle. She would organize dinner parties, get dressed for masked balls. . . .

As a hostess she was a delight, she would make everyone feel immediately at ease.

He leaned forward, noting in the semidarkness the contours of her face. The way her long exquisite fingers rested like an angel's, one hand on top of the other—the perfect nails, her tiny wrists. It was hard to believe that those long tapering delicate hands could become vicious claws.

Louis mulled over his conversations with Dr. Franks. Was he in some way to blame? In the stillness of the room he could honestly ask himself if he was guilty. Louis asked himself why the glimpses of sun in her life were so short-lived now, so rare, and why when she changed, there was such anguish.

He got up to stub out his cigarette. From the dressing table he looked at the still sleeping woman; she had not moved. He had to think not just of himself, but of Sasha, and the boys; they too had suffered, they had been forced to care for her, watch out for the signs. His eldest daughter had retreated into a busy social life that left little time for home. The boys had drawn very close to each other. The real hurt was to his younger daughter; she was so much younger than the others that she had seen fewer good periods.

Louis would perhaps never know the true extent of the damage to his children. He sighed. It would be easy, slip the pillow from the side of the bed, press it to her face, and it would be over. No one could say he had not been driven to it, that she did not deserve it.

She stirred, her hands fluttered, lifted a moment, and then rested again. She turned her head toward Louis, and slowly opened her eyes. He wondered if she knew he was there, wondered if anyone could understand what it was like to turn to someone you loved and face a stranger—and worse, be afraid. That awful moment of awareness when he knew it was happening. When the face he loved became distorted—the mouth he kissed pulled back like an animal— the voice he loved, snarled—and the gentle arms lashed out like steel traps.

Louis pressed his back against the dressing table and watched. Was he about to see the transformation now? The slender arms stretched, and she moaned softly, then smiled, with such sweetness.

"How long have you been there?"

"Not long," he lied, and sat on the edge of her bed.

"Where's Hilda?"

"She's having a break."

"She's so sweet."

"How do you feel?"

"Good, refreshed. Where's Helen?"

"I don't know, maybe shopping."

She sat up and shook her head. "We did my hair, Hilda and I. What time is it?"

She looked at her bedside clock, then threw back the sheet. "We can call Sasha and the boys."

He watched her slip her feet into slippers, and then yawn, lifting her arms above her head. "I feel hungry, I am ravenous!"

Louis hesitated, then told himself not to draw back now, to go through with it. "I'm glad you feel better, and hungry. Dr. Franks will be pleased, too."

He saw the catlike reaction as her eyes narrowed. He continued: "Franks is waiting for me to call him, he said that I should contact him as soon as you recovered."

"Really?" she said flatly.

"Yes. So, my dear, shall I call him?"

She pursed her lips. "Oh, I can't see him yet. I'm still too weak. Can you get Hilda for me?"

Louis opened the drapes, forced himself not to back off, not this time. "Shall I tell Dr. Franks perhaps tomorrow?"

"Oh, I don't know. Is Anne Marie in?"

Louis crossed over to her and took her hand. "Come and sit down. I'll get Hilda and Anne Marie, but first we need to talk."

She sat on the dressing table stool, looking up at him.

"I'm going to call Dr. Franks, right now. What shall I tell him?"

She hunched her shoulders. "I can't see him for a while."

He sighed and stuffed his hands into his pockets. "What does that mean? A day? two days? a week? How long do you expect us all to wait around here? This is the reason . . ."

She retorted angrily, interrupting him: "I know why we came, and I have agreed to see him, but not just yet!"

When Louis suggested they ask Franks to come and see her later in the afternoon, she snapped: "I have to rest."

Louis walked to the door, saying he would call him anyway.

"*I don't want* to see him, I've changed my mind. Besides I feel as if I am getting stronger. Without all those pills that wretched woman makes me take, my system is getting cleansed. I am detoxifying; it's a slow process, I am bound to have some withdrawal symptoms and . . ."

"That's right, keep on with the excuses, but this time I am not taking no for an answer. If you want to stay here a month I'll arrange it, but you are going to Dr. Franks."

"Don't be so nasty with me, why are you being so nasty?"

"For God's sake, I am not being nasty, you are being childish. I'll call him now."

"No."

He looked at her, opening the door.

"*I said no.*"

He slammed the door shut—hard. "*You* have no say in the matter, do you understand?"

"I won't see him."

Louis crossed the room and gripped her arm. "You will see him, do you hear me? You will see him, we agreed, *you* agreed and you cannot change your mind now."

"Why not? It's my mind."

He released her arm. "Right now it is! But for how long? I've told you, this is the last time, it's your last chance."

"Don't you mean yours?"

He had to control his temper. "We have nothing left, Bekki, you and I both know it. I am doing this for you—not for me, for you."

"Liar! You want me certified and dumped."

"I don't want to fight with you, Bekki, I want to help you. Can't you understand? That is all I have ever wanted to do—help you."

She stared at him, angrily. He kept his voice low, trying to be controlled. "You need help, you know it. If not for me . . ."

"Oh shut up! I've heard that one too many times." She mimicked him: "If not for me, do it for yourself."

She turned on him. "This is for you, Louis, I am here is this bloody awful country for *you, you* want to get rid of me, don't you think I know it? Well, one, I will not give you a divorce; two, I will go to see Dr. Franks when I feel up to going to see him, in my own time when I feel fit and well enough, and I will not be pressured by you, or by that whore Helen, I will not be forced into seeing this crank because *you* want to get rid of me and run off with that tart."

"You mean Helen? For God's sake, she is your friend, your doctor—and, Bekki, I am not running anywhere, I never have before, and I don't intend to now."

"But you are leaving me? . . . Aren't you? You've decided, haven't you?"

She plucked a tissue from its container and wiped her face, slowly removing her makeup. She had only dressed and made herself look pretty for him. She murmured under her breath about Helen again.

"Helen has nothing to do with any decision I make!"

She smiled. "Ah, you are making a decision all by yourself, are you? Well, that is a change."

He refused to be drawn into an argument, and their eyes met in the mirror.

"No, Bekki, you make the decision this time, it is up to you. If you refuse to see Dr. Franks, then . . ."

She held his gaze with a defiant stare. "Then what?"

"You cannot return to the children."

"They are old enough to make their own decision." She said it with defiance, but he could see her eyes were beginning to flick, to blink rapidly.

"Sasha is not!"

Her hands trembled and she began to twist the tissue, but she didn't look away from him.

"You can't do that to me! I love Sasha, she needs me."

"You give me no alternative. I've told you, this is your last chance."

He walked out. Even after he had closed the door, he felt as if her eyes were on him. He poured a brandy, his hands shaking as he lifted the glass. Would she begin throwing things, screaming, was she going to come hurtling out of the bedroom? The brandy hit the back of his throat, warming him. He poured himself some more, and then froze. The telephone extension rang once, he knew she was making a call, and he banged the glass down—breaking the stem. Was she calling Sasha? He hurried to the bedroom, about to fling open the door. He could hear her talking; he pressed his head to the door to listen.

Vebekka's palms were sweating, small beads of perspiration glistened on her brow. She gripped the telephone tighter, afraid she would unconsciously put it down.

"Dr. Franks? This is Baroness Maréchal, I . . ."

She could hear him breathing, then ask how she was, and she had to swallow once, twice before she could reply. "I am very much better . . ."

"Good, I am glad to hear it."

The sweating made her feel weak, her whole body shook. Her hair was wringing wet.

"Hello? Baroness? . . . Hello?"

Dr. Franks could hardly hear her, but he knew she was still on the line. "Are you experiencing any adverse effects? Any withdrawal symptoms? Baroness?"

"Sweating, I am sweating."

She gasped, and had to reach for the dressing table top to steady herself; she felt as if she were going to faint.

"That is only to be expected. You must drink, can you hear me? You must drink as much water as possible, keep drinking. Would you like me to come and see you?"

"No!"

Franks couldn't hear her. He asked again. "I can be with you in half an hour. Would you like me to come to see you?"

There was a long pause. He could not tell if she was still on the line or not.

She whispered. "I would like to come and see you."

"Pardon? I can't hear you?"

"I want you to help me, I want to come to you."

"That is good, I can arrange for you to have the entire morning. Shall we say nine in the morning?"

"Thank you." She replaced the phone carefully; it felt heavy. Her hands clasped tightly together, Vebekka felt nothing but fear.

✦ ✦ ✦

Louis was elated that Vebekka had called Franks herself. He had not expected her to have the strength. He called down to the desk to ask for Hilda to come to their suite immediately. He then called Anne Marie to check on his wife.

The baron was banking on Dr. Franks, as if on a miracle cure; it was naïve of him, and he knew it. But even if Franks could not help Vebekka, at least the baron could honestly tell himself that he had tried. And then he could, without guilt, have her placed in an institution. He no longer had regrets, it was the only choice he had.

From the open door to her bedroom, he watched for a brief moment as Anne Marie tended to Vebekka. He could see that her nightgown was sodden, her face dripping with sweat, and she was mumbling incoherently. The baron saw Anne Marie check his wife's pulse, then take her temperature. He continued to watch as Vebekka struggled a moment, her arms thrashing at her sides, and then she grew listless, still sweating profusely. He turned away as Anne Marie began to remove his wife's nightgown. Vebekka seemed unaware of the nurse, and when Anne Marie realized the baron was watching she hesitated, the gown half removed.

Louis bowed his head. "I'll be in the foyer if you need me."

He didn't go to the foyer, but to the small bar at the rear of the hotel's reception. There was no mistress for him to run to; instead, he sat hunched in the corner of the bar with a cognac.

Vebekka seemed grateful when Hilda bustled in and quickly began to help Anne Marie change the bed linen. They placed cold compresses on her brow. Bottles of mineral water were brought up. Hilda encouraged her to drink as much as possible. Vebekka began to shiver, and more blankets were piled on top of the comforter.

Hilda sat close by the bed, wringing out the cold compress. Vebekka had gone from shivering with cold to sweating with fever. At least she was sleeping deeply now, but Hilda grew more and more concerned. She gestured for Anne Marie to take Vebekka's pulse. It was rapid, but nothing to be too concerned about. Anne Marie felt the skin on the underside of Vebekka's wrist. There was a shiny area of skin, whiter than the rest of her skin, and she pointed it out to Hilda.

"What is that mark on her wrist from?" Hilda asked.

Anne Marie whispered: "She told me it was a burn, but it looks more like a skin graft." She continued whispering as she pointed out that it was the same wrist Vebekka had cut the night they had arrived. She smirked, suggesting that perhaps Vebekka had attempted it before. Hilda said nothing, she could see that the fresh wound was already healing, but the white, neat scar tissue was higher up, about four inches from the base of the baroness's palm.

✦ ✦ ✦

It was just after four when Vebekka woke, and she reached out for Hilda's hand, struggled to sit up, drank thirstily from a glass Hilda held, then rested back on the pillows. She looked to the window, asked for it to be opened, she wanted some fresh air. Hilda obliged. "Is this too much?"

"No, it feels good, has it stopped raining?"

"Yes, just! But there are dark clouds, I think there could be a storm."

Suddenly Vebekka's body went rigid and blinding colors flashed across her brain. Hilda rushed to her side. "What is it? What is it?"

The thin hands clenched the sheets, her body seemed caught in a spasm, and Hilda ran out to call for Anne Marie.

The colors screamed in her head, red . . . blood red . . . green . . . they were coming fast, flashes of brilliant reds, greens, and blues. When Hilda and Anne Marie returned, they saw Vebekka struggling to stand up, she kept repeating "*Up . . . Up!*"

They could not restrain her; she kept pushing them away. Then, as quickly as the spasm had begun, it stopped. She flopped back onto the pillows, clutching her head as if in agony. Hilda tried to put an ice-cold cloth on her brow but she swiped at her, screamed for her to get away, to stay away from her.

Hilda stepped back, frightened by the force of that skinny arm. Shocked, she looked to Anne Marie, who was standing back, nowhere near the thrashing figure.

"Should we call someone?" Hilda asked.

Anne Marie walked out of the room, warning over her shoulder for Hilda to stay away from the bed. Vebekka was rubbing at her hair, banging her head with her fists.

"Stop it. Stop it. Make it stop, please God make it stop!"

The colors hammered, flashed, and she couldn't get her breath. Panting and gasping, she reached out to Hilda, trying to get hold of her. Anne Marie came back with the straitjacket, unwrapping it from its plastic case. "The doctor should be here now, never mind her husband!"

Hilda stood by the bed, her arms open wide, protecting Vebekka. "*No . . . no . . . don't put that on her, I won't let you!*"

Anne Marie looked at the bed, and tossed the jacket aside.

"They shouldn't have taken her off the sedatives, this has happened before! Well, I am not taking any responsibility, she'll attack you."

Vebekka begged Hilda to get rid of Anne Marie, to make her get out of the room. Anne Marie looked to Hilda, as if to say *It is up to you!*

Vebekka wouldn't let Hilda go. "I'm here, dear, it's all right. Hilda's right here with you."

Anne Marie stormed out while Hilda stayed with Vebekka, calming her, stroking her hair, saying over and over that she was there, that she wasn't going to leave her. The thin arms relaxed and Vebekka rested her head against Hilda's shoulder.

"Oh God help me, what is it? What happens to me? Hilda, Hilda!"

Hilda coaxed her to lie back on the pillows, and Vebekka didn't struggle, she was too exhausted. She whispered, like a frightened child. "It is closer . . . it is so close, I can't make it go away."

Hilda made soft shushing sounds, as if to a little girl. "What is it? What are you frightened of? Is it something in the room?"

"I don't know. Something possesses me, controls me, and I can't fight it anymore, I'm so tired . . . so tired."

Hilda continued stroking Vebekka's hair. "What do you think it is? If you tell me, then maybe it won't be so frightening."

Vebekka turned away, curling her knees up, her arms wrapped around herself. How could she answer when she didn't know? All she knew was that it was closer than it had ever been before.

Hilda shut the window, drew the drapes, and in the semidarkness returned to the bedside, bending down to try to see Vebekka's face. She talked softly the whole time, saying she was there, nothing could come into the room, nothing in the room could frighten her. She stood by the bed, waiting, but Vebekka didn't move. Eventually, Hilda crept out, pulling the door behind her silently.

Hilda stood in the empty lounge, not knowing what she should do—stay or try to find the baron or Helen Masters. She looked at her watch—it was almost five—she looked to Anne Marie's closed door, back to the bedroom. The suite was silent, she could hear the clock ticking on the marble mantel, but outside the passing cars tooted, the noise of traffic drawing up outside the hotel was loud and intrusive, and she was afraid the sounds would wake Vebekka.

Hilda crossed to draw the wooden shutters closed. They were heavy and she moved from one window to the next before she lifted the fine white drapes to look into the street below. Hilda's hand was on the shutter when she saw a solitary figure. She could not see whether it was a man or woman, because a car drew up and obscured her view. The driver appeared to say something to the dark figure, who bent down, then straightened up, gesturing for the car to drive on. Hilda could tell now that it was a woman, but her hair was drawn back tightly from her face. The collar of her thick overcoat was turned up . . . but what caught Hilda's attention was the way the figure seemed to be staring toward the hotel, her head moving very slightly from side to side, as if looking from window to window, floor to floor. At any monent now she would face Hilda, and Hilda could catch a better view of her—but just then the doors to the suite were thrown open.

Helen Masters strode in, and asked brusquely if the baron was with his wife.

As Hilda turned back to close the shutters, the woman on the pavement below had vanished. "No, Dr. Masters, he is not."

At that precise moment the baron walked in. Helen smiled a greeting; the baron seemed a little unsteady on his feet.

"I called your room, have you been shopping?"

"No, Louis, you must come with me. I've traced a woman, a relative of David Goldberg's wife. She said she would see us."

"Excuse me, Baron . . ."

They both turned to Hilda, as if only then realizing she was in the room. When Hilda nervously related the earlier events, the baron slumped into a chair, then turned to Helen.

"She called Franks herself, this afternoon, said she would see him tomorrow!" Louis opened the bedroom door, went into the darkened room.

Helen asked if Anne Marie was with Vebekka, but Hilda shook her head. She was twisting her hands anxiously. Helen went to her side.

"Are you all right, did she frighten you?"

Hilda whispered to Helen that she would like to speak with her, that she did not mean to say more than she should, but felt Helen should know what Anne Marie's intentions had been.

Helen moved her further away from the bedroom, patting Hilda's shoulder. "It's all right, you can tell me . . . I want to know what happened, it's very important."

Briefly, and in a hushed voice, Hilda related to Helen the story of the straitjacket.

Louis bent down to try to see Vebekka's face; she appeared to be sleeping. He gave a featherlike touch to her head and then joined Helen. "She's sleeping."

Helen gestured for him to come close, repeated everything Hilda had told her. Louis strode to Anne Marie's room, knocked and without waiting for an answer, entered and closed the door behind him.

Anne Marie looked up from her book, flustered, trying to straighten her blouse.

"I would like you to leave, you can arrange a flight at the reception desk."

He opened his wallet, and before Anne Marie had time to reply, he left a thick wad of folded bills on her bed. She snapped her book closed, wanting obviously to discuss the matter, but he walked out. She stared at the money, her lips pursed, then counted it, looked at the closed door and swore under her breath.

◆ ◆ ◆

They were both sitting in the lounge when Anne Marie came out of her room, with case packed and coat over her arm. Her face was tight with anger. "Thank you for your generosity, Baron. Perhaps when you return to Paris, you would be kind enough to give me a letter of recommendation."

The baron threw the straitjacket at her feet.

"There will be no letter of recommendation."

Anne Marie stepped over the straitjacket, and crossed to the suite's double doors. She opened the righthand side, about to walk out without a word, but then she turned back.

"I would be most grateful for a letter, I will require one for future employment!"

Helen put her hand out to restrain Louis. Anne Marie looked at them both with disdain.

"I would be only too pleased to give *you* a letter of recommendation to have the baroness certified! She should have been, years ago! Dr. Franks is just another quack, another fool who'll take your money like the rest of them. There is no cure, it is a fantasy . . . your wife, Baron, is insane! She has been since I have been in your employment. She will kill someone, and that will be entirely your fault!"

Helen's restraining hand was pushed aside as the baron strode across the room. "You had better leave before I throw you out. *Get out!*"

"As you wish, Baron! I will collect my personal belongings from the villa."

He pushed her out and slammed the door shut. "I should have done this months ago."

At his feet was the straitjacket. He picked it up and stared at it. He seemed totally defeated.

"Don't give up, Louis, it isn't true. I believe in Franks."

He sighed, placing the jacket down on a chair. He kept his back to Helen. "Maybe she is right, maybe this is all a waste of time. I am so tired of it all, Helen."

His whole body tensed, his hands were clenched to his side. "I wish to God she were dead."

"That's not true!"

He turned to face her. "Isn't it? I was sitting by her bedside, earlier today, thinking if I had the guts I would put a pillow over her face and end it, for her, for me, then . . ."

"Then?"

He sighed, slumping into a chair. "She was lucid, understood that I cannot allow her to be with Sasha, and she called Franks, it was her decision."

Helen picked up her purse and took out her notebook. "I am sure he will help her, but I think we should at least talk to this woman. The more we know of Vebekka's background the better! Franks will need as much information as possible . . . Louis?"

He cocked his head and gave a rueful smile.

"Fine, whatever you say."

Helen picked up her coat, heading for her suite. "I'll have a bath and change. We can leave when Hilda returns to the hotel. I'll order some coffee."

Louis nodded, and then smiled. "Yes, I think some coffee would be an excellent idea."

The coffee arrived moments later, and Louis downed two cups before he felt sober. He carefully checked the time, first on his wristwatch, and then looked at the clock on the mantel. It was five-thirty.

He put in a call to this sons, and then spoke to Sasha for a while.

He said they missed her, and that he would tell her mama that she was being a good girl. The high-pitched voice hesitated before asking if her mama was being a good girl. He told her that everything was fine, and her mama would talk to her very soon. He managed to keep his voice calm and relaxed, but he was crying.

"Will she be coming home better, Papa?"

Louis pinched his nose between thumb and forefinger. "I hope so. She hasn't been very well for a day or so, which means we may be here longer than we anticipated." Sasha sighed with disappointment, but then changed the subject, talking about school and her new pony and telling him that she was practicing dressage, and entering a gymkhana—she was sure she would win a rosette this time. Angel—her pony—was living up to his name.

"Papa, we jumped a two-foot fence! He is wonderful!"

Louis congratulated his daughter, and then said he had to go, there was another call on the line. Sasha made kissing sounds, and he waited for her to replace the receiver before he put his down. He heard the click, then another click. He frowned; then replaced the receiver and walked into Vebekka's bedroom. She was propped up on her pillows, very pale, deep circles beneath her eyes.

"I will go to see the doctor tomorrow, Louis, even if you have to carry me there!" She sipped a glass of water, then replaced the glass on her bedside table. It took all her willpower to be calm, she needed something to help her, something to make her sleep, but she asked for nothing. She wasn't going to drug herself, not this time; she was determined she would see it through.

"I've dismissed Anne Marie. Hilda will be here shortly."

She leaned back, closing her eyes. "I never liked Anne Marie. Will you hold my hand?"

He sat on the edge of the bed, lifted her hand to his lips, and kissed her fingers; they were so thin, so weak.

"Will you promise me something, Louis?"

"Depends on what it is!"

She didn't open her eyes. "I understand what trouble I cause, and I know I am always asking you to forgive me, but I always mean it. If this doctor thinks I will get worse, that these good moments will get fewer, and you are right, that I shouldn't be with Sasha, I understand that, but you must understand, I never . . . I never intend to hurt anyone, I don't know what takes me over, but it unleashes such terrible . . ."

"I know . . . I know, but you must rest now, regain your strength."

She withdrew her hand, turning away from him. "Louis, if nothing can be done, you know, if after the hypnosis you find out things, I want no lies, no cover-ups, no new tests, because I don't think I can stand it anymore. I'm getting worse, I know that, hours go by and I don't know what I have done, who I've hurt, so promise me."

He knew what she was going to ask of him and he leaned over the bed to kiss her cheek.

"Sleep now."

She opened her eyes, they pleaded, they begged him. "Don't put me away, Louis, help me to end it—promise me?"

He kissed her again, tilted her chin in his hands, looked deep into her eyes. He didn't answer, and her eyelids drooped as she fell asleep, her chin still cupped in his hands.

They were still together like a loving couple when Hilda slipped quietly into the bedroom. Gently the baron drew the covers to Vebekka's chin, and Hilda saw the way he brushed her cheek with the edge of his index finger.

"She was so frightened, sir, of the dark. Frightened someone was out there."

The baron patted Hilda's shoulder. "Hilda, my poor darling is frightened of her own shadow. Thank you for your care and attention, good evening."

Hilda whispered "Good evening" as he quietly closed the door. She began to knit, then looked to the closed shutter and remembered the woman, the one she had seen outside that afternoon; she had been like a shadow, waiting, watching. The click click of her own knitting needles soothed and calmed Hilda.

Vebekka did not seem even to be awake, but her hand moved closer to Hilda, and she said very softly: "Ma . . . angel."

✦ ✦ ✦

While Helen was getting ready, the baron lit a cigarette, pacing the room, tormented by his wife's request. He picked up the late afternoon paper in the room, and a front-page article caught his attention: MURDERED MAN IDENTIFIED. He started to read the column. The man was called Tommy Kellerman, a dwarf, a circus performer, who had recently arrived in East Berlin from Paris. The Polizei requested anyone seeing Kellerman on or during the night of his murder to come forward.

Helen walked in refreshed and changed. Louis lowered the paper and smiled. "You look lovely!" He was about to toss the paper aside when he passed it to Helen. "Did you read this? A circus performer was murdered."

Helen glanced at the article.

"Yes, I was talking to one of the doormen, the hotel is only a few streets away from here. Apparently they have no clues, it happened late the same night we arrived. He was horribly beaten—the doorman was very keen to pass on all the gory details."

The baron put on his coat and said he would call down for a taxi. Helen opened the shutters to look at the weather, then felt a sense of déjà vu so strong she had to step back from the window . . . Helen saw Vebekka curled by the window. Helen recalled her exact words: "We have done something terrible" . . . and Helen remembered thinking she was referring to Louis. But now she recalled something else; she had seen a man, a tall man, passing in the street below. She was sure of it. "Good heavens, Louis, is there a description of the man they are looking for?"

Helen picked up the newspaper again, rereading the article. Something else jarred her memory, the word *Paris* leaped at her, and she turned to Louis.

"When we were at Dr. Franks's you said you remembered an incident with Vebekka and Sasha . . . something about a circus."

But Louis did not hear her, he was on the telephone. "There's a taxi waiting for us, I must tell Hilda we are leaving."

Hilda was told that should Vebekka awaken and need anything, she should call Dr. Franks. The baron thanked her profusely for being such a caring companion, and slipped some folded bills into her hand. She blushed, and replied that she was happy to look after the baroness. She added hesitantly: "I hope she will be helped by this Dr. Franks, that whatever demons torture and frighten her will be driven away."

The doorman ushered the baron and Helen into one of the regular hotel taxis: the same one that had just returned from the circus, having driven Ruda Kellerman back to her trailer. The driver kept up a steady flow of conversation about the price of the circus tickets, and said there were already lines of people waiting for them.

He was about to launch into telling them that an earlier occupant of his taxi was one of the star performers, but Helen and the baron began to speak to each other in French, ignoring him, and as he couldn't understand a word they said, he concentrated on driving to the address in Charlottenburg. It was a long drive, and he hoped the rain would hold off as they were about to get into the rush hour traffic. Suddenly, remembering that Ruda Kellerman had asked him to drive her the following day, he jotted down her name on his call sheet as he drove. The car swerved, but his passengers paid no attention. It was curious, he thought to himself, Ruda Kellerman had seemed just to want to stand outside the hotel. He'd watched her for a long time, standing almost as if she were listening to be called, a strange fixed expression on her face. She must have been waiting for someone, he thought.

7

AFTER RUDA KELLERMAN had identified her ex-husband at the morgue, Inspector Heinz returned to his run-down station in the slum area of East Berlin. He and Rieckert proceeded laboriously to type out all the information about the people they had interviewed.

Kellerman's immigration papers had not been found at Customs. All Torsen knew to date was that he had arrived from Paris, booked into the hotel, eaten a hamburger, and got himself murdered. Nobody seemed to have seen him, or seen anyone else enter his room, or leave it! Everyone who had known him from the circus felt his death was deserved. His ex-wife had not seen him since he had left prison, and was unable to describe the tattoo sliced from his left arm.

Rieckert put his typed report on Torsen's desk, and since it was almost one-thirty went to collect his raincoat.

Torsen watched him. "You know, a few nights we may have to work overtime on this . . ."

"I have a date tonight! You coming out for a sandwich?"

"No, but you can have a toasted cheese-and-tomato sent over for me, just one on rye bread—tell her I'll pay tomorrow."

Rieckert shrugged and walked out. Torsen completed his own reports, adding that the janitor from Kellerman's hotel should be questioned again. His stomach rumbled. He'd eaten nothing since breakfast, and he hoped Rieckert wouldn't forget his sandwich. He put the kettle on to make himself instant coffee and, waiting for the water to boil, he turned in his reports to the empty Polizei Direktor's office, and filed a second copy for the Leitender Polizei Direktor, who was away on holiday.

The coffee jar was virtually empty. He found some sugar, but no milk. He sighed, even thought about joining Rieckert when his cheese on rye was delivered, wrapped in a rather grubby paper napkin, but at least it was what he had ordered. He kept an eye on the delivery boy who hovered by the missing persons photographs, and not until he had left did Torsen return to his desk.

He chewed thoughtfully as he read the autopsy report. The heaviness of the blows indicated that more than likely they had been inflicted by a man—to have crushed Kellerman's skull took considerable force. Whoever killed Kellerman had also ground his false teeth into the carpet. A heel imprint, retained in the pile of the carpet, was still being tested at the lab. The print was of a steel-capped boot heel, again probably a man's because of the size. Samples of mud and sawdust found at the scene of the crime were also still being tested.

Torsen made a few notes:

a. Where did Kellerman go for his hamburger?
b. How many dwarfs performed at the circus?
c. Were any dwarfs missing from Schmidt's circus (just in case they lied about him not being employed there)?
d. Sawdust—was it from the circus?
e. Get the ex–Mrs. Kellerman to give a written positive ID so that burial may take place—(Rabbi).
f. Why was Tommy Kellerman in East Berlin?

Torsen wondered why Ruda still used Kellerman's name and not Grimaldi's. Then he remembered something that had been nagging at the back of his brain. He scrambled for his notepad and scrawled a memo to himself. "Check unsolved dossier—the wizard."

When Torsen's father had been detective inspector they had often discussed unsolved cases together. It had begun as a sort of test between the old policeman and his eager son, but the two men had eventually grown to enjoy discussing what they thought had happened, and why the case remained unsolved. One case they had nicknamed "The Wizard," because the murdered man had been an old cabaret performer. He too had been found brutally stabbed.

The Wizard—he could not even recall the man's real name—had been found in the Kreuzberg sector; he had been dead for many months, his decomposed body buried under the floorboards . . . and his left arm had been mutilated. It was suspected the mutilation had taken place because the discovery of a tattoo would have assisted police inquiries, might even have helped them identify him. They would have required a lot of assistance if his body had not been wrapped in a wizard's cloak. They had been able to trace him, but his killer had never been found.

It was, Torsen surmised, just a coincidence, but he could hear his father's voice, see that forefinger wagging in the air. "Never believe in a coincidence when you are investigating a murder, there are no coincidences."

Torsen picked up his notepad again.

1. Discover any persons residing in East Berlin or in the vicinity of the dead man's hotel recently arrived from Paris.
2. Call the Hospice Center.
3. Magician.

Torsen checked his watch, then demolished the rest of his lunch, carefully wiping the crumbs from his desk with the napkin. He sipped his coffee, draining the cup, and then, unlike anyone else at the station, returned it to the kitchen, rinsed it out, leaving it on the draining board. He had a quick wash and brush-up in the cloakroom before he went back to his office. He sifted through the work requiring immediate attention, and then checked his watch again. He had taken exactly one hour, no more, no less.

Rieckert was back late by a good fifteen minutes. Torsen could hear him laughing in the corridor. He snatched open the door.

"You're supposed to take one hour!"

Rieckert waved a new jar of coffee as an excuse, asking if Torsen would like a cup. "No, thank you. Now get in here!"

Torsen left his door open and began to gather up all his half-completed vehicle theft reports, at the same time shouting again for Rieckert to join him.

"I was just going to get some milk!"

"These are more important. Get them sorted, I want the lot filed and checked."

"But I'm off at five-thirty."

"You can leave when these are completed and not before. I have to go out later myself, so the faster we get through them, the . . ."

"Where are you going?" Rieckert interrupted sullenly.

"Kellerman's hotel. I am, in case you are unaware of the fact, heading a homicide investigation. I have to have further discussions with the manager and get hold of the register, find out whether the janitor saw anyone else leaving the hotel around the time of the murder. Perhaps I should have a look at the alleyway, the distance the janitor had been from the man he saw, if that is permissible with you!"

Torsen began furiously jotting down notes in his thick pad.

a. How did the killer get to the hotel?
b. Question taxi drivers.
c. Question bus drivers.
d. Question doormen at the Grand: very well-lit reception area outside, within spitting distance of Kellerman's hotel.
e. Discuss guests with hotel manager.

✦ ✦ ✦

Ruda had got soaked to the bone standing outside the Grand Hotel, yet nonetheless went to see Mamon before changing. As she turned to head toward her trailer, she saw Mike, and froze. He was still wearing Tommy Kellerman's black leather trilby. She swore at herself, at her stupidity for not remembering to dump it along with the rest of Kellerman's belongings. She watched Mike heading toward the meat trailer, but she couldn't do anything about it. She had to get ready to rehearse the act; she was behind schedule. When she reached the trailer Grimaldi was already there, with an open bottle of brandy.

"Why don't you stay sober, at least until I've worked the act."

"I just need something to warm me up, all right? I'm freezing. I looked all over the place for you— why didn't you wait for me? You just upped and walked out. Where the hell have you been?"

Ignoring his question, Ruda pulled on her old boots, and suggested nastily that all he had to do was try to retrieve the old plinths, then she slammed the door of the trailer. Grimaldi cursed her as she passed the window. Ruda didn't even turn her head, but gave him the finger. So much for thanking him for going with her to the morgue; he didn't know where the hell he was with her. "And you never have, you old goat!" he muttered to himself.

He really had not intended to get loaded, but he had just one more, then another, and then Tina tapped on the door.

She wore a raincoat over tights and a glittering bodysuit, and carried a feathered headdress.

"I hear you and the bitch went to see Kellerman this afternoon."

Grimaldi nodded, offered her a drink which she refused. Tina surveyed the broken crockery, the smashed pictures, and half smiled when she said, "Did you talk to her about us, then?"

"Yes, and it's settled . . . well, up to a point."

"What's that supposed to mean?"

"We discussed it, she's not going to be easy."

"But you knew that. Did you show her what we worked out?"

"I reworked bits of it, I can't just give her an ultimatum. She's worked her butt off for the act. It'll take a while to sort out."

"Take a while, *take a while!* You've been fobbing me off with that line for weeks. I'm pregnant, Luis, how long do you think I can get myself bounced around in my condition? You promised, promised you'd talk to her about it, about us."

He drained the glass. "And I just told you we talked about it . . . she's got a lot on her mind!"

"And I haven't? . . . *I am pregnant!*"

He sighed, opening his arms, but she wouldn't come near him.

"I want you to get it written down, on paper, I want her out of this trailer, I'm not rooming with the girls any longer."

He hung his head, his big hands clasped together. "After the opening, you and I can sort out the living accommodation."

"There's nothing to sort out—we agreed. You give her half, that's fair, it's your act, half those animals are yours, this is your trailer. Just see how far she can go without you and your name."

"She doesn't use my name—now shut up."

Tina hit the wall with the flat of her hand. "She just uses you, and I can't bear to see it, everyone laughing at you behind your back—and what are you drinking for? What are you getting pissed for at this hour?"

She was giving him a thudding headache. "I am not getting pissed, I am just having a drop to warm me up—I've been standing around a freezing morgue for half the fucking day, I've been wanderin' around lookin' for her, gettin' soaked to the bloody bone. She's been actin' like a bear with a sore arse. I dunno. Everybody is naggin' me, drivin' me nuts. So don't you start, just shut up! I dunno where she goes half the time, I dunno what she's doing . . ."

Tina sat down and began to pluck at the feathered headdress.

"Was it him, then?"

Grimaldi nodded. "Yeah, it was him."

"She must be sick in the head, how could she have married that grotesque, malformed creature?"

"Because he had a big dick!"

Grimaldi grinned, and she flung her headdress at him, but she smiled. "So have you . . ."

She went to him then, and sat on his knee. "I want us to be married, and with me behind you, you could take over the act."

He smiled ruefully. "You think so?"

"I know so. You were the best, everyone tells me, they all say at your peak you were the best in the world!"

"Ah yes—at my peak . . . that was quite a while ago, sweetheart, I've peaked and come up for air a few times, and I've plummeted. Maybe I'm too old."

Her heavy breasts were pushed up by her costume and he bent forward to kiss them. She was so young, too young to have ever seen him perform; he had been at his peak before she was even born.

"I want to have the baby, and then you can begin to train me, teach me what to do, I want to be in the ring, I want my face in the center of that poster."

He laughed a low rumble. "I bet you do . . . but it takes a long time."

"I'm young, I have time to learn."

He eased her off his knee and filled a glass. "She learned so fast, Tina . . . I have never seen anyone adapt to working with cats like Ruda."

Tina pouted. "Well, that was because she had the best to teach her, that's why I want you."

He smiled; sometimes she was so blatantly obvious it touched him. He leaned his back against one wall, staring at the posters. "See that one from Monte Carlo? That was her first solo performance. Then there's Italy, and France . . ."

Tina put her hands over her ears. "I don't want to hear about her, all I want is to know if you are ditching her, getting a divorce."

"Ditching her?"

"Well, separating, whatever you want to call it!"

The trailer door banged and Mike, wearing Kellerman's hat, popped his head round the door. "We're almost set up, sir, if you want to come over, we're ready to go in about fifteen minutes."

"Thanks, Mike! I'll be there."

Mike gave Tina a good once-over, and she glared at him as he closed the door. Grimaldi was checking some of the broken pictures. One was of Ruda with Mamon, she was sitting astride him as if he were a pony—she was laughing. "You know, she hardly ever laughed when we first met, was always so serious."

Tina swung one foot. "Oh please, no past glories, I get bored with all your past glories. All I am concerned with is the present, and the promises you make and don't keep."

Grimaldi replaced the broken frame, and hung the picture up without the glass. "I'll talk to her some more after rehearsal."

Tina clasped him in a hug from behind. "Will we keep him?" She pointed to a picture of Mamon.

Grimaldi shook his head. "No . . . she will never part with him."

She clung tighter. "I'm sorry I forgot, I'm sorry . . ."

He wanted to shrug her away, wanted her out of his way, but he stood there, her soft body curled around him, her pink young lips kissing his back, rubbing her nose across his jacket.

"You'd better go, I've got to get ready. We're trying out some new plinths—the cats could get tetchy!"

She slung her coat around her shoulders and picked up her headdress. "Okay, I'll be by later, can we have dinner?"

"Sure."

She stared at his back, waiting for him to turn, but he didn't. She sighed, opening the trailer door. "Be about nine, Luis?"

"Yes, nine's fine . . . see you then."

"I'll talk to her with you if you like!"

"No . . . no that won't be necessary, I'll work it out."

He sighed with relief when the door closed, and then bowed his head. "You stupid bastard, what the hell are you getting into!" he asked himself.

Another glass and the bottle was half empty. He stared at the wall of photographs. Tina was such a child, he was old enough to be her father, he laughed to himself, her grandfather even. He lit a cigar knowing he should be going across to the arena, but he couldn't move. The more he drank the more each photograph re-called his past. He glanced at Ruda riding Mamon, as if he were drawn back to that single memory more than the others. He leaned over and took it down, ran his fingers across her face, and then smashed the frame against the side of the table. "I've got to get to the arena," he kept on telling himself—but he couldn't move. It was as if the brandy were reopening the scar down the length of his body, opening it stitch by stitch until he felt on fire.

It had been late afternoon, in the winter quarters in Florida. He had watched her working the act, saw she was making extraordi-nary strides, knew he should have been in the ring with her. He saw her lifting the hoop, training Mamon to leap through it; the fire was lit on top, and Mamon jumped like the Angel she called him. Next, he watched her edging the padding for the flames further and further around the hoop, each time Mamon leapt through. Now the entire hoop was alight. Mamon hesitated, and then he jumped straight through it. She hugged Mamon as if he were a puppy dog! . . . and the hands standing around watching applauded and cheered. Mamon began a slow lope around the arena, and then on a command he moved closer and closer.

Luis had watched, genuine interest mingled with envy, as she held on to the massive creature's mane of thick black fur, and then sat astride him. One of the boys had taken the photograph, not Luis, but it was as clear a picture in his mind as it was in the frame. The way she had tossed back her head and laughed that deep, wonderful, full-bellied laugh; he had never been able to make her laugh like that, had never witnessed her so free, so exhilarated, and he was consumed with jealousy.

Mamon was Ruda's baby, Ruda's aggressive, terrifying love. She worshiped him, and Luis knew she was too close to him, that no trainer should get so involved with an animal. The danger was that the animal could become too possessive of her, that when she was working with the other cats, and she fondled one, or gave it a treat, the cat could become jealous and in his jealous rage he would attack.

Ruda and Grimaldi had argued about her training of Mamon. He had insisted she must refrain from treating him as if he were a pet. "He is a killer, a perfect killing machine—if you forget what he is, then you put yourself in danger."

She had smirked at him, insinuated that he was jealous because he was too afraid even to get into the ring with Mamon—he was jealous of the way she was handling him. He had turned to her angrily. "Wrong, Ruda. What I'm trying to do is to make you see. You treat Mamon differently—all the other cats you're working as I taught you, but with that bastard you constantly give in to him. What you refuse to see is that he is dominating you, and lemme tell you, the first, the very first moment he sees he has you, he will attack. You must not treat Mamon differently, because he will think he is stronger than you."

Ruda had stood in sullen silence before she had answered. "Mamon is different, I understand him, and he understands me."

Luis had shaken his head in disbelief. "You are being naïve, childish and foolish. He is not human, he is an animal!"

She had walked out, giving him one of her snarls, twisting her face. "Maybe I am one, too. . . ."

But Ruda knew Luis was right, and she made an effort not to be so familiar, not to spend so much time with Mamon. Still, he was the one she could train faster than the others.

They had introduced two more lionesses, and allowed Mamon to mate with both of them. Ruda watched him being released into the compound, she looked at his powerful body as he loped around the two lionesses, courted and showed himself off. The three disappeared into the huts, and she had sat outside all night, waiting. Luis had told her she should stay away from him the following morning, he would be all male, all animal—wild.

Mamon had sauntered out as the sun rose, his head low, his massive paws holding a steady rhythm. His eyes caught the sun like amber lamps and Ruda stood up, her hands on the netting. Mamon got up on his hind legs and roared, and she could feel his hot breath on her face. "You perform well, my love? You screw the arses off them, did you? Who's a beautiful boy!"

He brushed past her against the netting, and then loped off to drink at the trough, turning with water dripping from his mouth to see if she was still watching.

Both lionesses were pregnant, and Ruda watched over them until the births. Two female Bengals were pregnant, and one Siberian; she had her time cut out watching over the cubs, and began to see less and less of Mamon. He became distant, defiant, more and more uncontrollable. Luis blamed Ruda, but she refused any assistance. Working in the ring with sixteen tigers, two lionesses and two lions, she was still confident she could control her Angel.

Luis had been right behind her the first time she had taken over the main part of the act. Twice Luis broke up squabbles between two Bengals, but Ruda seemed to have the act under good control, until Sasha misjudged a leap and fell. She reared up as Jonah, a massive Bengal, tried to attack her, and Sasha fought back and somehow caught her right paw in the top of the meshing. Her claw held firm, and she hung, paws off the ground—open and vulnerable—as the tigers, only too ready for a scrap, moved in for a hoped-for kill.

Luis shouted for pliers to be brought—and fast—and helped Ruda force the rest of the cats back into their positions on the plinths.

The lions remained seated, with Mamon at the top of the pyramid, seeming to survey the situation. Luis kept up his commands as Ruda obeyed him. The clippers were brought and with Ruda moving in front of Luis to cover for him, he unclipped the wire caught in Sasha's claw. She was away fast, unharmed, lashing out a warning to the others not to come near her.

"Keep them in position, Ruda . . . Hold the positions, Ruda!"

She faced the cats, sweating, her whole body on fire with adrenaline. Sasha shook her head, became very vocal but moved back into position. The danger was over, and Luis at Ruda's side put his arm around her; he was smiling.

"Okay . . . you did okay . . . !"

That was the moment Mamon chose to make his attack. He sprang down from the twenty-foot-high plinth, his body seeming hardly to touch the ground as he sprang again. Both front paws caught Luis in the chest, he was thrown back against the railings, but he was up on his feet again fast. Mamon's right front paw ripped through Luis's shirt, cutting open his chest, before he dragged Luis forward. Luis's face was close to the massive jaws, and Ruda, clinging to Mamon's mane, screamed commands. She lashed out with the whip, and Mamon turned his attention to her, stalked her, but she commanded him to move off. Turning on her heels to keep the rest of the cats in her eyesight, she screamed out: "RED A-Gmamon . . . RED!"

Luis's hands clutched the open wound of his chest as he backed toward the trap gate. He managed to stay on his feet, still ordering Ruda to get the cats in line ready to be herded out, before he collapsed half in and half out of the trap gate. Mamon went for him again, Luis's own blood dripping down his jaws as, snarling, Mamon shook him like a rag doll, his teeth cutting through Luis's leather belt, ripping open his belly, trying to drag him like a piece of meat further into the arena. The boys got him out just in time.

When Ruda got the cats back down the traps to their cages, Luis was already aboard the ambulance and on his way to the emergency room. She arrived at the hospital shortly after he was brought out of the operating room. His wound had taken one hundred and eighty-four stitches: He had been ripped from his throat to his groin. He remained in intensive care for eight days, as the wound festered and he suffered blood poisoning.

Ruda was at his bedside when he regained consciousness. His voice was barely audible as he told her to shoot Mamon . . . that he had warned her that cat would do something like this. She had wept, promised she would get rid of him, had even lied to him at other visiting times, saying that Mamon was gone, that the most important thing was for Luis to get well.

Grimaldi had recovered slowly, very slowly; the wound constantly reopened and he suffered from persistent infections—caused by rancid meat caught between Mamon's claws. Luis's weight plummeted, he caught hepatitis, and then pneumonia put him back on the critical list. The hospital bills took every penny he had. Ruda worked as hard as she could, but nothing covered the costs of the feeding and winter quarters. Ruda began to sell off the cubs—sell anything she could lay her hands on; some of the cats were the prize of the Grimaldi act, but she had no choice. The bills kept on coming in, even though many of Grimaldi's friends rallied around and helped.

Grimaldi's chief assistant went to visit him in the hospital, and announced that he was quitting. It was a severe blow; they had been together for thirty years. It was not the fact that his wages had not been paid, that he could understand. What he could not deal with—and refused even to clean out his cage—was Mamon. Ruda, he told Luis, had never made any attempt to get rid of him—when buyers came, he was towed to the back of the quarters.

As sick as he was, Luis had ranted and raged at her: Why had she lied to him? Lost him a man he had worked with for all those years! Ruda had listened with eyes lowered so he couldn't see her expression, and then had said it was not Mamon's fault; he had been vicious because he had an abscess on his tooth, and since it had been removed he was as gentle as a lamb!

Grimaldi languished in the hospital as the bills mounted. Ruda came less often, claiming she was too busy trying to keep a roof over their heads. She did succeed in retaining nine of the cats—and Mamon, of course.

On his release from the hospital, she had driven Grimaldi back to the quarters. He was determined to see the cats, and with the aid of a cane he had walked from cage to cage.

"Where is he? . . . *Where is he?*"

She had stepped back, warning him, "Don't you touch him. I mean it, Luis, don't touch him."

He had pushed her aside, determined to find him, and she had stood guard over the cage, arms outstretched. "Please don't Luis . . . please, I have never asked you for anything in my life, but don't touch him."

Mamon was lying like a king, yawning, as Luis stared at him. Grimaldi turned away and limped to their trailer. Ruda called out that she would show him just what a sweetheart Mamon was, told him to watch from the trailer window. He got the shotgun then, could have shot him, but instead he had watched her, been afraid for her, loved her, and watched . . . until the fear crept up along the jagged scar, a fear that had crippled him since that time. He had never been in the ring since, and Mamon had proved him wrong. He had never mauled or attacked Ruda, but she had never forgotten Luis's words. She used everything he had ever taught her, and went beyond it, working out her own methods and her own commands. Even if Luis could make it back into the ring now, she would have to teach him a new act, the complete new set of commands she now used.

As for Mamon, he was both an obsession and a constant test of Ruda's capabilities. The controller and the controlled; theirs was a strange battle of wills that thrilled her beyond anything she could have imagined. Mamon was the lover she could never take, and they had achieved the perfect union, one of total respect. But she knew if she broke their bond, if she weakened, gave him an opening, he would attack her. She liked that.

✦ ✦ ✦

Luis stared in the mirror at his bloodshot eyes, began to clean his teeth, angry at himself for drinking so much. He heard the trailer door bang, and he sighed, hoping it wasn't Tina again.

"Yeah! What is it?"

Mike's voice called out, and intuitively Grimaldi knew something was wrong, he ran out of the small bathroom. The boy was panting, waving his hat around. "You'd better come over to the arena, she's having a really tough time. It's those new plinths."

Grimaldi ran with Mike across to the big tent, Mike gasping out that it couldn't have come at a worse time, the big boss was in, up in the gallery looking over the rehearsals.

Hans Schmidt, wearing a fur-lined camel coat, sat back in his seat, his pudgy hands resting on a silver-topped cane. Below him, way below, he could see the main ring, the cages erected and the caged tunnel. The spotlights were on, and Ruda's figure seemed tiny as she turned, calling out to the cats.

Mr. Kelm eased into the vacant seat next to Hans Schmidt. "You wanted to see me, sir?"

"This Kellerman business, has it been cleared up?"

"I don't know, sir, the Polizei were here, I told you. I gave them every assistance possible, but I heard they asked Mrs. Grimaldi to identify him this afternoon!"

Schmidt nodded his jowled head, his eyes focused on the ring. "Very disturbing, bad publicity . . . very bad!"

"Yes, I know, but I'm sure it'll all be cleared up."

"It better be. This is the costliest show to date. What do you think of the Kellerman woman?"

"She's stunning, I've seen parts of her act in Italy and Austria, she is very special."

"Doesn't look so hot now . . ."

Kelm peered down, and then told Schmidt about the new plinths, that the animals were playing up, they always did with new props. Schmidt stood up. "Jesus God, is that part of the act?"

Kelm looked down to see the cats milling around Ruda, he nodded his head and then waited as she did the jump, spinning on the tigers' backs. Schmidt applauded. "I have never seen anything like it . . . she must be insane!"

Kelm nodded again, his glasses glinting in the darkness. "She takes great risks."

◆   ◆   ◆

Ruda felt her muscles straining as she lifted one plinth on top of the other; the sweat was streaming off her, her hands in their leather gloves were clammy. She backed the tigers up . . . gave the command for them to keep on the move, and then tried for the third time to get them seated in the simple pyramid . . . they went up to the plinths, hesitated, and turned away.

"Goddamn you . . . HUP RED ED ED ED ED!! DDDDDDDDD! ROJA!" She knew if Roja obeyed her the rest would follow, but he was playing up badly. She was exhausted. Grimaldi moved slowly to the rails, asked if she was okay, and she backed toward him.

"The owners are up in the main viewing box, it's been mayhem . . . but I think I'm winning. Can you give me the long whip?"

Luis passed it through the bars. She took it from him without looking and began again, her voice ringing around the arena.

"RED-RED-BLUE SASHA BLOOOOOOOOOOOOot . . . good girl, good girl, ROJA UP . . . YUP YUP Red!!! . . . thatta good boy . . . good boy . . ."

Luis kept watch as she got them at last onto the plinths, leaving one vacant ladder to the top.

Ruda gave the signal, the tigers remained on their plinths as she gave a mock bow, looked to the right, to the left. The gates opened . . . in came one male lion, and a beat after she heard the click again and knew the second one was hurtling down the tunnel.

The two lions came to her, one to her right side, one to her left, and she herded and cajoled them onto the lower seats. They were unsure, backed off . . . but they were not as uneasy as the tigers.

She gave the signal, and Mamon, spotlighted in the long tunnel, came out at a lope. Ruda pretended she did not know he was there. Mamon was trained to come up behind her, to nudge her with his nose, and then in mock surprise she would jump—onto his back! She had a semicircle to go before she gave him the second section command. The act centered on Mamon's refusing to do as he was told; it was always a great deal of fun, the audience roaring their approval as Mamon played around.

Mamon refused, once, twice . . . Ruda called out to him but he swung his head low. Again she gave him the command: "UP . . . ma'angel up Mamon . . ."

Mamon refused the jump. He began to prowl around the back of the tigers. They got edgy, started hissing, and then two of them began to fight. Ruda called out "DOWN," herding them out, leaving Mamon to her right. They behaved well, moving back down the tunnel, but Mamon refused to leave.

Luis waited, watching, swearing to himself about the plinths, but it was too late now. Ruda gave the signal for Mike to lock on, to get the cats herded back into their cages. She was going to have to work Mamon with the new plinths, cajoling and talking to him, all the while trying to get him on the lower plinth. He refused, sniffing, unsure, smelling, circling, giving a low-bellied growl.

"Come on, baby . . . up up . . . YUP RED RED RED RED!"

Mamon lay down, ignoring her, staring at her. She stood with her hands on her hips. They eyed each other, and Ruda waited.

High up at the back of the main circle, Tina sat eating a bag of potato chips, watching as Ruda sat on one of the plinths, patting it with her hand, softly encouraging Mamon to come to her. He refused. Ruda checked the time, knew she was running over, and suddenly stood up. "Angel . . . ANGEL UP, come on—UP!"

Mamon slowly got to his feet, walked very, very slowly to the new plinth, sniffed it, walked around it, and just as slowly eased himself up and sat.

Ruda looked at him, "You bastard, now stop playing around . . . UYUP BLOOOOOOOO."

He shook his head, and then just as slowly mounted the blue plinth. He sat. Ruda encouraged him, flattered and cajoled him until he had sat on each plinth, sniffed it—twice he pissed over them. He was in no hurry, his whole motion was slow, leisurely, constantly looking to Ruda as if to say: "I'll do it. But in my time."

Ruda gave him the command for his huge jump down; he hesitated and then reared up and sprang forward, heading straight for Ruda. Tina dropped her bag of chips as she stood up, terrified.

Ruda shouted at Mamon, pointing the whip. "Get back . . . back! . . ."

Mamon paid no attention. Ruda spoke sharply to him—and suddenly he turned. Grimaldi gasped as the massive animal churned up the sawdust. Now he was not playing, now he was the star attraction. In wonderfully coordinated jumps he sprang from plinth to plinth, showing off, until he reached the highest point. Then he lifted up his front paws and struck out at the air.

By the time Mamon was moving back down the tunnel, Ruda had unhooked the latch to let herself out of the arena.

She slumped into a seat, taking the proferred handkerchief from her husband to wipe her face. He sat next to her and she could smell the brandy.

"That was tough going!"

"You said it, Luis. I am going to need double rehearsal time before we open, you could see! They're all over the place, they hate those bloody plinths. I hate them!"

"It was your idea to get new ones, I warned you but you wouldn't listen."

"I said get them the same *fucking colors. These are too bright!*"

They argued and Tina looked on. Her vision of herself taking over the act had paled considerably. She watched as Grimaldi and the boys began to dismantle the arena cages, then she went over to the horses and got ready for their practice. Grimaldi hadn't even looked in her direction.

Ruda was still in a foul mood, and exhausted, when she walked into the freezer trailer. She began chopping up the meat for the cats' feed. By the time Mike appeared, still wearing the hat, she had all the trays ready.

"The arena cages are stacked, we got two extra hours tomorrow."

"That's marvelous, this'll be a nightmare. You saw them, they were all acting up."

Mike shrugged, giving a funny cockeyed smile. "But you handled them. Word is that Schmidt was impressed! You want me to take the feed through?"

Ruda shook her head. "No, I'll do it, just double-check that their straw is clean, their cages ready."

"Okay, will you need me later tonight? I reckon if I get their night feed set out—me and a few of the lads want to go around to the clubs."

"I hope not in that hat. Where did you get it?"

"Oh, I found it, it was in here."

Ruda smiled. "Well, just leave it, will you? It's one of Luis's I kept here so he wouldn't wear it, it's disgusting."

Mike tossed Kellerman's hat aside. "Sorry, it was just that it was pissing down earlier. . . . Oh, about this guy Kellerman."

Ruda froze, staring at the blood-red meat.

"Somebody said he was a dwarf, used to work the circus, is that right?"

Ruda nodded.

Mike flushed slightly. "He was found in East Berlin, one of the lads told me he had been murdered."

Ruda lifted the trays. "Yes, he was, we had to go and identify him today. You ever meet him?"

Mike shrugged, shaking his head. "Nope . . . I don't know anything about him, just that I know he used to be your husband."

"Yes he was, a long time ago."

Mike watched her carry the trays down between the trailers, stacking them onto a trolley. She returned for the next batch and said sharply: "You going to stand watching me work or are you going to earn your pay?"

"Oh, sorry."

Mike began to place more feed trays out, and Ruda worked alongside him, until suddenly she banged down an empty tray. "Mike, if you've got something to say, why don't you come out with it?"

He flushed pink, unable to tell her what was bothering him. He was sure he had seen Kellerman the day he died, but he said nothing. She continued heaving out the hunks of meat. "Maybe you can feed Sasha and the two buggers with her."

"Okay," he said, already carrying out the second batch of feed. Ruda picked up Kellerman's hat and put it into her bag, then continued heaping the meat into the trays. Mike was still watching her and she banged down a tray.

"Okay, I married Tommy Kellerman—I needed a marriage certificate for a visa for the United States. Tommy offered it, I accepted, I went to the United States. End of marriage—or is that fertile imagination of yours working overtime?"

He laughed, and then paused at the open door.

"More kids arriving for the tour of the cages! Look at the little gawking creeps."

Ruda walked with Mike to the loaded trolley. Stacking the last of the big trays, she chatted nonchalantly. "There was one of those kids hanging around the cages the other afternoon, did you see me talking to him? Only came up to my waist, trying to put his hand into Mamon's cage. I had to give him a ticking off. Did you see him?"

Mike grinned. "I remember, yeah. It was a kid then, was it? I wondered, you know . . ." He went on with his business and called to her that he would return as soon as he parked the trays. Ruda returned to the freezer. Mike was now sorted out, he hadn't known it was Kellerman with her, and now that she had the little bastard's hat, she was safe.

Ruda stared at her hands, her red-stained fingers, the blood trickling down almost to her elbows. She was thinking of Tommy, seeing his crushed, distorted face on the morgue table, and she whispered: "I'm sorry I broke our pact, Tommy, but you just wouldn't stop."

It was as if he were calling out to her from the cold marble slab in the morgue, calling to her the way he used to when she teased him, but hearing his voice in her mind, hearing it now, made her feel a terrible guilt, like a burning heat it swamped her.

"Don't turn the light out, Ruda, please leave the light on!"

8

THE RAIN HAD started again, and the traffic jams built up, the journey to Charlottenburg becoming a long and tedious drive. The baron looked from his rain-splattered window and checked his watch. It was after six. Helen spoke to their driver in German. "I have never seen so many dogs!"

Their cab driver looked into his mirror.

"We Berliners love animals, bordering on the pathological. There are more dogs in Spree than anywhere else in Germany— they say there's about five dogs to every one hundred inhabitants."

The baron sighed, resting his head back against the upholstered seat. Helen stared from her window.

"Why is that? I mean why do you think there are so many?"

The driver launched into his theory, welcoming the diversion from the inch-by-inch crawl his car was forced to make.

"Many people living in the anonymous public housing complexes, many widows, a dog is their only companion. A psychologist described the Berliners' love of animals, dogs in particular, as a high social functional factor."

Louis grimaced, taking Helen's hand, and spoke in French. "Don't encourage him! Please . . . the man is a compulsive theorist!" Helen laughed.

They passed by the Viktoria-Luise-Platz, heralding the West Berlin Zoo, and their driver now became animated.

"The zoo, you must visit our famous Tiergarten. In 1943 the work of one hundred years was destroyed in just fifteen minutes, during the battle for Berlin. When the bombing was over, only ninety-one animals survived, but we have rebuilt almost all of it. Now we have maybe eleven or twelve thousand species—the most found in any zoo in the world!"

At last, they were near the center of Charlottenburg itself.

"*Bundesverwaltungsgericht,*" the driver said with a flourish, and then he smiled in the mirror. "The Fedeal Court of Appeal in Public Lawsuits."

Helen passed over the slip of paper with the address of Rosa Muller Goldberg's sister, a Mrs. Lena Klapps. The driver nodded, turned off the Berliner Strasse, passing small cafés and ale houses, and rows and rows of sterile apartment blocks, their shabby facades dominating the run-down street, before he drew up outside a building. He pointed, and turned to lean on the back of his seat.

"You will need me to get you back, yes?"

The baron opened his car door, said in French to Helen: "Only if he promises to keep his mouth shut!"

Helen instructed the driver to wait, and joined the baron on the sidewalk. They looked at the apartment numbers painted above a cracked wide door leading to an open courtyard. The numbers read 45–145. Their driver rolled down his window, pointing.

"You want sixty-five, go to the right . . . to the right."

The elevator was broken, and they walked up four flights of stone steps. Dogs brushed past them, going down, and one bedraggled little cross-breed scuttled ahead, turned and yapped before he disappeared from sight. There were pools of urine at each corner, and they had to step over dog excreta. Helen muttered that perhaps the residents were all widows. "Dogs are . . . what did he say? A social function? More like a health hazard."

There was a long stone balcony corridor, the apartments numbered on peeling painted doors . . . sixty-two, sixty-three was boarded up, and then they rang the bell of apartment sixty-five.

An elderly man inched open the door; he was wearing carpet slippers, a collarless shirt, and dark blue suspenders holding up his baggy trousers. Helen smiled warmly. "We are looking for Lena Klapps, née Muller? I am Helen Masters, I called . . ."

The old man nodded, opened the door wider, and gestured for them to follow him. They were shown into a room where good antique furniture was commingled with a strange assortment of cheap modern chairs and a Formica-topped table. The room was dominated by an antique carved bookcase, covering two walls, its shelves stacked with paperbacks and old leather-bound books.

The old man introduced himself as Gunter Klapps, Lena's husband, and gestured for them to be seated. He stood at the door with his hands stuffed into his pockets.

"She is late. The rain—there will be traffic jams. But she should be here shortly, excuse me!"

He closed the door, and Helen unbuttoned her coat. Louis stared around the room, looked at the threadbare carpet, then to the plastic-covered chairs. Helen placed her purse on the table. "Not exactly welcoming, was he?"

The baron flicked a look at his watch. "Maybe we should call the hotel?"

Helen nodded, and crossed to the door. She stood in the hallway, calling out for Lena's husband. The kitchen door was open, and he glared.

"Telephone—do you have a telephone I could use?"

"No, it's broken."

He continued to stare, so Helen returned to the room. The baron was still standing, his face set in anger.

"I hope this is not a wasted journey, I am worried about Vebekka, leaving her alone!"

"Their telephone is broken, shall I go out, make a call?"

He snapped: "No!" and then sat in one of the ugly chairs. Helen took off her coat, placing it over a typist's chair tucked into the table. She looked over the bookcase; some of the leather-bound volumes were by classical authors, but many of the books were medical journals. She was just about to mention the fact to Louis when they heard the front door open.

Lena Klapps walked in. She was much younger than her husband, but wore her hair in a severe bun at the nape of her neck. The gray hair accentuated her pale skin, and pale washed-out blue eyes. She spoke in German.

"Excuse me, I won't be a moment, my bus was held up in the rush hour traffic. May I offer you tea?"

The baron proffered his hand. "Nothing, thank you. I am Baron Louis Maréchal."

Lena retreated quickly, saying she would just remove her coat and boots.

She returned a few moments later. She wore a white high-necked blouse, a gray cardigan, and gray pleated skirt. Her only jewelry was her wedding ring.

"I must apologize for my husband, he has been very ill."

She shook Helen's hand, and nodded formally to the baron, gesturing for him to remain seated. She then withdrew the typist's swivel chair, lifting Helen's coat and placing it across the table. She seemed to perch rather than sit, her knees pressed together, her hands clasped in front of her.

Helen looked to the baron, but he gave a small lift of his eyebrows as an indication she should open the conversation. She coughed, and chose her words carefully.

"The baron's wife, Vebekka Maréchal—we are trying to trace her relatives, and as I said to you in my telephone call, we think she may have been your sister's daughter. Your sister was Rosa Muller?"

"Yes, that is correct."

Helen continued. "She married a David Goldberg? . . . and they lived in Canada and then Philadelphia, yes?"

"Yes, that is correct."

The baron cleared his throat. "Do you have a photograph of their daughter, of Rebecca Goldberg?"

"No, I lost contact with my sister before she left for Canada. I know they emigrated to Philadelphia, but we did not keep in touch. Her husband's cousin, a man named Ulrich Goldberg, wrote to me that she had passed away."

Helen bit her lip. "We need as much information as you can give us about Rebecca and obviously your sister."

Lena swiveled slightly in her seat. Her toes touched the ground, the folds of her pleated skirt falling to either side of her closed knees. She answered in English.

"I know nothing of . . . Rebecca, you say? I cannot help you."

"But Rosa was your sister?"

"Yes, Rosa was my sister."

Lena suddenly swiveled around to the bookshelf, reached over and took down a thick photograph album. She began to search through the pages of photographs. She spoke in heavily accented English, as if to prove a point—that she was aware of how uncomfortable they were.

"I find it somewhat strange that after forty years I am asked about Rosa! You say it is in reference to your wife, Baron? Is that correct?"

Helen went to stand by Lena. "The baroness is very ill, and we have come to see a specialist in East Berlin who may be able to help her. It is his suggestion that we should try and discover as much about her past as possible."

Lena nodded. "And this is Rebecca? Correct? . . . But there must be some confusion. She could not be my sister's child." She paused, turned back two pages, and then showed Helen the photograph.

"This was Rosa when she was seventeen, 1934."

Helen stared at the picture of an exceptionally pretty blond-haired teenager, with white ribbons in her hair, white ankle socks, and a school uniform. Next to her stood Lena, taller, fatter, and not nearly as pretty. She had been as stern-faced a teenager as she was now in middle age. Helen passed over the photograph album to the baron. Lena hesitated, her hand out, obviously not wanting the baron to take possession of the album. "That is the only photograph, there is no point in looking at any others."

"Lena, is there some way we could contact any of David Goldberg's friends or family, do you know if any of his relatives are still living in Berlin?" Helen asked.

"No. I did not know Rosa's husband, they met at the university. As I said, I have not spoken to my sister for more than forty years."

The baron turned over a few pages, and Lena got up and retrieved her book. She stared at the neatly laid-out photographs, some brown with age. "Berlin has seen many changes since these were taken. My family home—" She pointed to an elegant four-story house. "It was bombed, all our possessions, we lost everything but a few pieces, the other photographs are just my family, my mementos—nothing to do with Rosa!"

Lena held on to the book, touched it lovingly before she replaced it in the shelf, and then hesitated. "I agreed to see you, because I know Rosa was well off . . . as you can see, money is short—I thought perhaps she had made provisions for me. Obviously I was wrong." She stared from Helen to the baron and then, tight-lipped, remained standing. "I am sorry, but it seems very obvious that I cannot help you."

Helen reached for her coat, making as if to prepare to leave. "Rosa was a doctor? Is that correct?"

"She was a medical student, she did not finish her studies here, she continued in Canada, after the war." Lena folded her arms.

"Was her husband a doctor?"

Lena shook her head. "No, my father, my grandfather were also doctors . . ."

"But Rosa and David met at the university?"

"Yes, but he was studying languages, I believe. When they went to Canada, I heard he went in the fur business."

Helen looked at Louis, wishing he would say something, ask something; but he sat on the edge of his seat, obviously wanting to leave.

"Er . . . you said earlier that Rebecca could not have been Rosa's daughter . . . was she perhaps David Goldberg's daughter?"

"I don't know."

"But why are you so sure she could not have been Rosa's child?"

Lena pursed her lips, clenched her hands. She then carefully pushed her chair under the table. "Rosa could not have children."

Helen persisted. "Could you give me the reason?"

Lena faced her. "Because she had an abortion when she was seventeen years old, a backstreet abortion, paid for by that creature she ran off with and married. She nearly died, and she broke my father's heart. When he discovered her relationship, he would have nothing to do with her, he begged her to give David up, but she refused. He tried everything, he even kept her under lock and key to stop him from seeing her. She was obsessed by David and so she ran away, and my father never spoke to her again."

"This was when?"

Lena rubbed her head. "She ran off on the second of June, it was 1934, they ran away together, we discovered they had married."

"They went to Canada?"

"Yes, to Canada. His family were wealthy, they must have had contacts there to help him set himself up in business; they always help each other!"

Helen began to put her coat on. "Did they ever come back?"

Lena nodded. "I believe so, but not for a long time, not until after the war. The Goldbergs had property here!"

"So they came back to Berlin?"

"Yes, yes I believe so."

"And you didn't see him or speak to him?"

"No."

"Did you see Rosa when she came back?"

"No."

"And you cannot give us any clue as to any relatives?"

Lena stared hard at Helen, her eyes expressionless. "He had no one left, but a distant cousin, Ulrich Goldberg, who was already residing in the United States. Rosa never contacted her mother, never visited her father's, her brother's graves. As far as I am concerned, my sister died a long time ago, the day she ran away . . . . Now I should be grateful if you would leave."

The baron gripped Helen's elbow, wanting to get out, but she stood firm. "Do you think your sister could have adopted Rebecca when she returned to Berlin? Could she have adopted a child then, knowing she could not have children of her own?"

Lena pushed past Helen and opened the door. "I have told you all I know, please leave now."

Helen snatched up her purse and walked out, as the baron folded money and handed it to Lena. "Thank you for your time, I appreciate it."

He followed Helen to the front door. Lena watched them, her hand clenched around the thick wad of folded bills.

The stale smell of cabbage filled the hallway as they hurried along the stone corridor.

"She worked in a hospital for three months . . . I don't know where, I have told you all I know . . ."

The baron guided Helen down the stairs, holding her elbow lightly in the crook of his hand. "The family album was interesting! Did you get a chance to see any of the other photographs? The father was like an SS officer, the brothers were all in uniform too." He shook his head. "Can you believe it? She wouldn't see her sister for forty-odd years, and then thinks she may have left her something!"

Helen stopped, turned to him.

"We can get Franks to check hospitals, and we can contact someone from the Canadian embassy, see if they can trace a birth certificate—but you know something, I don't think they'll find one, I think they adopted a child here. God knows there must have been thousands of children needing help."

Louis snapped angrily: "Unless Rebecca was Goldberg's child! Don't get too romantic about this, we may have the wrong woman."

"You don't really think so, do you? She *was* Rosa's sister."

Louis continued talking as they walked down the stairs. "But we don't know if this Rosa was Vebekka's mother, adopted or otherwise; we are just clutching at straws."

They came out from the apartment building, and their driver tooted his car horn, having parked across the street. Louis slapped his forehead. "Dear God, I'd forgotten him! I don't think I can stand his guided tours all the way back."

But Louis did seem more relaxed, even good-humored, now that they had left the apartment. They got into the car and Louis asked the driver to stop at the nearest telephone booth.

They drove only half a mile before he went to call the hotel to check on Vebekka. Helen watched him from the window, and then leaned back closing her eyes. She was sure the jigsaw was piecing together. The Mullers had turned their back on Rosa not because she was pregnant, but because the father of her child was a Jew.

Louis returned and signaled for the driver to move on.

"She has eaten, she is resting, and Hilda says she is calm, sleeping most of the time!"

As they crossed into East Berlin, their driver became even more animated. "You know the communist regime may have tried to squash artistic freedom but, like the West, we always had circuses—you like the circus? At one time it was all provided for, classical music, opera, everything was funded by the state. Now we have no funds to sustain the arts, all our artists, our best talent and producers run to the West . . . now a leading ballerina from the East Berlin Ballet is having to find work as a stripper to cover her rent, it's true!"

Helen leaned forward, trying to stop the constant flow of monologue, and asked if he had heard about the murder, the dwarf found in the hotel not far from the Grand Hotel.

The driver nodded his head vigorously. "Yes, yes I heard, the crime wave is unstoppable here, we don't have enough police . . . maybe he was working at the Artistenschule, you know, teaching circus acts. We have many famous circus performers from Berlin, you know there is a magnificent circus about to begin a new season—if you want, I get you tickets, I have contacts . . ."

The car drew up outside the hotel, and still the driver talked. "I have many contacts for nightclubs, for shows, if you want something risqué—you know what I mean—I can arrange . . ."

He had exhausted them both. Helen rang for the elevator while the baron inquired at the desk for any letters or calls. He was handed a package, just arrived by Federal Express.

Standing next to the baron was Inspector Torsen Heinz, who gave him no more than a cursory glance; he was more interested in the contents of the envelope.

Torsen was mentally adding up the cost of the small salad he had eaten in the hotel bar. He'd never have another. It had not even been fresh or served well, but it had cost more than five times his usual cheese on rye at lunch.

Torsen had been waiting patiently over half an hour for the manager to give him a list of residents who had arrived at the Grand Hotel from Paris on or near the night of Kellerman's murder. The baron and Helen stepped into the elevator as the manager bustled across the foyer, gesturing for the inspector to follow him.

The manager ushered Torsen into his private office, then closed his door. "I have had to speak to the director of the hotel about this matter, I am afraid you place us in a very difficult situation. We do have guests, and they are from Paris, but whether or not I can ask . . ."

Torsen opened his notebook officiously. "I have been able to gain a positive identification of the murdered man, sir, and I will require from you the date these guests arrived. Does it coincide with the dates I gave to you?"

"Yes, yes, but these guests are Baron Maréchal, his wife, a nurse, and I think his wife's physician, a Dr. Helen Masters."

Torsen closed his book. "Could I speak with the baron?"

"I'm afraid that won't be possible, his wife has not been well, and she is resting in their suite. I really don't like to disturb them. Perhaps if you return in the morning, I will speak to the baron; he is not available right now."

"He just came in."

"Excuse me?"

"I said the baron just arrived at the reception desk, I saw him."

The manager tightened his lips, referred again to the conversation he had just had with the director, and suggested Torsen return in the morning. In the meantime, he would speak to the baron.

Torsen was ushered out into the elegant foyer, and checked the time on the clock behind the reception desk. He wondered whether he could squeeze in a quick visit to his father before interviewing the janitor at Kellerman's hotel. It had started to rain again, and the inspector decided he would treat himself to a taxi. He asked the doorman to call him one, but then he saw that one was waiting by the door.

The baron and Helen's driver was snoozing, but he jumped to attention when Torsen tapped on his window. Torsen gave the address of his father's nursing home, and was treated to a detailed account of the rise in price of facilities for the elderly. "This city will be in deep trouble—you know why?"

Torsen made no reply, knowing it would make no difference.

"The avalanche of poverty-stricken immigrants are heading this way. Our young have all flown to the West. I was telling the baron, he was in my cab today, I was telling him about the circus, the Artistenschule, once the most famous in the world for training circus performers. It'll close, mark my words, it'll close."

Torsen frowned. "Did the baron ask about the circus?"

The driver nodded. "We were discussing the murder, the dwarf, he was asking about the murder!"

Torsen listened, interested now, and instructed the driver to change direction, he wanted to go to the Artistenschule.

The driver did a manic U-turn in the center of the road. "Okay, you're the boss . . . I said to the baron, I said, they'll never find the killer."

"Why is that?" asked Torsen.

"Because we've got a load of amateurs running our Polizei, they never made any decisions before, they were *told* who to arrest and who not to, you can't change that overnight . . . This is it . . . main door is just at the top of those steps."

Torsen fished in his pockets for loose change, then asked for a receipt. The driver drew out a grubby square notepad, no taxi number or official receipt. "How much do you want me to put on this? Traveling salesman are you?"

Torsen opened his raincoat to reveal his uniform. "No . . . I just need to give it to my Leitender Polizei Direktor!"

The driver said nothing, scribbled on his notepad, and shook Torsen's hand—too hard, too sincerely. For a brief moment Torsen saw a fear pass over his face, and then it was gone—so was the Mercedes in a cloud of black exhaust fumes. In the old days he could have been arrested for slandering the state!

Torsen knocked on the small door marked OFFICE PRIVATE underlined twice. He waited, tapped again, and eventually heard shuffling sounds; then a rasping voice bellowed to an animal to get out of the way. The door opened, and Torsen was confronted by a massive man wearing a vest and tracksuit bottoms. Clasping his hand was a chimp, they rather resembled each other, the vest hardly hiding the man's astonishing growth of body hair.

Fredrick Lazars beckoned Torsen to follow him, saying he was just eating his dinner. Torsen was motioned to sit on a rickety chair, covered in dog hairs, as Lazars sat the chimp in a high baby chair. He brought a big tin bowl and a large spoon. He tipped what looked like porridge into the bowl, and then took out of the oven a plate piled with sausages, onions, and mashed potatoes. He offered to share his dinner with Torsen. It looked as if the man had already started dinner; the sausages were half eaten. Torsen refused politely, saying that he had just dined, and then added, "at the Grand Hotel!" He did not mention that it was just a small salad, and as Lazars didn't seem impressed, he dropped the subject. Lazars opened two bottles of beer and handed one to Torsen as the chimp flicked its spoon, splattering Torsen's uniform with porridge.

The chimp, only two years old, was called Boris, but was really a female—all this was divulged in a bellow from a food-filled mouth.

"Did Tommy Kellerman come to see you?"

The big hands broke up large hunks of bread, dipping them into his fried onions. "He did . . . the night he died."

Torsen took out his notebook, asked for a pencil, and Lazars bellowed at Boris, who climbed down and went to an untidy desk. The chimp threw papers around. "Pencil . . . PENCIL BORIS!" Torsen was half out of his seat, ready to help Boris, when a pencil was shoved at him, but Boris wouldn't let go of it and a tug of war ensued. Finally Lazars whacked Boris over the head and told her to finish her dinner. Boris proceeded to spoon in large mouthfuls of the porridge substance, dribbling it over the table, herself, and the floor.

"Kellerman came to see me about six, maybe nearer seven."

"Why have you not come forward with this evidence?"

"He came, he ate half my dinner and departed, what's there to tell in that?"

Torsen scribbled in his book. "So what time did he leave?"

Lazars sniffed, gulped at his beer. "He stayed about three quarters of an hour, said he had some business he was taking care of, important business."

"What did you do after he left? Or did you accompany him?"

"No, he left on his own, I stayed here."

"Do you have any witnesses to substantiate this?"

"Yep, about two hundred, we were giving a display, just a few kids trying out, but I started at eight-thirty, maybe finished around ten or later, then we had an open discussion . . . finished after twelve, we went on to O'Bar, about six of us, then we stayed there . . ."

Torsen held up his hand: "No, no more . . . if you could just give me some names who can verify all this."

Lazars reeled off the names as Boris banged her plate, splashing Torsen with more of her food. She started screeching for more, and when she got it she gave Lazars a big kiss as a thank-you.

"I love this little lady . . . mother died about a year ago. Well, she's moved in with me until I find someone to buy her."

Torsen asked Lazars what he knew of Kellerman's background, and the massive man screwed up his face, his resemblance to Boris becoming even more staggering.

"He was an unpleasant little bastard, nobody had a good word to say about him, always borrowing, you know the kind, he'd touch a blind beggar for money, but, well, he'd had a tough life . . . you forgive a lot."

"Did he ever work here?"

"Yeah, long time ago, I mean a really long time ago, early fifties I think. He turned up one day, sort of learned a few tricks, just tumbling and knockabout stuff, but he never had the heart . . . got to have a warm heart to be a clown, you know? Kellerman, he was different, he was never . . . I dunno, why speak ill of the dead, huh?"

"It may help me find his killer. Somebody hated him enough to give him a terrible beating."

Lazars lifted Boris up and carried her to the dish-piled sink. He took a cloth and ran it under the water, rinsed it, and wiped Boris's face.

"Look, Kellerman was a bit crazy, you know? Mixed up. He hated his body, his life, his very existence. Kellerman was somebody that should have been suffocated when he was born. He couldn't pass a mirror without hating himself. And yet when he was younger—it was tragic—he looked like a cherub. Like a kid. See, when he first came here he must have been in his twenties."

Torsen nodded, finishing the dregs of his beer. Boris, her face cleaned, now wanted her hands washed.

"I'm trying to train her to do the washing up!" roared Lazars, laughing at his own joke. "But she's too lazy!! Like me!"

Lazars sat Boris down, and cut a hunk of cheese for himself. "The women went for him, always had straight women—you know, normal size."

Torsen hesitated. "I met his ex-wife . . ."

Lazars cocked his head to one side. "She's a big star now, doesn't mix with any of us, but then who's to blame her, she's been world-wide with the Grimaldi act. He's a nice enough bloke, part Russian, part Italian—hell of a temper, nice man, but I'm not sure about Ruda . . . but then who's sure about anybody?"

Torsen flicked through his notebook.

"Did you know them when they were married?"

"No, not really. I don't to tell you the truth even know where she came from, I think she used to work the clubs, but don't quote me. Kellerman just used to turn up, we never knew how he did it. I think he was into some racket with forged documents, he seemed to be able to cross back and forth with no problems. We had a bit of a falling out about it, you know he'd come over here, check over the acts—next minute they'd upped and left. I think he made his money that way, you know—paid for fixing documents and pass-ports. He always had money, not rich, but never short of cash either in those early days, so I just put two and two together. He had a place over in the Kreuzberg district, so he must have had contacts. Not circus people, he was only attached to circuses because of his deformity—when he couldn't make cash on rackets, he joined up with a circus."

Torsen rubbed his head. "Did he have money when you last saw him?"

Lazars shook his head. "No, he was broke, told me he had been in jail but I knew that anyway. All he said was he had some business deal going down. Maybe he'd got in with the bad guys again, who knows? I do know he let a lot of people down . . ."

"How do you mean?"

"Promises, you know, he'd get them over the border, promise to get them work. They'd pay up front, end up over there, and no Kellerman—he'd pissed off. Any place he turned up you could guarantee there would be someone waiting to give him a hiding."

"Or kill him?"

Lazars had Boris on his knee; the chimp was sucking at her thumb like a tiny baby, her round eyes drooping with tiredness. Torsen reached for his raincoat; it was covered with animal hairs. "There is just one more thing, then I'll get out of your way."

Lazars stood up, resting Boris on his hip. She was fast asleep.

Torsen almost whispered, afraid to wake Boris.

"Do you recall a tattoo on his left arm?"

Lazars nodded, and the bellowing voice was a low rumble. "I remember it, they are the ones you never forget."

Torsen waited, and Lazars sighed. "Maybe that was why we all put up with his shit. Tommy Kellerman was in Auschwitz, the tattoo was his number."

✦ ✦ ✦

For once the rain had ceased and Torsen could take a bus to Kellerman's hotel. He sat hunched in his seat, making notes in his book. He wrote a memo for Rieckert and himself to visit Ruda Kellerman and question her again. He underlined it twice. She had lied about Kellerman's tattoo, she must have known what it was. He closed his eyes, picturing Ruda Kellerman as she touched the dead man's hair at the morgue that afternoon.

He spent the rest of the journey mulling over why she would have lied, but came to no conclusion. He stared from the grimy window of the bus at a group of punks kicking empty cans of beer along the street. They had flamboyantly blue and red hair; they wore torn black leather jackets, and black boots that clanked and banged the cans along the street. He felt old, tired out; bogged down, trying to find the killer of a man nobody seemed to care about. Was it all a pointless waste of time? The men at the station had inferred that it was; nobody else there would put in any overtime to help him.

He interrupted himself, swearing. He should have asked Lazars if the dinner he had shared with Kellerman was a hamburger and fries! He'd have to call in the morning, and again he swore—he couldn't call him before nine because his switchboard wasn't connected until then. He also wanted a telephone.

Torsen began another of his lists. He was going to start throwing his weight around—he wanted a patrol car for his own personal use, plus fuel allowance, and, as of tomorrow, he was going to work out a schedule, none of this nine-to-five from now on. They would work as they did in the West, day and night, around the clock.

The bus rumbled on, and Torsen sniffed his hands. They smelled of Boris, he smelled of Boris, and the remains of the chimp's food had hardened into flecks all over his jacket. The bus shuddered to a halt, and Torsen stepped down, checking the time, sure the janitor must have started work by now.

He headed for Kellerman's hotel, passing the ornate and well-lit Grand Hotel entrance, hurrying down the back streets, mentally tallying up how many girls he saw lurking in the dark, dingy doorways, even wondering if any one of them had seen the killer. But he didn't approach the girls because he was alone, and didn't want his intentions to be misconstrued. He made a mental note to add to his lists . . . check out the call girls. No doubt Rieckert would jump at the chance.

+ + +

The baron had ordered dinner in his suite, and the manager himself had overseen the menu. He bowed and scraped at the lavish tip. The baron thanked him for his discretion. He would of course speak with the director of the police. He shut the door, sighing, and turned to Helen.

"This place is unbelievable—they want me to meet with someone from the police, because we arrived from Paris on the same night that circus dwarf was murdered!"

Helen frowned, but said nothing; she was sifting through the package of letters and photographs that had just been delivered. She held up a small blurred snapshot.

"I am sure this is Rosa Muller, she's even got the same pigtails, and you can see where the photo's been cut in two, so maybe we were right after all . . . Louis?"

He sat beside her. "Yes, yes . . . I hear you."

Helen pointed out the cut edge of the photograph, sent by the baron's chauffeur from the United States. "I am sure Lena was on this photograph . . . it's very similar to the one she showed us, and just look at the other snapshot, Louis, I'm sure it's Vebekka."

Louis looked yet again at the snapshot of a girl in school uniform who was glaring at the camera. She had two thick plaits, her hands were clenched at her sides. And she was exceptionally plump, her face, even her legs seemed rounded.

"I just don't now."

Helen took the photograph. "We could always ask her, show it to her?"

Louis snapped. "No, I don't want her upset, I don't want anything to upset her, she's calm, she's sleeping, she's eating, she's going to see Franks tomorrow. You talk to him about it, see what he says, I just don't want these games we're playing to upset—"

"Games? . . . Louis, we're not playing games, for God's sake."

He shoved the papers aside. "I used the wrong word then, but we have come here to have Vebekka see Franks, she's agreed, now all this detective work . . ."

Helen pushed back her chair. "This detective work was, if you recall, specifically requested by Franks himself. I don't understand your attitude, you don't know anything about her past, and you have said it is your priority to find out whether there is any history of mental instability in Vebekka's family. But, Louis, unless we try and trace her goddamned family, how do you expect to find out?"

Louis rubbed his brow, his mouth a tight hard line. "Perhaps some things are best not uncovered. . . ."

"Like what?"

He stared at the ceiling. "I don't know . . . but all these photographs, this woman this afternoon, what have we gained? We still know nothing of Vebekka's family. Her mother or adopted mother is dead, her father or adopted father is dead—how can they tell us what, as you said, is my priority? And it is not just *my* priority, but my sons', my daughters'." He sighed. "Look, maybe I'm just tired, it's been a long day."

Helen carefully gathered the photographs together, the letters from Ulrich Goldberg, the lists of Goldbergs she had contacted to trace Lena, and stuffed them into the large brown envelope.

"Perhaps you're right. I think I'm tired too, maybe I'll make it an early night."

The baron poured himself a brandy. "Do you want one?"

"No, thank you, I'll look in on Vebekka if you like."

"No, that's all right, Hilda's staying overnight, she's using Anne Marie's old room."

"What time are the police coming?"

"First thing in the morning."

"I'd like to sit in on the meeting, if I may, just out of interest. What time will Rebecca be going to Dr. Franks?"

"Vebekka!"

"What . . . oh I'm sorry, what time is her appointment with Franks?"

Louis shrugged as he lit a cigar and began puffing it alight. "I doubt if it will be before ten, he has set aside the entire morning."

"Good night then."

He looked at her, then inclined his head. "Good night!"

Louis noticed she took the envelope with her; it irritated him slightly, but he dismissed it. He turned the television set on, and switched from channel to channel. Hilda came out of Vebekka's bedroom.

"She is sleeping!"

He smiled warmly. "Good, you are very good for her, and I am grateful for your assistance. Also for agreeing to stay. Thank you!"

Hilda crossed the room, head bowed, and slipped into Anne Marie's room. As she went into the small adjoining bathroom, she could hear a bath being run from Helen Masters's suite.

♦ ♦ ♦

Helen wrapped the thick hotel towel robe around herself, and then sat at the writing desk, taking the photographs out, studying them and staring at the wall. She picked up the photograph of the plump schoolgirl, turning it over. On the back was written, in childish scrawl, *Rebecca*.

She stared at the photograph angrily, and then let it drop onto the desk. Why was she so angry? Why?

She looked again at the photograph, and this time she took a sheet of paper and held it across the bottom part of the child's face, hiding the nose and mouth. They were Vebekka's eyes, she knew it!

♦ ♦ ♦

Inspector Heinz had to wait at Kellerman's hotel until after eleven o'clock for the janitor to come on duty. He stood waiting impatiently as the scruffy man rummaged through the trash bins in the alleyway. Eventually, and very disgruntled at his work being interrupted, he led Torsen to where he recalled seeing the tall, well-built man. He pointed from the alley toward the street—not, as Torsen had thought, the other way around.

"But it's well-lit, you must have gotten a good look."

"I wasn't paying too much attention, I'd just started work. I clear the trash cans at a number of hotels around this area, I don't start working until after ten, but I remember seeing him, and he was walking fast, carrying this big bag—a sort of carryall."

This was evidence not before divulged. The janitor was able after some deliberation to describe a dark hat, like a trilby, worn by the man. "It was shiny, sort of caught the light, yes, it was black and shiny."

"Did you see his face?" Torsen asked.

The janitor shook his head and asked if he could continue his work. Torsen nodded, standing a moment longer as the man turned on a hose and began to wash down the alley.

✦ ✦ ✦

It was almost twelve, but Ruda worked on. She cleaned around the sides of the sink, then rinsed out the cloths, filled a bucket of water, and carried it to the chopping table. She scrubbed the surface, shaking the brush, dipping it into the boiling water. Her mind raced. Had she covered all possible tracks, all possible connection to the murder? As hard as she tried to concentrate, she knew, could feel something else was happening. It had begun in the hotel, when she was sick in the toilets. Why did she feel the complusion to return to that hotel? She hurled the brush into the bucket, yanked the bucket up, slopping water over the floor and herself as she tipped it down the drain . . . white tiles, splashes of red, bloody water . . . white tiles. The same tingling started. Her hands, the nape of her neck, the dryness in her mouth. She rubbed her hands dry on the rough towel, then, as she threw it into the skip used for the laundry, she saw the bloody towels and cloths and caught her breath. It wasn't Tommy, it wasn't the murder, it was something else.

She swore, muttering louder, she must not allow this to happen. She had controlled it her whole life, she would not allow it to break into her mind, not now, and she punched out at the walls, punched with all her strength. But nothing would make the memory subside, return it to the secure, locked box in her mind. Her fists slammed against the wall, and she turned her fury to Kellerman: It was his fault, all his fault. . . . Why did he have to come back? Why now? But Ruda knew it was not Kellerman who was back. It was the past.

✦ ✦ ✦

Louis was sitting in a comfortable chair, a magazine in his hands;
he was wearing half-moon glasses, but he had been unable to concentrate. The glasses took Helen by surprise, she had never seen
him wearing them. It was a moment before he realized she was in
the room.

"Can't you sleep?" he asked softly.

Helen glanced at the clock on the mantel—it was after twelve,
she hadn't thought it was so late. "No, no I can't. I'm sorry, it's
very late but . . ."

He put his fingers to his lips, then indicated Vebekka's room.
He gave no indication of his surprise at Helen's intrusion, but he
was nonetheless taken aback; she was wearing only a rather flimsy
nightgown, her robe was undone, and her feet were bare.

"She's sleeping, she looks very well."

"Good, I'm glad."

Helen sat on the edge of the sofa. "Louis, I need to ask you
something, I am just not sure how to phrase it . . ."

"Do you want a brandy?"

"No, nothing thank you." She stared at his slippered feet, suddenly aware that in her haste she had not put on her own slippers.
"Vebekka has said repeatedly that she is afraid of hospitals, nurses,
and doctors in white coats, yes?"

He nodded, pouring a glass for her. He went over to the sofa
and held it out. "Here. It'll help you sleep."

Helen took the glass, cupping it in her hands. "So even though
she was afraid of needles, of doctors, she had plastic surgery—to
her nose, her face? I read it in Dr. Franks's reports."

He frowned. "Yes. It was not extensive, and I suppose when
she had it done she was well. I never thought of it. It was done in
a private clinic in Switzerland, the first time, and then I think in
New York."

"Were you with her on these occasions?"

He touched his brow, coughed lightly. "The first time, but not
the second. She had no adverse effects; quite the contrary—she was

very pleased with the results. She's always been very conscious of her looks."

Helen sipped the brandy. "The photograph is of Vebekka, Louis, the girl may be plump, fat, but her eyes—I recognize her eyes. She could never change her eyes."

He slowly stubbed out his cigar, his back to her. Helen took another sip of the brandy; she licked her lips. "But that is not what I wanted to ask you."

As he turned to face her, he removed his glasses, carefully placing them in a case.

Standing up, she put her glass down. "I think you were, to begin with, prepared to try and discover everything about her background until . . ."

He moved closer. "Until what?"

She looked at him, met his dark blue eyes. "Until you heard the name Goldberg . . ."

"What's that supposed to mean?"

Helen backed further away from him. "I know how important your family is, your family heritage, I know you have put up with your wife's illness because they would not approve of a divorce."

"They?" He said it quietly, but with such sarcasm. "My dear Helen, I am the family, I am the head of the family, and I can't for the life of me think what you are trying to say."

"I think you know, Louis."

He shook his head in disbelief, and then walked to the windows, drawing the drapes to one side. "You really think I would care?"

Helen cleared her throat. "I think the old baroness would have, perhaps your father; it was common knowledge he allowed the Gestapo to take over your villas."

He patted the curtains into place. "I think, Helen, you should try and get some sleep, before you say or insinuate anything else."

"You have not answered me."

He was at her side, gripping her arm so tightly it hurt. "You know nothing, nothing, and your inference insults me, insults my family."

She dragged her arm free. "It's always your precious family. I think you, Louis, hate the thought of your precious family being Jewish, as much as you hate the thought of producing more insanity!"

His slap sent her staggering backward, she cried out more with shock than pain. He rushed to her, touched her reddened cheek. "Oh my God, I'm sorry . . . but you don't understand."

Helen put her hand up to indicate for him not to come close. He flushed, and gestured another apology with his hands. "I am so sorry."

She watched as he took out his handkerchief, touched his lips, the brow of his head, and then crossed to the window and un-hooked the shutter. He remained with his back to her as he reached through the half-open shutter to the window.

"I don't care if Vebekka is Jewish, how could I? She's the mother of my children, I care only about their future." He opened the window, breathed the cold night air, but still seemed loath to turn and face her.

Helen twisted her ring around her finger. "Then surely you can understand my confusion—why don't you want to try and find out as much as possible, Louis? Please, look at the photograph, look at it."

He walked briskly to the table and snatched up the photograph where Helen had left it. He turned the photograph over, then let it drop back onto the polished wood surface. He saw the childish looped writing, the name *Rebecca*.

"Helen, if she is this little girl, if she is in some way connected to that dreadful woman this evening, to these people in Philadelphia, then we must do whatever you think is right. But please don't ask me to show enthusiasm. Show this photo to my wife, if you wish, or preferably ask Franks to, because if she looks at it and admits it is her, then she has lied to me, to everyone. Let Franks do it, but don't ask me to . . ."

"Don't you see, Louis? It is the reason why she has lied that may be important—it has to be, and when we discover why, maybe . . ."

He snapped then, his face taut with controlled anger.

"Maybe what? Everything will fall into place? Have you any idea, any knowledge of how often I have hoped for that? Let Dr. Franks handle this photograph and any further developments."

"As you wish!"

As Helen crossed to the door, he said her name very quietly, making her turn.

"I obviously appreciate all you are doing for my wife, and any financial costs to yourself will be met. I had no conception of how, well, how much we would be seeing of each other, or how much my own personal life would be placed under scrutiny. I ask you, please, to realize at all times you are privy to very private emotions, traumas—whichever terminology you wish to use. But please do remember that you are my guest, and that you are here because my wife asked you to accompany us. You are therefore free to leave at any time you wish to do so."

Helen felt as if he had slapped her face for a second time; his cold aloofness deeply embarrassed her.

"I arranged my vacation so that I could spend time here . . ."

"How very kind . . . but I will as I said make sure you incur no extra costs. Now, if you don't mind my asking, in future, if you wish to join me in my suite, you will be good enough to dress accordingly: Hotels are notoriously scandalous places. My wife has already managed exceptionally well in making a spectacle of herself since we arrived."

Helen gave a brief smile of apology. "Anything we have discussed is, and will remain, completely confidential. Good night Baron!"

He saw the glint in her eyes, and flushed, moving back to the shutters once more. He switched off the lights, leaving the shutter ajar, the streetlamps outside giving the only light in the spacious drawing room.

Helen would never know what a raw nerve she had touched, he assured himself. His mother had accused him of marrying not only a fortune hunter, but a Jewish bitch, with no breeding, no education, just a pretty face. She had ranted at him, shouting that men in his position took women like Vebekka as mistresses, never as wives, and the reason the bitch had never let him make love to her before marriage was because the promise of sex was all she had to lure him.

Louis could see his perfectly coiffured mother turning to gesture with her cane at the paintings, the tapestries. "Your father would turn in his grave . . . she is a tramp! And you cannot see it. What kind of name is Vebekka? Eh? Tell me that. I tell you, she is trouble. Marry your own kind, Louis, marry a woman who can run this estate, bring money to this estate, marry a woman who will make a wife."

Louis had ignored his mother and had married Vebekka. Later, when he had confronted her with a *fait accompli*—knowing it was too late for her to do anything about it—his mother had opened her Louis XIV writing desk and tossed a thick manila envelope at his feet.

"You should have checked on her background before you acted so rashly, now it's too late. You have made your bed, so you must sleep on it. I hope for your sake it works, because there can and never will be a divorce, I don't want the family name dragged through the courts and the press. I don't want to know about your private life, that is your business; my grandson must be protected, and if you want your inheritance, you will, in future, do as I ask."

Louis had known all those years she was really Rebecca Goldberg, but he had chosen never to confront her with what he knew. He had burned the contents of the private investigator's notes, and then left for a trip abroad.

Now the ghosts were catching up with him. His eldest son, wanting to marry, needed to know whether his mother was clinically insane. He also had to wait for the old baroness's inheritance to be released, to see whether he would be socially accepted by the family of his fiancée: She was one of the richest heiresses in France.

The entire family had always waited for the old baroness to die, most of all Louis. His fortune had not been released thus far.

Louis laughed softly; his whole life had been spent waiting. His mother had tied the bulk of the family fortune in trust funds for his children, leaving Louis an allowance for life. His second son was courting a daughter of a rich German industrialist, while his eldest daughter was engaged to a Brazilian multimillionaire. He laughed again, a soft humorless laugh. The promise of a massive fortune in the future was their cross in life!

Dear Helen, how very little she knew. Louis had been able to live in luxury and to create one of the finest polo stables in the world, only because of David and Rosa Goldberg's inheritance. It wasn't his money that he squandered so lavishly, but Vebekka's.

He yawned, and rubbed his hands. He felt chilly, the window was still open. As he reached to draw the shutters closed he saw a figure standing close to the brick wall opposite the Grand Hotel. He could not see if it was a man or woman, just a dark outline leaning against the wall, waiting. He paid no further attention, thinking it was probably a prostitute from the red light district.

✦ ✦ ✦

Ruda stared at the window, saw the light being extinguished. Her eyes flicked to the next window; it was dark. What had compelled her to return to this hotel in the middle of the night? What was here? She felt cold as she walked slowly to the taxi stand, and stepped inside a waiting cab . . . giving one last look at the dark window, the window with the shutters firmly closed.

Her driver was a small withered-looking man, who seemed delighted to have a fare at that hour. "Do you know what night it is tonight?"

Ruda lit a cigarette, and did not reply.

"Tonight is November the tenth. In 1938 Nazi mobs destroyed Jewish property, murdered a number of Jews, and arrested thirty thousand. They paved the way for the Holocaust. It was *Kristallnacht*—the Night of the Shattering Glass. And tonight, you know what is happening in Leipzig? Fighting! Hundreds arrested, the outbreak of violence is a nightmare. Some of my friends have gone there, for business, but me? Nobody will shatter the windows of my cab."

Ruda closed her eyes, she remained silent and motionless in the center of the backseat, aware of his dark eyes watching her in his mirror—suspicious, darting black eyes.

Back at the circus she paid him, leaning into his cab as he carefully counted the change. Suddenly she touched his cheek.

"Keep it. If they break your windshield, you get a new one . . . ."

9

GRIMALDI HAD BEEN drinking steadily all evening. He and Tina had gone out for dinner, and now they were about to make the rounds of some nightclubs. He had asked the taxi to stop when he saw a familiar street; very excited, he directed the driver to a doorway from which emanated loud music and around which a throng of kids were milling. He couldn't believe the club was still in existence. He had paid off the taxi before he realized his mistake; it was not the same club he remembered.

Tina moved down the murky stone corridor lit by a naked light bulb. She shrieked over the music that it was a terrible place. A young punk passed them, laughed at Tina, and then shouted to his friends. "What did he say?" shrieked Tina.

Grimaldi put a protective arm around her. "He said, 'Welcome to the Slaughterhouse!'"

The club was throbbing with kids where once it had resounded with the screams of slaughtered animals. Tina pushed and shoved her way to the bar. The music was so loud it was impossible to hear. Grimaldi felt his age among all these kids, dancing and drinking, smoking pot, and openly passing drugs. He suggested they drink up and leave.

Tina pouted. "Don't be so *boring!* This is the one night we have. Once the show starts, I won't be able to get out."

Grimaldi shrugged, made his way to a small alcove and a couple of crude benches. Tina sat on his knee as he squeezed himself onto the edge of a bench. She tipped back her bottle of beer, her feet tapping to the music. All around them young men and women prowled in black clothes, dark faces, white makeup. They shouted and danced while Grimaldi leaned back on the old white tiles, giving a shove to the girl behind him as she fumbled with her boyfriend's pants.

A young man asked Tina to dance. She kissed Grimaldi, gave him her purse and her half-empty bottle of beer, and dived onto the dance floor.

He sat waiting, getting hotter and hotter. He finished Tina's beer, and began to look around the crowd of thrashing kids to see if he could find her. He got up, looked over the heads of the dancers and saw her flinging her body around, dancing with her eyes shut, loving every minute of it.

Grimaldi made his way up the crowded staircase, and then pushed and shoved his way out. He heaved for breath on the pavement, and looked right and left. He was trying to get his bearings, sure the old club he remembered had to be close by. He grabbed hold of the beefy doorman, and shouting to be heard, tried to describe Tina in the event she came out looking for him. He told the doorman he had her handbag. He said that he was looking for a club called Knaast that had been in the area.

The doorman pointed down the street. Grimaldi walked for about ten minutes, stopped and turned this way and that, and was about to give up and return to the Slaughterhouse when he saw the club door. He grinned, and crossed the road.

The club looked the same, but the clientele had changed a lot. The club was now a leather bar; he had never seen so many chains and leather jackets crammed into such a small space. Beefy bar men, with T-shirts and muscles, wearing spikes and God knows what attached to their chests and throats, served customers, chained to bars. Some men were chained to each other, carrying on animated conversations, as if their chains were part of the decor.

Grimaldi pushed his way to the bar, asked for a beer, and turned to face the club floor. Only then did he realize that the patrons were all male! He was asked to dance by an aging homosexual in a strange leather helmet, a jockstrap and white tights. He downed his beer, and tried to edge his way toward the exit but it took a great deal of jostling. He shoved a large muscular man wearing an

SS hat, who turned and gripped Grimaldi by the testicles. "Don't push me!"

Grimaldi grimaced, the man's grip tightened. "I just want to leave, I am not looking for any arguments."

"You don't, cocksucker?"

Grimaldi was eye to eye with the SS officer's handlebar mustache. "I don't, but you will get in a lot of trouble if you don't get your fucking hands off me!"

"Make me," lisped the pursed lips through the mustache. Grimaldi backhanded the SS queen, then jabbed an elbow in his throat. He could feel his testicles burning as the man went sprawling.

Suddenly a blond-haired boy tried to swipe Grimaldi with his whip. Grimaldi snatched the whip and began to crack it, giving rise to a mixture of hysteria and applause. A bottle of champagne was waved at him from behind the bar, the chained barman screaming it was on the house, and Grimaldi abruptly broke up, laughing. The incident was so crass, so hideous, he had to laugh, and everyone joined in. He kept on saying he had only fallen into the place by mistake, he was straight. "Just get me out of here, somebody get me out!"

Grimaldi could hear his name being shouted, bellowed. *"Luis . . . Luis . . . Luis!"*

Grimaldi shook his head. His name was being yelled by a bloody chimp!

Boris was up on Fredrick Lazars' shoulders, the little animal's arms and legs virtually covering the man's face. Boris was pursing her lips; she looked as if she were the one calling Luis.

Grimaldi broke up in a roar of laughter, and the two men clasped each other in a bear hug as Boris whooped and screeched with excitement. Lazars introduced Grimaldi to friends and ordered drinks, dragging Grimaldi to a brick alcove.

✦ ✦ ✦

An hour later, Tina stood outside the Slaughterhouse club, in tears. She spoke no German, and her young dancing partner was still trying to persuade her to return to the club. She pushed him away, she shouted that she was looking for someone, but he began to pull at her arm.

"I'm looking for somebody . . . *leave me alone!*"

"I help you . . . I find for you, okay?"

Tina was so relieved he understood English, she hugged him, and kept tight hold of his hand as he talked to the doorman, who pointed down the street.

"Your friend, ze *big man* . . . go there, you come? I show you, come with me, yes?"

Tina teetered after her young friend, looking back doubtfully to the doorman, who gestured to the street with his hand. "Zat way . . . he go zat way."

While Tina was walking down the dimly lit alleyway, Grimaldi was staggering out of a taxi, with Lazars. Boris was on Lazars' shoulders; the two men were stumbling around the pavement. Lazars tried to get his wallet out of Boris's hand but Grimaldi took out a thick wad of notes and paid the driver. Tina's handbag was still hooked over his arm, though he seemed unaware of it. He was very drunk. Lazars bellowed for him to follow as he entered his apartment.

Lazars handed Boris over to Grimaldi, and opened two bottles of beer. He drew up two chairs, and then weaving slightly he spread both his arms, beaming. "She's a good girl, you won't regret this, and I'm giving you a good price!"

"I don't want a fuckin' chimp!"

"But you know somebody who would want her! You got lots of contacts, somebody'd want her. She's two years old, lot of years in her. She's intelligent, sharp, an' I've got all her papers, her certificates, her inoculations; it's a hell of a deal, I can't keep her here, shake on it! Look at her. You don't have a heart for human beings but a heart for animals. You don't have compassion. . . . I love her, my friend, but I am willing to let you have her."

Grimaldi shook his head. "I can't . . ."

"Put her in the act."

Grimaldi drank the beer, and banged the bottle onto the table. "Forget it, I don't want a goddamned chimp!"

Standing Boris on the tabletop, and pulling a worn old cardigan over the chimp's head, Lazars showed the little animal as much affection as if she were a child. "She's toilet trained. She could live in your trailer, heard it's like a palace."

"You been up to the grounds?"

"No, Tommy Kellerman told me, you know he's dead?"

Grimaldi yawned, scratching his head. "Ruda had to identify him!"

Lazars tucked Boris up in the old horsehair sofa, gave her a teddy bear to cuddle, pattted her head, and waited for her eyes to close before he opened two more beers.

"Do you remember the mad Russian, Ivan, the crazy horse?"

Grimaldi nodded. "He's a tough one to forget, you been over there? I hear he's still with the Moscow Circus."

"Yeah he's still with them, earning peanuts and working in that jungle of concrete and glass. He's got eighteen tigers, ten lions, and two panthers—act's good, he's good—one of the best, but . . ."

Lazars drank thirstily, and then stared at the bottle in his massive gnarled hands. "Not the way it used to be. Ivan took me to see the cages, steel cages on wheels, hardly enough room for the poor creatures to turn around in. You know, all my life I dreamed of working with big animals, but I never had the money or the breaks, and then—just like that!"

Lazars slapped the table with the flat of his hand. "I changed my mind . . . my whole outlook changed. I didn't wish it anymore. I talked to the Soviet Union's Society for the Protection of Animals, SSPA, I said there should be greater controls. You know, they lost three, *three* giraffes a few years back, they transported them around in railway carriages. They couldn't stand upright, hadda travel with their necks bent, crouched on their knees, for five days. But they told me they could do nothing against the power of the Soyuz-gostsirk—the organization that runs most of the circuses in Russia. It sickened me! For the first time I began to think we should reconsider, try again to find the heart of the circus."

Lazars opened more beer, and gulped half a bottle before he

continued. "Then, my friend, my eyes were opened. You ever seen France's Circus Archaos? You seen it?"

Grimaldi shrugged. "Yeah, but it's not everyone's taste!"

"They got chainsaws, punks, Mad Max, and *fire!* Rock music— it's new, its exciting!"

"*Bullshit.* What kids want to see clowns in dirty mackintoshes and rubber boots, *Bull shit!!*"

Lazars banged the table. "No, you are wrong, my friend. They have some of the finest performers. The heart of their circus are the jugglers and the trapeze artists. The shows have all been updated, they cater to the new audience, the kids, the teenagers that don't want to see fucking bears pedal bikes, chimps, like Boris, forced to become entertainers. They see through it, they know it's a fucking lie! You train a dog to sit and you've got to use force. Animals are no longer wanted."

"*Bullshit!* Don't give me this arty-farty crap about the French. They tried an animal-free circus in England and it flopped belly up, nobody came. You stand by the box office and you hear every other caller ask: What animals? *They come for the animals!*"

"No, not anymore. Luis, they see with their own eyes, they see man trying to prove he is top dog! They see man only wanting to dominate other species. They see the tragic animals hemmed into their cages, *they see . . .*"

"I should get back!" Grimaldi tried to stand up, and slumped back into his chair again.

Lazars took no notice, and handed him another bottle. "So, how is Ruda? She's come a long way, she's queen now, huh?"

Grimaldi nodded, and Lazars began to reminisce about the time when Grimaldi himself was a big star attraction. They swapped stories, recalling past glories . . . the two massive men seated on either side of the small table in the filthy cluttered kitchen. They laughed, they slapped each other's shoulders, and plowed their way through the crate of beer.

Suddenly they fell silent, caught up in their own private memories.

The first time Grimaldi had seen Ruda was with Lazars; Grimaldi was with a group of performers having a night out. He was drunk that night, had been drinking for the best part of the evening when they all stumbled to the basement club.

The city was bombed out. Abject poverty was everywhere, the only escape was in drink. The people were dazed, hungry; the aftermath of the terrible war hung like a sickening cloud. Memories of prewar times, of affluence, of dreams were pushed roughly aside; living and being alive was all that mattered, surviving the only priority.

Grimaldi had money then, one of the few who had. He was a young boy of fifteen when the war started, and had gone with his father to the United States, where his father died. It was in America that Luis learned his two brothers had been killed on the Russian front. He built up the act, and was one of the first performers to return to Europe after the war. It was the mid-fifties, and word had spread that young Luis Grimaldi was someone to watch. Those he was out with that night had all seen his performance, and everyone was slapping his back, toasting him. Then Ruda and the old magician had appeared on the cabaret stage in a puff of pitiful green smoke. This elicited general catcalls and yells, and a bottle was hurled at the old man while he attempted to continue the act.

The audience was called to attention by a taped drumroll. The old man asked for the patrons' participation. He was greeted with whistles and lewd remarks. Dressed in cheap black bra and panties, with laddered black tights and high-heeled shoes, Ruda appeared disinterested in her own performance, passing the tubes and hoops with a half-hearted smile on her face.

The magician had drawn from various pockets small silk handkerchiefs, red, blue, green. With great showmanship he had thrown them into the air, and urged the audience to hide the silks. Grimaldi's friends took a bunch of the squares, blew their noses with them, and tossed them aside, while Grimaldi tucked one into his right boot.

Ruda stood impassive, her head half turned from the blinding spotlights. Now the magician slipped a thick black blindfold around her eyes.

He began to thread his way through the audience. Ruda, in a low monotone, named the colors as each was retrieved.

"Red, blue, red, red, red, blue, green, red, blue, green . . ."

At one point she seemed ahead of the magician as the colored squares were caught and held aloft. She turned her head slightly as if listening, and yet kept reciting the colors. The audience had grown quiet, caught up in the act as the old man worked the club, gathering the squares; at times he had his back to her, it was impossible for her to cheat.

He stepped in front of Grimaldi. "Red . . ."

Grimaldi shrugged his shoulders, smiling, denying that he had hidden a square.

"Red . . ."

They had all cheered as he retrieved the red silk square from his boot.

Grimaldi and his friends had continued on to another club. It was almost dawn when Grimaldi hailed a taxi to go home. While waiting he saw her, standing on a street corner. She was still wearing her costume, but now she had an old brown thin coat around her shoulders. He saw her stop two men, and then shrug her shoulders as they moved on.

The taxi pulled up and Grimaldi got inside, the cab did a U-turn, coming to her side. She stared dull-eyed at the cab, and then stepped forward. Grimaldi wound down his window, about to say he had seen her act, when she stuck her head in the car and asked, "Do you want a blow job?" He shook his head, but she hung on.

"You can name your price!"

Grimaldi asked the driver to move on, but she still clung to the window. "Oh, it's you. It was in your fucking boot. You like to make people look like shit? . . . *Fuck you!*"

Grimaldi shouted for the driver to stop. He got out. She backed away from him, afraid. But he smiled and complimented her.

"You know, that was quite good. You should get rid of that old man, work up a real act, you're good! It has to be some kind of trick, but it works."

She hung back, pressing herself against the wall until he returned to the taxi and drove off. But the following morning she was there, hanging around his trailer.

"I'm looking for work."

Grimaldi had brushed her off, but nothing deterred her. She came by every day. He would give her a little money, get rid of her, but she still turned up. He would find her sitting on his steps, no matter what the weather, waiting; asking for a job, or peddling a blow job, masturbation. He ordered one of the stewards to keep her out, but she came back. If she wasn't hanging around his trailer, she would be waiting by the cages. She was always there, always in the same worn brown coat, and always hungry.

Grimaldi had been having an affair with a very attractive Italian trapeze artist. She screamed at him to get rid of the whore. He then became nasty with Ruda, physically shoving her away. Still, she came back.

There were only a few more days left on his contract before he was to travel on, and so he had given in. He became more pleasant, asked where she came from, if she had a home. She would shrug her shoulders. Then he did a foolish thing, seeing her huddled outside his trailer in pouring rain; he had asked her inside.

Once inside, she showed genuine interest in his photographs and reviews. He offered to take her coat, but she refused, sitting in the sodden coat, smoking.

"Will you take me with you when you go?"

He had laughed, saying this was impossible. He was going to Austria, then on to Switzerland, crossing back to Italy and then, he hoped, America.

She offered to be a groom, sweep, do anything. He had told her she would have to be hired by the circus bosses.

The next day, he found her sitting in his trailer. He chucked her out, but after his show she was back. Exasperated by her persistence, he said that if she had the right papers, passport and visas, he would see what he could do with the circus boss.

Later that night she came back, tapping on his window. He shouted for her to get the hell away, but she kept on tapping and in the end he had opened the door.

"Look, I said I don't want you around. If you got the papers leave them. I'll see what I can do, now go . . ."

Brazenly, she had walked past him into the small bedroom, taking off her filthy coat. She had on the black brassiere, black panties with a garter belt. The stockings were even more laddered.

"I've got someone with me, okay? Whatever you have to say, make it quick."

"I got no papers, I need you to help me, I need money."

He laughed at her audacity.

"My husband won't let me have any money."

"Your husband?"

"Yeah, the old man, I work for him, it's his act, you know, the magic man?"

Grimaldi hitched up the small towel around his waist. "Like I said, part of the act—the part with the colored silk squares—you should work it up. I mean I don't know what the signals are, but it's good."

"Signals? What do you mean?"

"Well, how you do it, how you get the colors in the right order, and so fast."

"Oh . . . that's no trick, that's just something I can do. I can do that easy, ever since I was a kid." She was looking around, peering into his bedroom.

"Well, it's good. The old guy's not so good, though. You should get a new partner."

Suddenly she was in his arms, coiled around him. She pinched his cheek with her finger and thumb. "You lied, there's no bloody woman here."

He didn't want to kiss her, or even touch her, but he stood there and let her go down on him. He let her take him in the middle of his trailer.

When it was over, she wiped her mouth with the back of her hand.

"That was for free! I'm going now."

He had felt guilty, and had thrust some money into her pocket.

She took out the bills and counted them, and then she had looked up and smiled. He had never seen her smile before.

"Next time I come, I'll have a visa, you can take me with you then. My name is Ruda . . . R U D A, you won't forget, will you? Thanks for the money."

He left the next day, but he didn't forget her—five years later when she turned up again, he recognized her immediately. It was in Florida; she was accompanied by her husband, Tommy Kellerman.

✦ ✦ ✦

Grimaldi woke up, he had no idea where he was. His head throbbed so hard he couldn't lift it. He felt something warm and hairy curled by his side, and as he lifted the stinking blanket he saw Boris's face.

"Whoop . . . Whoop."

Grimaldi let the blanket fall back over the chimp. Loud snoring was coming from across the room. In the darkness he could just make out the sleeping Lazars, his legs propped up on the table, his head on his chest, still sitting in his chair.

Grimaldi cursed. How in God's name had he got here? He couldn't remember. He sighed, and the strong hairy arm patted his chest gently. He inched up the blanket again, and the round bright button eyes blinked.

"What time is it, eh?"

Grimaldi tried to sit up—but slumped back again. Better to sleep it off, he doubted if he could stand up anyway.

✦ ✦ ✦

Ruda was wakened by a bang at the trailer door. She lifted the blinds, and saw a bedraggled Tina waiting outside.

"What do you want?"

Tina peered through the window. "Is he here? I can't pay the taxi . . . he took my handbag. Let me in!"

Ruda put on an old wrap, stuffed her feet into worn slippers. She got her wallet and opened the trailer door.

"You know what time it is? How much do you need?"

Tina was red-eyed from crying. "He just left me, he took my bag."

Ruda laughed. "That's my husband! Here, take this."

"Is he back? Did he come back?"

Ruda shook her head, about to close the door, her hand on her hip.

"I can't get into my trailer, the girls lock the door."

"What do you expect me to do?"

"Can I come back, after I've paid him?"

Ruda shrugged and left the door ajar, then returned to the bedroom and closed the door. She heard Tina enter, followed by the clink of cutlery. She stormed out. "Eh! What do you think you're doing?"

"I was making a cup of tea."

"Oh were you? Don't you think it would have been polite to ask? You wake me up, get money out of me, and now start banging around in my kitchen. You've got nerve, a lot of nerve."

"I'm sorry, do you want one?"

Ruda hesitated. "Yeah, white, one sugar."

Ruda got back into her bed, turned on the bedside light. It was after four; she leaned back, listening to the girl banging around searching for the tea, then she heard the rattle of teacups and her door inched open. Tina had a tray with two cups and a pot of tea, she'd got sugar and biscuits. She poured Ruda's cup, spooned in the sugar, then stirred it carefully.

Ruda took the cup, watching Tina pour her own, then she laughed softly. "Well isn't this cozy? You fancy keeping the baby in my room, do you? Little pink elephants on the curtains, frilly crib, white baby wardrobes?"

Tina edged to sit on a small stool in front of Ruda's dressing table. "I got really frightened, he was with me one minute and the next he just disappeared. He's got my handbag, my money, my cards, checkbook—everything. I'm worried about him, do you think he'll be all right?"

Ruda opened her bedside drawer, took out a bar of chocolate, breaking it into pieces. She sucked on a large piece, not offering Tina any. Tina took a biscuit and nibbled it. "I mean, he had been drinking."

Ruda said nothing, kept on staring at Tina.

"Actually, I wanted to talk to you, Ruda. Is it all right if I call you Ruda?"

Ruda took another bite of chocolate, and sipped her tea. She found it amusing to watch the stupid little bitch squirming.

"I know he's talked to you about the baby, and we've never really spoken, he said you'd agreed to a divorce."

Ruda licked her mouth, leaving a dark brown chocolate stain.

"I know how much the act means to you. I was watching you in rehearsal, I mean I was really impressed. I don't know all that much about training, but . . ."

"Impressed! Well, I am flattered." Ruda held out her cup for more tea, and Tina scuttled to the tray and poured, spooned in more sugar, and then started for the door.

"I don't want any milk, never have milk in the second cup, thank you."

Ruda smiled, and Tina sat down on the edge of the bed.

"I love him."

"You love him. How old are you?"

"Age doesn't matter."

"Doesn't it?"

"No, and I think I can make him happy. He's really excited about the baby."

"Is it his?"

Tina flushed. "That's a terrible thing to say. Of course it's his."

Ruda slowly put her cup down and leaned forward. Tina backed slightly, and then allowed Ruda to take her hand.

"What tiny little hands you've got, let me see your palm. Oh yes, really interesting, my my! What a lifeline."

Tina moved closer, allowing Ruda to press and feel her open palm. "Do you believe in that stuff? I think it's all mumbo-jumbo."

Suddenly Ruda gripped Tina's hand so hard it hurt, but she continued smiling, as if she were joking. "And I think everything you say is a load of crap—you little prick teaser. You don't love Luis. You don't love that big bloated old man, that drunken has-been, you want . . ."

Tina tried to draw her hand away, but Ruda held her in a viselike grip, pulling her closer and closer . . . and then, there was no smile. Ruda's face twisted with anger, and with her free hand she punched Tina's belly, pummeled it as if it were a lump of dough. Tina twisted and tried to break herself free. She started screaming—terrified, trying to protect her womb.

Ruda hauled Tina almost on top of herself. Tina kicked out with her legs, but Ruda dragged her closer, and covered her mouth. Tina could feel Ruda's body beneath her, and she twisted again, tried to turn.

"Don't struggle or I'll break your neck."

Tina began to cry, her body went limp. She knew she couldn't fight, Ruda was too strong.

"Promise not to cry out? Promise me? . . . *Promise!*"

Ruda jerked Tina so hard she gasped. "I promise! I promise! Just don't hurt me, don't hurt my baby, please . . ."

"If you scream or cry out, then I will hurt you, maybe even kill you." Slowly Ruda released her grip, easing Tina from her, and then rolled off, and leaned up on one elbow. She smiled down into the frightened girl's face. Tina was like a rabbit caught in a poacher's beam of light. Her eyes were wide, startled, and terrified. She was transfixed, unable to move, too scared to cry out. Now Ruda's strong hands stroked and caressed, with knowing assurance, gently easing down Tina's skirt to feel between her legs, her voice soft and persuasive, a half-whispered monotone, hardly audible.

"On nights when they held their entertainments, when they had their drinks, their music, we knew we were safe for one or two hours. We'd hear the laughter, we'd hear the singing, the applause, the shouting. . . ."

Ruda unbuttoned Tina's blouse, cupping the heavy breasts in their white lace brassiere. Her skin felt soft, so soft. Ruda had an overwhelming desire to hold Tina, as if she was some long-forgotten lover she wanted to protect. She no longer frightened her, she knew that, and she cradled Tina in her arms, drawing her closer, her lips close to Tina's face. She gave gentle, almost sweet kisses to her neck, to her ears. Tina felt the sadness sweep over her like a wave, a terrible sadness. She could not stop herself giving in return a childlike kiss to Ruda's neck. "Where were you?" Tina asked hesitantly, unsure what was happening, why it was happening.

Then Ruda rested her head against Tina's breast, while Tina softly stroked the back of Ruda's head, as if to encourage her to continue. "Where were you?" Tina repeated.

"Oh, I was someplace, someplace a long time ago. The older ones discovered there was a flap beneath the main hut, that we could wriggle beneath, hide under the trestle benches, hide and wait to see the show. . . ."

Ruda moved to rest her head on the pillows. Tina could easily have got up then, but she didn't move. The strong woman's sadness had mesmerized her.

"What was the show? Was it your first circus?"

Ruda sighed. "Yes, it was a sort of circus. They had animals, they had dancers, and they had hunchbacks, and giants. They had every imaginable human deformity, but they had chosen only the prettiest girls, they were thirteen, maybe a little older, but each one had her head shaved, her body hair shaved, and they wore coronets of paper flowers . . . red flowers, like bright red poppies."

Ruda's eyes stared at the ceiling, her face expressionless.

"They made the dwarfs fuck the giants; they made the hunchbacks fuck the pretty sweet virgins; they forced the dwarfs to ride the dogs' backs with their dicks up their arses. They clapped and applauded, laughed, and shouted for more. Then they began to beat the pretty, weeping girls, and they kept on beating them until their white bodies were red with their own blood, as red as the paper flowers on their scraped and scratched bald scalps. One of the trestles moved, cut into my leg. The others escaped, they crawled back under the feet of the bastards, inching their way out. But I couldn't. I was trapped, I had to keep on watching. When I shut my eyes, it made it worse because I could hear them, hear the cries, hear the dogs."

Ruda seemed unaware of Tina, who slowly inched away, and then slid from the bed until she knelt on the floor to pick up her clothes. Ruda made a strange guttural sound, half sob, half cry, and covered her face with her hands.

"Oh God, my poor Tommy, poor Tommy . . . !"

Tina slipped on her blouse. Ruda made no attempt to stop her from leaving. She wiped her cheek with the back of her big raw hand.

"Not until the show was over, not until they were too drunk to stand, too drunk to care, could I crawl back. Next morning, I saw what they'd done to the older ones. They were on the cart, the skin of their little bald heads burst open, clouds of flies stuck to their blood, purple-black rimmed eyes. They only wanted to see the show, to see what made everyone laugh."

Tina crawled toward her skirt. Suddenly Ruda rose from the bed, her hand outstretched. "Don't go. Please stay with me, just for a little while."

Ruda reached over and placed her hand on the unborn, the rounded belly of the young girl. "I will see that you have money to travel, but you must leave."

Tina backed away, the expression in Ruda's eyes made her afraid again. "You will leave, Tina, but without my husband."

Tina blurted out a pitiful: "No . . . no!" She would never forget the look on Ruda Grimaldi's face, the strange hissing sound before she spat out the words: "He is *mine!*"

The slap sent Tina reeling against the wall. At the same time Grimaldi eased open the trailer door, silently, so as not to wake Ruda. He heard the cry, went to Ruda's bedroom, and opened the door. For a moment he was unable to comprehend what he was seeing.

He slammed the door, burst out of the trailer, and began to vomit. He turned as Tina rushed out hysterically, half undressed, sobbing. She gasped. "My handbag . . . I want my handbag."

Tina snatched it from him and ran. She stumbled once, flaying the air with her hand, and then was out of sight.

Ruda was at the trailer door, looking at him . . . shaking. "You better get some coffee down you. Come on, I'll get Mike to clear up in the morning."

Grimaldi, dazed, allowed himself to be helped back up the steps, stood as she took his jacket, peeled off his shirt.

"Christ, you stink. What the hell have you been doing?"

"I met Fredrick Lazars, we got drunk . . ."

"Sit down and let me take your pants off, you stink like a dog!"

Grimaldi sat as she heaved off his boots, unbuttoned his pants.

"I slept with Boris, a baby chimp."

He curled up on the cushions. She brought a blanket, put it on him, then placed a bottle of scotch next to him for when he came around. She knew he would be unable to face the day without a drink. When she was sure he was asleep, Ruda returned to her room and slumped onto her crumpled bed, confused by the evening's events. What had she just done?

She rubbed her arms with revulsion, very angry at herself. She had told Tina, stupid little Tina, about a part of her life that she had never shared with anyone before. Why? She bit her knuckles. Tina had made her feel something, the girl's soft body in her arms had reminded her of a warmth, a loving, she had forgotten. But it wasn't the same. It was stupid to even think of it now. She had to get her mind straightened out, had to think straight. She had even offered to pay her money to leave—why? "Ruda, what do you want?"

Even if she didn't want him, was it the real truth that she didn't want anyone else to have him, either? That surprised her. "What do you want?" Ruda said aloud as she started pacing up and down the small bedroom. Her pace quickened, and she paused twice looking up at the cupboard. She could feel its pull, but every time she got close to it, she turned and walked back across the room. She paused by her poster. She pressed her hand against her own face, and then she couldn't stop herself. She stepped up on the small stool by her makeup mirror, and opened the small cupboard above. She had to balance on tiptoe to reach it, her hands pushing aside boxes and hats until she felt the cold sides of the black tin box.

She hugged it to her chest, secretive, like a child, and then got to her hands and knees, lifting the carpet until she found the key. She always felt a strange sensation opening the box—pain pierced her insides. The odd assortment of treasures, her secrets that meant so much to her, but were of no value to anyone else. She spent a long time fingering, touching her "things," unaware of the low humming sound she made, her body rocking backward and forward.

"Mine, mine . . . mine . . ." She licked the small oval gray pebblelike object, then replaced it, and looked to the poster of herself. "Mine, mine, mine." Her face in the center of the brightly colored poster became a distorted skeleton head. She could see the loaded truck, weighted down, being dragged through the muddy yard, teetering dangerously to one side. Beneath a hastily thrown tarpaulin, she glimpsed the stacked, bloated bodies, and from the crushed bellies of the corpses came the hideous hissing sound of escaping gas.

As the truck tilted a body slid from beneath the tarpaulin and fell to the ground, rolling to one side. The guards shouted to the orderlies to get the corpse back on the truck, but then in the darkness something glittered on the fat bloated hand with fat purple fingers. The guard tried to wrench the thick gold wedding ring free, but try as he might he could not release it. He picked up a spade and, holding it above his head, he brought it down blade first across the dead woman's hand. The fingers jumped, as if they had a life of their own, fingers like black sausages, and they rolled in the mud. The guard dug this way and that, swearing and shouting but unable to find the ring. He gave up and screamed for the truck to move on. An orderly unhooked his coat belt, made a loop, and flicked it over the dead woman. He dragged her by her neck back onto the truck, and then pulled the tarpaulin down. The guards and the *Kapos* began to push and shove the truck forward through the freezing muddy ground.

As it disappeared, the ragged men, hidden like nightmare shadows, appeared like a pack of dogs, scrabbling in the mud until one of them, on his hands and knees, found the ring. *"Das gehört mir!"* "Mine!" But the others tore at him and beat him. He screamed and screamed; *"Das ist der meinige, meinige, MEINIGE!"* The pitiful man clung to his treasure, fought like a demon, then desperate to save himself, he threw the ring and it shot through the air, sinking in a puddle two feet away from a tiny little girl, a little girl crying from pain in her leg, terrified by what she had just witnessed . . . a frightened Ruda, crawling between the alleyways of huts, safe from the shadow men, on the other side of the barbed wire fence. The man clung to the meshing with his skinny hands, his mouth black, gaping and toothless, like a starving jackal he screeched: *"Das ist der meinige, das gehört mir, das ist der meinige!"* Ruda had crept back to her hut, silently lifting the worn blanket, slipping in to lie beside her sister, needing her comfort, needing to feel the warmth of the tiny plump body. In her sleep, Rebecca turned to cuddle Ruda, to cover her with sweet, adoring, childish kisses. Ruda felt safe and warm. They had a prize worth a fortune. A golden ring. The music, the red paper flowers, the screams and the anguished faces blurred in her mind as Ruda, not old enough to comprehend the misery, felt only the burning pain in her leg, and repeated over and over in her mind: *"Das ist der meinige, das ist der meinige . . . meinige, meinige . . ."*

Ruda carefully relocked her treasure box, hid the key, and re-turned the black tin box to its hiding place. She knew she could not sleep, and as it was after five decided she would shower and get ready for the first feed of the day. As she soaped her body, turning around slowly in the small shower cabinet, she felt the tension in her body begin to ease. But she could not rid herself of her deep anger. She carefully wrapped herself in a clean soft towel, patting herself dry, then pointed her left foot like a dancer. There was still the small scar where the trestle bench had cut into her leg, so many years before. She poured some lotion into her cupped hand and massaged her leg. The wound had festered. She had been so frightened of telling anyone that eventually she had been taken to the hospital bay. They had put a paper dressing on it. Days, perhaps weeks later the pain had become so bad, she had been carried back to the hospital by an orderly. Lice had eaten into her leg beneath the pus-soaked bandage, and she had been forced into the delicing bath, screaming and crying out in pain. It was as a result of the festering wound that she came to the attention of Papa. She had been taken to see him that afternoon, wearing clean clothes, washed and cleaned, her hair combed, her wound well bandaged with a proper dressing. That was the first time she had been alone with him, the first time he had asked her if she wanted to play a very special game with him. He had sat her on his knee, given her a sweet and bounced her up and down. When she didn't unwrap the sweet, he had asked why not. He had smiled, she remembered, asking why she didn't want the sweet. He even playfully tried to take it away from her.

"Das ist der meinige!" The little girl's fist clenched over the sweet as she glared into his handsome face. Her determined expression delighting him, he smiled, showing perfect white teeth.

Ruda tossed the towel aside. She continued to rub the lotion into her body, then she dressed. The anger was gone now. Thinking of Papa always made the anger subside. It was replaced, as it had always been, with a chilling, studied calmness. Ruda braided her hair, gave a cursory look at her reflection. She passed the poster of herself and lightly touched it with her hand. The poster represented everything she had fought so hard to attain, and nothing would take it from her. She didn't even look at the poster as she passed, but she whispered quietly to herself, making a soft hissing sound: *"Das ist der meinige!"*

Luis was still asleep where she had left him. She drew the blinds, pulled the blanket around his shoulders, and opened the door. Outside she picked up the hose and washed down the trailer herself. Then she began to whistle, stuffing her hands into her pockets as she strolled over to the cages. She looked skyward, shading her eyes. It still looked overcast.

Ruda passed between the trailers, calling out a brisk good morning to the early risers. There was movement now, some trainers and performers were heading to the canteen for breakfast, some like Ruda were getting ready to prepare their animals' feed.

She made her routine morning check, passing from cage to cage, calling every cat by name, and then she stopped by Mamon's cage.

He was lazily stretching, he threw back his head and yawned. "You're mine, my love." She leaned against the rails, and he swung his head low, stared at her, and then threw his black mane back with a roar that never ceased to delight her. He seemed to roar her inner rage.

"Everything's all right now ma'angel!"

10

TORSEN WOKE REFRESHED. The moment he got into his office, he pasted up his memos, his suggested schedule for the men. It was still only seven-thirty; he had brought in fresh rolls and was brewing coffee. He typed the past evening's reports furiously and distributed them around the station.

At eight-forty-five when the men began to trickle in to the locker rooms, they saw a large memo requesting all station personnel to convene in the main room for a briefing.

Torsen was placing his notebook and newly sharpened pencils on the incidents room's bare table when he overheard Rieckert laughing as he entered. "It's not just a dwarf, but a Jewish dwarf and . . ."

Torsen gestured for Rieckert to join him. He kept his voice low, his back to the main room. "I hear you make one more anti-Semitic remark, in the station, in the car, at any time you are wearing your uniform—you will be out, understand?"

Rieckert smiled, said that he was just joking.

"I don't care, I don't want to hear it, now sit down. . . ."

Torsen handed out the day's schedule, and suggested that they should all review their on/off-duty periods. Anyone with any formal or reasonable complaint should leave a memo on Torsen's desk. He then discussed in detail his findings to date regarding the murder of Tommy Kellerman.

The meeting was interrupted by the switchboard operator, who slipped a note to Torsen. It was an urgent request to call his father's nursing home. Torsen telephoned, and the nurse informed him that his father was exceptionally lucid, and had asked to see him.

Torsen returned to the incidents room. "I will not, as listed, be on the first assignment; Rieckert and Clauss you take that, and I will join you at the Grand Hotel. Please stay there until I arrive."

Torsen had made clear that they must all remain in contact with each other throughout the day to exchange information and discuss findings. He declined, however, to tell them where he was going. After his pep talk, a visit to his ailing father should perhaps not have taken precedence over the murder inquiry.

✦ ✦ ✦

Nurse Freda, a pleasant dark-haired girl in her late twenties, was waiting for Torsen at the main reception. "He seemed very eager to speak to you."

"I appreciate your call, but I cannot stay long. I am involved in a very difficult case!"

He followed her plump rear end along a corridor, and into his father's ward. Nurse Freda turned, smiling. "He's been put by the windows today; it's more private, you can draw the curtain if you wish."

The old man looked very sprightly, with his hair slicked back; he had on a checkered dressing gown, and clean pajamas. A warm rug covered his frail knees, and his jaw looked less sunken: He was wearing his dentures.

"Took your time, took your time, Torsen. I don't know, only son and you never come to see your poor old father."

Torsen pulled the curtain, drew up a chair to sit next to him.

The old man crooked his finger for Torsen to come closer. "This is important, I woke up thinking about it and I've been worried stiff. Can't sleep for worrying. Then I had a word with Freda, and it clicked, just clicked."

"What did, Father?"

"You need a wife, you've got to settle down and have a couple of kids, you've got a good job, good pay, and a nice apartment— now Freda, she's not married, she's clever, she'll make you a good wife. She's got good, child-bearing hips."

Torsen flushed, afraid they would be overheard. "Father, right now I don't have a telephone."

"Why haven't you got a telephone? Did they take it out?"

Torsen sighed, they had had this conversation before. "No,

remember when you moved in here, I was given a smaller apartment. The telephone has remained in the old apartment, I was not allowed to take it with me."

"How can you work without a telephone?"

"With great difficulty. I have requested one months ago, and today I left a memo in the director's office. Today, in fact, I have instigated many changes, some I am quite proud of."

The old man stared from the window, plucked at his rug a moment, then turned, frowning. "No telephone?"

Torsen checked his watch, then touched his father's hand. "I am in the middle of an investigation, I have to leave."

The old man sucked in his breath and turned around, leaning forward to see the row of beds. Then he sat back. "Dying is a long time in coming, eh? . . . There are many here, waiting and afraid."

Torsen held the frail hand. "Don't talk this way, I don't want to go away worrying about you."

"Oh, I'm not afraid, there are no ghosts to haunt me, but the dying here is hard for some. They have secrets, the past is their present, and they remember. You understand what I am saying? When you pass by their beds, look at their faces, you'll see. You can hide memories surrounded by the living, but not in here. Still, soon they will be all gone and then Germany can be free."

Torsen wondered what his father would think if he saw the packs of skinheads with their Nazi slogans. "I hope you are right."

The old man withdrew his hand sharply. "Of course I am. We have been culturally and politically emasculated by Hitler, devastated by the Allies, and isolated by the Soviets for more than half a century. Now it is our second chance. The city will be restored as the capital of reunified Germany. We are perfectly placed, Torsen, to become the West's link to the developing economies of the democratic East. You must marry, produce children, be prepared for the future."

The old man's face glowed.

"Father, I have to leave. I will come by this evening."

"What are you working on?"

Torsen told him about the murder of Kellerman, and the old man listened intently, nodding his head, muttering: "Interesting, yes, yes."

Torsen leaned close. "In fact, I was going to ask you something. Remember the way we used to discuss unsolved crimes?"

The old man nodded, rubbing his gums as if his teeth hurt.

"There was an old case, way back, maybe early sixties, late fifties, we nicknamed it the Wizard case . . . do you remember? The body was found midway in your jurisdiction and I think Dieter's—there may be no connection, it was . . ."

"How is Dieter?"

"He died, Father, ten years ago."

The old man frowned. Dieter was his brother-in-law, and for a moment he was confused; was his wife dead too?

"Father, can you remember the name of the victim in the Wizard case?"

"Dieter is dead? Are you sure?"

Torsen looked into the perplexed face, and gently patted his hand. "I'll come and see you later."

Torsen drew the curtain back, waved to Nurse Freda to indicate he was leaving. His father began singing softly to himself.

Torsen proceeded to walk down the aisle between the beds. He paused, watching Freda finish tending a patient, then he waited until she joined him.

"I wondered if perhaps, one evening we . . . if you are not on duty, and would like to join me, for a movie . . ."

Freda smiled. "Your father has been playing Cupid?"

While Torsen flushed, and fiddled with his tie, she laughed a delightful warm giggle and then asked him to wait one moment. She disappeared behind a screen with a bedpan.

Torsen stared at a skeleton-thin patient, plucking frantically at his blanket, his toothless jaw twitching uncontrollably, his eyes wide and staring as if at some unseen horror.

Torsen turned and hurried out, unable to look, too agitated to wait and arrange a date with Freda.

✦ ✦ ✦

Rieckert was waiting in the hotel lobby. Torsen hurried to his side, apologized for his lateness, and then crossed to the reception desk to ask if they could go to the baron's suite.

The baron opened the doors himself, and pointedly looked at his wristwatch. Torsen apologized profusely as they entered the large drawing room. Rieckert gaped, staring at the chandelier, the marble fireplace—the room was larger than his entire apartment.

The baron had laid out his wife's and his own passports and visas on the central table; he then introduced them to Helen Masters, who proffered her own documents. Torsen leafed through each one, and then asked if they were enjoying their stay. The baron murmured that he was, and sat watching Torsen from a deep wing armchair.

Torsen noted that their papers were in order; then, standing, he opened his own notebook. "Would you mind if I ask you a few questions?"

The baron shrugged, but looked at the clock on the mantel. Helen Masters interrupted to say they were late for an appointment. Torsen smiled, said it would take only a few moments. He looked to the baron, and asked whether the baroness was feeling better.

"She is, will you need to speak with her?"

Torsen coughed, feeling very uneasy, and he drew up a chair to the central table. "If it is not too much trouble. But if it is not convenient for her I can return at a later date!"

The baron strode toward the bedroom, he knocked and waited. Hilda came to the door. "Is the baroness dressed?"

Hilda murmured she would only be one moment, and the door was closed.

Torsen directed his first question to Helen Masters.

"You arrived by car on the evening in question, that is correct?"

"No, I think we came just before lunch."

The baron sighed. "We lunched in the hotel restaurant, then returned to the suite. Then we left at about three o'clock for Dr. Albert Franks's clinic. We visited with Dr. Franks, and then returned back here. We dined in the suite, and remained in the hotel all evening."

Helen nodded her head, as if to confirm part of the baron's statement. Torsen looked to her, and she hesitated a moment before saying, "I had dinner with Dr. Franks, but I returned here about ten-thirty, maybe a little later."

Torsen asked if on the way back she saw anyone in the street.

Helen laughed softly. "Well, yes, of course, I saw a number of people, the doorman, the taxi drivers, and . . ."

She looked to the baron. "Your chauffeur, we have forgotten about him. He returned to Paris and then flew to New York, but he would have left before early evening."

"On your return to the hotel did you see a tall man, about six feet, wearing a dark raincoat, and a shiny, perhaps leather, trilby hat?"

Helen shook her head. Torsen looked up from his notes. "Did you see anyone fitting that description at or near the hotel entrance on the night in question?"

"No, I did not."

"Did you see anyone fitting that description in the lobby of the hotel?"

Helen gave Louis a hooded smile. "No, I am sorry. Is this man suspected of the murder?"

Torsen continued writing. "I wish to talk to this man about a possible connection to the murder."

Helen asked: "Do you have any clues to his identity?"

Torsen closed his notebook. "No, we do not. I think that is all I need to ask."

"What was the time of the murder?" Helen inquired.

"Close to eleven or eleven-thirty. We know he was carrying a large bag and that his clothes would have been heavily blood-stained."

Helen asked how the victim was killed, listening intently as Torsen described the severity of the beating.

Helen wanted to know if the victim was with the circus. Torsen gave a small tight smile, wondering why she was so interested, but at the same time answering that the victim was not, as far as he had been able to ascertain, an employee of any circus.

The bedroom doors opened, and Torsen rose to his feet as the baroness, assisted by Hilda, walked into the room. The baron sprang to his feet, crossing to his wife, arms outstretched. "Sit down, come and sit down, the car is ordered."

Vebekka wore a pale fawn cashmere shawl fringed with sable, a fawn wool skirt, a heavy cream silk blouse, and a large brooch at her neck entwined with gold and diamonds. She also had on her large dark glasses. Her face was beautifully made up, her lips touched with pale gloss. She held her hand out to Torsen.

"I am sorry to inconvenience you, Baroness. I am Detective Chief Inspector Torsen Heinz, and this is Sergeant Rieckert."

The baroness's hand felt so frail, he did no more than touch her fingers. She smiled to Rieckert. Hilda helped her to sit, and brought her a glass of water. Torsen noticed how thin the baroness was, how her body trembled, her hands shaking visibly as she sipped the water. He found it disturbing not to be able to see her eyes.

"I need simply to verify your husband's account of the day you arrived in Berlin."

She sipped, paused, sipped again and Hilda took the glass.

"What day?"

The baron coughed. "The day we arrived from Paris, darling."

She nodded, and then looked to Torsen. "What did you ask me?"

"If you could just tell me what you did, during the afternoon, and evening."

She was hardly audible, speaking in a monotone, as she recalled arriving, having lunch, and then going to see the doctor. She reached for the glass again, and this time Hilda held it as she sipped.

"We dined in the suite, I was very tired after the journey."

Torsen placed his notebook in his pocket, gave a small nod to Rieckert as an indication they were leaving.

"Why are you here? Has something happened? Is something wrong?"

She half rose, looking to the baron. "Is it Sasha?"

The baron hurried to her side. "No, no, nothing wrong; something happened close to the hotel the night we arrived, and the Polizei have to question everyone who booked into the hotel from Paris."

Torsen noticed he spoke to her as if she were a child, leaning over toward her, touching her shoulder as if shielding her from harm: "There was a murder, everyone in the hotel is being questioned."

"Is this true?" the baroness asked, and looked concerned to her husband. "But why? Why have we to be questioned? I don't understand, did I do something wrong?"

The baron patted his wife's hand, gently telling her they were asking all the guests in the hotel the same questions.

"You didn't happen to see anyone—perhaps while you were looking out of the window down to the street—at about eleven o'clock, a tall man wearing a shiny hat, carrying a suitcase?"

The baroness seemed unable to understand what he was talking about. She stared at her husband. "I didn't do anything did I? I was in the suite, I never left the suite."

Torsen shook Helen's hand and thanked her. He gave a small bow to the baron. His sergeant was already holding open the door. As they waited for the elevator, Rieckert whispered to Torsen, "She's a sicko. That doctor, Albert Franks, he's a famous shrink! Deals with crazies, hypnotizes them. That's what they must be here for. She's a sicko."

As Rieckert went to collect their patrol car, Torsen waited on the whitewashed steps. He saw the line of taxis waiting for hire, and recognized the driver from the previous night. He crossed over to his Mercedes.

The driver jumped out, started to open the rear door.

"No, no, I just wanted to ask you to spread the word around for me, ask if anyone saw a tall man, wearing a shiny trilby hat, dark raincoat, boots, carrying a bag, on the night the dwarf was murdered."

The driver stopped him with an outstretched hand. "I know

the night, we've all been talking about it. But I never saw anyone fitting that description, sir!"

Torsen persisted. "You ever pick up Ruda Kellerman? The lion tamer? Her husband is Luis Grimaldi?"

The driver nodded his head vigorously. "Yeah, picked her up from this hotel, yesterday, took her back to the West, to the circus."

Rieckert drew up in the patrol car, giving an unnecessary blast of the horn. Torsen and Rieckert drove off as the driver went from cab to cab asking if any of them had seen or given a ride to a tall man in a big trilby, with high boots—the killer! As he went from driver to driver his description became more melodramatic . . . scarred face, huge hands covered in blood. One cab driver did recall driving Ruda Kellerman from the hotel, but then remembered it was *after* the murder, so he didn't mention it, nor the fact that he had seen her standing on the opposite side of the road, looking up at the hotel windows. He didn't think it was important.

◆　◆　◆

Ruda was feeling a lot happier, the act had run smoothly, the animals seemed to be getting used to the new plinths. She saw to the feeds, checked that the cages were clean and the straw changed, and then, still in her working clothes, went to Tina's trailer. She rapped on the door and waited.

A big blonde with a gap between her front teeth inched open the trailer door.

"Is Tina in?"

"She doesn't want to see anyone, she's been very sick!"

Ruda stuffed her hands in her pockets. "Tell her it's me, will you?"

After a moment the girl returned, said Tina's room was at the end of the trailer. The girl went out as Ruda went inside.

The trailer was small and cramped. Girls' costumes and underwear littered the small dining area. Ruda stepped over the discarded clothes and pushed open the small bedroom door. Tina was huddled in a bunk bed, her face puffy from crying. She wore a flowered cotton nightdress.

Ruda hitched up her pants. "You seen him?"

"No . . . I can't face him. What did he say?"

Ruda shrugged. "Nothing much. Actually, he sort of suggested I come by, check on you. If you want, I can fix you something to eat."

"I'm not hungry, Oh God!" She buried her head in her hands and sobbed. "It was disgusting, I mean, I dunno why I let you."

Ruda began to tap her boot. "Look, I didn't come here to talk about last night. I just want to tell you something. He will never leave me, Tina, and I will never divorce him. He's old, sweetheart, he's an old man, he's washed up, and without me he's fucked."

Tina stood up, her hands clenched at her sides. "I don't want to hear any more—just get out, leave me alone."

Ruda leaned forward and pressed Tina's stomach. "How far gone are you?"

Tina backed away, her hands moving protectively over her belly. "Three and a half months."

"You're lucky . . . they don't like terminating after four months."

Tina gasped. "What did you say?"

Ruda smirked. "You heard me, now stop playing games and listen—"

"I don't want to listen to you—you are evil, you are sick. Get out—*get out!!*"

Ruda cocked her head to one side, kicked the bedroom door closed. "I am here to help you, you stupid little bitch. I can help you, I can give you names, good people you can trust, they'll take care of it."

"I want my baby! I want my baby."

Ruda shrugged her shoulders. "Okay, that's up to you . . . but I am going to make you an offer. Now listen to me. I am going to give you fifteen thousand dollars—dollars, Tina! You can leave Berlin, go back to wherever you came from, you can have the baby, abort it—whatever you want, but . . ."

"I don't want your money."

Ruda dug into her pockets. "It's the best offer you'll have, sweetheart—fifteen thousand dollars, in cash, but the deal is you leave before twelve. If you hang around, the money goes down every hour, so you got until twelve o'clock noon, Tina, think about it. I'll be in my trailer, okay?"

Ruda half opened the bedroom door, then hesitated, swinging the door backward and forward slightly.

"You know, I am doing you a big favor. I was married to an old man once, as old as Luis, decrepit, senile, pawing at me. You turn the offer down Tina, and I guarantee your life will be a misery. He's a failure, he's washed up, and you wouldn't last a season with any act he tried to get together. He's scared, Tina, he'll never go into the ring again—everything he's promised, all the lies, are just an old man's dreams."

Tina sat hugging her knees, rocking backward and forward. Big tears trickled down her cheeks. She cringed as Ruda stepped toward her, looked up, almost expecting to be slapped. Instead, Ruda gently brushed the girl's wet cheeks with her thumbs. "Take a good look around this hovel. Now, imagine a cradle, a little baby bawling and clutching at you, needing you, and your body all bloated, your face blotchy. You want to bring it up here? Get rid of it, walk away. It won't hurt."

Tina turned her face away. "I want my baby."

Ruda swallowed. Tina surprised her. "Then go home, Tina. Take the fifteen thousand and get out!" Ruda was almost out of the door.

"Make it twenty." Tina tried hard to meet Ruda's eyes, but they frightened her. She bowed her head, but quickly looked up again when she heard the big deep laugh.

"You're going to be okay, sweetheart. And you know something—I like you. It's a deal."

◆　◆　◆

Ruda whistled as she threaded her way between the trailers. When she reached her own, she eased off her big boots, stacking them outside. She looked up; the rain clouds were lifting. She let herself in silently, and eased open drawers as she collected the money, counting it. She slipped it into an envelope. She heard Luis stirring.

"Hi, how you feeling?"

He needed a shave, his eyes were red-rimmed. She gave a quick look at the bottle—it was a quarter full—and she crossed to him, pulling up the blanket.

"Sleep it off, then I'll fix you something to eat, eh? Rehearsal went well, they are calming down, getting used to the plinths. You were right, you said they'd work out okay."

"That's good," he mumbled. "Do you want a chimp? Lazars got a chimp."

She cocked her head to one side, handed him the bottle. "Here, is this what you want?"

He moaned, said he didn't want a drink, but he took the bottle anyway. She walked out and left him, ran a shower for herself, and began to undress.

The bottle fell from his hand, he stared at the ceiling, one arm across his face. In his drink-befuddled mind, he kept on seeing the fear on Tina's face, her wretched submissiveness. But worse, he couldn't forget the way Ruda had looked at him, because she had looked at him in exactly same way as when she had ridden on Mamon's back—daring him, mocking him. He tried to sit up, but the room began to spin, he couldn't get on his feet, couldn't stand. He sank back, then reached for the bottle. He held it by the neck, unable to focus.

He yelled: *"Rudaaaaaaaaaaaaaaaaaa, Ruda!"*

Ruda held the bottle out for him. He eased himself up, and stared at her. "Thank you."

Ruda was soaping herself when she heard the light tap on the door. She smiled, peeked around the shower curtain, it was almost twelve! She wrapped herself in a towel, was about to call out when she heard the main trailer door opening.

Tina walked into the trailer. It was dark, the blind drawn, she stood in the doorway, unable to adjust to the darkness.

"Want a drink?"

He was stretched out on the bench seat, his fly undone, his shirt hanging out. Tina edged further into the room as he held out the bottle. "Have a drink?"

Tina took a step back, whispered his name, and then in a half sob repeated it. She had somehow not expected him to be there.

"Chimp, got a three-month-old chimp, called Boris . . . *Boris!* . . ." He laughed, and continued to drink; he didn't even seem to realize she was in the room.

She jumped when she felt a light touch on her shoulder, and Ruda drew her close.

"Look at him, take a good look, Tina."

Tina squeezed past Ruda into the tiny corridor by the front door. "I did love him. I did."

Ruda pressed the envelope into her hand. "I know. I know you did, but you know as well as I do, it would never have worked out."

Tina fingered the thick envelope. "Because you would never have given us a chance. I'll take your money, Ruda, not for me but for my baby—Luis's baby."

The young girl's eyes stared at Ruda. This time she didn't look away. "We agreed twenty, don't make me count it. You said twenty."

Ruda smiled, touched Tina's cheek with her hand. "Don't push your luck, little girl. I have done only what I had to. It's called survival. You got off lightly, now get out of my sight before I kick you out."

Tina let herself out. Ruda shut the door fast, even faster than she had intended, because right outside the trailer she could see the wretched little inspector. She swore under her breath. Why had she been so foolish? She should have just smiled at him. She took a deep breath and waited. Was he coming to see her?

Torsen and his sergeant were looking at the pair of large boots outside the Grimaldi trailer. They had steel tips! Torsen gave Rieckert a few instructions, which he had to repeat, since Rieckert was distracted by the pretty girl who had just left the trailer. Then Torsen tapped on the trailer door.

Ruda inched open the door and smiled.

Torsen gave her a small bow. "Mrs. Grimaldi, could I please

speak to you for one moment—oh! are those your husband's boots outside?"

Ruda hesitated, and then drew her gown tighter around herself. "Yes, why, do you want to borrow them?"

"No, no. May I come in?"

"I'm afraid he cannot see you right now, he's indisposed."

Torsen cocked his head to one side. "It is you I wished to speak to, Mrs. Grimaldi!"

Ruda shrugged her shoulders and stepped back from the doorway. She gestured to her husband, still sprawled out, and then suggested they go into her bedroom. She tossed the duvet over the unmade bed.

"What is it this time?"

Torsen remained in the doorway. "It is with reference to your husband."

"He won't be able to talk sensibly for hours, maybe days. He's drunk."

"No, it is about Mr. Kellerman. You see, when I questioned you, both here and at the city morgue, I asked about the dead man's left wrist. You said you had no knowledge of a tattoo, and you repeated that at the morgue. I have subsequently discovered that the dead man was a survivor of Auschwitz, and the tattoo was his camp identification number. So you must have known what the tattoo was when I asked you. Now I ask you, why? Why did you lie to me, Mrs. Grimaldi?"

Ruda sat for a moment, her head bowed, and then slowly began to roll up her left sleeve, carefully folding back the satin, inch by inch, until her arm was bare. She looked at Torsen.

"Is this a good enough reason for not talking about it?"

She turned over her wrist, her palm upward, displaying a jagged row of dark blue numbers: 124666. Her voice was very low, husky. "When they reached two hundred thousand they began again—did you know that? They were confident that by that time there would be no confusion, no two inmates carrying the same number. You know why? Because they would already be dead."

Torsen swallowed. He had never met a Holocaust survivor face
to face. He had to cough to enable himself to speak.

"I am so sorry."

She stared at him, carefully pushing the sleeve down to cover
the tattoo. Her eyes bore into his face. In great embarrassment he
stuttered that she must have been very young.

"I was three years old, Inspector. Is there anything else you want
to know?"

Torsen shook his head, mumbled his thanks and apologies, and
said he would let himself out. He hurried to the patrol car, where
Rieckert grinned at him.

"I did it, took a shoe box, one of the performers gave it to me.
I filled it with mud, then pressed the boot down hard, we've got
two good clear prints. I took the right and the left because I wasn't
sure which heel we got the original print from."

Torsen started the engine.

"Left, it was the left heel, and they're Grimaldi's boots."

The car splashed through the mud and potholes and onto the
freeway. Rieckert opened his notebook.

"I got samples of sawdust from the cages, from all over the
place, got it all in plastic bags as they told me. So, what did she
say? Why did she lie?"

Torsen stared ahead. After a moment, he said, "She had a reason
for not wanting to remember. One I accepted."

✦ ✦ ✦

Ruda carried her boots to the incinerator, the one used for the
rubbish left after a show. She checked the grid. The fire was low,
it wouldn't really get going until after the performance, but she
tossed them inside anyhow, and waited by the open door to see
them ignite. They took a long time, the leather was tough and hard.
Gradually they began to smolder and to give off a heavy odor. She
slammed the oven closed.

For many years she had controlled the flow of images, fought
them, but the smells . . . they were the worst, they would sneak
up on her, and they were stronger because they were unexpected,

more difficult to repress; the pictures they conjured up were more powerful, more horrific.

Ruda walked blindly, her hands clenched, taking short sharp breaths. She made her way to the cages as if by instinct, until she arrived at Mamon's. He sprang to his feet, swinging his head from side to side, and she clung to the bars, gripping them so tightly her knuckles turned white. "Ma'angel . . . Ma'angel!"

Mamon's tongue licked her through the bars, rough and hard. She closed her eyes, comforted by his affectionate, heavy-bellied growl, and she answered him with a part howl, part scream of release, as the pictures faded.

✦ ✦ ✦

Vebekka was calm on her way to the doctor's. She was seated between Helen and Louis, holding their hands.

She clung to Louis as they went into the reception, where Maja greeted Vebekka warmly. Dr. Franks, wearing a green cardigan and an old pair of gray flannel trousers, sauntered in, kissed Vebekka, and suggested they talk in his sitting room.

"Sit where you will, my dear, and Helen, Baron—if you wish to stay with us, do. We are only going to have a friendly talk. . . ."

Helen touched Louis' arm; she knew Dr. Franks wanted them to sit in the adjoining room and watch through the glass. Vebekka seemed a little afraid when they left, but then sat down.

"And how are you?" Franks asked softly.

"A little better, still weak and thirsty. I keep on drinking as you asked."

"Good, good." He drew up a chair, and then he went to get a stool. "Now, let me get you some iced water, would you like a cigarette?"

Vebekka started to relax. He would not offer her a cigarette if he were going to hypnotize her, would he? She opened her case and he clicked open his lighter. She bent her head, inhaled and leaned back. Franks settled himself in his chair and propped his feet up.

"Tell me," he said quietly, "if you were to describe, in one word, how you feel mostly, what word would it be?"

She let the smoke drift from her mouth, and then cocked her head. "One word? . . . Mmmmmmmmmmmmmm—that is very difficult."

The room fell silent, Franks sitting with his arms folded over his chest, Vebekka cupping her chin in her hand.

She flicked the ash from her cigarette. "One word?" she asked again. He nodded.

She continued to smoke pensively for a while, then she sipped some iced water and put down the glass.

"Can you think of a word, Vebekka?"

She turned her face away from Franks and sighed.

"Longing."

He repeated the word, and then smiled. "That is very interesting, nobody has ever said that to me before . . . longing."

"I long for . . . always I feel I am longing for . . ."

His voice was gentle and persuasive: "What, Vebekka, what are you always longing for?"

"I don't know."

The clock was ticking. She could hear a soft voice telling her not to be afraid, that she had nothing to fear, and that perhaps she would like to lie down and rest for a while.

Helen and the baron saw Vebekka smiling and smoking, and then saw Franks help her lie down on the couch. He took a soft blanket and covered her. Her eyes were wide open.

Franks now flicked on the intercom connecting the two rooms, and looked to the two-way mirror. "She is under, I am going to begin now," he said.

11

DR. FRANKS STARTED with simple questions: what she liked to eat, drink. She answered coherently and directly. Then he referred to the doctors she had visited and asked for her reactions to the tests. Again she answered directly, speaking about the last diagnosis with sarcasm. Franks asked if she often felt afraid.

"Yes, I am afraid."

"Do you know what you are afraid of?"

"No."

"How does the fear begin?"

"As if someone I am frightened of were entering the room."

Franks changed the subject. He did not want to push Vebekka too far on their first session. He asked whether she liked to travel, what cases and clothes she liked to take with her. He was given a long list of favorite items from her wardrobe. She continued for ten minutes, and he saw that she was relaxed again, her hands resting on the top of the blanket.

The baron looked at Helen, raised his eyebrows, and sighed. He could see no point in the session whatsoever.

"Wait . . . just wait," Helen whispered.

"Now tell me about the cases, Vebekka."

She described her various suitcases, how she liked to pack everything with tissue paper. Franks asked her about her vanity cases, and she calmly listed her jewelry, her makeup, the photographs of her children, and her medicine.

"Do you feel these cases, or boxes, have also another meaning, the fact that you separate everything into compartments?" He received no reply. "Do you have similar boxes inside you?" he persisted. "For example, shall we say the makeup box is your head? Do you think that way at all?"

She hesitated, and then smiled. "Yes, yes, I do."

"Can you explain this to me?"

"I have many compartments inside me."

"Do they all have keys?"

"Oh yes!" She seemed pleased.

"Will you unlock them for me? Tell me what is inside. Can you do that?"

She sighed and shifted position.

"Well, there's the first compartment that holds my special makeup, makeup I use only on rare occasions."

"Tell me about the second."

"My children. I have their letters, their photographs, things I treasure. I have Sasha's first baby tooth and I have . . ."

"Tell me about the third box. What's in there?"

"My jewelry, all the pieces I am most fond of, the most precious pieces. There is an emerald and diamond clip and a bluebird made of sapphires and—"

"Go to the next box. Open the next box."

"Sleeping tablets, pills. I have them all listed."

"You make a lot of lists?"

"Yes, yes, lots of lists."

"Go to the next . . . open the next box."

Vebekka's hand clenched.

"Go to the next box."

"No."

"Why not?"

"Because it's private."

"Please, open it. Or does it frighten you to open it?"

"No, it's . . . just personal, that's all."

Franks waited; she was breathing very deeply. "Open it, Vebekka, and tell me what is inside."

"Rebecca."

Franks looked to the two-way mirror, and then turned to Vebekka.

"Rebecca?" he asked softly.

"*Yessssssssss,* she's in there."

"Do you have any more boxes?"

Vebekka was more agitated now, chewing her lips.

"Go to the next box, Vebekka . . . tell me about the next box."

"No . . . it is not a box."

"What is it?"

"Locked, it is locked, I can't open it."

"Try . . . why don't you describe it to me?"

"It's hard, black, it's chained, I don't have the key." She began to twist her hands. "Rebecca won't open it."

Franks talked to her softly, saying he was there to help her and whatever was in the box, he would deal with—all she had to do was open it.

"It's not a box."

"Whatever is there, we'll leave it for a while. No need to be upset, if you don't want to open it then we won't . . . but tell me about Rebecca, who is Rebecca?"

Her breath hissed, she seemed exasperated. "She guards it, she protects it, so nobody can open it, nobody must know."

"Know what?"

Franks could feel her strength, it astonished him. She was fighting his control. She began breathing rapidly, her eyelids fluttering, she was trying to surface, trying to come out of the hypnosis. Franks changed the subject.

"Vebekka, tell me about Sasha."

Vebekka relaxed and began to tell Franks about her daughter, that she liked to ride, had a pony. She described Sasha's bedroom, and her clothes, giving Franks a clear picture of the little girl.

"Tell me about Sasha's toys? Her dolls?"

Vebekka described the different dolls, where they had been bought. How many were for birthdays, for Christmas.

"Why did you destroy Sasha's dolls, Vebekka?"

"I did not."

"I think you did . . . you took all Sasha's dolls, you took their pretty frocks off, and you stacked them up like a funeral pyre, didn't you? You set fire to them, you burned them . . ."

"No . . . She did that!"

"Who? Who burned the dolls, Vebekka?"

She tugged at the blanket, her body twisted. "Rebecca."

"Who is Rebecca?"

Vebekka vomited, her whole body heaved and she leaned over the couch. Franks fetched a bowl and a towel. He rang for assistance, and Maja entered. She went to Vebekka's side as Franks put down the bowl.

"I am so sorry." Vebekka turned to face him, and then she looked away.

Franks checked her pulse, helped her to lie back on the cushions. He drew up his chair. She smiled and whispered again she was so sorry, then she closed her eyes.

Franks touched Maja's shoulder, whispered for her to clean up the room, and he slipped out. He joined the baron and Helen Masters.

"First . . . I must tell you I have never experienced this before, someone able to move into the waking cycle on their own. She provoked the vomit attack; her will is quite extraordinary, I had quite a hard time hypnotizing her . . . usually it's a matter of seconds, but she took much longer, did you notice, Helen?"

Helen looked at the baron, and then asked if she could speak to him privately. Franks seemed slightly taken aback, and then said by all means, he would wait in the corridor. Helen turned to the baron and said that, considering what Vebekka had related during the session, she felt they should tell Franks about the photograph.

Helen went to Franks, told him about the photograph, and gave him the black-and-white snapshot. He studied it, turned it over to read the inscription, then asked if Vebekka was aware of its existence. Helen was sure she was not. The baron came out into the corridor. Franks looked to the baron. "I must ask if you are sure your wife has had no hypnotherapy treatment before . . ."

"None that I know of."

"I ask because I feel that she is very aware, and I did not take her too deeply. But now, now I would like to try."

The baron gave a shrug of his shoulders. "You are the doctor, I will go along with whatever you suggest."

Franks returned to Vebekka. Helen and the baron took their seats in the viewing room once more. She whispered: "He was trying to find out if this is a case of a multipersonality. He took her via the boxes through various internal protective layers."

He sat tight-lipped, irritated when Helen added softly, "I was right, Vebekka is Rebecca!"

Vebekka sipped the iced water, resting back on the cushions, and Franks checked her pulse again. She was very hot; he removed the blanket. Returning to his seat he paused a moment, before he began to hypnotize her again.

"*Longing,* repeat the word to me, Vebekka."

She did, but it was hardly audible, and she did not resist him.

"So you feel a longing . . . yes? . . . Listen to me, Vebekka. Just listen to my voice, don't fight my voice, just listen. . . . You feel very relaxed, you feel calm and relaxed. You know no harm will come to you, and the feeling of longing . . . longing . . ."

She was under again. This time her eyes were closed, and she breathed very deeply, as if sleeping. Franks waited a few moments before he asked if he could speak to Rebecca, would Vebekka allow him to speak to her? She sighed.

"You don't understand!" She sounded irritated, as if he had asked her something stupid.

"Then help me, let me talk to Rebecca."

"I am Rebecca," she snapped.

"I'm sorry, you were right, I didn't understand."

"Oh that's all right, you wouldn't like her anyway. She's not very nice, she has very bad moods, very dark moods and a very bad temper. She is ugly and fat, always eating, always wanting sweet things. Rebecca is not nice."

"But you said you are Rebecca?"

Again there was the irritable sigh, as if his incomprehension of what she was telling him annoyed her. Her voice became angry. I *was* Rebecca, but I didn't like her. Don't you understand? I am Vebekka, I am not Rebecca anymore."

"I see, so which of you would you say was the strongest? Rebecca or Vebekka?"

She hesitated, then gave a strange sly smile. "Rebecca was, but not anymore."

Vebekka went on in a low unemotional voice, describing how she had made the decision to shut away Rebecca because she did not like her. She left home, left her parents and went to live in New York. Nobody knew Rebecca there, so it was very easy; she created a new person, someone she liked. She lost weight, became slim, and joined a modeling agency as Vebekka.

"How did Rebecca feel about this?"

"Oh, she couldn't do anything about it. I locked her up, you see, I shut her away."

Franks began to try to pinpoint dates and times, discovering that the change of name or personality occurred when Vebekka was seventeen. Subsequently, she did not want any connection with her old self, and as she became successful in her career, she started to travel on assignments, eventually securing work in Paris.

"When did Rebecca start to come back?"

Vebekka turned on the sofa, wriggled her body, her face puckered in a frown. "She started to get out. You see, she wouldn't stay locked up."

"I understand, but when did she become difficult to control?"

She held her hands protectively over her stomach. "My baby . . . she said there wasn't enough room inside me, not enough room for the two of us, she kept on trying to get out, but I fought her, she said terrible things, terrible things about the baby, she said it would be deformed, it would be deformed. . . ."

✦ ✦ ✦

Franks spent over an hour with her, and then decided he needed a break. He did not wake her because he wanted her to rest. He tucked the blanket around her, checked her pulse, and told her she would sleep for a while.

Helen poured a black coffee for the doctor. He sipped it, sighing with pleasure.

"Let me explain something to you, Baron. What you have heard may seem extraordinary to you, but it is quite common. At some time or other everyone's mind undergoes something akin to a split.

The easiest way to understand this is by way of an example: Let's say you've had a near-miss car accident—a voice will begin calming you, talking your fear down, telling you it's over, that everything is fine, that it was a narrow miss, et cetera, et cetera. . . . Your wife created Vebekka because Rebecca was as she described, moody, bad tempered, fat. In other words, she was someone she did not like, did not want to be associated with. We do not know as yet the reasons for Rebecca's moods, or why she needed to split her personality. All we know is that for Vebekka to be able to survive, to live normally, she had to lock Rebecca away. There will be a reason, it will surface, but it will take time. I will begin taking her back to her childhood, perhaps something occurred with her parents that instigated this dual personality."

The baron drained his coffee cup. "You mean she could have been mistreated?"

"Quite possibly. Often the safety barrier is created to shield the memory of sexual abuse. We shall find it out, but as you can see, it is a slow process, a step-by-step process to get at the truth."

Helen was excited. "If Rebecca began to resurface during her pregnancies, this ties in with what Louis has said, that her breakdowns began when she was three to four months pregnant."

Franks nodded. "We shall see. . . ."

Helen looked to the baron, then told Franks about the meeting with Vebekka's mother's sister, and that she was sure that Vebekka was adopted.

Franks shook his hand. "You must keep me informed, I have asked you to report any information, since everything could be of value. Did you receive the newspapers—the ones I asked for?"

"Not yet," said Louis.

"Please try and contact whomever you have working for you in New York to send you copies. And now I would like to be alone for a while. Do go out and have some lunch; when you return, you may go straight into the viewing room."

Franks walked out, and went to lie down in his office. But he did not sleep. He replayed slowly in his mind his exchanges with Vebekka. He was sure this was a case of severe child abuse, that had taken place over a period of years. What amazed him was that none of the many therapists and doctors who had seen Vebekka had diagnosed such a common trauma. However, he felt that there were more layers to be uncovered, he sensed that it was about something deeper—if not, he hated to admit it to himself, but he would be disappointed.

Vebekka slept deeply, totally relaxed. Maja checked her pulse, and drew the blanket closer around her. She emptied the ash trays from the viewing room, and then went to have a quick lunch, peeking into Franks's office to tell him she was leaving. He was fast asleep on his couch.

✦ ✦ ✦

Grimaldi slept like a dead man. Ruda had opened the trailer windows, thrown out the empty bottles, but he had not stirred. She prepared for the afternoon's rehearsal. In the evening there would be the dress rehearsal: in full costume, lights, ringmaster, and all. She still needed more time to get the cats used to the new plinths. She took out her costume, and got the ironing board ready to iron the jacket. She opened the blinds and looked skyward. The sun was still trying to break through, but more rain clouds had gathered. She crossed her fingers, hoping the forecasted storm would hold off, and then she left to feed the cats.

Grimaldi heard the door close, as if from some great distance. Slowly he opened his eyes, and moaned as the light blinded him. He lifted his head and fell back with a groan. His body ached, his head throbbed, even his teeth hurt. He let his jaw hang loose; his tongue was dry and rough. One hand gripped the edge of the bunk seat and inch by inch he drew himself into a sitting position. The room spun around and around; his heart hammered in his chest. He needed another drink. He looked around bleary-eyed, but could not see a bottle within reach.

He got to his knees, and then pushed himself upright. He fumbled in a cupboard for a bottle, knocking over glasses, sauces, cans of food. He began to retch uncontrollably and staggered into the shower. Turning on the cold water he slumped again onto his knees, and let the cold water drench him.

Grimaldi peeled off his soaking shirt and pants. He had such a pounding headache that he was seeing tiny white sparks shooting, dancing in front of his eyes. He moaned and swore, but now he eased off his pants and propped himself up under the shower, turning on the hot water. He began to feel the life coming back into his limbs, his chest, but his headache felt as though unseen hands were pressing his ears together. He could not remember how he had got into such a state and did not begin to piece it together until he sat down hunched up in a towel with a mug of black coffee. He hung his head and sobbed, but the movement made his head scream, so he gulped more and more coffee and a handful of aspirin. The pills stuck in his gut and he burped loudly. Weaving unsteadily to the sink, he looked at himself. His eyes were bloodshot; his face yellowish, unshaven. "Dear God, why do I do this to myself? Why?"

He began to shave, fragmented memories of the previous evening making him feel disgusted. Poor little Tina, he had to talk to her . . . and then he saw Ruda's face smiling at him, and saw Tina huddled half-naked against the wall, and he bowed his head with shame. He remembered now he had left her in the club, so aptly named the Slaughterhouse. In fact, he had led her like a lamb to the slaughter.

He got himself dressed, and the effort exhausted him. He sat morosely trying to find the strength to get himself out of the trailer and across to Tina's. He put on a pair of dark glasses, and, still unsteady, he crossed the trailer park, knocked on Tina's door and waited. He knocked again. A voice inside yelled for whoever it was to wait. Tina's girlfriend opened up, she was wearing jodhpurs and pulling on a sweater over a grubby bra. She looked at Grimaldi and tugged her sweater down.

"What do you want?"

"Tina in?"

"You must be joking . . ."

"Where is she?"

The girl went back into the trailer, and came out again carrying a rain cape. She slung it around her shoulders while he stood there like a dumb animal. The girl looked at him with disgust. "She's gone, packed her bags and gone, you bastard!"

He tried to reach for her arm, to stop her from leaving. "I don't understand, what do you mean she's gone?"

"Ask your wife, shithead, ask your bloody wife!"

"Gone where?"

"Home. She's gone back to the States."

"Did she leave a letter?"

"What you want? A forwarding address? Dickhead! She's gone—left, understand? You'll never see her again."

His mind reeled, and he leaned against the side of the old trailer. The girl sauntered off, calling out to two guys leading a couple of horses through to the ring.

Grimaldi walked a few paces and then stopped. He turned back to the trailer, sure the girl was lying.

"Tina? . . . *Tina?!*"

He kicked at the set of steps in a fury. He felt impotent, angry, unable to believe she would go away, leave him without a word. He turned toward the big tent and began to weave his way toward it, cursing loudly, striking out at the sides of trailers as he passed.

◆ ◆ ◆

Mike ran into the meat truck looking for Ruda. He was told she was feeding the cats. Mike took off, calling her name, dodging animals as they were being led into the ring.

Ruda was coming out of Sasha's cage and wheeling the feed trolley on to the next cage. Mike shouted for her; she turned to look in his direction. She entered the next cage and put down the food, talking softly to the tigers as they approached her. She rubbed their heads, tossing chunks of meat to them. Mike was still calling her. She let herself out, bolted the cage, maneuvering the trolley. "I'm here, Mike!"

He ran toward her, his face flushed. "It's the boss, he's screaming and yelling over at the main ring, you'd better get him. Mr. Schmidt is walking around, and a party of school kids has just arrived."

Ruda muttered, "I have to finish the feed."

"He looks kind of crazy, Ruda, he's breaking up chairs. No one can get near him."

Ruda picked up Mamon's big bowl and unbolted his cage. She stepped inside. "Be right with you. . . . Ma'angel . . . come on, dinner time, come on baby."

Mike leaned against the bars. "He's thrown a punch at Willy Noakes, kicked a hole in his trailer."

Ruda's attention wavered from Mamon to Mike, and the big cat snarled, swiping a paw at her, demanding her full attention.

"Get back . . . *No* . . . don't you dare! Here—eat."

She tossed another hunk of meat, and Mamon caught it in his jaw, then lowered his head to rip it apart.

"*Rudaaaaaaaaaaaaaaaaaaa . . . Ruda!*" Grimaldi bellowed.

Mike turned, startled. Grimaldi was heading toward them, carrying a pitchfork, dragging it along the cage bars. "*Ruda!*"

Ruda moved further into the cage. She faced Mamon, and tossed out more meat. She rested her back on the bars, turning to her right. She could see Grimaldi staggering along with the huge pitchfork.

"Mike, get him away from the cages!"

Mike, terrified of the big man, stuttered out to him to keep back.

"You want to make me?"

Grimaldi shoved the boy aside and came to Mamon's cage. "She's gone, she's left me, she's gone!"

Ruda threw another chunk of meat, but Mamon lowered onto his haunches, no longer interested in eating. He let out a low, rumbling growl. Ruda was trapped in the small cage; the exit door was behind Mamon. "Good boy, back . . . back off . . . GET BACK!"

Grimaldi banged the bar. "What did you do to her? *You bitch! . . . What have you done?*"

Mamon hurled himself against the bars, trying to slice through with his paws, snarling and snapping at Grimaldi. Ruda went around him and out of the trapdoor. She bolted it shut and ran to the front of the cage. "Get away from the cages . . . *Get away from the cages!*"

Grimaldi vented all his pent-up anger at the snarling and snapping lion. He pushed the pitchfork through the bars and caught him on the rump: The cat went crazy, lunging at the bars and roaring with rage.

Ruda struggled with her husband, trying to jerk the pitchfork out of his hands. They fought like two men, pushing and shoving each other.

"Let go, *Luis, let it go . . . !*"

"She's gone, she's left me. You did it! You did this to me!"

Ruda brought up her knee and slammed it into his groin. He gasped with pain, let go the fork, and doubled up in agony. She took the fork and pointed the sharp iron prongs at Grimaldi's chest. "Get back . . . *Get out of here!*"

He tried to grab at one of the prongs with his bare hand, but Ruda yanked it free—as she did, the prong sliced into his palm. He stumbled back, blood streaming from his hand.

Ruda tossed the fork to Mike and shoved Grimaldi with her hands. "Get out . . . go on, go back to the trailer—*back, get back.*"

He stared at her, yet moved back a couple of steps. "I'm not one of your lions, one of your cats. . . . *You pushed too far this time, you pushed too far!*"

Grimaldi turned on his heels and stumbled away. Ruda turned on Mike.

"What the fuck are you gaping at? Get that fork back onto the truck, and bring the feed trays—go on!"

Not until she had fed every cat did she take off for her trailer, but halfway there she was stopped by the administrator. Mr. Kelm asked that she go over to the offices immediately. The chairman wished to speak to her. Ruda followed, the sweat still dripping off her.

The big man was standing, his coat draped over his shoulders, his silver-topped cane propped against a large oval table. As Ruda walked in, he snatched the cane and brought it down with a crash on the highly polished table.

"We pride ourselves . . . understand me, Mrs. Grimaldi . . . we take pride in ourselves . . . in the fact that everyone working here is the best. The best in the world! We have millions riding on this show, millions in advertising—we have school groups coming through . . . I want every child to go home and say they want to come to the show, that's parents, sisters, brothers. And today those children witnessed a brawl—*a brawl!*—involving one of my top acts. . . . Now, if you and your husband have domestic problems, sort them out in private—*not* in a disgusting public display. You may be a top act, Mrs. Grimaldi, but I will not have the name of this circus damaged, even if it means ending your and your husband's contract. Do I make myself clear?"

Ruda nodded, furious at being spoken to like a child. She turned as if to leave.

"Every act is replaceable, Mrs. Grimaldi—remember that!"

She faced him. "Not every act. You show me one cat trainer, one act on a par with mine . . ."

"Yours?"

"Yes, mine, my husband no longer works in the ring."

"I see. . . . If your husband has a problem—get rid of it! Do I make myself clear?"

She nodded, and glared at him. He dismissed her with a wave of his hand. She turned and walked out, carefully closing the door behind her.

Schmidt turned to Kelm. "That woman is trouble! Any more problems and they both leave. We can hire the lion act from the Moscow Circus. Keep your eyes on the pair of them and let me know what's going on!"

✦ ✦ ✦

Ruda tore back to the trailer in a rage, only to find Grimaldi, his hand wrapped in a towel, clumsily loading one of his rifles. As soon as she saw what he was doing, she slammed the door shut and locked it. "Put that away. Luis, put it away!"

He turned, sneering, cocked the gun and released the safety catch. He then pressed the barrel to his neck. "I was going to shoot that beast, that crazy fucking animal. Then I decided I should kill

you . . . now, I think I'll blow my own head off, because that's
what you want, isn't it? . . . *Isn't it?*"

She sat on the bunk, forcing herself to stay calm. "If that's what
you think, then do it—go on, shoot."

He wavered, but did not put down the gun.

"Why do you think I want you dead?" she snapped.

"Give me one good reason you don't?"

She shrugged. "That might be tough, but if pressed I'd have to
admit that maybe I need you."

He lowered the gun. "You haven't needed me for ten years."

She watched the gun being lowered, with relief. She couldn't
deal with one more scene, not after that lecture. "I don't need you
for the act, that's true . . . but maybe I need you."

He slumped down, the gun loose in his hand. "Bullshit, you
don't need anyone, you never have—unless you want something,
then you pretend to need."

Ruda stared at him. "Why don't you give me that gun and stop
playing around? Come on, give it to me."

He cocked his head to one side, asked why she had done it.

"Why did I do what?"

"Make Tina go away."

She laughed, shaking her head. "I made her? . . . *I made her?*
You don't think maybe you had something to do with it?"

"I loved her, I loved her."

"You left her, without money, without anything. Left her in
the middle of the shittiest place in Berlin, and now you tell me—
you loved her? The only thing you love is booze, she came here
crying her heart out, all I did was comfort her!"

"Comfort? *You filthy whore!*" He lurched to his feet. "I saw you
together, *I saw what you were doing to my little girl!*"

"She wasn't your little girl, and don't think for two seconds
that baby was yours—she told me it wasn't. She came here asking
for money, threatened to tell that fat slob Schmidt about you, about
you screwing all the young kids, and you know what he just told
me? He told me that if you play around with any more teenagers
then you and I will be out, contract or no contract."

"I don't believe you."

"Ask him, go ask him. Kelm was there, he heard, I just got a lecture from the fat-assed bastard. Tina was a little tramp. I am telling you the truth, the baby was not yours—she admitted it to me."

Grimaldi leaned back, closing his eyes. "I don't believe it."

Ruda moved quickly, grabbed the gun from him, and put the safety catch on. He made no effort to stop her. He held his face in his hands, saying over and over she was lying to him, then he looked up. "I could have had a life with her, I could have started again."

"Doing what? Changing someone else's brat's diapers?"

"I could have been happy with her."

Ruda sighed. "And what would you have lived on? You know I would never have parted with the act. I tell you something, you would have had to shoot me to get them. This was just a fantasy on your part."

He got up and poured himself a glass of water. "I talked to Lazars, spent hours talking to him. We argued and yelled a lot, but he's changed, too, he's changed."

"I don't follow, can I have a drink?"

He handed her a glass of water, and then stared at the posters. "I tell you the circus, as we know it, it won't last, it can't last. You remember Ivan the Russian? He spent fifteen years training his tigers, he's been in the circus business since he was six years old, but he couldn't afford to keep them out of season. He shot the poor bastards, all twenty-four of them, so nobody else would have them . . . said they were of no use to anyone, and he wouldn't let a zoo have them, didn't think it was fair. He told Lazars he shot them because he loved them. Now what crazy mind is that?"

Suddenly he laughed his old rumble laugh, leaning back, his eyes closed. "Maybe I should shoot myself, can't be put out to pasture, can't get any other work."

Ruda's heart was hammering. She had never heard him talk this way, ever. She sat next to him, close to him. "Don't . . . don't talk like this."

"It's the truth, I've known it for a while. I see them cramped in their cages. I keep on telling myself that it was different when I was working the rings, that it was better, but I know it wasn't, if anything it was worse. You, we, are living on borrowed time, because the day will come soon when all wild animals will be barred from being used as cheap entertainment."

"No, no, I don't believe it. I love them, I care for them, I love every single one of them."

Grimaldi cocked his head, gave a slow sad smile. "No, you don't. You love to dominate, you like the danger, the adrenaline, but you don't love them."

"I do, you know I do . . ."

"Caged, locked up twenty-four hours a day, you call that love?" He stretched out his long legs, resting his elbows behind his head. "You know this little Boris, Lazars' little chimp? Well he got her from a troupe of Italians; spent his savings on her. Boris was too young to work in the ring, she was being trained. Lazars sat in on one of the training sessions, kept on watching the Italian rubbing the chimp's head . . . he thought it was with affection. But the little baby was very upset. After the rehearsal Lazars checked her over, Boris's head was bleeding. This so-called trainer, he'd got a nail sharpened to a point like a fucking razor—he wasn't patting her, he was sticking his nail into her head. . . ."

Ruda stared at her boots. "Lazars was always a second-stringer, a soft touch. You shouldn't listen to his bullshit."

"I haven't before . . . I just think what he's saying may be true, that acts like ours have a short time to go."

Ruda sprang to her feet. "I won't listen anymore . . . I've got to go and get ready to rehearse."

"Yeah, make them jump through hoops of fire—great, they love it . . . get their manes singed, they fucking love it."

Ruda paused at the door. "Will you give me a hand in the ring? They're still nervous about the plinths."

He looked up at her. "You don't need me, Ruda."

"What are you going to do?"

He turned away, unable to look at her. Unexpectedly, the big man's helplessness touched her. She hesitated, then went and slipped her arms around him. "You're hung over, go and lie down. I'll come by later and cook up a big dinner, okay? Luis?"

He patted her head. "Worried I'll run off, go after Tina?" She wriggled away from him, but he pulled her close. "You are, aren't you? Is it me you want?"

She tried to get away from him, but he wouldn't let her go. "Is it me?"

She eased away from him, her face flushed red. "I guess I'd miss you, I've got used to you being around."

He watched her reach for the door, unlock it. He gave a hopeless smile, he knew she didn't really want him but she didn't want anyone else to have him. The door closed behind her and he sat down, once again staring at the posters and photographs on the wall.

◆　◆　◆

The forensic laboratory had made a plaster cast of the heel taken from the Grimaldi boots. They were good impressions, very clear; but the print off the carpet was not. Even so, they were reasonably sure the impression had been made by the same boots. Torsen asked whether it could be used as a piece of evidence, whether it would stand up in court. He was told that it could not, since the print taken from the victim's hotel room was only of a section of the heel.

"But you think it was from the same boot?"

"Yes I do, but that is just my personal opinion."

Torsen sighed; it had been a long, fruitless day. The second disappointment was that the sawdust taken from the victim's hotel room matched the fifteen samples taken from the circus, all from different cages. The sawdust was also discovered to be similar to samples brought in from the Berlin zoo, the Tiergarten.

Torsen's next inquiry was at the bus station. The night duty staff had still to be questioned regarding bus passengers the night Kellerman was killed. The three drivers could not remember any male passenger fitting the inspector's description; two could not recall anyone getting off from a bus at or near the Grand Hotel; the third driver could only recall a female passenger who had picked up the bus from the depot and gotten off at the stop close to the Grand Hotel; but he could recall little else about her except her long, dark hair. He remembered that it had been a particularly unpleasant journey, the vehicle was mostly filled with Polish women and children who had been greatly disturbed by a group of young punks hurling bricks at the bus, shouting Nazi slogans. The driver spent considerable time berating the police, saying they should provide buses, drivers, and passengers with better security.

Torsen returned to the station, heated up a bowl of soup in the microwave and looked over his notes. He had a motive—the man was disliked by everyone he seemed to have been in contact with, possibly owed money to whoever killed him. But from there on it went downhill; no one person had seen a man fitting the description of the potential suspect.

The inspector sipped his soup . . . it was scorchingly hot, and he burned his lip. He almost knocked it over when his phone rang. It was Freda, she would be off duty at five, and wondered if she could see him, or if he could come to the hospital. His father had written a note which he had made Freda promise to deliver. Torsen suspected it was a ploy to get him to see Freda. He stuttered that he would try to pass by the hospital. He inquired about his father's health, and Freda laughed and said he was making snowflakes again. He did not find amusing the vision of his father plucking the bits of tissue, licking them, sticking them on the end of his nose and blowing them off again. He said that he would come by when he had a chance, but that he was very busy investigating a homicide.

"I know, his letter has something to do with it. Would you like me to read it to you? It will save you a journey."

Torsen fumbled for his notebook.

"Are you ready? Shall I read it?"

"Yes, yes, please go ahead."

Freda coughed, and then said: " 'One'—it's very much a scrawl—'no coincidences.' Does that mean anything to you?"

Torsen muttered that it did, and asked her to continue.

" 'Two'—and this is very hard to decipher, it looks like 'Wise man,' or 'wizard'—does that make sense?"

"Yes, yes, it does, please continue."

"It's a name, I think . . . Dieter? Yes?"

"Yes, yes, that was my uncle, is that all?"

Freda said she was trying to puzzle out the next few words. "Ah, I think it says . . . 'Rudi' . . . 'R-U-D-I' . . . Yes, it's Rudi and then there's a *J*. I think the name is Polish, Jeczawitz. Yes, I am sure it's Rudi Jeczawitz. Would you like me to spell it for you?"

Torsen jotted down the name, thanked Freda, and apologized for his brusqueness. She laughed and said no matter. She put down the receiver before he could pluck up the courage to ask to see her. He swiveled around in his desk chair to look at the photograph of his father, murmured a "Thank you!" and finished his soup. He had to think carefully how to track down the Jeczawitz records. He would have to go cap in hand to the West Berlin Police with some story in order to get this information.

✦ ✦ ✦

Torsen and Rieckert crossed the old border and drew up outside a new building housing a section of the West Berlin Police. The office was a hive of activity, the reception area alone busier than the entire station the pair had left. They were directed toward the records bureau through a long corridor. Outside the department was a counter at which a stern-faced woman heard Torsen's request for the records of a Rudi Jeczawitz. She checked his identification and handed him a formal request sheet to fill in.

They did not have to wait long. The station was fully computerized and the gray-haired woman returned with three sheets of paper clipped together.

They hurried back to their patrol car, Torsen skimming the pages as they walked. He got into the car, and continued to read. Rieckert waited patiently, having no idea why they had come to the station in the first place.

"Where next?"

Torsen lowered the paper. "Better head back to the station. I have to speak to the Leitender Direktor."

"He's still on holiday!"

"I have to speak to him . . . just drive."

Rieckert drove to their station, darting glances at Torsen who read, muttering to himself. His cheeks were flushed. The car had hardly drawn to a halt before he was out and running up the steps.

The records gave details of the dead man. The corpse had been found in a derelict building used for many years by vagrants, and considered "unsafe." His body had been squashed inside a small kitchen cabinet, not, as Torsen had thought, under floorboards. The body, because of the freezing temperatures, had been remarkably well preserved, yet Torsen was sure his father had described the body as badly decomposed. It was found almost intact, apart from deep lacerations to the left wrist and forearm. The skin had been hacked off with a crude knife with a serrated edge, but no weapon had been found. The victim was naked, apart from the cloak in which he was wrapped.

The police had been unable to identify the body for a considerable time, until a newspaper article requesting information on the identity of the deceased gave a clear description of the strange cloak found wrapped around him. A club owner had come forward, identified the dead man as seventy-five-year-old Rudi Jeczawitz, a one-time magician who had performed in his clubs. The man was an alcoholic, known to deal in forged documents. He had also been a procurer of very young girls, and shortly after the war had run a prostitution ring. The drinking destroyed him, and at the end he worked for little more than free drinks, using his wife as part of the act. His wife, a known prostitute, had disappeared; she had not been seen after the murder. It was supposed that she too may possibly have been murdered. No one was ever charged with Rudi Jeczawitz's murder; his case remained on file. A few more details were given; informants had said that he had been at Birkenau. He had survived by entertaining the guards with his magic act.

Torsen's heart pounded as he read and reread the name of Jeczawitz's wife: Ruda. Coincidence number one. Number two: Rudi, like Tommy Kellerman, had been involved with forged documents. And then there was the third: All three were survivors of concentration camps. He paused, the fourth: Both men had been tattooed, and both had had their tattoo slashed from their arms.

Torsen jotted down a list. He had to find out if they had been legally married, find out Ruda Jeczawitz's maiden name, see whether there still was anyone alive who had known the magician and could describe him. But most important he had to know whether Ruda Kellerman was Ruda Jeczawitz. . . .

Torsen was sweating, his lists grew longer. Next he wrote "boots"; he had supposed the boots had belonged to a man because of their size, had even asked Mrs. Grimaldi if they were her husband's boots. But what if they were her boots? Torsen let out a small whoop. He thumbed through his book until he found the page he was looking for. One of the bus drivers was sure no male passenger had gotten off his bus the night of Kellerman's murder, only a woman, described as . . . he stared at his scrawl, momentarily unable to read it, then he snapped the book closed. He knew he had to go back and interview the guy; all he had written down was: "female, dark-haired."

He grabbed his coat, shouted for Rieckert, his voice echoing in the empty building. He stormed through the empty offices and burst into the switchboard operator's cubbyhole.

"Where in God's name is everybody?"

She looked up at him in astonishment. "Tea break! They have gone across the street to the café for their tea break! It is four o'clock, sir!"

12

"'I AM GOING to take you back in time now, Vebekka. Can you see the calendar, the years are in red ink, 'ninety-one, 'ninety . . . can you see the date, Vebekka?"

"Yes, I can see it."

"Go back, 'eighty-nine, ten years before that, go through the dates . . . what year do you see now on the calendar?"

Vebekka sighed. "Nineteen seventy-nine. It is 1979."

Franks looked to the two-way mirror, then turned to Vebekka.

The baron tapped Helen's hand. "That was the year of the newspapers."

Franks continued. "Go to the morning in New York when you were reading the newspaper, sitting having breakfast with your husband. Can you remember that morning?"

She sighed, gave a low moan, and then nodded. "I am reading the real estate pages . . . Louis is reading the main section. I talk to him, but he pays no attention, I tell him . . . an apartment is for sale, but he doesn't listen to me."

"Go on . . ."

She sighed and her brow furrowed as if she were trying to recall something.

"Go on, Vebekka, you see something in the paper?"

She breathed quickly, gasping. "Yes . . . yes . . . Angel, *Angel,* ANGEL."

She twisted and turned, shaking. "They have found him . . ."

"Who, Vebekka? Whom have they found?"

She ran her hands through her hair. "It's in the paper, it's in the papers, I have to find all the papers, I have to know if it's true. Angel, the dark Angel of Death will find me, he put the message in the paper to find me."

"It's all right . . . it's all right, no need to be alarmed. Who is the angel? Is it the angel who makes you so frightened?"

She banged the sofa with her fists. "They will know what I have done. *He knows what I have done . . . Oh! God help me!*"

Franks raised his voice and told her to advance to the next morning. She calmed down, and said that the next day she remained very quiet, and didn't mention anything to anyone about what she had seen. She had had a nightmare, she had thought the Angel had come into her bedroom to make her tell, but it had been just a shadow, just the drapes.

Franks wrote down on his pad that they must trace the newspaper. He was certain he was dealing with a woman traumatized by an event in her childhood, but when he began to discuss her childhood she became very calm. She seemed relieved. When he asked if she was Vebekka or Rebecca she giggled, told him not to be stupid, she was Rebecca.

She began to talk quite freely. She described her home in Philadelphia, discussed her parents. She said they were kind, but never very affectionate toward her, she said that they were very close to each other, that she had often felt like an intruder.

"Did this upset you?"

"Not really. They always gave me what I asked for, they just seemed more interested in each other. My mother was often unhappy, she used to say she missed her home, her family, but they would never speak to her, they sent back all her letters unopened. She was often crying, and often ill: She used to get bronchial troubles, that was why they had moved from Canada—it was very cold there, and Mama had been very ill."

Franks asked if she loved her parents. She hesitated, and then shrugged with her hands. "They loved each other, and they fed and clothed me."

"So you never felt a great affection for them?"

"No . . . just that they kept me safe, they watched out for me, no one could hurt me while I was with them, they told me that."

"Who wanted to hurt you?"

"I don't know."

Franks asked her to recall her first memory of her mother. She pursed her lips and said, "She gave me a blue dress, with a white pinafore and a teddy bear."

"How old were you then?"

She seemed to be trying to recall her age, but in the end she shrugged her shoulders and said she was not sure. He asked if she was afraid of her parents, and she said very promptly that she was not. "They were afraid of me! Always afraid, afraid . . ."

"Had they reason to be afraid of you?"

"Yes, I was very naughty, had terrible tantrums."

"What did they do when you had these tantrums?"

"Oh, Mama would talk to me, get me to lie down and talk to me, you know, so I would calm down."

"Did they try and stop you leaving home?"

She laughed. "Oh no . . . they were pleased, I think they were pleased when I left!"

"Did you miss them when you left?"

"Yes . . . yes sometimes, but Mama helped me often, told me how to handle Rebecca."

"What did she tell you to do?"

"Oh, put her in a closet, throw away the key, forget her."

"So it was not your idea to change your name?"

"Yes, it was, it was all my idea, I never told Mama what I had done, and I never told Papa. I just did what Mama said, put her away."

"Is the other box inside you?"

She started to twist her hands, plucking at the blanket. "Yes, yes, that is always there."

"Did your mama put somebody in the box?"

"It's not a box!"

Franks was growing tired; he rubbed his head, checked his watch. "What is it then?"

She remained silent, her face taut as she refused to answer.

"Why don't you want to tell me about it?"

She seemed to be in terrible pain, her face became distorted.

She opened her mouth as if to scream, but no sound came out.

Franks stood by the couch. "It's all right, shushhh, don't get upset, I won't ask you about it anymore. It's all over. Unless you want to tell me. Do you want to tell me?"

She cried, her mouth wide open like a child's, her face twisted, and the blanket was wrung into a coil between her hands. He waited; in the viewing room the baron rose to his feet. He hated to see his wife in such pain; he pressed his hands to the glass. "Stop him, tell him to stop this. . . ."

She was clawing, trying to get up; Franks gently held on to her shoulders.

Her scream made him step back; it was a scream rising from a terrible depth, it was a howl. Her body shook.

Franks asked her over and over what was happening, but the torture continued, her body thrashed about, she was out of control.

"Vebekka, listen to me, the longing time, come back to the longing . . . Can you hear me? Longing . . . Come on, come on, wake up! Everything is all right, you've been sleeping, you'll wake up refreshed, relaxed."

But her body was stiff, he was not able to wake her. Once more he began to repeat the key word between them, but whatever it was, it held her, and she was fighting it, fighting to get it out of her.

The baron turned helplessly to Helen. "It's as if she were possessed. Can't he stop it? . . . Tell him to stop!"

Vebekka gasped, panting, saying she was coming up the stairs, rounding the spiral staircase, but she could not find the door. Franks was quick to pick up, he said the door was in front of her, she could open it. She began to relax, her breathing quieted down, and she sighed. He moved back as she sighed again and her eyelids fluttered.

Awake, she lifted her arms above her head and yawned, like a cat. She stretched her whole body, and then curled up.

"I am so thirsty. . . ."

Franks rang for Maja, and poured her a glass of water. She drank avidly, and held out the glass for more. He refilled it, and she drained it again. Maja came in, and smiled to Vebekka, asked how she was feeling and Vebekka laughed. "Good, I feel very relaxed and refreshed. . . ."

Franks was exhausted, Helen and the baron drained. They left Maja with Vebekka while they got together in the small office.

"She has been through deep hypnosis before—when I don't know, but she knows how to hypnotize herself, bring herself through the waking cycles. I had no control over her for some considerable time. I have never witnessed anything like it, it is quite extraordinary. But we must try and ascertain when this occurred, because she is in a dangerous state. You witnessed yourselves her own deep struggle. Whatever she has locked, she refuses to unleash. God only knows what she was involved in, or subjected to . . . the key to her lies in that box, chest, the thing that is so hidden inside her, with chains, locks, God knows what else . . . but it is inside her. It is imperative that we find out the nature of the hypnosis she has been subjected to on previous occasions. Somebody at some time treated her, made her lock away horrors, and what you have witnessed, Baron, what we have all seen here today, is the danger that can result. Vebekka, Rebecca has repressed a trauma, hidden it deep inside her mind, and it rears up. When this occurs, it brings her to the edge of a breakdown. If we find out what it is, your wife may, with time and therapy, be able to face and deal with the trauma. But we also must acknowledge that we are dealing with the unknown. Others may argue that she has survived only by locking this trauma away. It will have to be your decision whether we continue or not. I sincerely hope, however, you will agree to pursue these sessions."

The baron stared, nonplussed. He could not tell whether Franks believed he could help his wife. He turned helplessly to Helen, who looked away.

"It must be your decision."

"But what about Vebekka, doesn't she have a say in this matter?"

Franks stared at his shoes. "Your wife has no memory of what occurred in that room, none whatsoever. As her husband, it must be your decision."

"But what if she goes crazy . . . as you said, if you open up this trauma, and she cannot face it, then what?"

Franks still refused to look up. "Then she will continue as she has done. There will be sane periods, insane periods, spasmodic logic, violent moods. Who knows what will happen? All we know is that she has, in your own words, grown steadily worse. She has attacked your daughter, you, your sons. . . ."

The baron pinched his nose, looked again at Helen, wanting, needing confirmation—anything to assist his decision—but she turned away.

"What time would you like to see her tomorrow?"

Franks nodded. "Good, you have made the right decision. Let's say nine, to have an early start."

◆　◆　◆

Vebekka felt better than she had for a long time, even though she had taken no drugs for two, almost three days. She wanted to eat out, go to some of the clubs, and Louis agreed. But first Vebekka said they should go to the hotel to check whether there were any messages. Perhaps she would call Sasha. Then, after dinner, they would decide where to go. Louis was exhausted, had no desire to go to clubs; neither did Helen, but she giggled good-naturedly. The patient was full of energy, having slept most of the day! Helen suggested to Vebekka that maybe she should rest, take care of herself, but in reply all she got was a pinch on the cheek.

"Don't be such a fuddy-duddy, Helen. If my darling husband is too tired, then you and I will go; some of the Berlin clubs are the most famous in the world."

There were letters and two packages for the baron at the hotel desk. Helen went up in the elevator with Vebekka, but returned to her own suite for a shower. Louis read more material pertaining to his wife's background: names of schoolgirls who could be contacted, schoolteachers. . . . He knocked on Helen's door and entered with the papers.

Helen read over the letters, and then asked if the newspapers had arrived, and the baron nodded; they would have to look through them. Helen had already decided that she would see what else she could find out about Rosa Goldberg, née Muller. The baron asked Helen if they should dine in the suite or in the restaurant. She said she would prefer the restaurant. He booked a table for eight-thirty and returned to his room to shower and change. He heard Vebekka on the telephone talking to Sasha, and called out to send his love. He said they would be dining in the hotel restaurant at eight-thirty.

◆　◆　◆

Shortly before eight Louis went to see if Vebekka was ready, but she was not in her room. She had changed; the clothes she had been wearing were on the bed. He called down to reception to see if she had gone ahead to the restaurant, but she was not there. Helen came in and they searched the suite. Helen spoke to Hilda, who said she had helped Vebekka to dress and presumed she had gone to the restaurant.

The manager signaled to the baron as soon as he saw him get off the elevator. He gestured to the main foyer. "The baroness has just left."

The baron went pale. "Did she say where she was going?"

"No, Baron, I think she took a cab from the taxi stand outside, would you like me to inquire?"

The baron shook his head, gripped Helen by the elbow and guided her through the revolving door. He was angry and swore under his breath. As they stepped onto the red carpet, he curtly questioned the doorman, who told him that he had just missed the baroness.

"Do you know where she went?"

The doorman looked puzzled and ran to the taxi stand, signaling for the baron to join him by a waiting cab. The driver popped his head out.

"She asked to be driven around to some clubs, I heard her say. We can catch them . . . no problem."

The baron turned back to the hotel, and Helen hurried after him. "Louis, what are you doing? Don't you want to go after her?"

"I have been going after her all my life. She can do what she wants. I am hungry, I want to eat."

Helen hesitated; she knew that in spite of his words, Louis was very distressed. The baron went halfway toward the dining room before he stopped. "Perhaps I should return to the suite, have something sent up. I'll wait half an hour and if she has not returned I'll contact the police."

The walked to the elevator. Louis rubbed his forehead with his hand. "Why? Dear God, why is she doing this? I don't understand. She seemed so full of energy and . . . I had hope."

◆ ◆ ◆

Vebekka sat in the back of the taxi feeling like a truant schoolgirl. She wore her dark glasses, her sable cape, and a pale green cashmere top with matching slacks. She had taken great care in applying her makeup: thick eye shadow and a dark foundation. Her lips were outlined in a bright, unflattering crimson. This was makeup from her special box, makeup she used only on special occasions. She lit a cigarette and as she dropped the lighter back into her bag, realized she had no money. She tapped the glass.

"I have no money. Can you give me some?"

He stopped the car, turned back to her. "You want to go to the hotel? Yes? Get money? Yes?"

She shook her head. "No, you pay for me, okay? I am borrowing from you."

The driver turned and hit the wheel with his hand. "You must have cash! *Cash only, understand?*"

Vebekka opened her bag, took out her solid gold lighter. "Take this, *gold . . . good gold.*"

The driver looked first at the lighter, then back at Vebekka, and put the car in gear with a broad smile. "Okay. Where you want to go?"

Vebekka looked from the window. "Clubs . . . take me to some clubs."

13

TORSEN'S EYES WERE becoming bloodshot reading the screens; he had been at it for hours and still had not traced the Jeczawitzes' marriage certificate. Many of the files were incomplete, and the further back he went, the worse they were.

Torsen looked up as the woman in charge of the records department gestured to her watch. She wanted to leave. "The building is empty, Inspector, and the watchman has to lock up the main gates before nine."

He began to collect his belongings. She came to stand by his side. "You still have four more files on the J's . . . will you come back tomorrow?"

Torsen nodded. She promised to have the files ready for him.

"Not knowing the year this man was married it is very difficult, especially in the fifties, there were so many refugees, so many homeless people, you know the cost of the Nazi dictatorship."

They walked to the door, and she sighed as she turned off the overhead lights. "There were four million inhabitants, more, and you know how many were left? Only two million. This city was devastated, there were corpses everywhere, burned-out tanks . . . You are too young to remember, but the survivors were mostly children, old men and old women, making homes amidst the rubble, in cellars, in old bunkers. . . ."

They walked toward the main exit. On the way she stopped at a coat closet. "There was something so frightening about the terrible emptiness in the city; even the survivors crept about—no one believed it was over. I lost my father, my brothers, my family home—all my possessions. . . ."

Torsen waited while she collected her coat and hat and told the watchman to lock up. He took her arm, and they walked slowly across the courtyard.

"I began working here after the war, nearly all my life, recording marriages, births, and trying to trace the dead. The worst was trying to put the papers in order. You see the building had caught fire, there was nothing left. In those days the main priority was to find food, everything was scarce, and without documents people could not get food coupons. The black market trade flourished, there were forged documents galore, endless confusion. It still goes on. People from all over the world are trying to trace their relatives, they come back year after year to find out about a son, a daughter. . . . It is impossible, but we do what we can; that is all we can do."

Torsen paused and took out his notebook. "May I ask you a great favor, if you could, when you have a moment, see if you can find any record of Rudi Jeczawitz's wife. All I have is a Christian name, Ruda, I don't know her age."

They walked on. She seemed glad of his company. "Ruda? Is that Polish? Russian? We had so many refugees, they poured in daily, they were starved . . . many so young, all they had was their body. Now we have them again, refugees from the borders—they come every day, no papers, no money . . . it is getting bad, begging on the street, Gypsies—Romanian, Czech, Polish. Dear God, it seems it will never end!"

Torsen nodded. "I have been told she was a prostitute, perhaps they were not married legally, I don't know . . ."

"Many married for papers, they would marry for a name, for an identity. You know, many children roaming the streets in those days knew only their first name, nothing more—and some only a number. It was a terrible sight to see these young children everywhere, their shaved heads, their skeletal bodies. Now, when I see these punks . . . this new fashion stuns me, they do not remember . . . maybe, maybe it is best they don't, because it haunts the living, I know that."

Torsen continued walking. "My father has been saying the same things to me, he's in a nursing home. He said there were many who clung to life because their memories made them afraid of dying. . . ."

She turned to him, a tight smile on her face. Her blue eyes searched his for a moment, and then she pointed to a bus stop. "I leave you here, my friend, and I will do what I can, but no promises. I have enjoyed speaking with you."

They shook hands, and Torsen apologized: He did not know her name.

"Lena. Lena Klapps."

Torsen waved to her as she stepped onto her bus, and then caught one himself, going in the opposite direction. He was worn out, and wondered whether he had been wasting his time; the days were passing and he had made no arrest. He was behind in his regular duties. He closed his eyes. "There are no coincidences in a murder inquiry. . . ." As he opened his eyes he looked out of the window— and saw Ruda Kellerman stepping out of a taxicab. He craned his neck to look more closely, but he could not see her face because she wore dark glasses, and a fur draped around her shoulders. She was standing outside Mama Magda's—a notorious hangout for gay, lesbian, and mixed couples. He moved to the back of the bus to see more clearly, and watched her entering the dark, paint-peeling doorway. He was sure it was her. He wondered what she was doing in such a place, then returned to his seat, his mind churning over the day's events, asking himself if there was some connection between Ruda Kellerman and the two murders. Suddenly he realized he was almost at his stop, and as he rushed from his seat calling out to the bus driver he rang the bell. Hurrying along the aisle he came face to face with the driver he wished to question again. He asked whether he could hold the bus for just a few moments.

For privacy, they spoke on the pavement. Torsen asked for a fuller description of the woman who got off his bus near the Grand Hotel the night of Kellerman's murder.

The man removed his cap, rubbed his head, and tried to recall what he had told the inspector—while the disgruntled passengers glared at them from their seats.

"She was foreign, definitely dark-haired . . . and wearing a dark coat, no, a mackintosh . . . it was raining, and she was tall, yes, tall . . . taller than me, say about five feet eight, maybe a little more."

"That is very tall, are you sure she was that tall?"

The driver backed off and sized up Torsen, asking him how tall he was. They then stood shoulder to shoulder, until the man was satisfied he was correct.

A passenger descended the steps and asked angrily if they were going to stay there all night.

✦ ✦ ✦

Torsen let himself into his apartment, and turned on his electric heater. He looked into his empty fridge and swore, slamming the door shut. He brewed some tea, sat at his kitchen table, and began making laborious notes.

He had a suspect, one he underlined three times. Ruda Keller-man-Grimaldi—but what was the motive?

1. Motive: None.
2. Gain: None.
3. Alibi: Good.
4. Did she have help?
5. Could she have inflicted the hammer blows?

Torsen erased number five, then reinstated it. He recalled her handshake. She was very strong, she was very tall. Could she have been mistaken for a man leaving Kellerman's hotel?

6. Check if Ruda Kellerman has a trilby.
7. Check if Kellerman had a trilby.
8. Stock up fridge—coffee and milk.

The more he thought of food the hungrier he got, so in the end he went to buy some rolls from the all-night delicatessen. He ate standing by the window, at a small bar provided by the shop for their customers.

When he returned to his apartment it was after ten; a message was pinned to his door. Freda had popped by to deliver the note from his father. She had also left her address and phone number, and her schedule list of days on/days off, evenings on/evenings off. He liked that, liked that she was methodical and made lists. He decided he would call her in the morning, to ask for a date.

◆　◆　◆

That same evening, Ruda was ironing her jacket lapels. Luis woke up and sniffed. He loved the smell of freshly ironed clothes: They reminded him of his mother. He wrapped his dressing gown around himself and wandered in to see Ruda.

"How did rehearsal go?"

"Mamon is adjusting, but he still hates the new plinths. He's acting up, and I really have to push him."

Grimaldi looked into a large frying pan left on the stove. There were bacon, sausages, and onion rings, all of it cold. She turned off the iron. "I did call you, but decided not to wake you. There's a baked potato in the oven. Do you want a beer?"

He forked out some food and refused the beer, said he'd stick to water. He carried his plate to the table and sat down. She called out that he would have time to shower and change, the dress rehearsal was not until nine. She came in zipping up her tight white pants. "Ours is the last act before the intermission, and we open the second act. It's a good spot—well, the one before the intermission is. I'd like to close the show, but the manager won't let me have the time to reassemble the cages."

She put on her jacket, looked in the mirror, and then arranged her hair in a tight braid down her back. She pulled it back tightly from her face so that it looked sleek, almost Spanish. She leaned against him as she slipped her feet into her boots. He looked her over, and gave her a pat on the behind.

"Don't," she snapped, "your fingers are all greasy!"

"You look good," he said with his mouth full, and she did a small pirouette, then picked up the short whip and her stick. With a final glance at her reflection, she went to the trailer door.

"Get dressed, Luis, I want you on display, sober and looking good. Everyone heard about our scene, so let's put up a good front. It's almost seven-thirty."

He laughed. "This crowd thrives on what the Grimaldis do, what they said, who hit whom—tell them to go fuck themselves."

She picked up her hat, twisted it, and put it on. "Over and out, big man! See you in the ring!"

Grimaldi shaved and dressed, and looked at himself in the mirror. Even after a shave and a long sleep he looked beat: his eyes bloodshot, his skin puffy. He checked his hairline; he needed a tint, the gray was showing through.

He tightened his thick belt. His belly hung over the top, and he hitched the shirt up so it almost hid the extra pounds. And as he stared at himself in the long mirror, he asked himself where it had all gone wrong . . . he couldn't blame it all on the mauling. He was falling apart long before that.

He looked at the wall of photographs, saw his papa and his brothers, and remembered holding tightly to his dying father's hand. "You keep it going, you marry, you have sons, don't let the Grimaldi name die. Have many sons! . . . for your brothers, Luis, God rest their souls."

He thought about little Tina. It had been a foolish dream, and yet he had been thrilled to think at last he would have a son, an heir. He had even wondered what it would feel like to hold his son, he never considered it could be a girl: It was a son he had always wanted. Yet he had married Ruda. . . .

Luis opened a drawer and took out an old folder of small snapshots. He sifted through them, not even sure what he was searching for.

He inched open Ruda's closet, wondering where she had stashed all his albums.

He looked up: There was a row of cupboards on top of the closet. In the first she kept her show hats; in the second he saw an old winter coat and a plastic rain cape. He couldn't open the third, so he stepped up on a stool and pulled hard. He almost lost his balance as the albums tumbled out. Paper clippings and loose photographs spilled everywhere; he swore as he bent to retrieve them.

He sat on her bed and began to flip through the books, chuckling and smiling as the memories flooded back. He had had a wonderful childhood. But Ruda never talked of her past; she had said without any emotion that some things are best left buried. She had talked about her life with Kellerman, even, up to a point, about the old magician, but then she would change the subject, as if her life before that was not worth mentioning, or perhaps too painful to bring up, because when he had insisted, she had rolled up her cuff, and had thrust the scar in his face.

"I have this to remind me. I am reminded every time I stand naked, every time my head aches, that's enough. . . . Why talk about it? Why open up memories I have fought to forget?"

When she had been in one of her moods, when she had thrown one of her tantrums—because money was short or his drinking was out of hand—she would turn on him enraged, screaming that whatever pain he was in, she had known worse.

She would thrust her tattoo defiantly under his nose. "This is my proof, what is yours, Luis? What right have you got to complain about anything?"

She had taken over. Slowly he turned the pages, asking himself how he had allowed it to happen. The first time he had met her, he was the star, he had money—he had success.

He lay back on her hard pillow and closed his eyes, visualizing the Florida winter quarters, remembering how he had stood by the cages as the vet went from one animal to the next. He had been working in England, just before all the quarantine laws come into effect. His act had gone down well. He had traveled to Manchester, to Brighton, and then to Wembley for the big Chipperfield contract. In the early sixties he had been at his peak—what a time that had been—and then he had returned to America, at the invitation of a Barnum & Bailey scout.

With the winter season coming on he had arrived in Venice, Florida, ready to be an internationally acclaimed star.

Knowing he had the contract, Grimaldi spent freely, even bought two more tigers. Then the bombshell: First to die was his lead cat, a massive Siberian tiger trained by his father. The big animal began sweating, his eyes ran, and his coat quickly began to look dull. The vets diagnosed a virulent, dangerous flu, most likely contracted in England.

The flu spread like a forest fire. They were going down one by one; the act was disappearing in front of his eyes. He worked every hour God gave him, but no matter what care and attention he lavished on his beloved animals, they died. No injection could save them, his only hope was to segregate the animals. Then the second calamity struck; the surviving animals were poisoned by hay laced with a pesticide intended to kill rodents in the barn from which it came. The fittest of his remaining cats now became dangerously ill, and Luis worked himself into a state of exhaustion. He watched his beasts sweat and cough, their breath rasping as they choked and grew listless, eyes and noses running. Their paws sweat, they refused their food. They died in his arms. A pyre was built, and he stood by watching as the prize and pride of his life burned in front of him. He felt as if it were his own life blazing.

Out of eighteen tigers only four were left, plus one fully grown lion and a small, sickly panther. The cost of replacing the animals was astronomical, and no insurance covered the epidemic.

Then, when he believed nothing else could go wrong, a hurricane swept through the state. His trailer was destroyed and two more cats perished. His cages were wrecked, his props and plinths crushed.

Luis Grimaldi could not sign the contract, his most coveted prize; he didn't have the resources to buy new animals. He was finished. He moved into a run-down trailer given to him by the circus folk of the winter quarters. That's where his drinking began. For weeks his old retainers fed and cleaned the remaining animals, without wages, but eventually they were driven by necessity to seek work elsewhere. Only Johnny Two Seats was left, so nicknamed because of his wide, fat ass. He cared for Grimaldi as best he could, and saw that at least he ate the odd meal.

Winter came and went, the circus performers moved on, and Grimaldi remained. He had nowhere else to go and, out of pity, the owners and managers let him stay on.

One day Ruda Kellerman had appeared, in a rusty old Jeep, with her obnoxious husband. They were traveling on to Chicago, where Kellerman was to join a troupe of acrobats. She wasn't half starved anymore, but well filled out—twice the size of her diminutive spouse.

Kellerman was there only a few hours before he got into a brawl, and was asked to leave. He yelled that it hadn't been his idea to come to the run-down shithole, but his wife's, because she wanted to see Grimaldi.

Ruda appeared at Grimaldi's shambles of a trailer. She banged on the window. Hung over, unshaven, and stinking to high heaven, he had flung open the door, shouting to whoever it was to leave him alone. She was shocked to see him in this state, the man who had been her idol for years.

She brought him food, brewed some coffee, told him how she made pocket money doing astrology charts and reading palms. She had laughed at how easy it was to make money.

Grimaldi wasn't listening; he sat in a stupor, drinking the thick black sweet coffee. She dug deep into her old trouser pockets, took out a wad of dollars and stuffed them into his hand. "Here, you were kind to me once, I've never forgotten that. . . ."

Kellerman had banged on the door and yelled that they were on their way. She had shouted back for him to wait in the truck, and stood up staring at Grimaldi, concerned. "I got to go, you take care now, maybe I'll see you around."

She extended her hand, like a man, but he turned away, embarrassed at having taken her money, and yet unable to turn it down.

For the next four months Ruda and Kellerman had traveled around, stopping off at small-time circuses, never for long. Kellerman held on to his dream of working in one of the main venues in Vegas, but when they eventually arrived there they were so broke he had to sell all his so-called props. He had no act to sell, never mind one that would earn them any cash, and none of the high-class acts would even consider his type of performance. Ruda had to work as a waitress, at a roadside truckers' stop. She worked twelve-hour shifts to earn enough for them to live on.

The gambling bug took hold of Tommy: Slot machines attracted him like a drug, and he began to borrow more and more money. Then he made the mistake of getting in with loan sharks. He owed thousands, and gambled in a feverish panic to try and cover his losses. Three weeks after their arrival in Vegas, Ruda returned home, worn out after a late-night shift, to discover Kellerman had sold their mobile home at the trailer park—sold it, when they didn't even own it! But he had at least left word where he had bolted to and she tracked him down to a small, seedy rooming house. The only possessions he had been unable to sell were a few of her clothes. Ruda had told Grimaldi, albeit a long time after, how she had opened her cheap trunk, rummaged through her things, and then slammed down the lid. She had told him how angry she had been, demanding to know what Kellerman had done with her albums and notebooks. Kellerman, so Ruda had said, hadn't seemed to care, he had simply got out as fast as he could.

Grimaldi remembered asking Ruda if that was why she had left Kellerman, and she had told him . . . He frowned, trying to recall what reason she had given, then suddenly it came to him, he remembered exactly what Ruda had said:

"I was pissed off at him so much of the time, and the thought that he had left my boxes, the ones with all my letters, my customers' telephone numbers, that really got me mad." She had grown silent, and Grimaldi had asked about the boxes. Had Ruda got them back? She had shrugged, was dismissive.

"Yeah, the little shit had that much decency. Oh, Luis, I was so angry, I beat the hell out of him and I really went crazy when I found out he'd gone through them. He knew he wouldn't find any money there, but what got me so mad was that he couldn't even leave my boxes alone. It was the last straw that finally made me leave him. He didn't give me any respect. You see, they're mine. They're all I got."

Grimaldi could have no knowledge of the importance of the boxes to Ruda. He could not know that Kellerman had watched her check each item: the little pebble, a piece of string, a heavy gold wedding ring, and all the tiny folded squares of newspaper, some of them brown with age, their edges frayed from being opened and refolded so many times. Ruda had never told her husband of the fight that had followed.

Ruda was always placing ads in newspapers. In every city, every town, she would run the same, just two lines: "Red, Blue, Green, Ruda, *Arbeit Macht Frei,*" and then the box number where she could be contacted. Kellerman had given up trying to persuade her it was a waste of time; finally he had got so angry he had torn up the neatly cut square of newspaper, ripped it into shreds and screamed: "She will never contact you. She is dead, *dead,* DEAD!"

Ruda had looked at him, then calmly opened the kitchen drawer and taken out a carving knife. She flew at him from across the room, and he had saved himself only by crawling under a table. She kicked at him, and stabbed the knife into the wooden tabletop; her frenzied attack continued until she had slumped exhausted onto the floor beside him. She had let him remove the knife from her hands, and like two children hiding, they huddled together under the table.

Kellerman never brought up the subject again, or acknowledged how much it hurt him to see those words: *Arbeit Macht Frei.* These words were printed above each hut in the concentration camp. He knew, more than anyone else, the importance of the black box, but he had not realized it meant more to her than he did.

The morning after the fight, Ruda had given him some money she had earned as tips the previous night. He had promised he would not gamble, he would look for a job, but he hadn't even attempted to find one. He used Ruda's money to buy a gun.

Kellerman and two pals had planned a robbery together. They would go to a circus where he had once worked. Kellerman knew when and where the takings were counted.

The robbery, seemingly so simple, got out of hand and the cashier, a man who had himself lent money to Kellerman at one stage, was shot and died on his way to the hospital. Kellerman had planned to run away with Ruda, but he had barely arrived back at the rooming house with the money when the police came for him.

Ruda had been arrested along with him and held in jail, suspected of being his accomplice.

Perhaps one of the few decent things Kellerman had ever done in his grubby, miserable life was to deny adamantly that Ruda had played any part in the robbery. She was released. She went to see him only once, and had listened to him as he begged her to find a good lawyer. Then she had looked at him and asked how she was to pay for it. He had pleaded with her: "You've got to help me, Ruda, please. Help me get out of this!"

She hadn't even waited for the visiting time to be over; instead she had said, with a half smile: "No, Tommy. I'm through helping you. You see, Tommy, you should never have opened my box. It's mine."

Ruda never tried to contact Kellerman again. She read in the papers he had been sentenced to eight years. By this time she was already heading back to Florida, and arrived at Grimaldi's winter quarters on the same day he had been asked to leave. Grimaldi was broke: The people who had befriended him could extend their charity no longer.

Ruda acted as if he were expecting her, putting down her suitcase beside the table, picking up his notice to leave, and walking over to the manager's office. She paid over two thousand dollars in cash and asked if she could use Grimaldi's shack for fortune-telling. They all knew about Kellerman's arrest—the fact that he had stolen from his own people—but Ruda stood her ground, saying she had walked out and filed for divorce as soon as she knew what he had done.

Grimaldi had run up huge debts, and just to have the rent paid made Ruda's appearance acceptable. She promised that from that moment on she would take care of him, as though she had wished to substitute one loser for another. Luis asked himself why. Why had she come to him?

Ruda had returned to the run-down trailer and ordered Luis to get out while she cleaned the place up with buckets of water and disinfectants, washing and scrubbing as he sat on the steps drinking beer. She borrowed a van and carried the filthy sheets and laundry to a laundromat; she ironed and tidied, bought groceries and cans of paint. She was up at the crack of dawn, painting the outside of the old trailer, forcing old "Two Seats" to lend a hand. Grimaldi never lifted a finger.

Ruda slept on the old bunk bed in the main living area; Grimaldi had the so-called bedroom.

One morning, Grimaldi leaned against the open door, watching her work. She was sweating with the effort, it was a blistering hot day. He caught her arm as she was about to push past him.

"Where's Kellerman now?"

"In jail. We're through, finished. He's history." She released her arm, and went inside. It was dark, there were flies everywhere. She poured water from a bucket into the sink—they didn't have running water.

"We got a quickie divorce, only cost a few dollars. If I'd known how cheap it was to get rid of him I'd have done it years ago."

Grimaldi slumped into a chair. "So you married him?"

She turned, hands on hips. "Yeah, I married him. I had no way of getting out of Berlin—he was my way. That answer your question?"

He looked up at her helplessly. "I don't know what you want from me. Why are you doing all this?"

"You got somebody else?"

He laughed. "Does it look like it? I'm just trying to get a handle on what you want."

Her eyes were a strange color—amber—they reminded him of his cats, and even in his drink-addled mind he felt she was dangerous. She had moved close to him; it was not sexual, it was a strange closeness. She put out her hand and covered his heart.

"Marry me."

He had laughed, but her hand clutched his chest. "I'm serious; marry me. I'll get you back on your feet, I'll get you going again. All you need is money, I can make money, I can get enough so you can start again, but I want some kind of deal, and if I am your wife, that's a good enough contract."

"My wife?"

She returned to the sink, began scrubbing a pan. "Think about it. I don't want sex, sex doesn't mean anything to me. It'll just be a partnership."

Grimaldi grinned, not believing what he was hearing. "You got any idea how much cats cost? . . . and feed, and transportation? Then there's the training, it'll take months to get an act, any kind of a decent act together."

"Yeah, I'm sure it's a lot, but we can do it, and I am willing to learn. I can muck out, do anything you tell me to do. I've been around circuses now for long enough, I know the ropes, and I know it's hard work."

He sighed, shaking his head. "No way, I couldn't do it . . . I'm finished."

She threw the pan across the room. "You were the best, *the best,* and you can be the best again. I'm giving you a chance."

He grabbed her hand, dragged her out of the trailer, and crossed to the back of the sheds, to the pitiful remains of his once fine act. He shoved her against the bars. "Look at these animals, they're as fucked and as finished as I am. . . . You don't know what you're talking about, you have no idea of what an act, an act the likes of mine took, *years—my father, his father before him* . . . and that's what I'm left with. . . ."

She gave him one hell of a punch. "They'd turn in their graves if they heard you. Go on, get another bottle, go on, get drunk . . . you weak bum!"

He stormed off in a rage, wanting to hit her back, but wanting even more to hit himself. Alone, she had stared at the bedraggled unkempt cats, their filthy cages, their ribs showing through their matted coats. She grabbed a bucket of water and headed back to the trailer.

The water hit him in the face, then the bucket. "You bastard! You can get drunk, you can let yourself go, but what you've done out there is a crime . . . you're starving them to death."

"I have no money to feed them . . . I got no money, and nobody wants to buy them!!"

She rolled up her sleeve, shoved her tattooed arm under his

nose. "See this? I've been caged, I've been starved, I've been beaten, I've been to hell and back and I am still here. I am still fighting, and I have enough for the two of us, you got ten minutes before I take a gun and shoot what's left of those poor creatures, and then I'll leave a bullet for you. You won't let them suffer another hour, you hear me? . . . *You hear me?*"

She had slammed the door of the trailer so hard it came off its hinges. She went around to the cages. Never having been inside a cat's cage, she simply unbolted the door, stepped in, and took out the empty trays. She then rebolted the door and went back to the trailer. He was sitting, head bowed.

"What do they eat?"

"Meat, horsemeat . . . maybe I should put myself in there, let them have a go at me!"

Ruda stormed out and went into town. She came back an hour later, carrying a stack of boxes. She found Grimaldi mucking out the cages, Two Seats using a hose to wash them down. She cleaned out the bowls, and carried the fresh meat to the cages. Two Seats gave a toothless smile to Ruda, and he touched her hand with his gnarled, crusted fingers.

"I don't know what you said, but I thank God for you, young woman."

They fed the cats and went back into town for fresh bales of hay and sawdust. Neither of them brought up the question of marriage. Luis stopped drinking and began to exercise the animals. Two Seats collected the old plinths from the storage huts and dusted and washed them down. The heat was oppressive and the small trailer airless; they continued to sleep separately.

Four months after Ruda's arrival, Grimaldi took off for town. Old Two Seats sat on the steps glumly muttering that he doubted if the boss would come back that night, he'd be getting plastered at the local whorehouse.

Ruda flopped down on her bunk. "Shit! *Shit!*" She had traded one bum in for another. She was wondering if she had made the wrong decision when she heard Grimaldi calling her. Luis had re-turned, stone sober, and he put on the kitchen table an envelope and a small red box. It was a marriage license and a wedding ring. He said nothing, just pointed to the table.

He hovered outside the trailer, watching her from the window as she opened the envelope. He saw Ruda smile—she who so rarely smiled—and then slowly open the ring box. She snapped it shut, was about to walk out to him when she heard Grimaldi ask the old man if he had a suit.

"A suit! . . . You must be jokin', it's at the pawnbroker's."

"Well, get it out, and by Wednesday, 'cos you're gonna need it."

"What fer?"

"Wedding, you old bugger."

"What?"

"We need a witness, me and Ruda are getting married next Wednesday."

There was a loud guffaw, and then a lot of back slapping. She came to the door, and Grimaldi held out his big hand. She took it, gripped it tightly as the old man wrinkled his nose and then threw his hat up in the air with a yell.

"By Christ—that's the best news I've heard in years!"

✦ ✦ ✦

The wedding had been a small affair with just a few people from the winter quarters. They had lunch at a local restaurant, and then returned to feed the cats. Ruda had been very quiet, she had smiled for a photograph, but as the day drew to a close she continued to find things to do, anything to delay the consummation of the marriage, even though she was unsure if that was what Luis wanted. She had arranged a platonic partnership with Kellerman, but after six months he had demanded to have sex with her. Kellerman revolted her, but nevertheless the marriage had been consummated, insofar as it ever could be. Kellerman liked kinky sex, her physical problems had never bothered him. He liked her to give him blow jobs, liked the sight of her on her knees in front of him.

Luis had brought flowers and champagne, and she noticed that the bed linen had been removed from the couch she had always slept on. Luis was in high spirits. Having made the decision to marry Ruda, he was now more than willing to take her into his bed. He opened the champagne, and then produced a box, which he gave her with a flourish. She opened it, and the delicate night-dress, its lace and frills carefully snuggled in white tissue paper, made her bite her lips. She didn't even want to take it out of the box.

"Don't you like it? It's silk, the lace is from France, is it the right size? Take it out, go on take it out. . . ."

Slowly she had held the delicate nightgown against herself.

"You like it?"

She whispered that it was beautiful, and he asked her to put it on. She hesitated, and seemed so distressed he wanted to put his arms around her, but she stepped away from him. "Nobody ever gave me anything. . . ."

"So let me see you in it?" he said gently.

"You want this to be a proper marriage?"

Luis was confused, he said that he thought that was what she wanted, and she had turned away from him, hunching up her shoulders.

"I guess that is what I want, Ruda. I mean, maybe I've not been the best person to have around, not said the right things, but you wanted to marry me, didn't you?"

She nodded, but when he tried once again to hold her she fended him off. "I want to tell you something, I sort of thought you knew. . . ."

Again he tried to make her turn to him, look at him, but she pulled further away. "Don't, please don't touch me."

She lifted the soft silk to her face, almost caressing the gown. "Luis, I can't have normal sex. Something was done to me when I was a child. I can make it all right for you, but that is all."

Luis had a sudden vision of her as having had her sex changed: Was she really a man? He couldn't hide his revulsion, his confusion. "Jesus Christ, what a fucking time to tell me! Are you kidding?"

She turned to him, unbuttoning her shirt, her face rigid. "Do you think this is something to kid about? Do you?"

She began to undress in front of him, and he now backed away from her. She undid her blouse, took off her bra, and then started to unzip her trousers. "Look, Ruda, don't . . . don't, I can't deal with it, please, Ruda!"

She continued to undress, easing her pants down. She had on a pair of thick cotton underpants. Grimaldi was convinced she was going to show him a penis. Instead, he saw the terrible scars on her belly. He stared in disbelief.

Ruda then held up her wrist, showing him the tattoo. He looked from the row of numbers to her body; he couldn't look into her eyes.

"I'm surpised you've never commented on it before."

He swallowed, and gave a half smile, but his hands were shaking. "I guess I'm just not very observant. . . ."

She stood in front of him with such helplessness, such shame, her head bowed. He picked up the gown, and slipped it over her head. Then he stepped back.

"Now you look like a bride."

The small space between them was like a chasm he did not know how to cross. Seeing her standing there in the white negligee made him want to weep.

Her voice was husky, her head low. "I'll make up the bed on the sofa. . . . You don't have to be with me, I understand."

He gathered her in his arms and held her tightly. His voice was thick with emotion. "What kind of a man do you think I am? We said to each other for better or worse, didn't we? Well, I don't think you got such a great bargain, so maybe you're damaged too, that's okay, we'll make out."

Ruda had clung to him, her whole body shaking. When he cupped her face in his big hands, two tears rolled down her cheeks. He told her then that he loved her. Maybe it was those two tears, he had never seen her cry before, and he had carried her into the small bedroom and gently laid her down. He undressed, and then he got in beside her, and he reached out and cradled her in his arms.

"Don't ask me about it, Luis. You don't ever want to know what was done to me, because it might open up a darkness inside me that I could not control. It happened, and now it's over. . . ."

He had never felt as protective of any living soul. He kissed her head as she rested against his chest. "I will always take care of you, Ruda, nobody will ever hurt you again. You are my wife, this will be our secret, no one will ever know."

He made her feel secure, a feeling she had never experienced before. She felt warmed by this big soft man, and gently she stroked his chest, and then rolled over to lie on top of him. She smiled and then whispered that she could make him happy, there were ways, she would teach him how to make love to her, he would like it, he would be satisfied.

The old hand and the few workers left at the winter quarters gave knowing winks and nudges as a very happy Grimaldi greeted them the morning after the wedding. He was a man who appeared infatuated. Maybe it was indeed love.

◆　◆　◆

The big album dropped to the floor, and Grimaldi woke with a start. For a moment he was disoriented, couldn't even remember coming into Ruda's bedroom. "You're gettin' old, you old bugger, noddin' off. . . ." He yawned, and leaning back he became aware of Ruda's scent on the pillow. He nuzzled it, and then slipped his arm around it, sighing. "Oh Ruda . . . where did I go wrong, huh?"

He knew she would give him hell if she found him in her room, but he chuckled and eased himself into a more comfortable position. His last thought before he fell into a deep sleep was of Ruda. "What a bloody wife . . ."

◆　◆　◆

Ruda had intended to apply for a divorce from Kellerman as soon as she had the opportunity. That she had married Grimaldi biga-mously never worried her; with Kellerman in prison, he would not find out; by the time he was out she would have secured a divorce. She wished she had done it in Vegas, as she had told Grimaldi she had, but she had been in such a hurry to leave that divorce had been the last thing on her mind.

Grimaldi began to earn money by training other acts, traveling around the United States. He returned with gifts, and cash to buy new cats for his show. Ruda worked at the winter quarters. She learned how to groom and feed the animals, and they thrived under her care and attention. They began to breed the tigers and their first summer together as man and wife saw four new cubs born. Ruda was a doting mother, and was heartbroken when Grimaldi sold the cubs. He said they had to because they needed the money, but also he said the cubs were not a good color. He taught Ruda how to spot the best of the litters, how to test their strength. Health was always the main priority. Ruda was a willing pupil. She worked tirelessly, nothing was too much trouble. Everyone said that Grimaldi had found the perfect wife, that Ruda was getting him back on his feet.

Ruda continued with her stargazing sideline. The letters arrived every week, and she would spend hours every evening typing replies, making predictions. She typed very slowly with two fingers, deep in concentration. She had a dictionary beside her, always thumbing the well-worn pages. Grimaldi used to tease her, and at times was stunned when she asked him to spell the simplest of words. He believed at first it was because she was German and typing in English, but then watching her effort he understood she was almost illiterate. She had caught him observing her and had given him the finger. "I never went to school, dickhead, so no jokes!"

He leaned over her chair and began to read a letter. She tried to cover it with her hand, but he snatched it out of the roller.

" 'Dear Worried from Nebraska'—my God, what in God's name is somebody writing to you from Nebraska for?"

"I've done her charts, now give it back."

Grimaldi had waved the letter jokingly. "Her charts? What in Christ's name do you know about all this junk?"

He roared with laughter as he read Ruda's predictions. She folded her arms. "You laugh, but they pay ten bucks a letter, and they pay for the cats' feed. You got any better ideas how to make dough that fast?"

Grimaldi slapped the paper down and patted her head. "Keep working, keep working!"

She had carefully rolled the paper back into the typewriter, and he was about to walk out when he paused at the doorway. "You never did tell me how you did that scarf trick, you know, with that old magician?"

She began typing again, and without looking at him said that it wasn't a trick. He told her to stop pulling his leg, but she turned to face him. "That wasn't a trick. I'm telepathic."

"Oh yeah, prove it!"

She shrugged and said she didn't feel like it, but he insisted, teasing her, asking her to prove it. She sighed, then pushed the typewriter aside. She picked up the stack of letters she had received that week. She handed them to him, thumbing through them like a pack of cards. She then looked away and told him to turn up each envelope and she would tell him the color of the stamps. She repeated, in rapid succession: red, blue, red, red, green, blue, red, red, red, red . . . she then swiveled around in her chair and cocked her head.

"You knew . . . you cheated!"

She held out her hand and shrugged. "Yeah . . . Now can I get on with my work?"

"Don't let me hold you up, carry on!" But he remained leaning at the doorway watching her, until she looked up at him and made a funny face.

"Is it just the colors then? I mean, can you do anything else?"

She laughed. "If I were to say yes, what you gonna do? Set up a booth and make me wear a turban? Just get out, go on, don't you have anything to do?"

Grimaldi laughed. As he stepped down he called out: "I'll get myself a cloak like that old boy you worked with. Old Two Seats can bend over and give us a good fart, I'll set light to it!"

She could hear him laughing as he passed by the window, and then he stuck his head against the glass. "Did I tell you today how much I love you? Eh? Cross my palm with silver . . . and I'll tell you how much!"

She gave him the finger, shouted for him to "Sit on it!" and he gave his marvelous, deep-bellied laugh, and at last he went about his business.

Ruda began her laborious typing once more, but after a moment, she sat back and slid out from beneath the typewriter a slip of paper. It was another advertisement, in another place: Florida. She stared at the two lines, remembering how Tommy Kellerman had told her she was crazy. First she crumpled the paper, then changing her mind she straightened out the creases, and read and reread the two lines, "Red, blue, green, Ruda . . ." and the message Tommy had hated so much.

Ruda crossed to her dressing table, opened a drawer, and took out the small black tin box now fitted with a new lock. She went to get the key, hidden in the bookcase, and unlocked it. She looked at the stack of newspaper clippings. The last one she had inserted was in Vegas. This had been the longest pause between ads, perhaps because, for the first time in her life, she felt a sense of security.

Ruda locked away her secrets again, carefully hiding the tiny key, and returned to her typewriter. She sat staring at the white sheet of paper in the roller. She couldn't concentrate. She went into the bedroom and as she passed the door she slipped the bolt across, drew the curtains, until the small room was in semidarkness.

She sat in front of the dressing table and slowly drew toward herself the three-sided, freestanding mirror. She got closer and closer until she could see her breath form a tiny gray circle on the glass. She turned her head first to the left, then her right. Finally she stared directly ahead. She breathed deeply through her nose, until she felt the strange, dizzy sensation sweep over her. Her shoulders lifted as her breathing deepened . . . first came the red, as if a beam of red light were focused on her face. She breathed deeper, concentrated harder, until the red turned into a deep green, then a blue. The colors began flashing and repeating: red, blue, red, red, green. . . . They never fused, each was a clear block of single color. Her body began to shake, her hands gripped the edge of the table. The bottles of cologne vibrated, and the entire dressing table began to sway; she held on tightly for as long as she could, before she regulated her breathing again, bringing herself slowly out of the trance.

Her body felt limp, exhausted. Then she tilted her face forward to kiss the cold glass. Slowly she sat back, and traced with her fingers the faint impression of her lips lingering on the glass. She was consumed by an overpowering longing; the desire to feel warm lips return her kiss was like a pain inside her, a pain that, like her scars, would never heal. She could never give up, never, because on three occasions she was sure she had felt a contact.

She lay down on the bed and closed her eyes, waiting for sleep. But a nagging pain at the base of her spine made her feel uncomfortable. She turned on her side, but the pain grew worse, it began to feel as though something were being ripped out of her belly. Ruda was frightened as the pain intensified . . . she gripped her stomach, it felt swollen, and she began to rub her hands over it. As quickly as the pain had begun, it subsided. Ruda lay back.

Then the pain started again. Twisting in agony, she called out for Grimaldi. The rush of pain centered in her belly and as she tried to sit up, she screamed with all the power in her lungs.

Grimaldi was working in the barn. He paused and listened. "Did you hear that? Eh, you toothless old bastard, was that one of the cats?"

Two Seats shrugged. Grimaldi stood for a moment longer, listening intently. Hearing nothing more he resumed his work, but after a while he tossed down the pitchfork and walked back to the trailer. He peered in through the window, then crossed to the door, dragging his feet on the grid to wipe off the mud. He was just about to enter when he heard the bolt on the door drawn back.

"Ruda? You okay? Ruda?"

She opened the door, her face pale, shiny with sweat.

"What you lock the door for?"

Ruda gave a weak smile. "I just didn't feel too good. I think it must be something I ate. I've been sick."

"You running a temperature?"

He reached out to touch her face and she stepped back. "No, I'm fine now, you get on with your work. I'll lie down for a while. Go on."

"I'll check on the cats, I swear I heard screaming. Did you hear anything?"

"Get back to work, you lazy old so and so. I'll bring over some food. It was just something I ate, now off . . . off you go!"

He smiled, walking back to the barn, calling her a slave driver. He didn't notice that she held on to the door for support.

As soon as Grimaldi was out of sight, Ruda inched back to the table and slumped into the chair by her typewriter. She had felt this same pain before, although she couldn't remember exactly when, but the pain had been the same. She tried to type, forcing herself not to think about what she had just been through because it frightened her. She was terrified of doctors; hospital doctors in white coats made her shake with terror.

She felt her energy returning, and with great determination she forced herself to continue working, jotting down the week's itinerary for the work she had lined up for Grimaldi. Almost immediately she felt better.

With Ruda pushing him, Grimaldi continued taking on more training work. As the money came in, they began to buy more and more animals. Weekends he would train them, and she sat and watched his every move. Gradually she began to work alone when he was away, putting into practice everything she had seen him do.

They bought a new trailer and a truck and then one night, he sat her down.

"I know your injuries, the scars, but I was wondering, with you being here, and me away working until we have enough finances, that maybe this would be a good time . . ."

"For what?" she had asked, dragging out the typewriter.

"Maybe we should see a specialist. They have all kinds of newfangled equipment now, and maybe we should go see someone about having a baby."

She continued picking up papers, stacking them neatly at the typewriter, carrying her boxes of mail to the table. Over the past few months her little sideline had grown into a lucrative business. Having a semipermanent address helped, and she worked each evening after the animals were settled. Grimaldi sometimes sat and watched her, although he never read any of the letters, he was never that interested.

Tonight, though, he wasn't prepared to sit. He didn't want her working, he felt this was too important.

"Ruda, listen to me. Maybe, just maybe, you can have this done medically, you know, artificial insemination. We could at least try."

"I have enough work cut out for me, without bringing up a kid."

"I want a son, Ruda. I mean, we're breaking our backs to get an act back together, so why not? We'd have a hell of a boy, Ruda. Don't you even want to give it a try?"

She rolled a sheet of paper into the typewriter and started to type. He came and stood behind her, massaging her shoulders. He felt her shoulders shaking. She tried to type, and then folded her hands in her lap.

"If it hurts you, then we walk away. I don't want anything to hurt you, but we should just go see somebody."

He kissed the top of her head and left her. Slowly she began to type: "Baby-baby-baby-baby . . . MY BABY. MY BABY. MY SON . . ."

She stared at the word until it blurred. She touched the paper, the word *baby*. Nothing had prepared her for this, for Luis wanting a child. She whispered: "My child, he would be mine. My baby."

It had never occurred to her that there was a way. The more she thought about it, the more excited she became. Would it be possible? Dare she think it could be?

She ran out of the trailer, shouted to old Two Seats asking if he'd seen Grimaldi, and he pointed to the barn. She ran, calling for him, and hurtled into the barn. He was using a pitchfork, heaving the bales of hay. She threw herself at him, backing him onto the bales.

"Luis, Luis . . . I want a baby! *I want a baby . . . I want I want I want!*"

They kissed, and held each other tightly. She was excited, almost feverishly so, and asked him to fix an appointment. She would do anything necessary, and then she had leaned up on her elbows, looking down into his delighted face. "You love me, don't you? You really love me!"

Luis knew what it meant to her to learn she could not conceive. She had not spoken a word since they had returned from the clinic, and he was incapable of comforting her, needing comfort himself. Even when he tried to reach out to her in bed she had turned her back on him.

"Don't touch me, please leave me alone."

He was almost grateful that he had to leave for a two-week stint in Chicago.

After he left she didn't want to get up. She didn't even open the blinds, but remained in the darkened trailer. She remembered Eva then, a girl she had hardly known, a girl much older than herself. Eva had been in the camp too, like Ruda had survived. After the liberation, when Ruda had been taken to the mental institution, she hadn't known Eva was still alive—not until she saw her in the ward. Eva had a beard now, like a man. The teenage girl who had always had stories and jokes to tell the little ones now sat on a stool with her head bowed and her face covered with hair. Her eyes stared to some distant place.

Like Ruda, Eva had not spoken since she had been found, but Eva was docile, while Ruda showed signs that she was greatly disturbed. They had to sedate her. Ruda found it impossible to utter a word, impossible to believe it was over. Every night she waited for the men in white coats to take her back to the hospital ward in the old camp. She forced herself to stay awake; the screams and weeping from the inmates didn't frighten her, she was used to those sounds. What she was terrified of was being taken back, back to the camp. A key turning in the door sent bolts of terror through her. She could not verbalize her fear, could not cry. When the doctors tried to comfort her, she was sure it was a ruse; when they spoke kindly to her, she was sure they had some hidden motive. She spat out the pills they gave her, refused the food. Suspicious of everything, everyone, from the moment she had arrived in the institution, her paranoia grew in intensity when she saw Eva. Now she was certain it wasn't over, and she knew she had to escape somehow, because any day, any hour it would be her turn and she would become an animal like Eva.

In the end, Ruda made herself think her inability to conceive was for the best. Maybe she could only produce a monster, an Eva. She would not think of a baby, her baby, anymore: She would forget. As it was, the entire episode had taken her back to the darkness of her childhood. She was angry, determined that nothing would ever drag her back again.

Ruda had no real concept of how long she had been unreachable, how many times Luis had attempted to embrace her, show his love and concern. She wasn't aware he had slept on the couch, tried to tempt her to eat, or that she had kicked the tray from his hands. She was oblivious of the fact that when Luis had tried to tell her that he had to leave for a few weeks, she had told him to fuck off, go wherever he liked, she didn't care.

Grimaldi had discussed her behavior with old Two Seats, who suggested that all Ruda needed was time. She was just hurting, he said, and this hitting out at Luis was her way of dealing with it.

"She's just like one of 'em cats, Luis. They get injured, and by Christ you'll know it, they'll go fer you! She's just hurtin'."

Luis punched the old man's shoulder, said perhaps he was right. He never mentioned to her his own hurt; he had wanted a son. And he had left. She hadn't said good-bye because he hadn't wanted to disturb her. Ruda had been sitting on the bunk bed, with her old tin box.

◆ ◆ ◆

Luis sighed, his face still pressed into Ruda's pillow. He rolled over, awake now, and he sighed again. "I wanted a boy, a son so bad, Ruda . . . but most important, I wanted him to be ours!"

He sat up and ran his hands through his thick hair and he got out of bed and straightened the bedcover. The photo album had fallen open at an old picture of himself with his father. He picked it up, touching the picture lightly with his finger. "Ah, well! Maybe the circus days are numbered, an' maybe I'd get a kid who wouldn't want to go into the ring, it happens. . . ."

Luis stepped up on the stool, still talking to himself. "The Karengo brothers got a kid who's studying law! Mine'd probably end up in jail someplace, who knows? . . . Can't all be warriors, eh Dad?"

About to shut the cupboard door, he saw the box, the old square black tin box at the back. He stretched and reached, then stepped down with it. He tried to open it—it was locked. He went into the kitchen and took a knife, but when he tried to pry the box open, he buckled the lid. He swore as he wrenched and pulled, but it wouldn't open.

The trailer door banged, Luis turned guiltily: He was behaving just like Kellerman—had he reached this point with Ruda, too?

Mike called out that they were on in ten minutes.

"Ruda said to get over to the ring, the big boss is in the viewing room, and he's got a scout from Ringling Brothers' circus with him. We're all set to go."

Luis shouted that he would be right there, and quickly hid the box under his mattress. Mike was waiting at the door, and raised his eyebrows at seeing Grimaldi; he admired the old man's resilience. There he was all done up like a Christmas dinner, and not long before he had been good and plastered.

"Your hand okay?" Mike asked as they walked toward the big tent. Grimaldi gave a big rumbling laugh and hooked a huge arm around Mike's slim shoulder.

"Son, I've been slashed by a lot more dangerous species than a pitchfork!"

Mike laughed, then lifted the tent flap. "She's all steamed up as usual, pacing out there like a panther. . . . Mamon's acting up, I hope to God he'll play ball tonight. It's those plinths, he hates them . . . did I tell you the Ringling scout is in?"

"Yeah you told me, son. You know once I had a contract with them, some years back, but they offered me a . . ."

Mike had gone, and he was alone, talking to himself. He stood in the semidarkness staring at the empty rows of seats. A juggling act was going through its paces in the ring, the performers' spangled costumes catching the spotlights. He looked to the lighted viewing box; Schmidt was talking with a man sitting next to him, gesturing down to the ring. Then Grimaldi saw a third man, seated just behind Schmidt. He shaded his eyes to get a better view. It was Walter Zapashny, probably one of the finest animal trainers in the world. Grimaldi wondered why he was up there; it made him feel uneasy.

Grimaldi inched down the aisle; he saw one of the hands standing by to erect the cages around the ring and moved quietly to the man's side.

"Have you seen who's in the viewing tower?"

The man nodded. Everyone knew, he whispered, it was the big Ringling scout; the word was out that he great Gunther Gebel Williams was about to retire. It meant that the most lucrative circus job in the world, a possible ten-year contract with the Ringling Bros. of New York, was coming up for grabs. Williams had dominated the bill as one of the greatest showmen for almost twenty years.

Grimaldi's heart was pounding. What he had dreamed of all his adult life could now be Ruda's. He felt a rush of pride.

"Tell Ruda I'm here, tell her to make this the best show she has ever done . . . hurry!"

14

AS RUDA PREPARED to begin her act, Vebekka sat at the dingy bar, its red light giving the customers an eerie pink tinge. It was only nine, the club was almost empty; three girls wearing miniskirts and tight lace tops chatted quietly at the end of the plastic-covered bar. Vebekka had gone from club to club until she found Mama's. The bouncer came out of the toilet, looked at the elegant woman sitting alone, and gave her a careful once-over; he was sure she was after young blood—male or female. She'd get it, if she had enough money. He went under an arch, its green and red beaded curtain held back by a ribbon, and started up the stairs leading to the main entrance, then flattened himself against the wall as Mama began her heavy descent. He saw the swollen ankles first, the fat rolling over her gold sandals, as the tiny feet moved down one step at a time.

Mama Magda Braun's massive frame bumped into her bouncer, but she didn't acknowledge him. She was talking loudly to a small man who was following her, clutching her poodle. "I am sick to death of those ugly bastards, I don't wanna see those bitches stealing my girls' jobs. The smell of them! Emptying the store shelves, bringing crime and bad taste, I hate them! Everything used to be under control, now, Jesus Christ what a mess!"

His high-pitched lisping voice squeaked behind her. "Now, Magda, the shops are doing a roaring trade, you know it, I know it."

He was referring to Magda's sex and porn shops in East Berlin. She was making money hand over fist, but hated it when the girls from the East tried to come to her clubs in the West. Magda was the biggest porn shop owner in the West. Now with the wall down, she had been quick to identify the new market; the sex-starved Easties, as she called them, needed an injection from the Westies, and she was giving them what they wanted—but they didn't have to come swarming over into her clubs. Magda Braun owned four nightclubs, she was a multimillionairess.

Magda's peroxide curls turned bright pink in the red light, her diamonds glittered, as did the large beaded necklace dangling over her huge bosom. She gave a bad-tempered look around at the few customers. It was early, but she hated it when it was empty. This was her main club, the one in which she had her small, cramped office. Eric, her diminutive husband, called out to the girls, waved to a few couples, followed Magda to a door marked *private*. The effort of walking across the small dance floor had exhausted what little breath she was able to squeeze through her nicotine-polluted lungs. Her chest heaved, and she gave a phlegmy cough. She could still be heard coughing as the door closed behind her.

Magda checked the day's earnings on the computer, a cigarette in her crimson-painted lips. Years of smoke had tinged yellow one side of her jowled face. "Our take is down again this week. You think those bitches are at it again? I tell you Eric, you have to watch them like hawks, give me a barman any day, I trust men better than those tarts. . . ."

Eric was peering through a small peephole. "You seen the class act at the bar?"

Magda paid no attention, continued working on the accounts. The boys handling the girls over in the East were shortchanging her, she knew it. They'd have to be taught a sharp lesson.

"I'm gonna check what the deal is with this woman, be back in a minute."

Magda picked up a pencil and dialed, hooking the phone under her chin. "It's Magda, can you get over here, send a couple of the boys, yeah? . . . Yeah he'll do, no! . . . Give me another." She listened and agreed to three of the names supplied by the caller, then she replaced the phone, sighing. They never learn their lesson, they should know you don't get to be near eighty and rich without learning every trick in the trade.

Eric scuttled back, gestured for Magda to come to the spy hole.

"She's asked for water, just sits there, she may be a fruitcake—

you want to take a look? She's wearing good jewelry, that's sable on the edge of her wrap. Magda?"

"I don't give a fuck, if she's paying, then what's the problem?"

"That's just it, she's been here for over half an hour, says she's got no money, just wants to sit. She didn't pay at the door, the bouncer wasn't on duty . . . Magda!"

Magda shoved him aside and peered through, her heaving breath seeming to stop suddenly. She straightened up. "I just seen a ghost . . . fuck me!"

She laughed, and sank down into a wide cushioned seat. "Eric, bring me a bottle of champagne, good stuff, and ask the lady to come in."

"You know her?"

Magda nodded. "I know her, she may look like class now, but honey, believe you me, that was one hell of a whore. You know something, Eric? They always come back . . . one day, they come back, maybe to see where they came from, or how far they've gone . . . but they always come back to Mama. Get her in, this one I've been waiting for so long now I can hardly remember."

Eric crossed to Vebekka, asked if she would join Madame Magda for a drink. He pointed to the office, the door left ajar. Vebekka hesitated, looked toward Magda, who was smiling, gesturing for her to come in, but Vebekka shook her head.

"Thank you, no . . . I don't speak German."

Eric asked if she was English, she told him she was French, and he attempted to repeat his invitation in French.

"*Ruda!* Come in here, Ruda!"

Suddenly Vebekka felt strange, a little faint, as the fat woman kept calling, waving her over. She slid from the stool. "Excuse me, I must go . . ."

Eric ordered champagne, took Vebekka by the elbow. "Please, you come."

"No, thank you, no . . ."

"*Ruda! . . . Ruda!*"

Eric insisted, holding her arm firmly, as one of the girls carried a tray with a bottle of champagne and two glasses across to the office. Vebekka was ushered into the small room, and the big woman held open her arms. "Come here . . . *Come and give me a kiss!*"

Vebekka stepped back, repelled. Eric pushed her further into the room, the waitress squeezed out, and Magda waved Eric away. "You, too, get out . . ."

Disappointed, Eric walked out. He went to the bar and ordered a martini. He noticed she had left behind her purse.

Magda poured the champagne and handed Vebekka a glass, but she shook her head. "No, I don't . . ."

Magda smiled and set the glass down and lit a cigarette from a stub, offering the case to Vebekka. She took one, and Magda flicked a Zippo lighter across the desk. "You look very good, I didn't recognize you at first . . ."

Vebekka remained standing. "I am sorry, I don't understand, I don't speak German."

Magda smiled, shrugged her plump shoulders. "What then?"

Vebekka spoke in French, introducing herself as Baroness Maréchal, asking if they had met before. Magda looked steadily at Vebekka, she observed her heavily made-up eyes, the mascara so thick the lashes were spiked. "You want to speak in French, Italian, Spanish, that's okay by me . . . you been away so long, huh? . . . that long?"

"I don't understand, I am so sorry, but I think there is some misunderstanding. I don't think we have ever met!"

Magda leaned her fat elbows on the desk. "Okay, I'll play, have a drink, sit down."

Vebekka eased herself onto the proffered chair; she felt very uneasy, but she sipped the champagne. Magda suddenly reached out and took Vebekka's left wrist and turned it over. Vebekka tried to withdraw her hand, but the old woman, for all her heavy breathing, was as strong as an ox. Her long nails scratched at Vebekka's wrist, turned her palm upward, and traced the fine skin graft with the tip of her nail. She let go, and smiled.

"Why did you do that?" Vebekka rubbed her wrist.

"So I know for sure. Drink, drink—it's good, the best money can buy," Magda answered in French.

Vebekka sipped the champagne while the old woman scrutinized her. Magda said that the work was good, she looked good, looked young. She asked where she was staying, why she was in Berlin, and Vebekka said she was with her husband.

"And you couldn't resist it? Had to come back and see Magda? And now you are a what? A baronness? Well, well—face changed, name changed, what did you call yourself? Vebekka? What kind of name is that?"

Vebekka smiled, a sweet coy smile, and sipped more champagne. Magda picked up her vodka, drank heartily. "I still take it neat, with ice, but now I have a warehouse full! Times change, huh? Times change, Ruda . . . little Ruda, just look at you, and married to a baron! Does he know you're here?"

Vebekka began to feel uneasy, frightened. Why did the woman keep on calling her Ruda? But all she said was that her husband did not know.

"I bet he doesn't . . . so you got to America? I heard you had, and then what? You met a prince and a baron—all the same thing. Is he rich?"

Vebekka drained her glass, and Magda poured her another. She asked again if her husband was rich. Vebekka shrugged. "I suppose so, I don't know, I never think about money. . . ."

Magda laughed, her body shook. She had a coughing fit that seemed to subside after a drag on her cigarette. "You don't think of money . . . I do, every second of every day, I count it every night on this little computer."

The two women drank in silence. The sounds of Madonna could be heard from the club, the low murmur of voices and shrill laughter. Magda's eyes watered. "You know, it hurt, Ruda, it hurt when you ran off—I never thought you would steal from me, not after all I did for you. I never thought you would do that to Mama, maybe that's why I have never forgotten you . . . you forget lovers, forget husbands, forget children even, but when someone hits your pocket, you don't forget. I never forgot you, Ruda, and maybe I just guessed one day you would come back."

Vebekka listened, her head cocked.

"I don't understand what you are saying, but I know I have never met you before. . . . I am not this—Ruda? You are mistaken. . . ."

Yet Vebekka felt a strange sensation when she pronounced the name *Ruda,* it rang through her brain like an ominous bell. Magda pulled herself to her feet and looked at Vebekka with distaste. "Don't play games with me, I am a master player, honey. You don't speak German? We've never met? Who the fuck do you think you are kidding, eh? Because you got fancy clothes on, and call yourself a baroness?"

"I don't understand . . ."

Magda was losing patience, she slapped the desk with her fat hand. "Don't make me angry, it's been many years, a lot of changes, Ruda . . . I run this city, hear me? You stop this act right now—*I have had enough!*"

Vebekka gulped. "I have never met you before! Please, there is some misunderstanding, I must leave . . ."

Vebekka started to go but Magda pushed her back into the seat, looming over her.

"You want something to refresh your memory? Huh? I didn't want to do this, I was prepared to be hospitable, maybe forget, but me? Never, I forget nothing . . . no one, you owe me a lot, Ruda, you owe me!"

Magda waddled to a large built-in cupboard and gasped for breath as she opened the double door. The cupboard was stacked with boxes and files, she looked up and down, reached in for a box, and then withdrew her hand. Suddenly she yelled at the top of her voice: "Eric . . . *Eric!*"

The club was in full swing now, Madonna blared from the speakers.

"Just sit, sweetface, I'm gonna jog that memory of yours."

Eric came in, looked at Magda, Vebekka, then asked if everything was all right.

"There was a box, old cardboard box from the Kinkerlitzchen, taped up, big brown cardboard box . . ."

"What about it?"

"I want it. Where is it, it used to be stashed in here, in this cupboard, where is it?"

Eric stood by the cupboard doors. "I haven't moved anything in years; everything you wanted brought over should still be here, unless when we computerized somebody threw it out!"

"I never gave permission for one thing to be chucked out!"

Magda's chest was heaving, and Eric got down on his hands and knees to look for the box. "Shit, this palce is filthy, it's dusty down here."

Magda stood behind him. "Just find the fucking thing."

Vebekka looked from one to the other, not understanding what they were saying. Eric suddenly pulled a box from beneath a stack of files. "Is this it?"

Magda peered over his shoulder, and told him to put it on the desk. Eric dumped the dusty box on the table and then restacked the files as Magda tore open the box. She rooted around, hurling things to the floor, and then took out an old torn thick envelope. "Put it all back and get out!"

"Shit, Magda, I'll have to take all the files and restack them again, it won't fit now."

Magda yelled for him to leave, she would sort it out later. Eric tripped over the dog, who yelped and scuttled under the desk, and then slammed the door shut.

Magda filled Vebekka's glass again, then settled herself back on her cushions, lighting another cigarette. "You don't remember Mama, huh? You don't remember what I did for you, what Mama did to help Ruda? Well tell me, do you remember this, sweetface?"

Magda tore the envelope and pulled out an object wrapped in old newspapers.

Ruda? The name puzzled her. She suddenly looked behind her, she had the sensation there was someone else in the room, close to her; but there was no one. *Ruda,* she repeated to herself, no longer listening to Magda. She sipped the champagne; it was chilled, it tasted good. She had not been allowed to drink for years. She turned again, sure that someone was there, but as she did so she saw Magda watching her, and she laughed nervously.

"I have not been allowed to drink! I had forgotten how lovely it tastes. Are you all right?"

Magda was coughing, ripping the newspaper. She withdrew an old wood-handled carving knife, a knife with serrated edges, and snarled: "You forgotten this?"

Vebekka looked at the knife. "I don't understand?"

"You don't understand, and you are not Ruda? . . . And you didn't come crying to Mama? Didn't come begging me to help you clean up? Help you to strip him, help hide him? You couldn't lift him, you had to come running to Mama? That perverted piece of shit still moaning and begging us to save him, begging you, begging me, but you couldn't do it, so you started begging Mama—*you remember Magda now, tart?!*"

Magda staggered, gasping for breath again. Vebekka began to shake, both hands clasped around her champagne glass. She could hear Louis shouting at her, he was dragging her to their car while she was trying to button her blouse. Where was it? Was it here? She couldn't remember, all she could hear was his voice as he pushed her roughly into the car. "You tart! . . . *You cheap tart!*" He had driven off fast, the tires screeching, his face white with anger. He was shouting that he had been searching for her. Then he had pulled over and had punched the steering wheel with his hands. "Why, why do you do this?"

"Answer me, tart!"

Vebekka's head began to throb, she gulped the champagne. "Did my husband tell you?" she asked Magda. She felt hot, the cramped office was stifling.

"Water, could I have a glass of water?"

Magda leaned back, clinking the ice cubes in her vodka glass. "What have you done to your face? You've done something to your face, you had a nose job? That's what's different, you had some work done, sweetface?"

Vebekka touched her face. "Yes, yes . . . I had, er, surgery."

Magda chuckled. "I knew it, I knew it. I can always tell . . . Ruda."

"Please, I need a glass of water!"

Magda reached over to the champagne bottle and banged it down in front of Vebekka. "You want a drink?"

Suddenly her fat face twisted. She leaned forward and threw the contents of her glass into Vebekka's face. The vodka burned her eyes, and she knocked over her chair as she sprang to her feet, her hands covering her face.

Magda waved the carving knife in front of her. "Get the hell out, and think about this! Think about this, Ruda, then come back and see me! You owe me, maybe now's the time to pay me off, out—*get out!*"

Vebekka stumbled to the door and fumbled, trying to open it. Magda pressed the button at the side of her desk. The door buzzed open, and Vebekka ran out as Magda picked up the phone and screamed for Eric to come in.

Magda was sweating, her eye makeup running. She didn't even give Eric time to walk in before she snapped at him to follow the tart, find out where she was staying and report back. "I want to know everything about that one, you understand me? Go on, get out!"

Eric straightened his silk tie, smoothed his hair, and made his way quickly to the club exit. He stomped up the stairs and looked for the bouncer. He saw him examining two kids' driver's licenses. "You see a woman come out, dark-haired woman, few seconds ago?"

He nodded, jerked his thumb along the street, and Eric took off, swearing loudly that he should have put on his overcoat. It started to pour; the bouncer cursed and huddled in the doorway.

Magda opened up the soft leather clutch bag. It contained only a gold and diamond embossed compact, a matching lipstick, and a gold cigarette case. There was no wallet, no credit cards, nothing. She sniffed the lining; there was a faint smell of perfume. "You sure it was hers?"

The bartender nodded, said the woman had left it at the bar when she went into the office. "Okay, you can go."

The bartender left as Magda took a magnifying glass from a drawer and examined the compact. She squinted, then lifted her eyebrows; it was gold, so the diamonds must be real. She checked the cigarette case; it too was eighteen-carat. Maybe the bitch wasn't lying, maybe she was a baroness. Magda laughed, lit another cigarette, then turned the cigarette case over in her hand. She'd hang on to it and the compact; they would cover what the little bitch had stolen all those years ago. Hell, she thought, nowadays the leather bag alone would cost two hundred dollars. She opened a drawer and put the bag inside, slamming it shut. It was funny, but she hadn't meant to turn nasty, she hadn't wanted her debt repaid, so much water had passed under the bridge.

Magda sucked on her cigarette. The room stank of smoke. It was the way the bitch refused to admit who she was that really pissed Magda off; who did she think she was kidding? All the handouts she'd given, all the helping hands to the young punks, yet they always turned around and slapped you in the face. She thought about the girls and the pimps she had set up, buying their trailers, even the bitches' clothes, all they had to do was stand outside them and pick up customers. She paid off the police, she, Big Mama, covered everything—and they still robbed her when they could.

Magda reached for the carving knife. The blade was eight inches long, the handle carved but worn; Ruda had probably stolen even that, or found it in one of the bombed-out houses. In those days it was surprising what you could find poking around in the rubble. Magda ran her fingers along the serrated edge, now brown with rust.

She gulped her vodka, slowly calming down as she remembered the good times. The Americans, the English . . . those soldier boys wanted women, young, fat, thin, they wanted them, and Magda filled their needs. She tried to accommodate every sexual preference: even for underage kids, boys and girls. Children roamed the streets, hundreds of them, hungry and homeless; they'd turn a trick for a meal, for a crust. That's how she got her nickname "Mama," even that bitch Ruda had called her Mama.

Magda closed her eyes, and saw Ruda as clear as yesterday. Ruda, no more than eight or ten years old, infested with lice, dressed in rags, her skinny legs covered in open sores. She was like a stray dog, no matter how often Magda and her boys sent her packing, she returned, hand out, begging. Magda had taken pity on her, let her scrub out the cellars Magda had started to convert into makeshift brothels. She clothed her, fed her, and the child never said a word. For weeks they didn't know her name, or was it months? She couldn't remember how long it was before the girl had started talking, and when she did she had an odd, gruff voice, and used a strange mixture of languages: Polish, German, Yiddish. They never found out her real nationality; but they could see because of the tattoo that she had survived one of the camps—which camp they never discovered.

They nicknamed her Cinders, after Cinderella, and wondered if she was deaf because she spoke so little. Then one day, she hit one of the young boys who tried to mess with her. She hit him with a broom and knocked him unconscious. Mama Magda had been called to attend to him. Ruda was huddled in the corner, clenching the broom, and then in her odd gravelly voice she said that her name was Ruda. Magda had slapped her hard, told her she had to behave if she wanted to be fed.

"My name is Ruda."

Magda asked if Ruda had a last name. She was worried about the police rounding up her kids. At every bomb-blasted corner there were long notices of missing children; Magda always read these lists in case one of the missing children was working for her. If any were, she got rid of them fast, even dragged them to the depots. The families could cause a lot of aggravation. Soldiers, doctors, and nurses from the many orphanages being set up tried to get the kids off the streets. It seemed like a hopeless mission; no sooner were some picked up and housed than others took their places—the pitiful bedraggled aftermath of war. Some kids, diseased and sickly, simply died on the streets. The ones who knew their way around landed with Mama Magda.

Magda often asked Ruda if she had a last name, but the child acted dumb. Once she had shown Magda her wrist, as if the number were a surname. Maybe it was that gesture that had touched Magda, maybe that was what made her take such an interest in the skinny wretch. Magda let her work in her own apartment, washing and cleaning. She was all fingers and thumbs, but the good thing about Ruda was she didn't talk, just got on with her work. She put on weight, her hair became free of lice, and her sores healed. She was not a pretty girl, but she had something, and Magda's men friends soon started to take an interest in her.

Magda would probably have kept Ruda on as a maid, had she not been visited by health inspectors, who regularly checked on missing kids. They had a long list of kids who had escaped from orphanages. Magda listened to the names and shook her head. "I look over the lists, I make sure none of them are around here. If I find one, you know me, I drag them to the depot, I'm known there."

Then they asked if she'd come across a girl called Ruda. They had no last name, and they were still trying to trace any living relative. Ruda had arrived at Auschwitz but had been removed to Birkenau until her release. She had been kept in a mental institution for four years right after the war. She was a survivor of Birkenau, could be recognized by her tattoo; they described her as possibly eight to twelve years of age. They had a place for her in an orphanage but she had run away.

Magda said she had no child of that age working for her. She was sorry she couldn't help, but she would keep her eyes peeled. For a moment she was scared they were going to search her apartment, but they folded their papers.

"I hope, Magda, you don't keep any underage girls, because if you do, we'll keep on coming, and we'll bring the police with us."

Magda had given them a black market bottle of scotch. Laughing and joking, she told them she drew the line at kids. "You think I'd use kids?—what kind of a woman you think I am?!"

They had no illusions about her, but what could they do? They had no search warrants, no time to really look, there were too many children. . . . Even the threat of bringing in the police was an empty one, but they had to make a show, at least try to salvage some of the children roaming the streets. They took the scotch and left.

After they had gone, Magda had to look for Ruda, guessed she must be hiding. She went into her bedroom and opened the wardrobe. Ruda was crouching inside. "Don't send me back there, Mama, please . . . please don't."

"I can't keep you here, sweetface, they'll shut me down. I don't want trouble; I said I didn't know you. They find out I lied and I won't get them off my back."

Ruda had clung to her, sobbing. It was the first time Magda had seen her shed a tear. "I can't keep you here, but I'll see what I can do."

Even though she now knew Ruda's age, she got one of the older girls to take her around to the brothels, got her to break her in. But then, after a few weeks, Magda was told that there was something wrong with the girl's vagina. She couldn't have straight sex. Magda had shrugged; she was still a kid, maybe too tight. She suggested they teach her a few other tricks, to get her working. "Just don't bring her back, I don't want her here. If she can't earn her keep, kick her out."

Ruda was taught about oral sex. She was grateful it didn't hurt her insides. She would do anything not to be sent back to the mental institution or orphanage. She learned fast, and was given a small percentage of the money she earned. She ate well, and started living with a few of Magda's whores in a run-down house. The customers often asked for her, since she was exceptionally young. But she was forever stealing; no matter how often she was beaten she still stole wallets and food coupons. Magda turned her loose on the streets, to see if that would teach her a lesson—out by the bomb sites, giving head wherever there was a dark corner, a derelict truck or car. It was worse than Magda's filthy cellars, at least they had mattresses there, but now Magda never knew just how much she earned, even though she sent her thugs around to collect. Ruda could always lie, hide a percentage of her takings, even up her price.

Ruda worked the streets for almost three years, scrimping and saving money, never buying the black market clothes the other girls coveted; she couldn't care less. Over her underwear she wore the same old brown coat Magda had given her, opening it as a come-on to the soldiers. The few items of clothing she bought secondhand were neatly folded in a battered case she got as a tip. She had found a derelict house to share with a few prostitutes, girls so low down they didn't even have a Magda to look out for them. These girls fought and clawed each other to safeguard their territory, be it a lamppost, doorway, or wrecked car.

Ruda's house had no electricity or running water but her room was dry, and she slept on a burned mattress she had retrieved from the rubble. She began to bring in clients, but then one night a U.S. Marine had wanted more than oral sex. When she had said she couldn't have straight sex, he had tried to rape her. Unsuccessful, he had forced her to have anal sex. It had hurt her, made her bite the edge of the mattress to stop herself from screaming, but when it was over, he gave her a handful of dollars, tossing them onto her naked body. The pain dissipated as she counted the money. She realized she could ask more, she could do more.

Ruda would buy a bath a week at the local bathhouse. She paid for a private, number one bath—this meant she was the first to use the water. This was her only luxury; she hoarded her earnings, dreaming of going to the United States one day. She plied any American soldier she met with questions about America. She was naïve enough to believe that when she had enough money saved she would simply buy a ticket and go.

When Ruda discovered that without documents, visas, and a passport she would never go anywhere, she remained secluded in her hovel for two days, then went to talk to Magda.

"You want papers? Visas? You any idea how much that kind of thing costs, sweetface? There's lines, hundreds, thousands lining up waiting . . . go find somebody with papers, marry him—that's the fastest way you can get a legitimate passport. You'll have to wait, but you'll find one eventually."

Ruda begged Magda to help her—where was she going to find anyone who would marry her? Magda asked how much she had saved, Ruda admitted to half the amount she actually had; she knew that Magda would be suspicious. Even so, Magda accused Ruda of holding out on her, it was a lot of money. Ruda had opened her coat. "I have no clothes but these, I don't cheat on you, not any-more. I don't smoke, I don't drink, Jesus Christ, Magda, I hardly fucking eat, I save every cent, I wanna go to America."

"What's so special about America?"

Ruda buttoned her coat. I need some surgery, I have trouble peeing straight, it hurts all the time. I'm not going to a hospital here, they'd drag me off to a mental hospital, but in America they can help me."

Magda arranged for Ruda to meet with Rudi Jeczawitz, a cabaret artist who knew people dealing in forged papers. Jeczawitz had survived Auschwitz, maybe he'd be prepared to help her.

Magda made a deal with him; he needed a girl to help him with his act, and she made a deal with Ruda. She asked for half of her savings. Ruda was pleased she had not told Magda the right amount she had stashed away. In some respects, Magda was relieved she had got rid of her. Within the hour, she had found another girl to work Ruda's territory. She knew Jeczawitz had contacts, but whether he could get Ruda to her beloved America or not didn't concern her. Magda just pocketed the money; she did nothing for free.

Jeczawitz worked the clubs, and those in need of forged papers went through him. He then forwarded the requests to a man named Kellerman, a dwarf.

Jeczawitz took Ruda into his act and for the rest of her savings agreed to marry her. That way she would have a marriage license and a last name. Ruda paid, believing that it would be only a matter of time before her husband got the visas and documents necessary for her to leave for New York.

Rudi Jeczawitz was in his late sixties, and crippled with arthritis. He had lost his wife and children at Auschwitz. He made no sexual advances toward Ruda. She cooked for him, and washed his tattered belongings, and he moved into her derelict room. He owned a battered cardboard suitcase filled with hoops and magic tricks, which he had been allowed to keep even in the camp. He had stayed alive by entertaining the officers; they had found him a cloak, and a wizard's hat. The suitcase represented everything to him, and he guarded it obsessively. He kept his hat in the case and always wore his cloak.

It was Ruda's job to hand him the hoops, hats, and silk handkerchiefs he dragged from his sleeves, night after night. The clubs were seedy and run-down; most of them employed him only because of his contact with Kellerman. If they were caught trafficking in illegal papers, they could be closed down; but by using Jeczawitz as the go-between, they could always plead innocent: He had agreed to take the blame. After every show there would be a number of desperate figures waiting to speak to him.

One night, just before a show, he had been arguing with Ruda about the order of the handkerchiefs, when she had grabbed them, called out the colors, and stacked them in a heap. He began to notice how quickly she had caught on; he tested her a few times, holding them up to her, then behind his back—she was always able to guess the order of the colors. If he spread them on a table, she needed to look only once before telling him each color in rapid succession. He asked how she did it. She had shrugged and said they used to play games in the camp. It was a test they did. . . .

He stared at her. "You played games? . . . My babies died, my wife died, thousands died—and you played games?"

That was the first time he beat her; he took a stick and kept on hitting her. She took the beating, she was used to it. She simply shut her mind off and waited for the old man to exhaust his rage. Bruised, she had gone onstage, hating him, and holding him to his promise of papers.

From then on Jeczawitz beat Ruda regularly; afterward he would weep inconsolably, calling out the names of his wife and children.

Jeczawitz was as pain-wracked as Ruda; his mental wounds would never heal. He had no peace, but he lived somehow, day to day, dragging his old suitcase to clubs and brothels. Every night he heard the pitiful pleas, collected the folded money, remembered the names. Some nights he became so drunk she had to help him to their room.

On one evening when he was too drunk even to make it to the club, Kellerman arrived at their hovel in his flashy clothes, and Rudi offered Ruda to the dwarf for the night.

"I don't want your whore, hear me? I want names, the money that's been paid to you."

Ruda had followed Kellerman out of the house and offered herself. He turned and spat at her; he never paid for women, he didn't want a whore.

"I want papers," Ruda said. "Can you get them for me? My husband said you could, I have money. . . ."

He had stuck his thumbs into his suspenders. "I can get anybody anything they can pay for. You got the money, I'll get you the visas, passport—anything you want."

"I've got my marriage license, I've got proof of who I am."

He had laughed in her face, told her he needed only money. He would supply a name, get tickets for anywhere in the world—all she had to have was money!

When she learned how much, her heart sank; still she tried as hard as she could. But then Jeczawitz's drinking got out of hand, they lost two cabaret spots, and she had to get him sober enough to keep the third. That night their audience was a rowdy bunch. They were performers from the big circus, she was told.

Ruda had found out who the big man in the audience was, and she even tried to pick him up after the show, but he had virtually knocked her off her feet before his taxi drove off. Later, she had gone looking for him because she was certain he could get her out of Berlin. She had pushed her way into his trailer and he had given her money, told her he was leaving, that he couldn't get her a job.

When she got back to her room she found Rudi huddled on the bed.

"Kellerman's been here. He's not coming back, they kicked me out of the club, Ruda." He opened his arms up to her, wanting comfort, but she slapped his face.

"He was my only hope. You've ruined everything, where is he? Tell me where I can find him!"

Rudi lay down again, said there was no way Kellerman would do business with her, he hated whores.

She went to her hiding place, to look for her tin box. It was gone, as was all the money she'd saved.

"Oh no, please . . . please tell me you didn't take my money, please tell me you didn't."

He hung his head, shamefaced. "I owed Kellerman, I had to give him money, it had been paid to me . . . I'm sorry, I'm so sorry. . . ."

She punched him, and he tried to fend her off. He screamed out that Kellerman lived in the Kreuzberg district, that was all he knew. He never went to his place, Kellerman always contacted him. He started to cry, covering his face with his hands, blubbering his children's names.

"Shut up. I don't want to hear about your fucking children, your wife, your mother, you survived, *you're alive!*"

He sat up. "No. I am dead, I wish to God I were dead, like my babies, my wife . . . Oh God help me, why did they have to die?"

Ruda smirked at him. "You made them all laugh, didn't you, playing out your stupid tricks, Mister Wizard? What else did you do, huh? You had to do something else at the camps. You think I don't know? *You named names . . . You gave those bastards names . . . You killed your own babies, you bastard!*"

"So help me God I did not!"

Ruda danced around him. "Liar, why would they let an old man live?"

He reached for his stick, but she snatched it from him, started thrashing him, and he fought back, kicking at her. He raged at her, screaming: "You played games, you were *his* children, in your pretty frocks. I saw you all, I saw you all fat and well fed . . . my babies died, but you . . ."

Her rage went out of control. How could he know what they had done to her, what they had forced her to do? She kept on hitting him with the stick, over and over. She hit his head, his weak, bent body. She was panting, gasping for breath. At last he was silent, and she began to panic. She felt for his pulse—and then ran.

✦ ✦ ✦

Magda could hardly understand what she was saying. Ruda was on her knees, begging her to help, asking what she should do. She had to have somebody help her. "Mama, please, he lied to me . . . he took all my money, and he never got me papers . . . all my money . . . please, please help me. He said he would go to the police, tell them about you, tell them about the forged papers, he's really sick."

Magda sighed, threw on her coat, said she would come and see the old bastard, get a doctor if he needed one. "This is the last time Ruda, you don't come to me for anything, understand?"

Magda took the old man's pulse. He was alive, just, but she doubted that he would last long. She told Ruda to strip him and stuff his clothes into his case. Ruda did as she was told. Magda collected all the pitiful possessions around the room, scooping everything into an old sack. She then opened a cupboard. Jeczawitz moaned, his eyes opened, and he begged Magda to help him; she gestured for Ruda to grab his legs, and they heaved him into the closet, drawing his legs up, pushing and shoving him into the tiny space.

"He's alive, Magda, he's still alive, what if he gets out?" Magda snatched a piece of rag, stuffed it into his mouth. "Hold his nose, *hold his nose so he can't breathe, you stupid bitch!*"

Ruda pinched his nose as he twisted and made weak attempts to push her away; then his chest heaved, once, twice. . . . Still Ruda held on to his nose, then he gurgled, and there was no more movement. He was dead. Magda looked around the room, saw the old knife, and picked it up. "Use this, cut it out."

Ruda was panic-stricken, not understanding.

"The tattoo, his number, they can trace who he is, cut it off his arm, and hurry up. I'll take his case, dump it, just clean everything up, cover him up, shut the door."

Ruda averted her face as she sliced into his frail arm, hacking at the skin. The knife was serrated, it seemed to take a long and terrible time. Magda tied a knot to close the sack, and shouted for Ruda to hurry. "Gimme the knife, come on!"

Magda left Ruda, telling her to make sure to leave nothing that could be traced back to her. Ruda pushed the cupboard door shut, pressing her body against it. But his hand was caught, and she had to open the door again. It was then that she saw his old cloak and threw it over his head, slamming the doors shut. She got a block of wood and dragged it against the cupboard, then bricks, anything she could lay her hands on. She scrambled in the filth and dirt. Ripping up newspapers, she lit a fire, stacking wood on top of the papers. She closed the heavy door to the room, and prayed the fire would ignite.

The fire smoldered, and it was the smoke that eventually drew the attention of a passerby. The fire was put out, having only partly gutted the room. Anything of value still intact was swiftly taken. A new occupant was ready to take over the squalid room, but the police boarded it up. The dead man remained undiscovered for weeks.

Magda was almost surprised when Ruda showed up; she poured her a vodka, straight. Ruda was still shaking as she thanked Magda. She told her she would work for free, she would do anything Magda wanted. Magda laughed, told her she just wanted her gone, and to clear out fast.

"I've no money, I've nothing."

"That's how you came sweetface, so that's how you leave. I reckon I have done more for you than for anyone else in my life, why I dunno, but I'm a Gemini . . . what star are you?"

"I dunno, I don't know when I was born, we were in hiding when they took us, my sister . . ."

Magda cocked her head. "You got a sister, sweetface?"

Ruda felt icy cold, as if her body were slowly freezing. She couldn't speak, the room began to spin. "Sister? . . . sister?"

When she came to Magda was sitting next to her, on Magda's red satin bedcover.

"Jesus Christ, sweetface, where in God's name have you been? You went out like a light. I've had smelling salts under your nose, even lit a feather . . . you gave me a fright, I thought you were dead!"

Ruda smiled weakly, and reached for Magda's hand. Magda held the dirty skinny hand in hers. "You got to go, Ruda, I can't let you stay here, I want no more troubles than I got. You can have a bath, get some food from the kitchen, but then you are out!"

"Don't throw me out Mama, please . . . please, I need you."

Ruda had reached up, held the big fat woman, smelled her heavy perfume. She wanted to lie in this woman's arms, wanted her to comfort her, and Magda rocked her gently. "I can't let you, it's too much of a risk, just get yourself cleaned up, like a nice good Mama's girl."

Magda had cupped Ruda's face, and then on an impulse kissed her lips. She thrust her tongue into Ruda's mouth. She started smothering her. She took Ruda's hand and put it under her skirts, between her big fat thighs. "Oh yes . . . yes, push your fingers inside me, Ruda, yes . . . yes!"

Magda sweated and moaned, and Ruda pressed and could feel the wetness dripping from Magda, seeping down her thick thighs. She began to moan and groan as she climaxed, and then she sighed . . . her body shuddered. Ruda prayed it was over, she could hardly breathe.

Ruda had to wait for Magda to finish bathing before she could wash. Magda tossed her a few clothes from a trunk, and told Ruda she could have them. They were good clothes, hardly worn, and Ruda clutched them tightly. Magda dressed in one of her tents, slipped on some gold bangles, and redid her makeup. "Go on, sweetface, get yourself all cleaned up and out of here. When you're through, come into the office. I'l give you some money, don't expect a lot, I need every cent I earn, but I'll see you have enough to get to another big city, maybe give you a few contacts."

Ruda slipped into Magda's bathwater, it was still quite warm. She soaped her body and leaned back. She dreamed of the lion tamer, Luis Grimaldi. She had to get to America, she had to find Kellerman, she had to find Luis Grimaldi wherever he was.

Ruda buttoned up the dress, it was too short, and the neckline gaped on her thin shoulders. She had been given a pair of under-pants, the crotch hung very low, they were many sizes too large, but they were silk. She put on a nice plaid coat with padded shoulders, then she went to the dressing table to brush her hair and see if she could find a safety pin to close up the neckline of the dress.

She looked over the dressing table dusted with powder, there were pots of cream and makeup jars everywhere. There was a large box full of beaded necklaces and cheap bangles, but no safety pin. Ruda inched open the small drawer under the mirror; in a leather jewel box she saw rows of rings. She picked one up and squinted; it was gold. She looked over the rings again. They were Magda's famous diamonds, the rings she wore on every finger.

Ruda took a handful and started for the door. Then she went back and took a necklace, stuffing it into her pocket. Her heart was pounding. She opened the door and crept down the stairs, past the kitchens and the rest rooms. She saw no one, but as she reached the entrance to the club, she heard voices. Magda was giving the barman hell because he was not watering the drinks enough.

Ruda ran out and down the street in a panic, not sure which way to go, or where. She kept putting her hands into her coat pockets, making sure the rings were there.

She went to a club she had worked at with Rudi and spoke to the manager, who gave her the once-over. She was looking very classy . . . he touched her coat. "Found yourself a rich American, have you?"

Ruda smiled. "No, something better, I got people, a family with money, and they want a contact for passports."

The manager shrugged and said he couldn't help her, he knew of no one dealing in foreign documents or currency.

"Kellerman. I want to talk to Kellerman, I know you know him, and I know he's somewhere in the Kreuzberg district. Now you tell me, or I tip off the authorities, I know this club is a contact drop."

Ruda found Kellerman sitting in a bar playing poker. It had been a long walk. She didn't have money for a taxi, even for a bus.

Kellerman didn't recognize her, and she didn't remind him where they had last met. He took her into a back room and looked her over, leaning against the wall as if he were some American movie star—all three feet of him.

"So what do you want?"

"Visa, passport, tickets to America."

He laughed out loud. "Oh yeah . . . what makes you think I can get them?"

Ruda sat down and swung her leg, her legs were good, and she inched up her skirt.

"Friend told me, I got something to trade!"

Kellerman touched her knee. "Baby, if it's your cunt, forget it. What you want costs a lot more than a fuck!"

"Maybe I've got a lot more."

Kellerman shoved his hands into his tiny pockets. "Let's see what you got."

Ruda was no fool, she had stashed the bulk of the stones under a broken-down truck outside the bar. She took out only a couple of rings, and held them in the palm of her hand. Kellerman picked one up, examined it, then prodded her palm with his short squat finger. "Good stones . . . but this isn't enough."

"I have more, a lot more, and I've got a marriage license."

"You'll need birth certificates, inoculation, visas, passport, then tickets . . ."

Ruda felt her heart drop. How much was this going to cost? She held out her hand again. "I've got more, a necklace, diamonds . . . how much do I need?"

Kellerman touched her palm again, and then he pushed back

the sleeve of her coat and saw the tattoo. She tried to withdraw her
wrist, but he held on to her. "S'okay, I won't hurt you . . . where
were you?"

Ruda bowed her head. "Does it matter?"

"I guess not, all that matters is you survived, eh? I'm not
prying—see, I got one too."

He lifted his sleeve. Then he flushed and pulled his cuff down.
"I don't show it to anybody . . . I was at Birkenau."

She virtually whispered it. "So was I."

He looked up into her face, and reached to touch her cheek with
his short stubby hand. There was no need to speak, there was mutual
understanding in their eyes, it was not compassion, or love, it was
a kind of solidarity. Ruda kneeled, and Kellerman cradled her in
his arms. Still they did not speak, and it was Kellerman who broke
the embrace. Stepping back he said, softly: "Never get down on
your knees for anyone. Look at me, show me a fist, show me some
fire in those eyes . . . I'll get us out of this shit. Get up, up on your
feet, girl." He began to pace up and down, short, blunt steps.

"We got to find a buyer first, sell the stones, turn them into
cash, then we can do the deal. If you got more like the ones you
showed me, we can get enough."

"We? I don't understand, why we?"

He gave her a cheeky wide smile. He had perfect white teeth,
and his face was cherubic under the thick black curly hair. "Yeah,
that's the deal—Ruda, you said your name was?"

"Yes, Ruda—" She could not say her recently acquired last
name.

"The deal is, Ruda, I get the documents, make all the arrangements, but I want to come with you. We both go to America, and
I'll get us a license. We get married, you go as Ruda Kellerman,
it'll make it a lot easier. I already got my papers, I just never had
enough dough to get out of this shithole."

She hesitated, then smiled. He looked up at her. "You know
when you smile, it changes your whole face."

"Same could be said of you."

He chuckled. "I guess maybe we've neither had too much to smile about, but have we got a deal?"

She nodded, but then held her hand up. "But it's just a marriage of convenience, right? And where the stones go, I go? Agreed?"

He laughed, and then swung the door wide with a flourish. "Let's go, partner. America here we come!"

✦　✦　✦

It had taken two nerve-wracking months. Ruda and Kellerman stayed in his small rented room. He never made any advances toward her; instead they played cards and he taught her how to read and write. They felt safe together and they liked each other. He found out about the magician, and said she would come to no harm, he would take care of her. And he did. He pocketed a lot of the money for himself, but he kept his promise, he got them to America.

Magda had sent all her boys searching for Ruda, sure she would turn up on some street corner. The days turned into weeks, months, and Magda had to admit she was wasting her time searching for the little bitch. But she never forgot Ruda; every time she slipped a ring onto her finger she remembered her. She had never told anybody of her part in the murder, but she had kept the knife—as a memento, a warning never to turn soft on any of her tarts, or on anybody else for that matter. The knife had traveled from apartment to apartment, club to club, until she had stowed it away. Somehow she knew that one day Ruda would come back, one day she would see her again . . . and when she did, she would think about cutting her throat open.

✦　✦　✦

Magda ran her nail along the serrated edge. She had been right, she had come back. But when she had seen her, it was strange . . . she hadn't hated her, she had really wanted to talk to her. She had been ready to forgive, but Ruda had played a stupid game, pretending she couldn't understand German, that she didn't know Magda. Well, the baroness, or whoever Ruda pretended she was, would be sorry. This time she wouldn't be able to hide, there would be no place in Berlin where she could take refuge. Remembering it all made her head throb, she searched for aspirin.

Eric rushed back into the office. He was soaked. "I lost her, she was going from club to club, she was very drunk. Then I went in one door, and she must have walked out another; she disappeared."

Magda hurled papers from her desk. "You fucking little queen . . . all you had to do was follow the bitch!" Her face was puce with rage.

"I followed her up and down the fucking streets. I'm soaked— it's comin' down in torrents out there!"

"Get out of my sight, you useless piece of shit!"

Eric leaned on her desk. "I'm all you've got, you big fat cow. You haven't got a friend in the world, Magda. I am the only person who can put up with you."

"There's the door, Eric, and that thing attached is the handle. Turn it and walk. Go on, I don't need you, I don't need anybody— I never have. I have never depended on anyone or anything but me! Because that's all I've ever had, *me, I made me and my money is mine!*"

Eric hesitated, and she laughed—her heavy phlegmy laugh. How many years had he put up with her? But he had no place to go, and he did have an easy life. Besides, she couldn't last many more years. She was eighty, maybe even more. So he laughed, and she held open her arms, her mammoth body shaking.

"Come on, make up, give me a hug."

He let her embrace him, her beads clanking against his head. He could hear the rattle of her chest, the hideous breathing he had lain next to for fifteen years. She settled back on the cushions and said she'd start calling the clubs, she'd soon trace her.

"Who is she? I mean what's so important about her?"

Magda dialed, and waited. "She stole from me, Eric. I was like a mother to that girl, and she pretended she didn't know me. Well— she's going to know who I am."

Eric eased off his tie, removed his Gucci loafers. They were encrusted with mud around the edges. Magda made call after call, club after club, getting angrier as she described Vebekka in minute detail, down to the cape with the sable trim. She kept on saying it was urgent, she had to find her.

Eric took off his socks, his feet were cold. He was so intent on inspecting his feet he didn't even observe anything strange; he only looked up because the room was so quiet. She sat well back in her chair, her head almost touching her bosom, a cigarette still burning in her fat hand.

"Magda? . . . Magda?"

Eric walked around the desk, peering at her. The poodle suddenly started pawing at her leg, wanting attention. Eric took the cigarette from her fingers, stubbed it out. He called her name again, then felt her pulse. He withdrew his hand, and gave her body a small push—she slowly sagged to one side, and her arm slid from the desk and hung limply over her chair.

He gave a small, dry laugh like a hiccup, and quickly covered his mouth. He shooed the dog away and it scuttled beneath the desk. He was about to rush out of the office when he remembered he was in his bare feet.

As he slipped his feet into his loafers, he had another good look at Magda, and giggled. It was his club, all his now, and he wanted to hug himself.

The phone rang. He hesitated, deciding whether or not to answer, and in the end he snatched it up. It was the barman at the Vagabond Club returning Magda's call. The woman she wanted to know about had just walked in. "It doesn't matter, Magda's dead," said Eric. He heard the shocked voice asking how and when, and he beamed, but kept his voice to a hushed whisper. "I have to go, I have to get the police."

"Jesus Christ, what happened?"

"Heart attack, I think . . ."

"My God, when?"

"Oh, about five minutes ago."

"Oh shit, will you be closing the club?"

"No . . . no I don't think so, she wouldn't have wanted that. Nothin'll change, just that I'll be running the show from now on . . . so, if you'll excuse me . . ."

Eric carefully replaced the receiver, looked at the peroxided head of his wife. He couldn't see her face, he was glad about that. He whistled to the dog, and grabbed it by the scruff of its neck. "Your life, sweetface, hangs on a thread. You had better be very, very nice to me." Eric didn't even notice the carving knife on Magda's desk as he walked out of the office.

15

VEBEKKA EASED HER way to the bar, the third she had come to. The champagne had dulled her senses, she was confused and disoriented, and she wanted something—anything—to wake her. The rain had begun again, a downpour. Her hair was wet, her cape soaked, but she pushed her way through the customers, calling to the barman.

Vebekka felt a man brush up against her. He smiled apologetically and then signaled to the barman, snapping his fingers impatiently. His heavy gold bracelet and thick ring shone, and his cheap suit and white polyester shirt gleamed in the fluorescent light.

"Is it raining again?" he asked, smiling, his teeth as white as his shirt. She could see speckles of dandruff on his shoulders, and she giggled.

"I don't speak German, I'm American—or French."

He spoke in pidgin English, leaning his elbow casually on the bar. He asked her if she would like a drink and she nodded, asking for champagne. He hesitated, and moved closer.

"It's very expensive here."

She looked at him with a half smile, and asked for a cigarette. He patted his pockets; she leaned against him and slipping her hand into his pant pocket, she withdrew a cigarette pack and giggled. Confident, he slipped his arm around her shoulders, and then as the barman came over he asked for champagne.

She drank the entire glass in one go, and banged it onto the bar.

"Let's sit down."

She shrugged and wandered off. Taking her by the hand he guided her to a booth, she tossed her cape onto the seat.

"What's your name?"

"Vebekka."

She drank another glass, again gulping it down as if it were water. He moved closer to her; his hand began to feel along her thigh.

She suddenly felt sick, and pushed his hand away, mumbling that she needed to go to the bathroom. He touched her thighs and behind as she eased past him. She stumbled, and he caught her.

"Maybe you need help . . ."

They headed toward the door marked TOILETTEN, and by this time he had one arm around her, the other feeling under her sweater. The door led into a small corridor, ladies' and men's toilets on either side.

Vebekka staggered into the ladies' room. She vomited into the bowl and as the room began to spin, her legs collapsed under her. She swore, pushing herself up against the wall. She began to pant, trying not to be sick again. The cubicle door opened, she hadn't bothered to lock it.

"You okay?"

"I have to go . . . can you call me a taxi?"

He closed the door behind him and locked it. "Sure . . . in a few minutes."

She didn't even attempt to stop him from pulling down her panties and heaving up her sweater, she just leaned against him. He undid his fly, and pulled her hands down to his penis. Her head lolled against him, and he dragged her panties further down, ramming her against the wall. She half laughed, she felt like she was on a train, her back rocking against the wall. She kept on half laughing as he rammed himself inside her . . . it was over, and she laughed louder. He buttoned up his fly, listened in case anyone had come in, and then unlocked the door.

"You call that a fuck? When's the next train through here?" She laughed loudly, and then slowly slid down the wall, her underwear around her ankles. The tiles felt nice and cool, she inched down, rested her cheek on the cold tiles.

She was hauled to her feet semiconscious; the man literally had to drag her out. He dumped her in the corridor and went back into the club. He crossed to the bar, told the barman there was a drunken woman lying outside the toilets, went back to the booth, snatched his champagne bottle and made his way out.

The barman had crooked his finger to the bouncer hovering at the main club entrance.

Vebekka was thrown out of the club and fell into the gutter. She staggered up and stumbled away. She managed to pull her pants up, but she had lost her cape and her sweater was half off. She walked in the pouring rain. She stopped and looked up, opening her mouth to catch the water . . . she felt almost happy.

Three skinheads passed, and began pushing and shoving her until she slid down against a wall. She put up her hands in a pitiful attempt to protect herself, but one kept kicking her, calling her a filthy whore. Finally they left.

Vebekka sat hunched for a while, and then slowly stood, supporting herself against the wall; she was violently sick again.

✦　✦　✦

The baron slammed the taxi door shut. Helen instructed the driver to go to the next club: So far they had been to four, each one more tawdry than the last. They sat in silence. Suddenly, Helen leaned forward and asked the driver to stop. Helen shouted: "I see her!"

She was the first out, catching Vebekka in her arms before she fell again. The baron took off his coat and wrapped it around her. "Put her in the back!" he commanded.

Vebekka rested her head against Helen's shoulder.

"Dear God, look at her face. Have you got a handkerchief, Louis? She's bleeding."

He handed her one. "Aren't we all . . . here!"

Helen gently dabbed the cut on Vebekka's forehead.

"She's been drinking!"

"Clearly!"

They arrived back at the Grand Hotel, Louis and Helen holding, almost carrying Vebekka between them. The manager rushed forward, but the baron brushed him aside.

"My wife fell. She is all right, just call the elevator please."

The bellboy stared; the woman was so drunk she could hardly stand. He eased open the grid and stepped back. The baron scooped

Vebekka up in his arms and Helen hurriedly opened the doors to their suite. Louis dumped Vebekka on her bed. She moaned, and turned her face into the pillow.

Helen knocked on Hilda's door. She would be only a moment, she needed to put on her clothes.

"It doesn't matter, Hilda, just put on a robe. It's the baroness, she . . . she's had a little accident!"

Helen rejoined the baron, who stood staring down at his wife. "Look at her, take a good look Helen . . . so much for your damned doctor."

He was so furious that he had to walk out. Helen followed him, closing the door behind her.

"Hilda's bathing her, her stomach's bruised, as if she's been kicked. Louis? Did you hear what I said?"

He stood with his back to her, his hands clenched at his sides. "She stinks like a whore . . ."

Helen poured a drink and asked if he wanted one, but he shook his head.

She sighed. "I blame myself. The moment we knew she had left the hotel we should have gone out and searched, we wasted time . . ."

He whirled around. "Have you any idea how many times, how many nights I've had to go looking for her? Searching every seedy run-down club, every red light district. . . . She's been found in alleys, in back rooms, she's been fucked for the price of a drink, and tonight was probably no different. You smelled her, she stinks of sex and booze and vomit—she sickens me, disgusts me, she's been picking up men . . ."

"You don't know that!"

He looked at Helen as if she were an idiot. "I don't? She has played these games for years, *for years!*"

"I don't think she knows what she is doing. Are you asking me to believe she likes what she has been doing? Likes to be beaten up, kicked?"

He snapped. "That's what she goes out for, Helen, she *wants to be treated like a whore, she likes it—she is a whore!*"

"Don't shout at me, Louis, I am right here, okay? And no woman likes to be treated like a whore, that is a ridiculous statement! Women who work the streets don't necessarily like what they are doing."

"Oh, please, Helen, don't . . . don't give me your psychoanalytical theories, I don't want them tonight, I don't want them—period."

"It is not a theory, it's a fact: No woman likes to be beaten, but if you beat her long enough, you will . . ."

He gripped her tightly. "I have never beaten, struck, or hurt her, I have had reason to, God knows I have had reason, you don't understand . . ."

"I am trying to."

The scream made them both freeze. Helen ran to the bedroom as Hilda came running out. Her face was stricken.

"It is happening again . . . please . . ."

Vebekka was rigid, her hands in fists, her teeth clamped together. The colors were flashing across her mind, terrible, bright colors, reds, greens . . . they kept on coming, blinding her, she felt as if her brain were going to explode.

Helen tried to talk to her, but the pain was so intense Vebekka didn't know she was there, all she wanted was for the pain in her head to stop. Louis went to the other side of the bed, leaned over his wife, and she rose up. Her scream was low, her hands were like claws as she hit out, clawing at the pain.

Louis backed away, his hand to his cheek. She had scratched his face, drawn blood. Helen ran to the door, shouting that she would call Dr. Franks. Vebekka was thrashing in the bed.

Hilda, terrified, hung back by the door, shaking. Helen called Franks, who said he would be there within half an hour. Helen slipped her arm around Hilda and whispered that she should go back to her room. Hilda clutched her hand. "She bit me, she bit my hand!"

Helen forced Hilda to show her her hand, and was shocked—the teeth marks were clear, deep red bruises were already forming.

"Dear God . . . run cold water over it, Hilda, and I'll get you a bandage."

Louis stood a few feet from the bed, searching his pockets for his handkerchief, then remembered he had given it to Vebekka in the taxi. He drew out a tissue from a box on the dressing table and dabbed his face. He stared at Helen's reflection in the mirror.

"Franks will have to take her into his clinic. I'm through, Helen, this is it."

Helen nodded. "Yes . . . yes, I think so too. I'll pack her things, maybe if I call him back now I can catch him before he leaves. Maybe he will be able to make arrangements tonight."

◆ ◆ ◆

The first number had made even Schmidt stand and applaud. Ruda was in perfect form—she was brilliant. She had been flushed with excitement as Grimaldi helped her change. Ringling's scout's in, did you know, Luis?"

He told her he did. "You got them on their feet, it was the cartwheel, you should have seen Zapashny's face, he was open-mouthed—I could feel his envy!"

She began to freshen her makeup. "Zapashny? What's he doing here?"

Luis laughed. "Getting jealous! I've heard Gunther Gebel-Williams is retiring, they must be looking for someone to replace him at Ringling."

She turned in a panic. "Oh God, he's not here to replace me, is he?"

"Don't be silly, you'll see them coming here in droves to get to Ringling's man—get him to see their acts, bribe him, you know the scene."

Ruda brushed her hair, her hands shaking. Luis held out her black shirt, but she pushed it aside, pulling up her tight black jodhpurs. She stamped into the gleaming, polished boots, then she held out her arms as he eased the shirt over her head, careful not to mess her hair. She buttoned the collar. "God, I'm so nervous . . . this is supposed to be a dress rehearsal!"

"Everyone else is nervous, too, you can bet on it. You look wonderful! Now—make them get on their feet for the next number. You pull it off and we'll be in New York, I guarantee it!"

Ruda checked her appearance, tightened the wide black leather belt. She breathed in deeply, forcing herself to relax. All in black, her hair drawn away from her face, her eyes thick with black eyeliner, she looked like a cat herself, her strong lithe body taut with nerves.

"Okay, I'm ready . . . how long have I got?"

Luis checked his watch and told her she had plenty of time. All the acts were running over, everyone was playing up to the visitors, pulling out all the stops. She tucked in her shirt, and gave herself a nod of approval. "Okay, I'm ready."

Luis stood back and smiled. "Good luck! I'll be right by ringside. You'll need an umbrella, it's pouring."

Ruda took out a black umbrella and carefully sidestepped the big puddles as she hurried to the ring. Luis ran from the trailer, entering the big tent via the audience flaps. He made his way to ringside, and sat waiting. The clowns were chasing and tumbling after each other, skidding on the plastic floor covering—an electric car burst into flames as they reached the finale. The lights dimmed . . . it was strange to end in silence; usually the sound of thunderous applause accompanied the clowns, along with shrieks of laughter from the children.

Luis looked up to the viewing box. The Ringling Bros. scout stood with his back to the ring, talking animatedly to someone drinking champagne.

The crew moved like lightning, clearing the props, rolling the floor covering, raking up the sawdust. The ringmaster announced the Polish group of bareback riders, and they virtually stampeded into the ring—twelve of them, wearing brilliantly colored American Indian headdresses, whooping and screaming. The lights followed the riders, picking them out as they formed a fast-moving semicircle. Luis watched his boys getting ready to erect the safety cages around the ring.

✦ ✦ ✦

Dr. Franks, carrying a small medical bag, waited impatiently by the elevator at the Grand Hotel. He barely gave the bellboy time to open the gates before snapping that he wanted the Baron Maréchal's suite. As the elevator ascended, he checked his watch, silently hoping the ambulance would arrive quickly.

Helen opened the doors, and they hurried to Vebekka's bedside. "She's been quiet for about fifteen minutes."

Franks nodded, and Helen closed the bedroom doors. "She left the hotel, she's been drinking."

Franks felt Vebekka's pulse. "How did you let that happen?"

Helen flushed. "She seemed so well, we were going to dine in the restaurant, and she was dressing—the next moment she had left. . . ."

Franks drew back the bedclothes. "Have you given her something? Anything to sedate her?"

"No, nothing, she was acting up, as if she were having some kind of epileptic fit, and then she calmed down."

Franks took out his stethoscope and checked her heartbeat. "How did she get these bruises?"

"We don't know . . . we found her in the street."

Vebekka moaned softly. Franks sat on the side of the bed. "Are you awake? It's Dr. Franks. Well, what have you been up to, huh?"

"I went out . . . I had too much to drink!" She looked past Franks to Helen, and turned away.

"Would you please leave us alone, Helen?"

Franks waited until Helen had left the room, and then he leaned close. "What were you up to?" he repeated.

✦ ✦ ✦

The baron sat impatiently in a chair, his foot tapping, waiting for Franks to come out of the bedroom.

"What in God's name is he doing in there?"

Helen looked toward the bedroom. "They're talking."

The telephone rang and she answered it. The ambulance was waiting downstairs.

Franks came out and closed the door gently.

"The ambulance is downstairs."

He nodded, placing his bag down. "She's sleeping now, she's exhausted."

The baron kept his voice low. "I want her out of here, to-night."

Franks sat on the edge of the sofa. "She remembers everything she did, where she went, even the name of the clubs—Mama Mag-da's!! Notorious old woman. She remembers, Baron."

The baron pointed to his cheek. "She knew she did this?"

Franks shook his head. "No . . . she remembers up to the point she was brought into the hotel. Would you like me to look at the . . ."

The baron interrupted: "Mine is just a scratch, but she bit Hilda's hand. Don't you think maybe you should call whoever is necessary and take my wife away?"

"I am not sure . . ."

"I am, Doctor. I want her out of the hotel, tonight."

Franks turned to Helen and asked what she thought. She hesi-tated. "If I hadn't seen with my own eyes, seen how violent she was, how incredibly strong, neither of us could hold her down . . ."

"I see," Franks interrupted. "You know I hate to put her in a hospital, be it mental or otherwise. I really think some interesting things came out of the session today, and I would very much like to continue."

The baron stood up. "I refuse to take any further responsibility for my wife. If you wish to take her to your clinic, that is up to you, I want her out of here."

"Out of your life, Baron?"

"*Yes . . . yes!*"

Franks looked at his watch. "Very well, I will take her. She can stay at the clinic."

He opened his bag and sifted through some papers. "I want you to read these and sign them before you release Vebekka into my charge. This will mean it will be my decision to certify her, if, and only if, I feel there is nothing more I can do. Of course, you will have to cover all financial costs for her to be sent to . . ."

"Doctor, just give me the papers." The baron took them to the desk and searched for his pen. Franks looked to Helen, raised his eyebrows slightly, and then went into the bedroom.

Vebekka was lying with her hands resting on the cover. She turned to him, and smiled. "I'm hungry."

Franks took her hand. "Vebekka, I am going to take you with me to my clinic. There is no need to be afraid, but I think it will be for the best."

She closed her eyes. "Oh God, what did I do?"

Franks kept holding her hand. "Nothing too bad, but you need to be cared for, need to—" Her hand began to grip his tighter, he was astonished at her strength.

"It's coming back. . . ."

Franks could not release his hand. Her body twisted, he tried to stand, but she was so strong she pulled him down beside her; she was panting, her body began to go into spasm. The pain in her head . . . she saw them coming again, the bright lights, the colors. Frank wrenched his hand free and ran to the door. He shouted to get the ambulance attendant up immediately, then returned to the bed. She looked at him helplessly, opening and shutting her mouth, unable to tell him what was hurting her. . . . Her hands were shaking as she touched her temples. On and on went the piercing flashes of color.

Franks leaned over her. "Tell me. Tell me. What is it?"

Her mouth was open wide, but her face was frozen with terror, like a mask; the cement was creeping upward, reaching her knees, her stomach, pressing down on her chest. Any moment it would reach her neck, and though she could hear Dr. Franks, could see him, she could not communicate, could not tell him the oozing, thick whiteness was inching up into her throat, suffocating her. Franks saw her eyes glaze over, her hands became rigid. He turned with relief as the attendants arrived with the stretcher.

The baron watched from the doorway as they wrapped blankets around his wife, eased her stiffened hands to her side, and then strapped two thick leather belts around her.

✦   ✦   ✦

Luis moved closer to the arena. A single spotlight followed Ruda. The tigers moved in a circle around her in the darkness. She gave the command for the circle to break, for the tigers to form a pyramid on the stacked plinths.

Ruda was sweating. She issued a command to Roja, but he kept running, picking up speed. "ROJA UPPPP UPPP . . . BLUE . . . BLUE . . ." Roja suddenly sprang back, and Ruda continued the commands as, one by one, the tigers moved to their plinths. Blue, red, green . . . the spotlight widened and they were all in position. Ruda shouted "Up!" and they sat back on their haunches, their front paws swiping. She gave the command "Down" and they perched. With her left hand she gave Mike the signal to release the lionesses. They came down the tunnel within seconds, and she had to repeat her commands over and over again since they refused to get on the plinths.

Luis could feel the sweat trickling down his back; he gripped the steel bars, swearing at himself. . . . It was his fault, she was right, the new plinths were throwing them off. Luis raised his eyes to the viewing room. Zapashny was speaking to the Ringling Bros. scout, pointing to Ruda, then at himself. No doubt he knew she was in trouble, and would be only too pleased to give his professional opinion, only too eager to tell the scout how much better his act was.

The lionesses were on their plinths. Ruda gave them the command to rest their front paws on the pyramid above them. Once, twice, they refused, snarling and growling. The tigers hissed, but they stayed in place. Mike got the signal to let the two massive male lions enter the tunnel.

Three positions at the top of the plinth were still to be filled. Two lions ran on either side of Ruda; as rehearsed she looked toward the tunnel, bent down toward one of the lionesses as if asking a question, then turned to the plinths: three places, only two animals. She walked to the tunnel, followed by one lion, and whirled around to admonish him. Then, she looked down the tunnel, she got a nudge from him. She turned and wagged a scolding finger.

The children would be screaming by now, hysterical with delight watching the big cats tease her. Ruda put her hands on her hips in mock anger, and ordered the two lions to get up on the plinths.

It happened again. Both refused to jump, once, twice. Grimaldi wanted to scream out, but Ruda held her own, she was calm. Again she gave the command: They obeyed and Grimaldi sighed with relief. He looked up to the viewing box, the Russian was watching intently; he had to appreciate the exceptional training required to assemble a pyramid constituted by sixteen tigers, four lionesses, and two lions, all seated.

Ruda gave the signal for Mamon to be released, and he came down the tunnel at full run. He came to Ruda, as if he were late, and lay down in front of her as he had been taught to do. He rolled over, legs in the air. Ruda stamped her foot, pointed to the plinth, and Mamon rolled and rolled.

Unrehearsed, two tigers started to swipe at each other. She moved in their direction and shouted, and they turned on her. She yelled once more and they calmed down. Now she began the carefully practiced routine with Mamon, pointing to the twenty-foot-high plinth. He looked up and shook his huge head, she wagged her finger at him, and he whirled around and pretended to run back down the tunnel. Ruda grabbed his tail and began to pull him back.

Mamon and Ruda had a tug-of-war; throughout, she continued to issue commands to the cats on the plinths. Mamon appeared to be in good form, he didn't hesitate over a single command. To an onlooker, he seemed to be performing faultlessly, but Ruda could sense his impatience; like any star, he seemed to be pacing himself. He followed the routine very well, right up to the final command when he was to jump to the highest peak of the pyramid. The rest of the cats were seated, under control, and waiting. Ruda called out again, and then again. "RED—YUP . . . MA' ANGEL UP, UP!"

Mamon tossed his head.

Luis knew Ruda could not hold the pyramid formation much longer. The other cats were beginning to sense Mamon's unrest.

Suddenly he backed away and stared at Ruda, then crouched low on his haunches.

Up in the viewing box, all three men were on their feet, looking down into the ring. Ruda glared at Mamon. "RED-RED-RED . . . MA' ANGEL!"

Suddenly he leaped forward, as if he were going for her, then like lightning he veered off and sprang from one step to another, up and up, until he was on the top plinth, up on his haunches. At a command all the cats rose. They formed a mountain of brilliant colors. Then, in perfect order, they jumped down. Roja, in the lead, took them down the tunnel.

As rehearsed Mamon held his position at the top. Ruda now slapped the bottom plinth with her hand, ordering Mamon down. He shook his head. Ruda sat down with a shrug of her shoulders to the audience while, behind her, Mamon moved down plinth by plinth. Ruda was issuing commands—"RED-GREEN-BLUE"—pretending she did not know he was directly behind her. At this point, urged on by the ringmaster, the children would always scream out, *"He's behind you!!"*

Mamon leaned back, balanced himself, and then gently put his front paws on her shoulders. Ruda mimicked surprise and swiveled, virtually in his arms. Mamon was fully balanced on his own haunches—Ruda would not have been able to sustain his weight—it only looked as though he were resting against her. Slowly she slipped her arms around him in an embrace. The spotlight narrowed and zeroed in on them, until it framed them like lovers, Mamon's huge body overwhelming Ruda's. She gave a command that told him she was stepping away; at that point, he came off the plinth. As she took her bow, she extended her left hand toward his mouth. This was very daring—more dangerous than if she had put her head into his mouth: That was done by the trainer placing his hand over the animal's nose—the animal certainly wouldn't shut his mouth if he couldn't breathe! Mamon, however, held her hand gently in his mouth as she continued her bows. Finally, she pretended he was dragging her to the tunnel. . . .

The lights dimmed while the men ran to dismantle the arena. When they came back on, Ruda took her bow. Grimaldi looked up to the viewing box. The scout from Ringling Bros. was applauding. Grimaldi punched the air with his fist.

Ruda made sure the animals were back in their cages, fed and settled for the night before she made her way back to the trailer. Luis had helped first dismantle, then stack and prop up the cages for the following night's show. He returned to the trailer with a bottle of champagne.

Ruda came in, her shirt soaked in sweat, and he swept her up into his arms. "They were applauding, they were cheering you!"

She smiled, and slumped onto a bench. "They asked to see me right away, but . . . get me some bandages and the disinfectant, quick!"

Luis looked puzzled.

"Just get it, I have to be over there in a minute."

Ruda unbottoned her cuff and removed the protective wad under her sleeve. There were deep teeth marks on her arm. Dark bruises were already forming.

Luis brought the first aid box and knelt down beside her. "Jesus Christ! Did he break the skin?"

"No, no, it's just bruised. It was tough out there, they were all acting up."

Luis looked up at her, and carefully pushed her sleeve up her arm. "You mean your fucking angel was, you'll have to cut that part of the act. Jesus God—he could have taken your arm off."

"But he didn't. Just put some antiseptic over it, then find me a clean shirt."

She put on an identical black shirt. The old one was torn, Mamon's teeth had ripped the silk. She flung a coat around her shoulders while Grimaldi went to get his, to accompany her, but she patted his cheek.

"They just want to talk to me, Luis, you wait here. I won't be long."

He stepped back, flushed, saying he understood. He'd wait, maybe cook up dinner. She smiled, said that she was hungry and left. He watched her holding the coat over her head against the steady rain.

Luis knew her arm must hurt like hell. She never ceased to amaze him . . . all the cuts and knocks she'd taken during training, but she had never complained. He put away the first aid kit, and then remembered the tin box he had taken from her wardrobe. He had better replace it before she discovered it was missing. She'd know he had taken it because he had damaged the lid.

Luis was about to try to press the damaged lid back into shape without opening it when his curiosity overcame him. He took a screwdriver and inched the lid open. There was their wedding ring; she had worn it only for a year, then she had taken it off, saying it cut into her finger. There was also another wedding ring, probably the one Kellerman had given her. Luis picked up their wedding license, still in its envelope. Under it he saw, tied up in a pale blue ribbon, a pile of neatly folded newspaper clippings, brown with age. At first Luis thought they were reviews. He untied the ribbon; the clippings smelled musty, the frayed creases almost splitting in two. Carefully he unfolded the first, and stared at the headline. MENGELE STILL ALIVE IN BRAZIL. He checked each clipping; every one referred to Josef Mengele, the Angel of Death. One article described how Mengele had made sure the chimneys of Birkenau were always heated by thirty fires. There were 120 ovens; each one could burn three corpses at a time. Three hundred and sixty corpses could be disposed of every half hour; 720 people per hour, 17,280 per day. Dr. Josef Mengele made sure the ovens were filled to capacity; he alone had the power to choose who lived and who died, to direct the terrified masses to the gas chambers with horrifying efficiency.

Luis felt his blood grow cold, as he read the dates and was faced with the magnitude of the horror: May 1944, 360,000; June 1944, 512,000; July 1944, 442,000.

In her childish scrawl, Ruda had written on some of the articles: *Josef Mengele, Papa.*

Grimaldi refolded the scraps of newspaper. Some of the clippings described the diabolical experiments the Angel of Death had performed on small children, with or without anesthetic, depending on his mood or the availability of medication. Article after article described Mengele's passion for furthering the Aryan race. He had embraced cruelty beyond a sane person's credibility, he had been a madman. A piece of newspaper was wrapped around a small pebble, or stone, he couldn't tell; as he opened it, the cracks split the paper in two, as if this particular piece had been read and folded many times.

The article reported the alleged death of Dr. Josef Mengele. His body had been found on a beach in Brazil; the paper was dated 1976. The article discussed the possibility that the body found was not that of the real Josef Mengele; forensic scientists had left for Brazil to begin tests.

Luis began to restack the clippings the same way he had found them. He tied them with the worn ribbon. Ruda had kept them as carefully as treasured love letters. He replaced each item in the tin box, rescrewed the back, and put the box back in her wardrobe. As he stepped off the stool, he remembered things she had said to him in rage . . . how he would never know the pain she had suffered, that her worst scars were inside. He bowed his head and sighed. True, he had never even attempted to understand, but, he told himself, Ruda had always been very reluctant to talk about her past.

He looked around the kitchen to see what he could cook, wanting to do something special for her. He decided to go out and buy groceries from one of the all-night shops. He wanted to start afresh, a second chance. If she secured the Ringling contract, they could have a new life. He wouldn't fight her anymore, he would fight for her.

He passed the meat trailer. The lights were on, and he went inside.

"Mike? I'm going out for some groceries. If you see Ruda, tell her I won't be long!"

Mike grinned, said the word was already getting around, the Ringling Bros. scout was having talks with Ruda. Grimaldi winked, and told him not to count chickens before they were hatched. He looked out, the rain was still pouring. "You got a spare umbrella, Mike?"

"No, Boss—I dunno where they all disappear to, but I got a rain cape you can borrow!"

Grimaldi shook his head, pulling up his collar. Mike continued chopping and said that his hat was around someplace, in fact he had borrowed it.

Grimaldi held out his hand. "Okay, I'll take your hat, I'll give it back later."

Mike shook his head. "No, I said I used yours, that old black leather trilby. Ruda said she hated it, so she stashed it in here someplace. She caught me wearing it!"

Mike searched under the table. "I dunno where it is now. I tell you what. Wrap one of the rubber aprons around your head!"

Grimaldi laughed, hunching his shoulders. "I'll wrap it around yours, son. Never mind, I'll make a dash for it."

Grimaldi ran to their Jeep and started to drive out. He passed the lighted administration offices and slowed down to look in at the window. He could see Ruda with the boss and the Ringling scout. They were drinking champagne, talking, and the Russian was with them. He stared for a while. He couldn't help feeling hurt, even rejected, but then he punched the wheel. "Go get dinner, go cook for your woman . . . come on, get your fat ass into gear!"

He was about to drive off when Ruda shouted out to him. She ran from the administration office, leaping over the puddles like a young girl. She yanked open the passenger door.

"I did it, Luis! . . . *I did it!! They want me to go to New York straight after this contract ends . . . !*"

She spun around, hands up, face tilted to the rain. "*I did it . . .* I did it . . . !!!"

"And if you stay out there any longer you're gonna catch pneumonia . . . come on—get in the Jeep!"

She dived inside and slammed the door, flung her arms around him. "Luis, I did it . . . he loved the act, he thought it was great!"

Luis said he would drop her off at the trailer, and go on in to pick up groceries, maybe some champagne.

"I've had champagne . . . just take me to the cages!"

"But you're soaked."

"I don't care, I want to see my baby . . . I want to tell him!"

Grimaldi drove her to the animals' tent, and she was out before he'd even stopped the truck. "Get me chocolate . . . *black chocolate!*" She turned back as he started to roll up the window, and cupped his face in her hands. "I told you Mamon was a good guy, didn't I?"

He had thought she was going to kiss him, he'd hoped she would, but then she was off. Mamon bared his teeth as she pressed close to the bars. "Angel . . . Ma'angel—what's the matter, huh?"

His eyes ablaze, he ripped his meat apart, his whiskers and jaws bloody. She rubbed her arm, suddenly conscious of it. He had held too tightly; tomorrow they would have to rehearse again; she would rework him, remind him she was stronger than he was. She remembered Luis's instructions: Never let them know how strong they are, never let them know their own power. Ruda stared hard at Mamon. "Until tomorrow, My Angel."

16

VEBEKKA'S ATTACK WAS unlike any Dr. Franks had witnessed. He was convinced it was not an epileptic seizure. He looked through her files and saw a report from a doctor dated 1979: "Periods of loss of consciousness . . . with serious convulsions. Epilepsy brain scan negative." Franks rechecked: The date of the attack coincided with the newspaper incident. He called Helen Masters.

She informed him that the newspapers were still in the package that had just arrived. Franks asked her to read the papers and look for clues, and call him first thing in the morning. Helen replaced the phone. Seeing Vebekka taken away looking so defenseless had upset her more than she liked to acknowledge, and yet she couldn't talk to Louis, he had asked her to leave him alone. The newspapers were in Louis's room; she would have to wait until morning.

She sat for a long time deep in thought, going over the meeting with Frau Klapps, and then she shook her head and went to her desk. Neatly written side by side on a piece of paper were Ulrich Goldberg's number in Philadelphia and Frau Klapps's office number in Berlin. Though it was very late, Helen Masters decided to dispense with proprieties and call Lena Klapps. The phone rang four times but no one answered. Helen decided that it would be best if she were to wait until morning.

She waited up, pacing the room and reading, until two o'clock in the morning. She decided then that the time difference would allow her to catch Ulrich Goldberg early in the evening. She excused herself for intruding, but explained that the baroness, Rebecca, his cousin's daughter, was very ill, and they needed to know as much about her background as possible to help her recover. Ulrich hesitated; he did not understand what assistance he could give.

"My cousin and I were not on friendly terms. It is a personal matter that I would rather not speak of with a stranger."

"Rebecca is *very* ill, Mr. Goldberg."

There was a long silence; then he told Helen that the rift was over religion. His cousin's wife, Rosa, had never converted to Judaism, and the couple made no attempt to bring up Rebecca as a Jew. This became a matter of bitter contention. Also, David Goldberg had achieved financial success, whereas Ulrich had failed. When he had asked David for help, it was offered only on condition that they accept Rosa into the family.

"Most likely you cannot understand what this would have meant, to me, to my wife and my sons. My wife is the daughter of a rabbi, and one of my sons was to be ordained. My cousin left me no option but to sever ties. It was a sad day . . ."

"Can you tell me about Rosa?"

Ulrich paused, and then said sharply, "She was very cold, aloof. Exceptionally intelligent, but deeply disturbed. She thought we were persecuting her husband when nothing could have been further from the truth. She was quite cruel to me and my wife about a small debt. For the last fifteen years of her life she was bedridden. I would say she was a deeply unhappy woman."

When Helen asked about Rebecca he took his time to answer. "They had a great deal of trouble with her in Canada, I was told, but she seemed to settle down in Philadelphia. All in all I've seen her maybe three or four times."

"Was she adopted?"

Ulrich Goldberg coughed, and asked her to repeat the question.

"Were you aware of the fact that Rosa Goldberg couldn't have children?"

"Yes, I guess."

"Then you *knew* Rebecca was adopted?"

"I was never told."

"Was it perhaps because she may have been adopted illegally?"

"As I already told you, we were not close and in Philadelphia we didn't see one another much. I was not privy to his affairs."

"Mr. Goldberg, I am very grateful to you for talking to me. If you think of anything which may be of help to my patient, please contact me. May I give you my number at the hotel?"

Helen gave him the information and then, almost as an afterthought, asked how well he knew Frau Lena Klapps. She was surprised to hear that he had never met her, he had traced her only via Rosa Muller's address book. The sole telephone number he found for her was at work, at the bureau of records. After the death of his cousin, he had wished to contact anyone who might know his cousin's heir. Not being in touch with Rebecca, he did not even know if she was still alive.

"My cousin left everything to Rebecca, and it was at his funeral that I last saw her. She refused to let me go into the house. At the funeral she spoke to no one. She left almost immediately after she was told she was the only beneficiary of David's will. We were disappointed, had a misguided hope that David would forget our differences . . . but he left everything to her. We knew he was rich, but the fortune was much larger than we could have guessed. Rebecca's husband's lawyers settled the sale of the house and business."

Helen hung up and began to pace the room once again. Louis had remarked on a number of occasions that Vebekka had inherited her father's estate. What he had never disclosed was that it was vast. If his lawyers had settled the estate, he had to know. . . . Clearly he had lied about not knowing her true name. Helen found herself wondering whether Louis wanted to divorce Vebekka, or simply have her institutionalized so as to gain full access to her money—or had he access to it already?

Helen's mind reeled. She knew she had to speak to Lena Klapps, but now it was truly far too late to call her. She decided the best thing was to see her before Frau Klapps went to work.

Helen jumped when she heard a knock at her door. It was Louis, he said he couldn't sleep, and excused himself by saying he had seen her light was on. He was hesitant. "I feel in need of some company."

Helen smiled, and said she was glad that he had come in because she was anxious to read through the papers. Louis looked puzzled for a moment, and then remembered the package. "Oh, yes, of course."

"I promised Dr. Franks I would look through them before to-morrow. We can do it together."

Helen followed Louis into his suite. He asked if she was hungry, and she realized that she was. "Yes, maybe a sandwich." Louis picked up the phone and asked room service to send up some seltzer water and chicken sandwiches, then he went to get the newspapers.

They sat at the large oval table. Louis took out five newspapers and chose *The New York Times.* "I was reading the first section, and Vebekka had the real-estate section. Helen? . . . Helen, did you hear me?"

Helen stared at him, her arms folded. "Why didn't you tell me? You've known all along she was Rebecca Goldberg! I just don't understand why you have lied to me!"

Louis looked for his glasses. Finding them, he slipped them out of their case. "Haven't we been through this?"

"No. Why did you never tell me Vebekka was an heiress?"

His eyes flashed angrily over the half glasses, but he spoke with detachment. "Perhaps, my dear, I did not think it was any of your business."

Helen was stunned. "Not my business? I see. Why am I here, Louis?"

He opened the paper. "Because at your suggestion, we brought Vebekka to Dr. Franks."

"And you didn't think it was *important* that I know her real identity? Louis, Ulrich Goldberg told me about the money, he said your lawyers settled the estate."

"They did, and very well. They have cared for my finances since I was a child."

The room service arrived and the seltzer water and sandwiches were placed on the table, but Louis continued to look through the paper, not acknowledging either the waiter or Helen as she poured his drink and put it by his elbow. She sat opposite him, and reached for the newspaper.

"If Vebekka is institutionalized, will you have access to her fortune?"

Louis still did not raise his head. "It's immaterial, there isn't much left. I presume the costs of keeping her in any kind of nursing establishment will eat into what little remains."

He continued turning the pages, muttering that he couldn't find anything that could possibly be of significance. His reluctance to look up and speak to her directly infuriated Helen. Suddenly, she reached over and snatched the paper from his hands. Louis tried to retrieve it, and in so doing knocked over the glass—it spilled over him and he sprang to his feet, snapping: "That was a bloody stupid childish thing to do!"

"Was it? . . . *Was it?!*"

He stared at her coldly. "Yes, it was." He removed his glasses, picked up a napkin, and began to wipe off his dressing gown.

Helen patted the table dry with a napkin. "I am trying to understand you. You knew all along Vebekka was the daughter of David and Rosa Goldberg, but you never told me, you simply stood by as I kept making inquiries like an idiot. You wasted my time! Now I find out your wife inherited millions—another small fact you deliberately withheld."

Louis burst out in fury, "Leave me alone, just leave me alone!!" Helen watched in exasperation as he retreated into his bedroom.

She collected herself and started to gather the newspapers. The front page of the *Times* had fallen on the floor. Helen bent down and picked it up. It was wet and she dabbed at it with her napkin. Her eye fell on a small article at the bottom right-hand corner. ANGEL OF DEATH FOUND. Helen glanced over the single paragraph: Josef Mengele, the most wanted Nazi war criminal, had been found dead on a beach in Brazil. . . .

Frenzied, Helen was looking through the other papers, searching each page, when Louis returned, shamefaced.

"Helen, I'm sorry. . . . You are right, perhaps we should talk."

She turned to him. "I think I've found it. Remember you told Franks how terrified she was of a dark angel? You said you heard her sobbing that night, just after the newspaper incident. Look at the bottom of the front page."

Louis took the stained paper in his hands. "What am I looking for?"

Helen leaned over his shoulder and pointed. "Angel of Death . . . Josef Mengele, it's mentioned in two papers, small paragraphs, but they seem to be a possible link to her screaming; to her nightmare of the dark angel!"

Louis read the articles while Helen paced up and down. "If she was adopted in Berlin, perhaps this is the connection. Louis, I am sure she was adopted . . ."

"I did not know she was adopted, believe me, I didn't know. Where is all this leading us? If you think there is a connection, what should I do?"

"Just be honest with me, trust me. You must trust me, because if you don't, then there is no point in my being here."

He took her hand in his and gave her a small bow. "I apologize. I am grateful to you. I don't really know how I would have coped without you."

His hesitancy was touching, he seemed so vulnerable. "I know what you're thinking, Helen. But my mother gives me a small allowance; everything is tied up in trust funds for my children. When Vebekka came into her money, it was a relief, it meant I could care for her and continue to live as I always had. My decision to have her institutionalized is in no way connected to her fortune—it's gone. In fact, I will be dependent on my sons for the upkeep of the château, the apartments."

"And your life, Louis? What about your life?"

"I still have my allowance, and I can sell the polo stable. It will break my heart, but if it comes to that, then so be it. . . . I think it is time we went to bed, if you will excuse me. . . ."

He slipped his arm around her shoulder. "Good night, Helen." He gave her a light kiss on the cheek.

She walked toward her bedroom, not even turning as she said: "Good night, Louis."

She was certain that one could be very easily drawn into a life of luxury, of Rolls-Royces, of fabulous restaurants, flowers and expensive gifts. Louis was a very handsome man, his light, almost careless kiss made her all the more aware of how much she was attracted to him, and how easy it would be to take their relationship one step further. Helen knew he had mistresses, but she also knew that such a life was not for her. Suddenly she faced her own loneliness. She had always justified being alone, thinking to herself it was her choice; she even considered herself a very private person.

"You are so private, Helen, that no one even knows you exist!"

She said the words out loud, to her own reflection in the bathroom mirror. She brushed her teeth, washed her face, and returned to her bedroom—everything was neat and tidy, the bed cover was turned down in anticipation. She lay for a long while staring up at the ceiling. It was time she returned to Paris. She had given enough of her time, and with very little thanks. But then she remembered Vebekka. It had been at her instigation that Vebekka had come to Berlin. Helen was too deeply involved to extricate herself. But from now on she would distance herself from Louis.

Helen left the hotel very early the next morning. She did not wake Louis, but left a note saying she would meet him at Dr. Franks's and to be sure he took the newspapers to the clinic.

Helen looked along the taxi stand and saw the chatty driver who had taken them to Charlottenburg. He was dozing in his Mercedes. She tapped the window, and got in beside him.

"Same address?"

"Yes, the same! Frau Klapps, I want to get there before she leaves for work."

"No problem, there's no traffic at this hour."

✦ ✦ ✦

Inspector Heinz was at his desk by seven-thirty and began to plow through the vast amount of paperwork. He worked on until eight-thirty, then opened the morning paper. There was a large article on the front page with a picture. MAMA MAGDA DEAD. He read the piece, turned to the next page, and then flicked back. Now *there* was a coincidence: He had seen Ruda Kellerman entering Mama's club on the same night Mama Magda had died. He scribbled a note on his ever-ready pad and continued to read, checking on the time because he wanted to be at the records bureau when it opened at nine.

Rieckert came in with a black eye and a Band-Aid on his cheek. Torsen looked at him, and asked what kind of trouble he had run into. Reickert sat down. "Acting on your orders, sir, we tried to disband the hookers working off from the trailers. We warned them and told them to move their trailers. Out of nowhere, four big bastards jumped out, armed with iron bars, and they bloody beat us up. Kruger is in the hospital."

"Did you make any arrests?"

"You must be joking. We hardly made it into the local station's courtyard. We radioed them to open the gates for us. The bastards chased us, were on our tail for miles, their car was a hell of a lot faster than ours: a big four-door Mercedes! When we got there they banged and hammered on the gates. Have you heard about the damage they did?"

"This is madness, are you telling me the pimps *chased . . . chased* the patrol car?"

"Yeah! . . . overtook us twice, it was a near miss, one got me through the window—I had to have a stitch, cut my head open!"

"Could you recognize them?"

Rieckert sat bolt upright. "I'm not going back there, they'd bloody kill me. They're huge, muscle guys!"

Torsen's attention returned to his desk. He looked down at the paper. "There will be war out there. Mama Magda's died, last night. Most of those trailers are hers, so God knows what's going to happen!"

Rieckert leafed through the newspaper. "She must have been worth millions, I'm surprised nobody bumped her off before."

"It was a heart attack, she was over eighty . . . and the size of an elephant."

Reickert made himself more comfortable on the seat. "They open tonight, will you be using your ticket?"

"Excuse me?"

"The circus, they gave us free tickets, remember? They open the big show tonight."

"I'd forgotten . . . yes, yes, I think I will use my two."

Reickert left for the kitchen and Torsen called the nursing home and asked to speak to Nurse Freda.

"I have tickets for the circus . . . tonight, I'm sorry it's short notice, but I was wondering . . . if you aren't on duty, if you would care to . . ."

Freda giggled that she would love it. She acted so pleased that Torsen blushed with embarrassment. They arranged to meet at seven.

Torsen issued his orders for the day, and said if he was needed he could be found at the records bureau. He left, taking one of the few patrol cars in good condition.

Tommy Kellerman was buried by a rabbi from the Oranienburger Tor area. His body was taken to a run-down quarter where Eastern Jews lived. No one attended his burial. The plain black coffin was taken from the morgue before sundown, as Ruda Kellerman had requested. The costs were forwarded to the station, and Torsen planned to pass them on to Ruda Kellerman, care of the circus.

✦ ✦ ✦

Vebekka had slept soundly, and had even eaten some breakfast. She found herself in a small, white-walled room, with an old iron bed frame painted white. The chest of drawers was also white, but a bowl of flowers provided some color. At the center of the door there was a keyhole, but no handle on the inside. A white tiled bathroom was off the room, but it had no door and no mirror. There was no telephone.

Dr. Franks drew up the only chair in the room.

"How are you?"

"I'm fine. Do I have to stay in this room?"

"Only for a little while, then we'll go into my study. You remember you were there yesterday?"

She nodded. Franks told her that her husband had called and he would be in after breakfast. If she felt like it she could have a bath and get dressed. If she needed help, all she had to do was ring the bell by her bed, and Maja would be with her in no time.

She put her head back and said: "They should never have brought me here, it's very closed in, I feel it. . . ."

Franks cocked his head, and held her hand. "Feel what?"

"I don't know, a presence. I've felt it before, but not this close."

Franks threaded his fingers through her long perfect slim hands. "Maybe we will find out what this presence is, make it vanish."

She gave him a sad smile. "They've sent me away this time, haven't they? Ah well . . . I suppose it had to come."

"You are not away, Vebekka, you are here, in my clinic, until we sort things out. You do want me to help you, don't you?"

Tears welled in her eyes. "I don't think anyone can help, I hoped . . ."

He came closer to her. "I want more than hope, my dear. I want what you want, I want you to get well, I want you to help yourself, and for you to help me help you . . . okay?"

He returned to his office and picked up his notes, carefully transcribed from the day before. He had underlined two passages:

1. Get me to lie down and talk to me, so I would be calm.
2. Put her in a cupboard and throw away the key.

These were Vebekka's own words, describing what her mother had done and had told her to do. Franks was sure that the key Vebekka's mother had told her to throw away was at the root of her problems. He was so engrossed in thought that he hadn't noticed right away that his phone was blinking. The baron had arrived, bringing the newspapers. He told the receptionist to show the baron in, a little irritated he was so early.

✦   ✦   ✦

Frau Klapps opened the front door while eating a piece of toast. She was about to slam the door in Helen's face, but Helen put her foot across the threshold.

"I know this is an intrusion, but I have to speak to you. Please, I won't take more than a few moments."

Lena turned and walked into the hall, pulling the door open. She led Helen into the living room.

"I have to leave for the bus in fifteen minutes!"

"I understand. I'd be happy to give you a lift to the bureau in my taxi."

Lena walked out of the room and returned carrying a cup of coffee, but did not offer Helen one. She stood with her back to the large bookcase.

"I told you everything I know. I don't see how I can assist you any further."

"You have worked at the records bureau for many years? Is that correct?"

Lena nodded. She picked at a stain on her skirt with her fingernail, the same gray pleated shirt she had worn on Helen's previous visit. She sat in the typist chair, looked to Helen as if to say, "You may continue."

"I have checked the hospitals for any record of your sister. You mentioned that she worked at one of the large hospitals just after the war, when she came back to Berlin. They all referred me to the records bureau. You head the bureau, don't you?"

Lena continued sipping her coffee. When Helen asked her just how long she had worked in the bureau, she swiveled slightly in the seat.

"You have no right to pry into my affairs, Miss whatever-your-name-is. I have told you all I know. Now please I would like you to leave."

"If you won't help me then you leave the baron and me no choice but to go over your head at the bureau. I want to know whether your sister adopted a child, and I want to know the background of this child. I don't care, Frau Klapps, if the adoption was legal or illegal, all I am interested in is to try to help a woman who lives in a nightmare."

Lena stared into her empty coffee cup; a small muscle twitched at the side of her mouth.

"We all have our nightmares."

"No, no, we don't. Are you telling me that a sister, a sister you grew up with, didn't make contact with you when she returned to Berlin, that she didn't try to see you?"

Lena looked up, her eyes filled with hatred—whether for Helen or her sister, Helen couldn't tell. She banged the cup down on the table.

Helen was losing patience; she didn't mean her voice to rise but she couldn't help herself. "All I want is to know more of Rebecca's background, I am not interested in yours . . ."

Lena whipped round. "Please keep your voice down, I don't want my husband to hear you!"

She clasped her hands together. "No one has ever been interested in me. When we were children it was always Rosa this, Rosa that. She was the beautiful one, the clever one. She had everything, looks, brains . . . everything. And you know something else? She was always happy, always smiling, as though she had some secret, something filling her life. My father doted on her, worshiped her . . . she broke his heart."

Lena tightened her lips. Helen remained silent.

"She refused to listen to him. He pleaded with her to break off her relationship with David Goldberg, it was very embarrassing for him, for all of us. My father was a very well-respected scientist, with many connections, my brothers—" She lifted her hand to her forehead, as if unable to continue. She turned her back to Helen and faced the bookshelves. "When Mama died, I cooked and cleaned and waited hand and foot on him. But he wanted Rosa, always wanted Rosa. She made a fool of him, a fool of us all, but she refused to listen . . . and then, then she became pregnant."

Lena remained with her back to Helen, her arms wrapped around herself.

Helen had to know more. "You told me Rosa had an abortion, but I need to . . ."

"It was not an abortion."

Helen half rose to her feet: Rebecca was their daughter after all?

"My father and my brothers locked her in the house, and my father . . . he performed the operation himself, he sterilized her."

Helen sat back, shocked.

Lena's hand shook as she patted the coiled bun at the nape of her neck, but she looked defiantly at Helen. "Rebecca is not my sister's child."

Helen's face remained neutral, but she pressed her hands firmly against her thighs.

Lena moved closer, and stood in front of Helen. "I lied to you, I did see my sister again. She was working at the main refugee hospital with children picked up from the streets, from the camps, from everywhere. It was my job to keep a record of how many, of their names—that is if they knew their names. My father and my brothers were dead. I lived in the cellar, in the rubble of our old home, for years . . . and I hoped, hoped she would come back one day."

Lena repeated the same dismissive wave, as if she were shooing away a fly. "One day, smiling, she drew this child forward, she said . . . 'This is my daughter, Lena, this is Rebecca.' "

Helen stood up. "You have a record? . . . the child's last name? . . . the adoption papers?"

"There were no papers, no documents. The child couldn't even talk. She came from Birkenau."

Helen closed her eyes, and pressed her fingers to her eyelids. Suddenly she heard a loud banging, and her eyes flew open. Lena was hurling books from the bookshelf.

"She left me, she left her family, and all I have are these . . . these, and a broken-down man! Rosa was happy, she was always happy!"

Helen reached for her handbag and picked up her coat. Lena began to weep uncontrollably. "Why, why did you come here? Go away, leave us alone."

Helen asked gently if she could offer Lena a ride; Lena shook her head, wiping her face with her hands. "No, just go away."

One of the large medical books had fallen by the door to the living room. It was an old volume, and it had opened to a picture of a brain, with diagrams pointing to the front lobe. *The World of Hypnosis*.

Helen picked up the book. "Hypnosis? Frau Klapps, do you

know if your sister was ever . . ." The book was snatched out of her hand before she could say another word. Lena held the book close to her chest.

"This was my father's, this was my father's book, go away . . . *Go away!*"

Helen left, the door slamming shut behind her. She ran down the steps to the waiting taxi.

* * *

Ruda was in high spirits, singing in the shower. She washed her hair and tied a big towel around it. She called out to Luis that she would be only a moment longer. He shouted back that coffee was on the table, he was going over to check the meat delivery truck, it had just arrived.

She whistled as she sat down to breakfast, fresh rolls and black coffee; the newspaper lay folded on the table with a large bunch of flowers. Luis had printed a card with "Congratulations!" scrawled across it; she smiled and poured herself a cup. She bit into the bread and opened the paper—then slammed it onto the table: MAMA MAGDA DEAD.

Ruda read the article, and then leaned on her elbows, staring at the fat woman's face. Then she laughed, it was very fortuitous. With Kellerman dead, it was as though luck were suddenly on her side. She had a contract with Ringling Bros., the show was to open that night, and she was feeling good. Even Luis had remained sober and seemed as pleased at her success as she was.

She finished her breakfast, then took a pair of scissors and cut out the article. Folding it neatly, she got up and went into her bedroom. She pulled up the stool, and stood on it to find her black box. She felt around the cupboard and took it out, putting it down on her dressing table. She bent down to fold back the carpet and get the tiny key. When she straightened up, her eyes fixed on the old box. She turned it around, and saw the scratches on the hinges, the indentation where Grimaldi had tried to force it open. She had replaced the lock after Tommy Kellerman had broken it, now Luis had done the same. It could be no one else. Luis.

She unlocked the box and knew immediately that the contents had been touched. Her heart hammered inside her chest as she took out the small ribboned pile of clippings. She slipped the new cutting under the ribbon, then relocked the box. She felt as if the contents were burning into her hand . . . the memories began, like scars opening, bleeding. . . .

✦ ✦ ✦

Inspector Heinz checked his watch, it was after nine. He asked the receptionist again if he could go into the records room, and she apologized. Frau Klapps was never late, and she was sure she would have called in if she was not coming. She suggested Torsen have a cup of coffee somewhere. Torsen scribbled a note asking for both records to be ready for him, together with any record of a marriage license between T. Kellerman and a woman of the same name, Ruda.

Torsen headed for Mama Magda's; he wanted to know who was taking over the club and to discuss the problem of the influx of prostitutes.

Eric was checking over an order for flowers while examining swatches of fabric for redecorating the club.

Torsen pushed through the beaded curtain, getting one string caught in his lapel. Eric looked up fleetingly, then returned to his color charts.

"I am Chief Inspector Torsen Heinz from the East Berlin sector."

Eric turned and sighed. "Not another one . . . the police have already been here this morning, and last night there were more police than customers. What do you want?"

Torsen asked if there was some place they could talk privately. Eric led him into Magda's office. It smelled of stale tobacco, as did the entire club. Eric perched himself on Magda's cushions and Torsen sat on the chair opposite the untidy desk.

"I would like to talk with you, since you are taking over the clubs. We must try and stop prostitution from getting out of hand. I believe Magda controls the . . ."

"Did. I am her principal beneficiary, Inspector, I was her husband, so let's get down to business—how much do you want?''

Torsen frowned. "I am issuing a warning, I am not here to be bribed, it is against the law. You were not attempting to . . .''

Eric screwed up his face, trying to recollect if he had ever seen this one with his hand out. He sat back and listened as Torsen said that four of his officers had been attacked and chased. Eric interrupted him.

"I'm sorry, I don't follow, you say your men were chased?''

Torsen elaborated. His men had been chased by four men in a high-powered Mercedes; the license plate was being checked. He was there simply to warn the new management that he would not allow such things to continue.

Eric pretended to be greatly concerned, and agreed that he would personally look into the girls and the pimps he knew that were working in the West.

Torsen was about to leave when he remembered to offer his condolences. Eric murmured his thanks with downcast eyes, and then regaled Torsen with the details—how he had been sitting exactly where the inspector was when she keeled over. . . .

"It was a strange night, there was this woman Magda insisted she knew, and the woman insisted she didn't know her. I think it was this woman's fault she had a heart attack, Magda really got agitated about her, screaming and carrying on, as only Magda could do. . . .''

Torsen rose to his feet, hand outstretched. Eric jumped up.

"Ruda, that was her name . . . shot out of here, and Magda hit the roof, wanted her boys to grab her, you know the way Magda was, but I'd never seen that woman before.''

Torsen hesitated. "Ruda Kellerman?''

Eric shrugged. "Don't ask me, but she put Magda in one hell of a mood . . . eh, I shouldn't grumble—she's dead, and I don't mind telling you, telling anybody, I've waited a long time for that to happen.''

Eric continued talking as he led Torsen out of the club. Torsen headed up the stairs and back to his car.

Eric returned to the bar, and snapped his fingers at the barmaid.

"Get me Klaus, I need to know who we've got working over in the eastern sector, how many girls et cetera. Do you think this plum color would look good on the wall?"

Not waiting for a reply, he returned to the office to order the fabric. It was a coincidence that Torsen had been sitting barely two feet away from the carving knife which had sliced through Jeczawitz's arm.

✦　✦　✦

Torsen waited as Lena put down the file disks for the rest of the J's. She then handed him two more files on Kellerman.

"Thank you, this is very kind of you!"

She nodded, but walked out without saying a word. Torsen followed her with his eyes, and then turned his attention to the files. Perhaps she had had a bad morning.

Two hours later, his back aching from straining forward to see the screen, Torsen got lucky. He found the registration of the marriage license between Rudi Jeczawitz and a Ruda Braun. Stamped across Ruda's name was NO DOCUMENTATION AVAILABLE. She had signed her name with a strange childish scrawl.

He was even luckier with Thomas Kellerman and his wife, also Ruda Braun. He took copies of both licenses and matched the handwriting. Ruda Braun's signature was identical to Ruda Jeczawitz's. His heart was pounding in his chest as he looked from one document to the other. He gathered the papers to put them into his briefcase. As he did so, he realized his newspaper was tucked inside; he was about to throw it away when he looked again at the MAMA MAGDA DEAD. The first line of the article now leaped out at him. "Last night one of the most well-known women of West Berlin's red light district, the infamous Magda Braun, know as Mama Magda . . ."

Torsen's head was spinning thinking of all the coincidences as he made his way back to the station. He was sure he had enough evidence to interrupt his director's holiday and ask for permission to arrange a warrant for the arrest of Ruda Kellerman.

As usual, the station was virtually empty, most of the officers having taken off for lunch. He had to wait five minutes before they opened the yard gates to let him drive in. Once in his office he began to lay out all the evidence he had accumulated to date. He had to make sure he didn't commit any errors. Ruda Kellerman was now an American citizen—and a famous performer. This would be his first arrest for murder, he could not afford to make a mistake. He ran his fingers through his hair, flicked through his streams of notes, and then tapped with his pencil. He should have commandeered the boots. He still didn't know if they were Grimaldi's or Ruda's, or if they were in this together. He swore, checked his watch; it was almost one o'clock. He needed to get a search warrant.

His phone rang, he snatched it up. It was the manager from the Grand Hotel, who wanted to discuss the nightly invasion of prostitutes outside the hotel entrance; they even walked into the foyer of the hotel! Torsen said he would send someone over straightaway. He was then caught up in endless phone calls: There were more burglaries from tourists' cars than they could deal with, but the backlog of work would, Heinz knew, eventually be finished. The rabbi called, asking when he would be paid for Kellerman's funeral. Torsen diverted the calls to the operator, and then told her that he had to go to the circus.

"Yes, I heard you and Rieckert have free tickets!"

"I'm going on business, I'll be using the patrol car, contact me directly if need be. Have you got someone to take over from you?"

"We've got three candidates, but this is a very old board, you have to have experience . . ."

"I want someone on that switchboard day and night, is that understood?"

The receiver was slammed down and Torsen stared at his phone; he hadn't had any lunch and it was already two o'clock. He picked up the rabbi's bill; he would use it as an excuse to talk to Ruda Kellerman, and then ask if he could take the boots. If he waited around for a search warrant, it could take hours.

✦ ✦ ✦

Grimaldi was looking for Ruda, he'd not seen her since breakfast. She was late for feeding time; since she always fed the cats herself, he was worried that something had happened to her. When he saw the inspector making his way around the puddles, he hurried toward him. "Is something wrong?"

"No, no, I was just coming to see you, or your wife. I have the bill for Kellerman's funeral costs; you recall she said she would pay it."

Grimaldi shrugged. "I don't know where she is, but come on inside."

Torsen stepped into the trailer, wiping his feet on the grid, noticing the boots weren't there. He sat on the bench turning his cap around and around, as Grimaldi opened the rabbi's envelope. He examined the bill briefly, and delved into his pockets. "I'll pay you—cash all right?"

The inspector nodded. Grimaldi counted the notes, folded them, and handed them over. "Not much for a life, huh?"

Torsen opened his top pocket, asked if Grimaldi required a receipt. He shook his head, and then crossed to the window, lifting up the blind. "This isn't like her, she's never late for feeding, I wonder where the hell she has gone."

Torsen tried to sound nonchalant, but he flushed. "Perhaps she went to Mama Magda's funeral."

Grimaldi stared. "Who the hell is she?"

Torsen explained, embarrassed at his attempt to be a sly investigator. "She was a famous West Berlin madam; she died last night at her club, Mama's . . . I believe your wife was there."

"What are you talking about?"

"She was at Mama Magda's—I was told about nine, nine-thirty."

"Bullshit! She was in the ring, we had a dress rehearsal. You got the wrong girl!"

Torsen pointed to the newspaper on the table. "It was in the papers this morning, Mama Magda . . . photograph."

Grimaldi snatched the paper and opened it. "I've never heard of her, and why do you think Ruda was there?"

Grimaldi looked at the paper, but the article had been cut out. He said nothing, tossed the paper back onto the table.

Torsen was extremely nervous, the big man scared the life out of him. "Do you mind if I ask you a few questions? I'm sorry to inconvenience you."

Grimaldi sniffed, and rubbed his nose. "She's never late!"

"Do you have a leather trilby, or a similar hat—a shiny black hat?"

Grimaldi turned. "Do I have a what?"

Torsen stuttered slightly as he repeated his question. Grimaldi shook his head. "No, I never wear a hat."

"Does your wife?"

"What? Wear a hat? No, no."

Torsen explained why he had asked, that the suspect in the Kellerman murder wore a shiny black hat. Possibly it was Kellerman's own hat, worn as a disguise.

Grimaldi sat on the opposite bunk, his legs so long they almost touched Torsen's feet. "So you think I had something to do with Kellerman's death? Is that why you're here?"

Torsen swallowed, wished he'd brought someone with him. "I am just following a line of inquiry . . . an unidentified man was seen leaving Kellerman's hotel."

Grimaldi nodded, his dark eyes boring into Torsen. "So why do you want to know if Ruda's got a trilby?"

Torsen tugged at his tie. "Our witness could be mistaken. Perhaps the person leaving, er, the man with the hat, was in fact a woman."

Grimaldi leaned forward and reached out to hold Torsen's knee. His huge hand covered the entire knee, and he gripped tightly.

"You suspect Ruda? I told you, she was here with me all night, I told you that, and I don't like these insinuations."

Torsen waited until Grimaldi released his kneecap.

"We also have a good impression of a boot, or the heel of a boot. Would it be possible for me to . . . to check the . . . if I could look at your boots, and your wife's boots?"

Grimaldi stood up, towering above Torsen. "The only boot you will see is mine—as it kicks your ass out of my trailer, understand? Get out! *Out! Fuck off out of here!*"

Torsen stood up, closed his notebook and stuffed it into his pocket. "I just need to check your boots for elimination purposes. If I am required to return with a warrant, then I shall do so."

Grimaldi loomed closer, his voice quiet. "Get out . . . come back with your warrant and you'll fucking eat it—get out."

Torsen slipped down the steps as the door slammed shut so fast behind him it pushed him forward. He returned to his patrol car, his legs like jelly. Next time he would get a warrant, but he'd send Rieckert in for the boots.

✦ ✦ ✦

Grimaldi went over to the meat trailer. All the trays were ready, Mike and the other young hands were finishing the preparation of the meat. Grimaldi leaned against the chopping board. "She still not shown up?"

Mike said nobody had seen her, but the cats were getting hungry. Grimaldi glanced at his watch, said to leave it another half hour. Then he looked at Mike.

"Eh, where did you say you put my hat?"

Mike chopped away, not looking up. "Mrs. Grimaldi took it from me, I dunno know where it is."

Grimaldi stood at the open door, cracked his knuckles. "You ever meet that little dwarf, the one that got murdered?"

Mike flushed slightly, because he knew that Mrs. Grimaldi had been married to that dwarf. He covered his embarrassment by carrying the trays out to the waiting trolley. "No, I never saw him."

"I think I did," said another voice.

Mike jumped down, not hearing the other young hand who was running water into buckets. Grimaldi turned, easing the door half closed.

"What did you say?"

The boy turned off the taps. "Day we arrived, I think it was him, I dunno, but he came in here, well, came to the steps, asked for Ruda, she was out by the cages."

Grimaldi leaned on the chopping table. "You told anyone this?"

The boy started to fill another bucket. "Nope, nobody's asked me!" He turned back to Grimaldi.

"I saw him later talking to Ruda, so I presumed she must have said he was hanging around here. Have they caught the bloke that did it, then?"

Grimaldi rubbed the boy's shoulder with his hand. "Yeah, they got the bloke, so don't open your mouth, we don't want those fuckers nosing around here any more than they need to . . . okay?"

The boy nodded, and Grimaldi went out. "I'll see if I can find that bloody woman."

Grimaldi walked through the alley between the cages, and then he stopped. She had lied, Kellerman had not only been to the circus, but he had talked to her! He shrugged it off; maybe she just didn't want anyone to know she had been married to him. He thought about the hat, and then his heart began to pound. He remembered seeing her in the meat trailer, the night of Kellerman's murder . . . she had been covered in blood, it was all over her shirt and trousers. Shit! He remembered asking why she wasn't wearing one of the rubber aprons. . . . He stopped again, dear God, he had been so drunk that night he wouldn't have known if she was in the trailer or not!

Grimaldi ran back, slammed the door behind him, and went into Ruda's bedroom. He opened the wardrobe, searching for the shirt, trying to remember what clothes she had worn that night, but gave up, he couldn't remember. He rubbed his head. What did that little prick want to check their boots for?

The sound was half moan, half sob, but low, quiet, it unnerved him. He looked around, heard it again. He inched open the small shower door; she was naked, curled up in the corner of the shower, her arms covering her head, as if she were hiding or burying herself.

"Oh, sweetheart . . . baby."

He had to pry her arms away from her head, her face was stricken, terrified. She whispered, "No . . . please . . . no more, please no more . . . red, blue, red, red, red . . . blue, green . . ."

Grimaldi didn't know what to do, she didn't seem to recognize him, see him. Her voice was like a child's. He couldn't understand what she was saying. Some sort of list of colors, the plinths? Then he heard distinctly:

"My sister, I want my sister, my sister, please . . . no more . . ."

He took a big bath towel, gently wrapped it around her, talked quietly, softly, but she refused to move. He tucked the towel around her and closed the door. The cats needed to eat if there was to be a show, their routine had to be maintained. He went back to the trolley, and for the first time in years he fed the cats. They were very suspicious, snarling and swiping at him, but they were hungry and the food was their priority . . . except for Mamon.

If Grimaldi even went near the bars, Mamon went crazy. He couldn't get within arm's length of the cage to throw in the meat. Grimaldi swore and cursed him, then got a pitchfork and shoved the meat through the bars. Mamon clawed at the fork, his jaws opened in a rage of growls and he lashed out with his paws. He didn't want the meat, he never even went near it, but prowled up and down, up and down, until Grimaldi gave up trying and returned to the trailer.

She was in exactly the same position, curled up, hiding now beneath the bath towel. He knelt down, talked to her, keeping his voice low, encouraging her to come out. He was talking to her as if she were one of the cats. "Come on out, that's a good girl, good girl, give me your hand . . . I'm not going to hurt you, that's a good girl."

Slowly, inch by inch she moved toward him, crawling, retracting, and he kept on talking, until she allowed him to put his arms around her. Then he carried her like a baby to the bed, held her in his arms and began to rock her gently backward and forward.

"It's all right, I'm here . . . everything's all right, I'm here."

He wanted to weep, he had never seen her like this.

"Sister, I want my ssssister. . . ."

She felt heavy in his arms as he continued to rock her, and then he eased the towel from her face; she was sleeping. He was afraid to put her down in case he woke her; he held her as he would the child he had always wanted, sat with her in his arms, and said it over and over.

"I love you, I love you, love you. . . ."

Then he saw the box on her dressing table, saw beneath the old ribbon the newspaper clipping, "Angel of Death," and he whispered, "Dear God, what did they do to you? What did they do to you, my baby?"

17

HELEN ARRIVED at Dr. Franks's apartment just as he was on his way out to see a patient. Helen asked if he could direct her to a library. He gave her a quizzical look when she told him what books she wanted to find. "My housekeeper will make you comfortable and bring you some coffee," he said. "I think you will find what you want in my library."

Helen was shown into Franks's living room. The comfortably furnished room was dominated by bookshelves. Helen moved slowly along the shelves, neatly alphabetized, until she found what she had been looking for.

Helen turned the pages slowly, sickened by what she read. At Birkenau Josef Mengele had used shortwave rays in an experiment to deter the rapidity with which cancer cells reproduced. Plates were placed on the female victims' abdomens and backs. The electricity was directed toward the ovaries, the doses were huge and the victims were seriously burned. Cancer invariably developed and subsequently the victims were sent to the gas chamber. The women suffered unspeakable agony as the shortwaves penetrated the lower abdomen. The bellies of the women and female children were then cut open, the uterus and ovaries removed to observe the lesions. Then the victims were left, with no medication or pain relief, to determine how long they would stay alive.

Mengele paid particular attention to women and young girls. His experiments purported to discover the fastest means of mass sterilization, which he would then describe in an impressive report he planned to send back to Berlin. His experiments had no apparent order, no rules. So-called gynecologists used an electrical apparatus to inject a thick whitish liquid into the victims' genital organs, causing terrible burning sensations. This injection was repeated every four weeks, and was followed each time by a radioscopy.

Sometimes the victims, selected women and young female children, were injected in the chest. The physician injected 5 cc of a serum—no one has ever discovered what it contained—at the rate of two to nine injections per session. The injections caused swellings the size of a grown man's fist. Certain inmates received hundreds of these "inoculations." Children were often injected in the gums, because Mengele wanted to speed up the reaction.

The Germans experimented with sterilization in other camps too. Once victorious, they could ensure that they would never again be threatened by a new generation of an inferior race.

Typhoid swept through the camp, then malaria. When Mengele realized Greeks and Italians were the carriers, he sent thousands of them to the gas chambers on the pretext of curbing the disease.

Mengele's experiments were of no scientific value, his actions were replete with contradictions. For instance, he would take every precaution during childbirth, only to send mother and newborn infant to the gas chamber.

Helen had to stop reading, she simply could not take in any more. She checked her watch, and began to gather the books. One book she had not had time to read was a slim volume, written by an Auschwitz survivor; it chronicled the work and brutality of Josef Mengele, and Helen was about to put it back on the shelf when she saw the words "Angel of Death." The nickname had been given to Mengele, she read, because he was always charming, smiling as he sent thousands to their deaths. Mengele wore white gloves, and his uniform was specially designed by expert tailors. He was exceptionally handsome, dark-eyed with high cheekbones.

She stared at his photograph. It was very unnerving; Mengele had Louis's haughty stare. But Mengele was a monster with no morals, no feelings; he sent babies to their death as easily as he sent men, women, even pregnant women. No one escaped him, except . . . twins, identical twins.

Helen looked at her watch again, she could not stop reading. Mengele had one passion, the author wrote, an experiment that he pursued in the privacy of his deathly hospital. Telepathy. He wanted to discover the powers of human telepathy, and he focused his experimentation on identical twins. Twins of both genders were taken from their families and placed in a camp hut. They were well fed and, according to the author, treated kindly.

Many desperate mothers pretended their children were twins, in a desperate attempt to "save" them, unaware of the sickening experiments that were awaiting those selected. Mengele personally inspected these children, and rewarded those guards who had "salvaged" twins from the gas chamber. Soon, guards would scream out at the tragic new arrivals, demanding whether there were any twins among them.

Mengele became frantic if a twin died during his experiments; he would send the other to the gas chamber, but only after he had dissected and matched the internal organs of the dead with the living twin. He operated on these children, sometimes without anesthetic; he switched their organs. When both were still alive he would starve one and overfeed the other to watch their reactions. Eight thousand identical twins passed through the camps. Only seven hundred children survived.

✦ ✦ ✦

Helen walked to the clinic, needing to breathe fresh air. But when she sat down with Franks in his office, she was close to tears.

"I'm sorry, perhaps everything I have told you, you know already. It's just—to see it written down in black and white, to read it, to know it happened, to read him described as 'kindly' . . . it is beyond my conception of a human being . . . I'm sorry."

Franks gave Helen a steady stare, and in a soft quiet voice said: "People in the camps lived one day at a time. To live through each day . . . one needed such courage, such toughness, and perhaps most of all, luck. Anyone who collapsed physically would die fast, or was finished off by the *Kapos,* block seniors, and the SS men— all experts in brutality. The ones who remained alive were, as a rule, young. Some of the older men who survived became used to camp conditions, got by as best they could. It was always worst for the new arrivals, since they had no idea what a concentration camp meant. The key was to discover the art of staying alive, and it was an art, Helen, unless you were exceptionally lucky. The survivors were mostly men with no scruples, those men were able to advance rapidly inside the camp. The most important thing was to ensure your survival: You filled your stomach with stolen rations, you became cruel and ruthless; if not, the hopelessness of your position gave you only one alternative, to run at the electrified barbed wire fences.

"Helen, I was one of those whom fate spared. But it was many, many years before I could come to terms with what I had been forced to become, simply to survive, many years before I was able to hold my head up high. . . ."

His eyes met Helen's before he looked away, clasping the carved wooden arms on the old desk chair. "I think the worst thing is that we forget—Germany, every German, should carry the cross of what was done. But memories fade, scars heal; and today's adolescents were not even born when this took place. This city, this country, is a monument to a savagery that still makes one weep with shame. But—life goes on. . . ." He hesitated a moment, as if about to continue, then decided against it. He motioned to the newspapers on his desk.

Franks told Helen the baron had brought them, they had spent time with Vebekka, and now he was gone for a bite to eat. He gave a half smile and a shrug of his solid shoulders. "He is very confused, guilty, I think, and perhaps frightened. Perhaps you would like to see her before we start, it'll give me a few moments to get something to eat. Are you hungry?"

She shook her head, picked up her purse. "I'll see her, I'd like to." She then reached over and touched his hand. Franks smiled.

"We all have our secrets, Helen, but thankfully for me, they are no longer a nightmare, but a reality. Whatever is in Vebekka's past must also become her reality."

It was a few moments after Helen had left the room before Dr. Franks looked to the old framed photograph on his desk of his parents and grandparents, his brothers and sisters. He was fourteen years old, it was his parents' wedding anniversary. There he was, leaning against his mother's chair, smiling to the camera and wearing plus fours, a hand-knitted sweater, and hand-knitted socks. He could remember their color, a mixture of brown and green wool. His shoes were dark, highly polished brown laceups. It was the only photograph that remained, just as he was the only member of the entire family who had survived.

✦　✦　✦

Vebekka was dressed, sitting on the edge of her bed staring out of the window. She didn't turn when Helen entered, but seemed to know it was her. "I'm glad you came, come and sit beside me."

She seemed very calm, very rational. "I asked Louis that if things don't go well for me, I asked if he'd make sure I had some sleeping pills. Of course he won't, he may think about it, but in the end he won't be able to help me, so, I'm asking you."

"Please don't ask me, I could not do that."

"I couldn't bear to be locked up in a little room like this for the rest of my life . . . and I know that is a possibility. I know, Helen."

She got up from the bed and walked around the small white-walled room. "You know what is so awful? I never know when it will take me over . . . and now, I can't stand it any longer, to see the fear in that sweet-faced Hilda, the same fear in my children's eyes, I can't tell you what that does to me, to know I've hurt them, but not to know what I have done."

Helen twirled her ring around her finger. "Do you remember what you did last night?"

Vebekka giggled. "Yes, I got very drunk, and I think I got screwed in a toilet, but that often happens to sane people, they get drunk and screw, don't they?"

Helen laughed softly. "Yes, I suppose so."

Vebekka was working her way gradually toward the door, and was directly behind Helen. Helen suddenly felt wary; and spun around. Vebekka was leaning against the wall, her eyes to the ceiling.

"I met this big fat woman, and she kept on calling me by somebody else's name. It was strange, frightening, because I knew I didn't know her, and yet I was sure I had been there before. Do you ever feel that way?"

"You mean déjà vu?"

"Yes, yes, that you are in a place that you have been to before."

Helen nodded, said she did sometimes, and Vebekka flopped onto the bed delightedly. "I feel it all the time!"

She rolled onto her back, her arms spread out wide. "You know Louis loves me, he told me so, he's like a child, like a schoolboy. I think he's . . . he's afraid, Helen."

She sat up and wrapped Helen in her arms. "Take care of him, please, and Sasha, look after my baby for me."

Helen hugged her tightly. "Now, don't! You talk as if you were going away, but you're not."

Vebekka rested her head on Helen's shoulder. "I feel as if I am, Helen, I am so frightened, please don't let him open the trunk, please tell him not to do that."

Before Helen could answer, Dr. Franks walked in. He bowed his head a little and gave Vebekka his arm.

◆   ◆   ◆

Torsen waited for the director to come to the phone. He cleared his throat in preparation for his speech, but the rasping voice impatiently asked him what the hell he wanted; this was his holiday, the first he had taken since he had been married . . . whatever it was had better warrant the interruption of his lunch.

Torsen began his labored explanation of the investigation into the murder of Tommy Kellerman, including the evidence he had gathered and his suspicions. At last he finished, turning to the last page of his copious notebook.

"And that's it? . . . Sounds as if it's all supposition to me. The woman has an alibi, she has no motive. She's an American citizen. You need more, you need an eyewitness, the one you've got says he saw a man not a woman, you're going on a fucking imprint of a boot! That's your main evidence, isn't it? Have you got the boots? Do you know if they're hers?"

Torsen stuttered out that he required a search warrant to get the boots.

"So you haven't got the boots? As far as I can tell you've got fuck all—and you've seen too many American movies."

Torsen asked the director what his next move should be. He was instructed brusquely to wait. The director told him that the woman was not going anywhere, she was performing at the circus, so until he had more concrete evidence, he should wait.

The director slammed the telephone down. Torsen was about to replace his extension when he heard the click from the switchboard, and knew the operator had been listening. He tore out of his office and stormed into her booth.

"You were listening to a private call! Don't ever do that!!"

She made a great show of removing the wires and plugs.

"I have a call for you, I was simply trying to put it through. This exchange is old, sir, and we need an extension buzzer . . . would you like me to place the call through to you now, sir? It's the manager of the Grand Hotel."

Torsen snapped at her. "Tell him I am busy, and to call back." He burst into his office, kicked the door shut, and swiped at his desk. His accumulated lists scattered, his notebook fell into the wastebasket, and his report sheets, neatly typed up for the director to inspect on his return, received the dregs of his morning coffee. "Shit! . . . *Shit!*"

He sat in his chair, refusing to clean up the mess he had just created. He knew Ruda Kellerman was guilty of murder, knew it, and he should have taken the bloody boots. . . . He opened his desk drawer, fished around for the free tickets. At least he had got something out of all the hours he had put in. Attached to the tickets was an advertising leaflet, a colored picture of Ruda Kellerman with the lions grouped behind her.

Torsen stared hard at her face, and then grabbed his coat. It was a shot, a long shot, but if he could break Ruda Kellerman's alibi for the night of the murder, then he knew he had enough to charge her, with or without the director's approval. His one hope was that the bus driver who had described the woman passenger the night Kellerman died might recognize her from the leaflet.

✦ ✦ ✦

The baron slipped into the viewing room, and Helen turned and smiled, patting the seat next to her. Through the glass they could see Vebekka lying on the sofa, eyes closed, a blanket covering her body.

"Rebecca, I want you to tell me about your mother, the way she used to say lie down, lie down and talk to me, so you could feel calm. Do you remember that?"

Franks waited. It had taken much longer this time to put her under, but now she was deeply hypnotized. He leaned forward a fraction. "Tell me about your mother, Rebecca, how she used to encourage you to—"

She interrupted him. Her voice sounded strangely tired.

"Yes, it was in the study, in Papa's study, the big couch, he used to sleep on it, when he was working late."

Franks waited again, then coaxed her to continue. "What did she used to say to you?"

"Close your eyes, listen to my voice . . ."

"Do you know why she asked you to lie down?"

"Yes, because of my nightmares."

"Did she get you up from your bed to talk to you?"

"No, we called them my nightmares, but I would not be asleep, they happened during the day."

"Can you tell me about one, about what happened?"

"Oh, Papa was playing his records, and . . . it started, I was very bad, I broke Mama's china, all her precious china, every single piece. It was the music."

"What kind of music would make you break your Mama's china?"

"I remembered it."

"What music was it? Do you know the name?"

"Wagner. He never played it again."

"Why do you think Wagner upset you so much?"

She whispered conspiratorially, "Uncle played it all the time!"

Franks looked to the glass, gave a shrug of his shoulders, and then remembered. "Your Uncle Ulrich?"

"No, no . . . Uncle, Uncle! My papa, papa!"

She tugged at the blanket, very distressed. Franks waited, and then gently told her to listen to her mama's voice, to stay calm. She sighed deeply. Franks leaned forward and checked her pulse. "Can you hear me, Rebecca?"

"Yes." She sounded very distant, very quiet.

"What did your mama mean when she said put her in the cupboard, and throw away the key?"

"Me."

Franks asked if Rebecca was in the cupboard. She grew agitated again. "No, it was my other me."

"You mean the one who broke your mama's china?"

"Yes, put her in the cupboard, lock away the key, forget her, foget the bad Rebecca, she was a bad girl, she did bad things."

"Is Rebecca locked up, is Rebecca in the trunk with chains on?"

She started to struggle. Again he told her to listen to her mama's voice, to stay calm. Again she calmed down, and he checked her pulse. She was going deeper and deeper.

"What is it in the trunk that frightens you so much?"

Her face crumpled like a child's as she started to cry; kindly he repeated his question again. She tossed and turned, and mumbled something that he didn't understand. He asked again, and this time the pitch of her voice was higher.

"My sister's in there."

"Why is that so bad?"

"Because I ate her."

"You hate your sister?"

"No, no, I ate her."

She twisted her body, squirming, and then she began to sob, and her words tumbled out. . . . She had eaten her sister, they told her she had eaten her, that was why she was fat, she had eaten her alive.

Franks told her again to listen to the calming voice of her mama, and slowly she rested, her head leaning forward.

"But you know that is impossible, people don't eat each other."

Her voice was strong, it took him by surprise.

"Hah! You don't know, you don't know . . . they stack the

babies up, big piles of babies, and they put them in the ovens to eat them. *Hah!* See, you don't know . . . !"

"Did you see that, Rebecca?"

"Yes."

"And this person, this person inside you, did she see that?"

"Yes, we see it, we see it."

Franks looked to the two-way mirror, and gave a small shake of his head. "Does this person . . ."

"Sister, she is my sister."

"Ah, yes, she is your sister?"

"Yes! . . . Yes!"

"And she is inside you because you think you have eaten her?"

"Yes. Yes . . ."

"Does she have a name?"

"Yes . . . Yes!"

"Will you tell me her name?"

Vebekka's face contorted with pain. "Ruda . . ."

Franks looked toward the one-way glass. Both Helen and the baron stared back at him though Franks couldn't see them. Helen jumped up and left the room. She called Maja, asking her to give a message to Franks. Maja asked her to write it down, and then she put her fingers to her lips and entered the study area.

Helen returned to the viewroom and stared at the glass. Maja gave Dr. Franks the note. He looked to the glass and smiled.

"Is Ruda your twin?"

"Yes! Yes, Ruda and me, me and Ruda . . . !"

"I see. I understand now, and Ruda is inside you?"

"Yes! Yes . . ."

She tugged at the blanket, her brow furrowed.

"What are you doing? . . . Rebecca? Can you hear my voice, tell me if you can hear my voice? Rebecca?"

She was in a dark airless room, it was so cold outside, but in this room it was always hot.

"Hot, I'm hot . . ."

"Where, can you tell me where you are?"

She replied without hesitating, as though she were reciting, "Hospital Wing C Thirty-three, Hut Forty-two."

Franks removed the blanket, but she didn't seem to notice.

She was watching the white gloves lay out the cards, one by one. She could smell him, he was telling her to concentrate on the cards. "Remember the cards, Rebecca, keep on looking at the cards, remember the cards. . . ."

Franks asked Rebecca to listen only to his voice, but she sat up, bolt upright, and her head began to swing from right to left and back again.

Franks asked what she was doing. She didn't answer. He told her to hear her mother's voice, to stay calm.

She kept on shaking her head from side to side, a set expression on her face. She saw the white gloves move to the curtain. She wasn't ready, but the curtain began to move slowly back, and then she saw Ruda, held up by the woman. Ruda gave Rebecca a tiny wave of her hand. She was so thin, her body was covered with sores, and Rebecca had to remember.

Franks became concerned—Vebekka was still sitting upright, tugging and pulling at her clothes.

"Rebecca, listen to me, can you hear me?"

Again she did not answer. She had to get the colors right, she had to get the colors right. The same persuasive voice spoke to her again, "Feed your sister the colors, feed them to her, make her call out the colors and she will have sweets, she will have toys . . . come along, my pretty one, the curtain will be closing, I am closing the curtain."

Vebekka lay stiff. Franks checked her pulse, it was very fast. She was not responding to him, she seemed not to hear him.

"Rebecca, listen to me, move forward in time, listen to my voice!"

She spoke in German, still paying no attention to Franks. Her words came out like small rapid bullets:

"*Red, red, blue, red, green, blue, red, blue, red, red, red, red, red, blue, green . . .*"

Franks pressed his emergency button for Maja to enter. Vebekka continued to call out the colors as Maja moved to his side. She carried an electrode box.

The baron looked to Helen. "Dear God, what is happening in there?"

Helen, though unsure, tried to calm him. "It's all right, he knows what he is doing."

"*Red, blue, green, red, red, red, green, blue, red, green . . .*"

Vebekka suddenly became quiet, her voice trailing away, her head slumped onto her chest.

"Rebecca, *Rebecca,* can you hear me?"

She murmured, and he signaled to Maja that he didn't need the electrode box. He moved close to the sofa, held Vebekka's hand and spoke softly to her, bringing her back to consciousness. She seemed drugged, her voice slurred. "Yes, I can hear you."

Franks asked where she was. She remained silent; he asked again, telling her to listen to his voice, her mama's voice was gone, just to hear his, he wanted her to recall what she had just been telling him, it was important she remember. . . .

They watched her as she slowly came to, and then Dr. Franks held her hand. "Sleep for a little while now, sleep and when you wake up you will feel well, you will be able to discuss everything we have talked about, do you hear me?"

"Yes, I can hear you."

"Who am I?"

"Dr. Franks."

"Who are you?"

"My real name is Rebecca, but I call myself Vebekka."

Franks relaxed; he dabbed his head with his handkerchief. He asked Maja to sit by the sofa, then walked out.

Helen and the baron joined Franks in his office. "Well, now we know . . . your wife had been hypnotized by her mother to forget something, possibly in an attempt to help her. But the outcome, as you more than anyone else know, has been catastrophic. She will need many sessions, we have just begun."

Helen could not sit, she started to pace the floor. "As you know, Mengele experimented with tiny children, in particular on identical twins, preferably females, but first he had to establish which twin was most responsive."

Franks took down a number of books from his shelves. "We will need to study all the records of Mengele's tests. Rebecca was repeating some kind of code—the colors were spoken not in French or English, but in German! Yet she has maintained she does not speak German."

The baron was visibly upset, and sat in a state of complete confusion. Not being able to stand it any longer, he blurted out: "I don't think you have any idea what you are doing. How can you go on with this? Don't you think she has suffered enough as a child? Now you want to take it a further step. I refuse to allow this, I refuse!"

Franks stopped him gently but firmly. "You cannot wish this, you cannot leave her in limbo. We have brought to the surface some of the horrors inside her and she will need extensive therapy to be able to control them and come to terms with . . ."

"*No,* I refuse!"

Franks looked at Helen. "Perhaps you need to discuss this in private."

Franks walked out of the room. The man needed some time to come to his senses. They had made incredible progress, and he was sure with therapy Rebecca could come to terms with her past.

He walked down the corridor to his study. Vebekka was sitting up, her feet on the ground, but her hair looked tousled, as if she had been deeply asleep.

"How is my sleeping beauty?" he asked gently.

"A bit shaky, but she's still here."

He opened his arms and held her. Her voice was muffled. "I want my sister, I want my sister."

He stroked her hair. "I know. . . I know, and you've hidden her away for all these years, haven't you? But you know now, you didn't hurt her, it wasn't you, Vebekka. It was not you."

She gave a sad smile, and asked for a glass of water. He went to a side table, and poured some iced water. "Your husband is very afraid for you . . . he wants to end the sessions."

She took out a cigarette and he lit it for her; she inhaled deeply. "Do you think this longing I have felt always . . . is it for Ruda?"

"Of course, she was part of you, she was your twin!"

She sat silently for a while, and then said, "I feel a terrible sense of loss."

"That is understandable, you have lost your safety net, your trunk, the one with all the chains, the one you were so afraid to open."

She stubbed out the cigarette. "What did they do to me?"

He crouched down in front of her. "We'll find out, we'll find it all out, my dear, and gradually you will understand. But it will be hard going."

She nodded. "I don't remember . . . I don't remember."

He smoothed her hair away from her brow—she felt hot. He stood up. Drink up, drink some water."

"I'm tired."

"You can sleep in here, no need to go back to the other room."

Franks tucked the blanket around her and waited as she lay with her eyes open. "Don't try and remember, just rest. We will take it stage by stage, year by year, until all the pieces are back in place. You have a lot to catch up on, your mama—"

"She wasn't my real mama, I know that."

He smiled at her. "I think you will repossess your past, I sincerely believe it, and there will be no more rages, no more violence. . . . You locked Ruda away, but she wouldn't lie quiet. Now you will be able to give her peace."

"Peace," she repeated. Her eyes closed. Franks let himself out, quietly. He asked Maja to remain close by and look after Vebekka.

Maja went to her office exactly opposite the study. She was just about to sit down when Helen called out to her.

"Do you have some aspirin? Baron Maréchal is feeling ill."

Maja went into the medicine cabinet, took out a bottle of aspirin, and got a glass of water.

The baron was very pale. He thanked her profusely. She smiled kindly and said it must have been a very difficult afternoon for him. She had been gone from her desk no more than five or ten minutes. When she sat down she saw that her purse was missing. She looked around her office, then in the reception area. She was sure she had left her purse by her desk, but went in the viewing room just in case. It wasn't there. As she looked through the glass into the study she realized with a shock that Vebekka was gone.

Maja ran back to the office. She called Helen, her voice in a panic. "Is she with you?"

Helen came out to the corridor.

"She's not in the study."

Helen ran into the reception. "Has the baroness been through here?"

The new young nurse looked up and smiled. "Yes, about five minutes ago."

"Did she leave the building?"

"Yes, yes, she said her taxi was waiting. Is there something wrong?"

Dr. Franks ran into the reception. "Maja has just told me. Is it true? Vebekka has gone, just walked out and nobody stopped her?"

Helen said that she could not have gone very far. She had no purse, no money on her. Then Maja explained that her purse was missing.

Louis looked up, his head pounding, as Helen walked in.

"We have to look for her. Vebekka just walked out. Nobody knows where she has gone, she's taken Maja's purse. We'll get a taxi and start searching the streets, Dr. Franks will stay here."

✦ ✦ ✦

Vebekka got out of the cab at the Grand Hotel. She handed Maja's purse to the driver. "Would you return this to the clinic— but in about an hour—they'll pay the fare for the delivery, thank you."

Vebekka walked to the reception desk and asked for her key. She hurried to their suite, locked the door and ran into her bedroom, took out a purse and then rifled through Louis' bedside table for some cash. She raced to the lobby where she asked the doorman to call her a taxi.

"Magda's, Mama Magda's, quickly please, I am in a great hurry."

She knew they would be looking for her, she had little time before she would be found, but she had to know why the big fat woman had called her Ruda. . . . She knew Ruda was free now, she had released her, and she felt a strange new sensation. The feeling of loss was disappearing because, she was sure, Ruda was alive.

18

LUIS HAD LET Ruda sleep, sitting by her at first, almost as if guarding her. He kept an eye on the clock; she had already missed the chance to have a pre-show rehearsal. He had explained her absence by saying she had a migraine. Would she be capable of doing the show that evening? Her first spot was eight-forty-five, and he knew that if she did not feel any better, he would have to withdraw the act.

"Luis? What time is it?" She stood in the doorway, her face very pale. She was shaking badly. He rushed to her and helped her sit down. "You've missed the rehearsal, sweetheart, but don't worry . . ."

"Oh God!"

She let her head droop as he slipped an arm around her shoulders. "They've been fed, and after last night's workout they won't need a run today. You just rest, I've made you a hot chocolate."

She closed her eyes, leaning on the bench cushions. He held out the steaming mug. She smiled, and pushed it aside with her finger. "You always burn the milk."

He crouched down in front of her. "What happened?"

She sipped the chocolate, and gave a wan smile. "Ghosts."

"You want to talk about it?"

She shook her head. He went and sat opposite her. "Will you be fit enough for the show tonight?"

"Try and stop me!"

He chuckled, but he was very concerned; she seemed to have no energy, her body was listless, her eyes heavy.

"Is it about the box? The tin box? I wasn't prying, I was looking for my old albums. I found it, I know maybe I shouldn't have opened it, but to be honest I didn't think you'd find out."

"You shouldn't have opened it, but you did, so that is that."
She put the mug down. "I'd better check on the cats."

"No, I've done it, there's no need, and the boys are there. You
just rest, gather all your strength for the show."

She nodded. He was disconcerted; it was unlike her to agree to
anything he ever suggested. He snatched a look at his watch; there
was still time. She stared through him, beyond him, her eyes vacant.

"I found you all curled up in the shower, I carried you in my
arms like a baby. Bet you haven't let anybody do that to you for a
long time, huh?" He was trying to make light of it, attempting to
draw her out.

"Nobody ever held me when I was a baby, Luis, nobody,
only . . . only my . . ."

He waited but she bowed her head. "Sister?" he interjected.
"You said you wanted your sister. I've never even heard you talk
about a sister before. I mean, were you dreaming?"

Ruda shuddered, and she clasped her arms around herself, staring
at the floor, her voice so soft he had to strain to hear her.

"You know when we went to the Grand Hotel, after we'd been
to the morgue? Something happened inside me. I had a feeling . . . so many years, Luis, I've tried, tried to find her, but—she
was called Rebecca. We were taken in a train, hours and hours on
a big dark train. Rebecca slept, but I kept guard over her, I watched
out for her, she . . . she didn't talk too well, I used to talk for her."

She leaned back with her eyes closed, remembering the noise
of the iron wheels on the rails. She could hear the rat-tat-tat of the
wheels and everyone crying, howling, screaming . . . they were
crushed and pushed and trodden on as the big doors were inched
back. Had it been days or hours? She lost count, but at last the rat-
tat-tat had stopped.

Rebecca was crying because she had messed her panties, done
it in her panties, she cried for Mama, but they had no Mama, she
was gone, and then they heard the voices, screaming.

"Women to the left, men to the right, women and children to
the left, men to the right. Neither of us knew right from left."

"Any twins . . . twins over here, twins here, dwarfs, giants . . . twins . . ."

Ruda was picked up and thrown into a group of shrieking women. Rebecca fought and shouted to her sister, and the guard had picked Rebecca up by her hair and tossed her across to another group. The screaming went on and on. Pushed and kicked, they were herded toward a long path, at the end of which were gates, big high gates. Fences, with barbed wire as high as the sky, surrounded hundreds and hundreds of huts.

Ruda dodged between legs, squeezed under the weeping women and screeching children. At the gates she caught up with Rebecca, holding a strange woman's hand. A guard started shouting orders, Ruda tugged at his sleeve.

"My sister, my sister!"

The guard looked from one to the other, then grabbed them and hauled them into the back of a truck, just inside the perimeter of the gates. *"Twins . . . Twins!"*

The truck rumbled and swayed over potholes and ditches, a truck filled with children, boys, girls, all shapes and sizes, identical faces clinging in terror to each other.

Luis sat next to her, he wanted to hold her, comfort her, but she kept leaning back with her eyes closed. He heard only part of what she was saying; she lapsed into silences, and then odd words came out, some in Polish, Russian, Czech, and German. She was seeing with her adult's eyes what she had seen as a tiny child: the carts of skeletons, the strange eerie women with their shaven heads . . . the screaming women giving birth on a stone slab, and the babies snatched away, the afterbirth still covering their tiny bodies, thrown onto a seething mass of dying babies . . . the weeping and wailing never ceased, and the cold icy wind never stopped, the snow and ice freezing the memories like crystals.

They clung to each other, slept together, and played together. They had no mother, no father, no brothers, no religion, no surname; all they knew was that they were sisters, Ruda and Rebecca. Protected by being a pair, they fought as one.

In comparison to the other inmates, the twins were fed well. They were given not only clean clothes but toys, and their childish laughter tore into the tortured minds of the rest of the inmates. Men and women clung to the wire meshing that segregated these special children and screamed abuse at them. They hated them because they were playing. Some mothers clung on in desperation to see the faces of their children, and some crept out into the freezing night, and twisted their rags into ropes to hang themselves with.

But the twins who were old enough to understand knew it would only be a short time before the innocent laughter stopped. They knew what was to come. They had seen the twins carried back to their bunks in the dead of night from the hospital. They had seen the tiny, broken bodies lifted from the stretchers, disoriented by the drugs and chemicals that had been pumped into their young veins. Those who knew wept in silence, because they knew that one day it would be their turn.

Gradually even the new inmates, the fresh arrivals, the ones as young as Ruda and Rebecca, began to understand. When the nurse called out the numbers to go to the experiment wing, they trembled in fear.

Papa Mengele had a particular liking for the two tiny girls; he singled them out regularly, to the jealousy of the other children. They had sweets, occasionally even chocolate.

Mengele was fascinated by the way they interacted. Rebecca, slow to talk, began a sentence and Ruda completed it. They often spoke and moved in unison. Their closeness absorbed him, and for many weeks he simply watched them play together.

Ruda reached out and held Luis's hand, clenching it tightly, as the words and sentences were dragged painfully from her memory. At times her voice was so low he had to bend over to hear her.

"She was always smiling. He even let her play with his precious white gloves; she would sit on his knee and hug and kiss him, and he said she could call him 'Papa.' But his eyes, Luis, his eyes were like the Devil's, and he would stare at me . . . I was afraid of him, I tried to warn her, I didn't trust him, and he knew it, too. I was always afraid of him, but Rebecca had no fear, and then, one day, he said he was going to show her something pretty. I tried to stop her, and she slapped me, said to leave her alone, she was going with her papa to see something nice, and she held his hand, and left me. . . ."

Ruda got up, went to the window and stared out, her hands hanging limply at her sides. "She didn't come back for three days. For three days my body burned, my head ached, I screamed with pain. I knew . . . I felt every single injection they gave her. They were hurting her. Eventually they brought her back, the nurse carried her in, pushed her onto the bunk bed. Her eyes were glazed, she was burning hot, and she just lay there. I didn't know what they had done to her. Her face was bloated, her belly distended, her cheeks were flushed. They didn't call us for a long time. I stole what food I could, slept with her in my arms, warmed her with my body . . . and just as she was better, able to get up, they came back for her. When they called her number, I took her place. But they knew me, and I was punished for trying to fool them."

Ruda covered her face with her hands, she couldn't tell Luis what they had done to her . . . but what had been worse was not being with Rebecca, and each day they had promised she would see her soon. They gave her no food, and every day they administered the interminable agonizing X rays, the electrodes attached to her head, the drugs. They burned her insides, kept on asking her questions she didn't understand, the same question over and over: "Tell us what your sister is doing, tell us . . . if you tell us you will be given sweets."

Ruda sobbed, wringing her hands. "I didn't know what they wanted, I didn't understand. I hurt so much, I was in such terrible, terrible pain, all I did was cry . . . Luis, they hurt me so much, and then . . . then they took me to this little room, locked me inside, all alone, nobody came to see me, nobody gave me any food . . . and then fresh pains began, my head, my arms, my knees were on fire. I screamed, louder and louder, begging them to stop, to stop hurting her."

Luis leaned closer. "I don't understand . . ."

She almost screamed it, her face purple with rage: "I felt what they were doing to her, I felt every pain. I knew what they were doing to her, because *I* felt it." She gave a sobbing laugh, and began pacing around the trailer.

"Papa was very pleased with me. They came to me then, and I was carried into another room. They gave me hot milk and cookies, and kept on telling me what a good girl I was."

Ruda stared from the trailer window, then pressed her head against the cold windowpane. "They bandaged my knees, put ointment on my legs and stomach, dressed me in clean clothes. Then they took me into his office, and made me sit in front of him, he had . . . a—" She turned back to Luis: "telephone, and he was smiling at me. They were playing music on a gramophone. He spoke to someone, told them to begin. Oh, Luis, I screamed out— my head, I said they were hurting my head, then my stomach. The more I cried out in agony, the more agitated he became, shouting into the phone, again . . . again, until I fell to the floor. Then he replaced the phone, picked me up and sat me on his knee, told me what a good girl I was. Then she came in . . ."

"Your sister?" asked Luis.

"No. Papa's assistant. She came in, and he said to her: This is the strong one. Say hello, Ruda, say hello to . . ."

Ruda slumped onto the bench, unable to continue. Luis reached out and drew her into his arms.

"Did you ever see her again?"

She whispered: "Through the glass window . . . they used to show me Rebecca through the glass. Her face was like a stranger's, she was fatter, more bloated, but she still tried to smile at me. Then they would draw the curtain, and she would be gone. The nurses told me that if I was a good girl, if I could tell them what Rebecca was thinking, they wouldn't hurt her anymore."

Luis held her close, his cheek resting against hers. She kept staring ahead, whispering. "You remember the silk scarves? The old magician? That's where I learned it, Luis, they said they wouldn't hurt her if I could name the colors, and I used to try so hard, try to tell them what they wanted to know, but they would never let me see her . . ."

"But why, what did any of it prove?"

"They wanted me to read her mind, they showed her all these color charts, cards, and . . . and I failed, I couldn't get it right. So many, they wanted so many. When I failed they would burn me, make me try again, and I did, because then they didn't hurt her; if they had, I would have known, but she wouldn't concentrate. I'd always been able to think for her, talk for her, but she didn't concentrate hard enough. And then one day I could see them clearly, one color after another. Papa applauded and shouted, and they let me see her. They told me I was a good girl, that I had saved my sister and if I continued to be a good girl she would not be hurt."

"Did they continue to torture you?"

She nodded. "Not so much—but they would not let me hold her. I was kept all by myself, but you know, I knew she was being taken care of, so it was all right. But then, I got so tired I couldn't, I couldn't do it. They took her away, it was my fault." Her voice was hardly audible. "They hurt her . . . but all I could feel was her terror."

Luis felt so inadequate, he held Ruda tightly. "You listen to me. From now on, when something hurts you, when you remember, you tell me. Because no ghost is going to touch you. I love you, Ruda, do you hear me? You have done no wrong, you have done nothing wrong, you can't blame yourself, you were just a child."

She broke from him, and gave him a strange look. He could feel her mistrust.

"It's true, Ruda, you have done nothing wrong! You have to believe that!"

She reached the door leading to the small hallway. "I had better rest before tonight."

"You sure you will be all right?"

She nodded. "I do care for you, Luis, you know that. I think I always have. Maybe, in my own way, I . . ."

She couldn't say the word.

"Ruda, maybe it's taken me a long time to realize just how much I need you, that I'm nothing without you . . . but I understand that you need me too, Ruda, and it makes me feel good."

"Don't tell anyone what I have told you."

"As if I would . . . but, remember, you have nothing to be ashamed of."

She gave him that look, her eyes slightly downcast. "I didn't tell you all of it, some things you can never tell anybody. You know why? Because nobody could really believe it ever happened."

"May I ask you something? Did you know Kellerman at the camp? Was he at the same place?"

"Yes, Kellerman was also at Birkenau. I didn't know him there . . . he had it bad, they made him fuck dogs for their entertainment—and you thought it was funny to make jokes about the size of his dick, didn't you? See, look at you, you don't really believe it, do you? Kellerman the clown, *haw haw* . . . they degraded him, defiled him, and treated him like an animal, haw haw. Kellerman was not a clown, not in his heart."

"You did see him, here in Berlin. Didn't you?"

She looked at him straight in the eyes, without a flicker of hesitancy to indicate she was lying. "No. I suppose he came to try and squeeze money out of me, but I didn't see him. Look, I'd better go and rest, then I'll check on the animals."

She closed the door of her bedroom. Grimaldi put her half-finished mug of hot chocolate in the sink, then strode across the trailer and rapped on her door. She pulled it open. "What?"

"That little prick of an inspector was here, he wanted to know about the night Kellerman died, something about a pair of boots, the ones he'd seen outside."

She shrugged, gestured to her closet. "He can take whichever ones he likes. Is that all you wanted to say to me? I got a lot to do . . ."

"I'll go and check the props—and Ruda, if you still have Kellerman's hat, get rid of it. They asked about that, a leather trilby . . . Mike borrowed it, he said that you had said it was mine. Get rid of it, Ruda." Grimaldi slammed out of the trailer.

Ruda kicked her door shut. "Damn! . . . Damn!"

She paced up and down. She had gotten rid of everything, she was safe, they couldn't link her to Kellerman's murder. Then she realized maybe the police had not made the connection, but Gri-maldi had. She stood with her hands clenched at her sides. "Damn!" She calmed down, ordered herself to remain calm.

✦ ✦ ✦

Torsen hovered around the bus station, checking his watch. He had to get back to his apartment, bathe and change, and collect Freda; he wouldn't make it if the bus didn't come soon. There was a sound of a car backfiring, and Torsen looked out. He hurried toward the driver as he slammed the door shut. "Eh, you'd better be careful, slam it too hard and the engine'll fall out."

Torsen smiled. "Could I have just a word?"

The driver nodded, but said he would have to make it quick since he was late. Torsen produced the leaflet. "Can you look at this, it's not a proper photograph, but it's a good likeness of the person we think may have been the passenger on your bus the night the dwarf was murdered. Remember we spoke about it?"

Again the driver nodded. "You know it's been a while now. I dunno if I can remember her, let me see . . ." He squinted at the picture.

"I'm sure I've seen this before . . ."

"But is it of the woman on your bus that night?"

"I have definitely seen this woman's face before, but whether it was her or not, I couldn't honestly say. I just took her fare, I didn't have a conversation with her. It could be, but I couldn't say it was."

Torsen slipped the picture back into his wallet. "Thanks for your time. Have a good night!"

He returned to his car, was unlocking it as the bus drove past. On the side of the bus out of Torsen's sight was a large poster—Ruda Kellerman's face about a foot high was posted up on the wall of the bus terminal.

Torsen threw up his hands. So much for a valued eyewitness. He drove back to his apartment. On the way he called in for messages by radio, and stated that he would be using the patrol car that evening. Rieckert radioed back to Torsen asking if he could pick him up. There was just his girlfriend and himself. Torsen snapped that he thought he was giving the tickets to his wife and kid. Rieckert laughed. "Na, they hate the circus . . . see you about seven, over and out!"

✦ ✦ ✦

Mama Magda's was empty when Vebekka walked in. She called out and, receiving no reply, descended the dark unlit staircase. She passed through the arch with the beaded curtains, called out again, and walked toward the office. Eric opened the door.

"I came to see Magda."

Eric squinted in the darkness, unable to see her face clearly.

"I want to talk to her."

"That would be very difficult. Who are you?"

Vebekka introduced herself, and Eric opened the door wider.

"Please, it is very important I speak to her."

Eric gestured for her to come in. "You're twenty-four hours too late. She died last night."

Vebekka leaned on the doorframe. "Oh no . . . no please, no!"

Eric offered her a chair, but she refused.

"Can I be of help? I've taken over the club . . . sit, please sit."

"She called me Ruda. . . ."

Eric saw how distressed Vebekka was. "Look, I'm sorry I can't help you."

Eric watched her leave, then remembered the purse. If she was who she said she was maybe she could cause trouble. He opened the drawer, picked up her purse and ran after her.

"You left this last night, your purse . . . no money, there was no money in it, okay?"

She stared at the bag, disinterested. Eric thrust it toward her.

"It's yours, eh, are you okay?"

She took the purse. She seemed close to tears. "It was perhaps just a coincidence, you see . . . Ruda, Ruda was my sister. The big woman called me Ruda."

"I can ask around for you, what's her last name?"

"I don't know."

Eric backed away; she was a nut. "Well I can't help you then, good-bye. Any time you're passing, drop in. . . ."

He made his way back, and heard a screech of tires. She had walked out into the street and a car had narrowly missed her, but she kept on walking, not even turning to the shocked driver.

✦ ✦ ✦

Helen turned to see the baron, who was out of breath, having run up from the reception. "She came to the hotel, went up to the suite, and then took a taxi. The driver has just come back. He said Vebekka went to 'Mama Magda's' and he's waiting to take us there now."

When they reached the club, Eric explained that the baroness had been there; he swore he had returned the handbag she left there the previous evening.

"We are not interested in that, all we want to know is where she went."

Eric explained she had come asking about her sister, someone called Ruda, and the next minute she had almost got herself killed walking across the street, straight into the traffic.

Eric followed them out to the sidewalk, and watched them as they, too, ran across the street amid blaring horns. He shook his head. Crazy foreigners, all crazy.

✦ ✦ ✦

Vebekka walked on, bumping into passersby. She turned into a churchyard, unaware of where she was going. Fragmented pictures kept cropping up in her mind. She walked into the church and sat in a row at the back. Rosa used to take her to church on Sundays, but her adopted father never accompanied them. Vebekka closed her eyes, remembering. She used to call Rosa "the woman"—she didn't know the name of the woman who worked at the hospital where they had taken her after the camp was liberated.

The woman had been very gentle. She had explained she was just examining her, to see if she needed any medication. She asked her if she remembered her name, but Rebecca was too terrified to speak; any moment she expected them to stick needles into her arms. When the needles didn't come, she lived in terror they would bring the electric pads, and she hid beneath the sheets for long periods of time. The woman would come every day with little presents, but Rebecca would refuse to take them. She knew it was a trick. After a few weeks, maybe even months, she began to believe she was safe; until they had taken her to the X-ray department, and she had screamed and screamed.

Rebecca had spent six months in the hospital before she was sent to an orphanage; she had yet to speak a word, but she had begun to get used to the nice woman's visits. The woman had explained to Rebecca that she lived in Berlin with her husband, that she was not a doctor, just helping in any way she could. She had held the frightened girl's hand, saying she wanted to help her, and that she would come to the orphanage to see her, if Rebecca wished. Rebecca had slowly nodded her head.

In the orphanage, the older children would steal her things, and pinch her. She was so fat—they called her a pig, a fat pig. They were too young, too bruised themselves to know she had been injected and tortured, to know that they had all suffered. Rebecca rarely spoke. She missed her sister, cried for her every night. Then, one day, the nice woman arrived with her husband. She asked Rebecca if she would like to live with them.

✦ ✦ ✦

There were many children to choose from, but Rebecca had touched Rosa deeply; she was also outwardly the most healthy of the children, and Rosa was confident that, in time, Rebecca would be able to overcome her terror.

They had tried to trace Rebecca's family to no avail; she could not remember her last name. They knew her first name only because one of the children told them. Rebecca left with the Goldbergs a year and a half after her release from Birkenau, but it was months before she started to believe they were not going to hurt her.

Rosa made the decision never to speak of Birkenau. What she had heard about the camp was too much for her to accept and she felt it was better for Rebecca to forget the past. They had a plastic surgeon remove her tattoo, and although the doctors and nurses had terrified her, Rebecca recovered remarkably quickly.

Three years after the adoption, Rosa was beginning to despair. Rebecca still hid food, peed on the floor, and wet her bed every night. She remained suspicious and noncommunicative, retreating into sulking silences for so long that Rosa began to despair. And she had suffered from nightmares: Virtually every night Rebecca woke screaming hysterically and would let no one near her.

At school she disrupted classes, had no friends, fought, spat, and kicked. She stole children's toys and lunch boxes.

She alternated between refusing food for days on end and gluttonous horrific binges; Rosa would find her sitting on the kitchen floor eating everything in sight—mustard, jam, raw eggs—anything her hands could reach she would stuff into her mouth.

Rebecca wore Rosa Goldberg down. No care, no love seemed to break through to her. She was as cruel and vicious to pets as to the smaller children at school. The Goldbergs began to think they had adopted a monster.

Therapy sessions followed, and partly helped; through therapy they discovered she had a twin sister.

Rosa had tried to trace Ruda in a desperate bid to help Rebecca, but it was a long, fruitless, financially exhausting search. Ruda, it was presumed, had died in the camp. There was no record of her leaving Birkenau, no record in any orphanage; she had, like thousands of others, perished.

David Goldberg was at his wits' end. Under the strain of caring for Rebecca, Rosa became a nervous wreck. As a last resort, when they arrived in Philadelphia, Rosa arranged a session with a hypnotherapist.

For the first time Rebecca calmed down. Rosa soon read every book she could find on the subject. She trained at a local hypnosis clinic so that she could hypnotize Rebecca at home. Gradually she began to erase from the child's mind the memory of the past.

Rebecca did not change overnight. There were setbacks when she remembered Ruda. But Rosa found a solution: She talked Rebecca into locking her sister away, so she would not come out and would not make her do bad things. She would lock her away and lose the key. From then on Rebecca was able to study and she caught up with the other children.

◆   ◆   ◆

Vebekka sat back, staring at the altar. She understood now why she had been so afraid for her babies, afraid they would be born with two heads, born twisted, with ropes. She had been too young to know about umbilical cords. She had seen the twisting baby ropes cut with rusty knives. With the fascination of a young child she'd watched the skeletal women deliver. She saw once again the hundreds of rows of jars containing deformed fetuses in the hospital.

In the silence of the church Rebecca remembered, too, the relief and joy she had felt in holding her babies, and in touching their perfect little bodies. Her voice echoed softly around the dark empty church. "I'm so sorry." She had never meant to hurt them, it was beyond her control.

She thought of Sasha, and for a moment was panic-stricken: sweet innocent Sasha. She remembered wanting Sasha to see what she had seen, but then, she had not understood why. She wanted Sasha to see the burning babies in the hidden compartments in her mind. She had wanted Sasha to understand. Rebecca let out a long moan, remembering how she had frightened her daughter, frightened Louis, poor dear Louis. He was such an innocent, how could a man who had led such a pampered, charmed existence be expected to understand? He had only wanted her to love him—but Ruda's pull was stronger.

She sat back, feeling the hard wood of the church pew against her back. The red, green, and blue panes of the stained glass window sparkled in front of her. She stared at the colors . . . she heard his voice, that soft persuasive voice and the music. . . . He played the same Wagner recording over and over, he even whistled it as he walked through the camp, he used to hum it to her when he laid out the cards. . . .

"Clear your mind of everything, look at the cards, red, green . . . look at the cards, there's a good girl, now more cards. . . ."

The white gloves snapped down the colored cards. At first she had liked the game—it was fun, and Papa Mengele had kissed and cuddled her when she remembered each one. When she could transmit the exact colors to Ruda he rewarded her with chocolate, breaking off pieces, popping them into her mouth.

Then the games had become frightening. She was forced to transmit more and more colors. At first it had begun with just three cards, next day six. She found it hard to concentrate, she was hungry. Once she said she couldn't remember them because she was hungry, then she had been force-fed until she was bloated. Now, he had told her, you are full. Now show me how clever you are. This time there were twenty cards, this time, because she was frightened, she had concentrated as hard as possible. These sessions went on every day and gradually Rebecca was able to transmit telepathically to Ruda up to twenty-five colors.

If Ruda made a mistake, she would be punished. They told Rebecca that it was her fault, that she was hurting her sister. One day Papa displayed fifty cards, and Rebecca started to cry. Papa drew back the curtain then and made her see what she had done to Ruda. Ruda sat on a high chair with things clipped to her head. A nurse held her up.

Vebekka rubbed her temples, staring at the stained glass. It began to blur, her head throbbed. She was trying to reach Ruda, just as she had done as a child. Vebekka started to cry. She could not hope to reach out to her, it was too late. If only Rosa had understood, had not been afraid, if only she had allowed Rebecca to open up the past, then she might have been able to find Ruda. Instead, she had buried Ruda alive.

✦   ✦   ✦

Ruda double-checked the props. Next she went to the meat trailer and asked if all the cats had eaten. She was on her way to Mamon's cage when she remembered the time. The public would soon be starting to line up. As she started back to the trailer, suddenly her head felt as though it would burst open. She gasped with pain and leaned against the side of a trailer. Ruda forced herself to carry on, telling herself she hadn't eaten. That's what it was, she had to have something to eat.

✦ ✦ ✦

Torsen arrived at Freda's apartment building, ran his fingers through his hair, and rang the bell. She opened the door before he had finished buzzing. She had her coat over her arm, and her purse in her hand. Freda asked whether his use of the patrol car meant he was on duty. He shook his head. As they drove off he explained they were to pick up his sergeant and a girlfriend.

The two couples talked animatedly, looking forward to the show.

"How was my father today?" Torsen asked Freda.

"Well, he was very well at breakfast, but then it was snowflake time again."

Rieckert asked what she meant, and Freda explained, pulling a little bit of tissue from her purse, licking it and sticking it on the end of her nose, then blowing it off. "He does it for hours until the floor looks like there's been a snowstorm."

Rieckert laughed, nudged Torsen, and said it could be hereditary.

Torsen seethed. He would have to speak to Freda about this snowflake business, it wasn't funny. As Rieckert started to mimic his father in the backseat, Torsen got more and more uptight.

"If it were your father, you wouldn't think it was funny! It is *not* funny!"

Rieckert blew a fragment of tissue off his nose. "I agree! But it's one hell of a hobby!"

✦ ✦ ✦

As the baron and Helen continued walking, they passed one of the circus ads. Helen stopped dead and looked at the face surrounded by lions. Louis turned back as she pointed to Ruda Kellerman's name. "Ruda," she repeated, and then ran to hail a passing taxi.

Louis was a step behind her. "Why a taxi? The man said she was walking!"

Helen bent down to the driver. "The circus, please take us to the circus!"

✦ ✦ ✦

The parking lot was filling up: Crowds walked from the train stations and buses deposited parties near the fenced perimeter. Children waited impatiently to have their photograph taken while they sat on top of the elephant. Clowns passed leaflets and sold balloons. Speakers blasted music, and two majorettes in red sequined costumes paraded up and down banging their drums.

Ruda sat in the bedroom wearing her boots and white trousers. Her body wouldn't stop trembling. She pressed her hands together. They were wet with perspiration. She had never felt this way before, and she was beginning to get frightened. Luis ran into the trailer.

"Standing room only, it's pandemonium out there. Come and see the crowds, they're about to use the laser beams, it's one hell of a sight . . . come and see!"

"Luis, something's wrong with me, look, I'm shaking, I don't know how to stop it!"

He took her in his arms. "It's just nerves. They are coming to see you, Ruda. Look—your face is on every poster, your face, your act."

Ruda heard the roar of the crowd as Luis opened the trailer door.

"*Jesus Christ,* Ruda! Look at the laser beams. My God, I've never seen a show like this, that old bastard knows how to draw the crowds!"

High in the sky, in brilliant colors, the lasers wrote:

RUDA KELLERMAN,
THE MOST FAMOUS FEMALE WILD ANIMAL TRAINER
IN THE WORLD.
RUDA KELLERMAN, RUDA KELLERMAN, RUDA KELLERMAN!

Rebecca quickened her pace, buffeted along by the crowds heading toward the circus. Even if she wanted to turn back she would find it nearly impossible. She had an overpowering urge to run. Suddenly, the stream of people ahead began pointing upward to the laser beams. They gasped and called out, still surging forward, now with faces tilted skyward. But all Rebecca saw was the name RUDA. She could hear a child's voice calling out, screaming "I'm here, I'm here, I'm over here." Lost among the milling people, a little girl screamed for her mother, but to Rebecca it was a sign, a symbol. She had to get to the front of the crowd. "Let me through, please, please let me pass. . . ."

◆   ◆   ◆

Ruda stood in the open door of her trailer, staring at the sky. Slowly she looked back to the crowds. Thousands of people were milling around, eating cotton candy, carrying balloons, surging toward the massive triple-ringed tent. There was someone else there, too. She could feel it with every nerve in her body.

◆   ◆   ◆

Rebecca stood with her face pointed at the sky, her head spinning at the blazing name: RUDA KELLERMAN! She began to head frantically toward the trailer park. A man at the gate was about to stop her, then waved her through with an apology. He thought she was Ruda Grimaldi.

◆   ◆   ◆

Luis looked up with a proud smile and turned to Ruda. She stood motionless in the open doorway.

"Are you okay, honey?"

She stared ahead. He asked again if she was all right, but she didn't answer, she couldn't. She didn't hear him, because standing within yards of her was Rebecca.

Rebecca could not move, she could hear no sound, no voices, nothing. All she had eyes for was Ruda, framed in the doorway. The sisters had not seen each other in forty-four years.

Luis was not sure what was happening. He could see the tall elegant woman, but from far away he couldn't really distinguish her features. "Who is it?" he asked, as Ruda stepped down from the trailer. He watched as the woman moved closer and closer. She moved into the lights of the trailer windows.

Shadows played across her face, but he caught a glimpse of her eyes. They were Ruda's eyes, and he knew then. He was dumb-struck. All he could do was stand and look on as Ruda and the woman approached each other, oblivious to everything that surrounded them.

There was one step between them. They were the exact same height, but Ruda was more powerful. Her body blocked Rebecca from Luis's view. He moved sideways, but all he could see was Ruda's back. It was as if she were protecting her other self.

They did not speak as their hands moved to touch each other's face. But they said each other's name in their minds, in unison, as they melted into each other's arms.

Way past their heads, past the parking lot, out on the road leading to an entrance, Luis saw the ominous blue flashing light of a police car. "Please, dear God, no," he thought. "Please don't let them have come for Ruda, not now, not tonight."

19

THEY LAY TOGETHER like long-lost lovers, devouring each other's face with their eyes.

They felt the wild beating of their hearts. They had so much to tell each other, to ask, and yet they could not break from the embrace. Little by little Ruda released her hold on Rebecca, then rolled over to lie on her back. She felt Rebecca shudder.

"No, don't, don't cry, please don't."

It took all Ruda's willpower to let go of her sister. She moved away from the bed and reached for one of the posters on the wall. She turned to Rebecca, holding it up for her to see.

"This is me, Ruda Kellerman."

"I am . . ." Rebecca's lips trembled. She couldn't say her name.

Ruda held out her hand. "Come. Come with me!"

Hand in hand, they looked at the photographs on the walls. Ruda pointed, speaking softly, in odd descriptive sentences, and then their psychic communication began.

"Chicago, London, Florida . . ."

Rebecca nodded. Ruda would begin a sentence and Rebecca would finish it.

Their voices took on a childish lilt, and their words were no longer spoken only in English but in a mixture of languages: German, Polish, Czech, even in their own private language. Every movement was mirrored by the other. When Rebecca put her hand to her cheek, Ruda automatically touched hers. They were in a world of their own.

But the outside world was closing in. The showground was a heaving mass of bodies. The parking lot was jammed to the bursting point. There were lines of people waiting to buy ice cream and circus souvenirs. More lines formed by the ladies' and men's toilets, and the mass of ticket-holders surging toward the big tent entrance was four to five abreast.

Luis pushed his way toward the stream of cars. He could still see, about half a mile ahead, the police car with its flashing blue light. He had made up his mind what he had to do and say. He ran toward Inspector Heinz's patrol car.

Torsen was red-faced. Twice he had turned off the flashing light, but Rieckert had shouted that unless they used it, they would not make it in time for the opening parade. Rieckert was as excited as a child, urging Torsen on, poking him in the shoulderblade. "Go on, put the siren on, make them pull over."

Torsen banged the steering wheel. "Look, there are hundreds ahead of us. They won't start the show, it's not due to begin for another three quarters of an hour. We just have to wait like everyone else!"

Freda turned to the backseat. "He's right—we'll get there. They won't start the show before everyone's seated. Look up ahead, you think they won't let everyone inside first? Just sit back and enjoy the fireworks!"

Their car inched forward. It was frustrating to see passersby go past on foot. Then the line came to a complete standstill. Up ahead a car had overheated, and there were roars of laughter and calls of abuse as four young boys tried to push the car over to the side.

Far back in the long line of cars was a taxi. Louis and Helen began to think they should turn back; after all, it was a long shot. Yet Vebekka was looking for her sister Ruda, and a Ruda Kellerman was starring in the circus. There was a good chance. . . .

Helen suggested they get out and walk. Louis agreed, but the driver argued, since he could not turn back. Louis gave him a generous tip, and the well-dressed couple began to hurry alongside the cars.

The rain started, lightly at first, but after a while it began to come down steadily, so now umbrellas added to the crush. Torsen could see Luis Grimaldi coming toward him, and he lowered his window. Luis was soaked, his hair wringing wet, and he was out of breath as he called out:

"Inspector! Inspector!"

Torsen smiled, and turned to Freda. "This is my friend Freda, I think you know Sergeant Rieckert."

Rieckert leaned forward to shake Grimaldi's hand. "I keep telling him to put his siren on, just to get us through the crowds. Will they start on time?"

Grimaldi looked puzzled, but then Torsen waved his tickets. "We have complimentary seats, Mr. Grimaldi, front row. Will everyone get in, do you think?"

"Yes, yes. There are always enough seats or, if not, there's standing room. The show may be held ten, fifteen minutes—it's not usual. So . . . you are just here for the performance?"

Torsen nodded, slammed his foot on the brake as they almost ran into the back of the vehicle in front. "I am looking forward to seeing your wife's act."

Grimaldi walked away, relieved, and hurried back to the trailer. He churned over how narrowly he had avoided making a fatal mistake: The inspector wasn't coming for Ruda, he was there for the show. He gave a mirthless laugh. As he scraped the mud from his boots, he remembered again Torsen's query regarding Ruda's old boots. He sighed. Best, he told himself, just to ignore it.

Luis banged on the door and let himself in.

The women turned toward him. Ruda smiled. "This is my . . ."

"Sister," said Rebecca.

Ruda's cheeks were flushed, her eyes brilliant. Her mouth was tremulous, quivering.

They spoke as one: "We are sisters."

Luis found the way they moved together and spoke in the same high-pitched singsong voice disconcerting.

"We are twins."

"Twins," repeated Rebecca. They both lifted their right hand, touched each other's cheek, and laughed.

Luis looked from one to the other. "But—you're not identical."

They sat down at the same time. Crossed their left leg over the right. Ruda leaned forward, Rebecca leaned forward. "We were, but Rebecca . . ."

"I had my nose done."

Luis poured himself a brandy. When he offered them a drink, they shook their heads and said "No," in unison. For a moment he wondered if they were playing some kind of game.

"Just remember, Ruda, you've got a show to do!"

They talked together, heads very close. They made soft shushing sounds and words he could not make out. Then they both looked toward him.

"Rebecca wants to see . . ."

"The show."

Their eyes were identical in color. So were their lips, their cheeks.

Luis felt uneasy. "I see the likeness now. I see it."

They nodded, smiling as if very pleased.

Luis looked to Rebecca: "How did you find Ruda?"

Ruda answered. "She went to the church in the city."

"The lights . . ."

"Yes."

There followed a conversation that Luis could not make heads or tails of. He heard them say the name "Magda," then watched as they both put their hands over their faces and laughed.

Luis leaned forward. "Ruda, keep an eye on the time." She ignored him. Luis got up and looked out of the window. "The lines are thinning out."

Their eyes seemed to follow him around the trailer. He sat down again, then half rose. "Do you want to be alone?"

He saw the way they pressed closer and he sighed, looking at Rebecca.

"Ruda must get ready."

They stared back, with their identical wide eyes. He sipped his brandy. "Where are you from? I mean, do you live in Berlin?"

Ruda answered that Rebecca was staying in a hotel. "Her husband is called . . ."

They both said "Louis!" and then giggled, bending their heads.

They were beginning to irritate Luis. He drained his glass. "I'll go and check on the boys."

As he opened the door, he asked, almost as an afterthought: "Do you work in a circus, Rebecca?"

"No," said Ruda. "Mother," they both said.

"I'm sorry?" Luis didn't understand.

Ruda said her sister was a mother. Rebecca nodded, and shrugged her shoulders. "I am just a mother."

Luis had his hand on the door handle. He wanted to leave them, and yet there were so many questions he wanted to ask. "Does she know where your parents are? I mean, if they're alive?"

They both looked to him, turned to each other, then back to him.

"For God's sake, stop this! You're acting crazy, Ruda. I mean, can't she speak for herself?"

"Yes," they both said, and Luis yanked the door open.

Then Ruda answered solo.

"She was adopted after the war," said Ruda firmly.

"After the . . ." Rebecca's voice trailed off.

Luis sighed. It was too much for him. "Well, I'm glad you've found each other." He didn't mean it to sound so hollow, so lacking in warmth, as if they had been apart for only a few hours—not a lifetime. He forced a smile. "You have a whole life to catch up on, I'll leave you alone, but don't forget you have a big show to do, Ruda."

They stood up, hands still held tightly. "Nothing will ever separate us again." Then they turned and held each other.

Luis closed the trailer door behind him. A feeling of dread enveloped him. He knew he should have stayed, made sure Ruda got herself ready.

The rain was pouring down now and Luis had no raincoat. He muttered to himself. It was stupid, all he had to do was turn around, walk back, and get one. But he didn't want to see them again, not just now. He looked at his watch. Then he looked over toward the main tent. A few stragglers stood at the box office now, and the last cars were being directed toward the private parking lot, the attendant in his bright yellow cape making authoritative, sweeping gestures.

Luis passed by the lighted window of his trailer. He peered into it, but the blinds were down. He could see nothing. The laser beams continued to spell out the acts, and he looked up. Suddenly the sky blazed with the words: RUDA KELLERMAN.

Luis prayed that the reunion would not overwhelm Ruda. He knew just how essential it was for her to have her wits about her. He plodded through the sodden ground and made up his mind that, just in case, he would bring a loaded rifle to the ring tonight. Suddenly he stopped, oblivious to the rain.

"I love her." He said it out loud, to no one.

The realization of how little he really knew about Ruda and of her past shamed him. "I love her," he repeated to the air.

Of course he did. Hadn't he been prepared to tell the inspector that *he* had killed Kellerman? He could have been in cuffs by now. It was sad that after all the years they had been together, it was only now that he realized just how *much* he loved her. He shook his head, smiling to himself, and then chuckled.

They would be on the move soon, out of the country. He had time to make up for the bad years. Luis wondered if Rebecca would be coming with them.

"I love my wife," he repeated. Anyone who had witnessed his slow progress from the trailer would have concluded he was drunk, talking away to himself in the rain, without so much as a coat on.

✦   ✦   ✦

The ground was slippery; Louis held Helen's elbow tightly to ensure that she did not fall. They stepped onto duckboards leading to the administration offices.

At first the secretary thought the baron was trying to get invited to the small champagne party the owners had organized. She asked them to wait while she tried to reach one of the managers.

The baron gave her a winning smile and said that he did not wish to disturb anyone, that he didn't want tickets for the show, but that he wished to speak to Ruda Kellerman.

The girl beckoned the baron over to a map of the trailer park. "There is where she lives, but whether she will agree to see you, sir, I can't say. She is getting ready for the show."

The baron thanked her, and ushered Helen out, back down the slippery boards.

✦ ✦ ✦

Mike showed off the meat trailer, the freezers, and the massive carcasses to Torsen and his party. Before he left them, Grimaldi had said they could park in the artists' area. Mike had been the one Torsen had first approached to inquire about parking.

As they began to head toward the main entrance, Mike offered to show them a shortcut. He led them behind the trailers, pointing out the ones owned by the big acts, and then offered to show them the meat trailer. Until the show started he had nothing else to do.

Torsen checked his watch, worried he would miss the opening parade, but Mike assured him there was plenty of time. He told them that the "Big Boss" would make sure every single ticket was sold before the parade began. "You always think they'll never get everyone seated in time, but they always do. Maybe five, ten minutes late—never more. Besides, I'll show you the artists' entrance. If your tickets are for the front row, it'll be much easier."

As they peered into the freezers and looked over the cleavers and hammers, Vernon came in, already in costume. He was Mike's assistant, a trainee keeper—the Grimaldis never paid much and Vernon was only eighteen years old. Mike made the introductions, and was about to suggest they follow him to the big top when Torsen asked nonchalantly if Mike had ever met Tommy Kellerman.

Mike said he had seen him the day he was murdered—seen him briefly, up by the lions' cages. Torsen repeated his question to Vernon. Vernon flushed, shrugged his shoulders, and muttered that he was not sure whether he had seen him or not.

"You know he was brutally murdered," said Torsen. "So if you saw him, anything you can tell me could be of great importance. I am heading the homicide investigation."

Mike gave Vernon a warning glance, then checked his watch. "I'd better go change!"

Vernon said that since he was already dressed, he could show Torsen to the tent, and Mike, after another warning look to Vernon, skipped off.

As they hurried across the muddy ground Torsen asked again about Kellerman. Vernon said nothing, holding open the tent flap and instructing them to turn right through the main arena entrance. "I hope you enjoy the show."

Torsen smiled and was about to step inside when Vernon called out to him. He turned. The boy held the umbrella down, the rain glanced off the black-soaked canvas. "I did see Kellerman, sir, but only for a brief moment. He was standing talking to Mrs. Grimaldi, up by Mamon's cage. It was early afternoon on the day he was killed." Vernon was not one hundred percent sure, but no one had deemed him even interesting enough to talk to—so he had the inspector's full attention.

Torsen stepped closer. "Was it a friendly chat?" He felt water trickle down his neck, and inched under the umbrella. Vernon was a little scared, wondering if he should have just kept his mouth shut. "I don't know, I couldn't hear, sir. In fact, I thought at first that he was one of the kids, you know, from one of the school groups. They take them around the cages. She looked as if she was telling him off. She was in one of her moods, Grimaldi was on one of his binges, so he was pretty useless and she'd had to do everything . . . and the plinths, the new pedestals were wrong. She's got a temper, Mrs. Grimaldi does, and she's always telling the kids off for getting too near the cages, but then I noticed his hat!"

Torsen stepped further under the umbrella. "His hat?"

"Yes, sir, it was a trilby, a black leather trilby."

"How did you know it was leather?"

"Well, I saw it again, in the meat trailer. Well, I think it was his hat—Mike was wearing it."

"Mike?"

Vernon was shaking, sure he had really made something out of nothing. "Yes, sir, the other helper, sir. He said he'd found it in the meat trailer, but Mrs. Grimaldi took it from him, she said it was her husband's, but it looked like the same hat I saw Kellerman wearing. Dunno why I remembered it, but then everyone around here's been talking about the murder, so it sort of stuck in my mind, you know, wondering if it was him I had seen."

"But you said you did see him?"

Vernon was really nervous now. "Well I don't know for sure if it was Kellerman, sir. Just, well, he wasn't with this circus—I know that. He wasn't with any of the acts, or I would have recognized him."

They heard a loud fanfare, and Torsen looked to the tent.

"The parade is starting, sir, you'd better hurry or they won't let you to your seat."

Vernon sighed with relief when Torsen seemed no longer interested in him, or his theories, but at the same time, thinking it over again, Vernon was sure it was Kellerman he had seen.

✦　✦　✦

Grimaldi had seen them all leaving the meat trailer, had followed Vernon and Torsen toward the big tent and watched them huddle under the umbrella. As Vernon hurried away, he stepped out and caught the boy by his coat.

"I want to know what he asked you. What did he want sniffing around the freezer truck like a stray dog?"

Vernon backed off, terrified.

"He said you'd told him he could park in the artists' car park, then he asked about the cats. Mike brought him in and offered to show him the trailer. That was all, sir."

Grimaldi patted Vernon's shoulder. "I'm sorry, son, just that I'm a bit on edge tonight. It's a big occasion. Have you seen Ruda?"

Vernon said that he had not, and was relieved when Grimaldi started to walk away.

"Oh, Vernon, tell Mike. I'll be watching the cages tonight."

"Yes, sir."

Grimaldi looked back, his eyes narrowed. "You sure that prick wasn't asking questions about Tommy Kellerman?"

"Yes, sir."

"Cats all ready, are they?"

"Yes, sir, I'll double-check them before we go in."

Grimaldi waved his big hand to indicate to Vernon he should carry on with his business. In truth he was not sure what he should do himself. He looked at his watch; there was still a good three quarters of an hour before it was time for Ruda to go on, but she had to be dressed for the parade. He didn't want to go back to the trailer yet, so he walked around, making his way toward the cages. He heard his name called and turned to see Mike waving to him.

"Boss, there's a guy and a blond woman. They've been asking the way to your trailer. They went toward it about two minutes ago."

Grimaldi hurried to Mike. "They say who they were?"

"Yeah, I think the guy was a baron, maybe one of the celebrity guests. There's a bit of a bash in the main conference room over in the administration block."

Grimaldi shrugged. There were always stars at these big openings. He ran his hands through his soaking hair. "Screw 'em. Oh! Mike, in future you want to show any people around the freezer and meat trailers, you get permission, okay, son?"

"Yes, sir."

They walked on to the covered tent where the animals were housed.

"What did he want to go in there for anyway?"

Mike was uneasy. He knew he should have got permission, so he lied. "Oh, he asked us a few questions, you know, if we'd seen Kellerman, Mrs. Grimaldi's ex."

"I know who he was!" snapped Luis.

"It was raining, so we took cover in the trailer."

"What did you tell him?"

Mike wiped his face. "Nothing, sir. I'd better see to the props." He tried to move away, but Grimaldi held on to his arm.

"The cats all settled and in order?" Grimaldi asked.

"Yes, sir, everything's in order."

Grimaldi walked from one cage to the next. As always, the cats filled him with awe. Their wild, menacing beauty affected him deeply. He checked each cage, and then he heard the low heavy growl, the dull rumble. Mamon's eyes glinted, his head hung low, feet splayed out. He sensed the man's fear.

✦   ✦   ✦

Their voices spoke in unison. "Sasha! Sophia! Jason, Luis . . ." Four
of Ruda's cats had the names of Rebecca's children. They hugged
and laughed at the coincidences. Grimaldi hid behind Mamon's cage
as the women approached, watching them. They walked in step.
But from a distance, Grimaldi could see that Rebecca was just a
fraction behind Ruda, as if the movement was not instinctive, but
copied. Because Rebecca was so slender she appeared, in the low
lights of the animal arena, to be Ruda's shadow.

They had not yet caught up on the lost years, they could not
in so short a time. Only sections of each other's lives had been
snatched and clutched at. Ruda knew Rebecca was married with
four children, Rebecca knew Ruda was married and was an animal
trainer. There were many layers to uncover, many questions to ask,
but all they wanted now was this closeness. They studied each other,
touched each other, to make sure they really were reunited.

Rebecca showed no fear of the cats, only an extraordinary excitement. She wanted to touch them, put her hands through the
bars, but Ruda had to hold her back, whispering that it was too
soon.

"Too soon, yes, too soon," repeated Rebecca.

Ruda's physical strength made Rebecca weak with adoration.
Ruda's powerful body and rough hands made her want to be
wrapped in Ruda's arms. Ruda felt Rebecca's need and it awoke in
her a gentleness, a protectiveness that made her body tingle. She
showed off her animals with pride, wanting Rebecca to see her
loved ones, and to see her perform.

"This is everything I dreamed . . ."

"Yes, you dreamed this, and I want . . ."

"You to see me, with my children."

"Yes, they are my children," Ruda paused, and gave a strange
half laugh. "Sasha, your last daughter is twelve, yes?"

Rebecca nodded. Ruda recalled the pains she had felt at the time
of each birth. Sasha's birth pains she remembered most clearly.
They coincided with the time she had been told she could never

carry a child. As if she understood this, Rebecca clasped her sister's hand. In some ways it was as if they had never been apart. Rebecca accepted Ruda without question. In that one hour, the relationship had reverted to the way it had always been. Ruda was dominant, Rebecca passive. Ruda was born first, she had preceded Rebecca by two minutes.

The music became louder, and Grimaldi watched Ruda lead Rebecca toward the artists' entrance. He was soaked and made his way back to the trailer to change for the show.

The noise was deafening. Torsen couldn't see Freda or Rieckert anywhere. Apologetically, he edged his way through a group of jugglers waiting to enter.

Torsen moved cautiously along the tiers of seats. He stood at the edge of the ring and looked around the audience. He could see walls of lights and thousands of seats. He didn't have his seat number—all he knew was that he was in the front row. He squinted through the semidarkness, searching the sea of faces. Beyond the small ring was the vast main ring, beyond that the third ring. Suddenly the huge big top was plunged into darkness. The crowd murmured, sensing the show was about to begin. The fanfares blared, once, twice: *"Ladies and gentlemen, Schmidt's World Famous Circus welcomes you! Three rings, hundreds of artists. We welcome you to a night of unparalleled extravaganza! From Argentina, the world famous bareback riders—The Comancheros. . . ."*

Torsen, his eyes at last accustomed to the darkness, made out Freda's and Rieckert's faces at the side of the main ring's entrance. He scurried into his vacant seat just as the horses thundered into the ring.

Freda clasped his arm. "Isn't this exciting? I have never been to a circus before!"

Torsen inched off his wet coat, and Freda moved close to him, slipping her hand through the crook of his arm. Torsen touched her fingers.

"I am glad I asked you to come with me."

She looked in awe at the ring as the Argentinian riders screamed and called out at the top of their voices. Twenty-five horses, groomed and gleaming, galloped around carrying a sparkling banner.

The bareback girls whooped and yelled as they bounced and bobbed, leaping to stand upright on the horses' backs with nothing more than a glittering red ribbon for a rein. The smell of the horses, the sawdust, and the resin added to the excitement.

Torsen was happy. His father had been right. Freda was lovely.

✦   ✦   ✦

Grimaldi was buttoning the high collar of his clean shirt when he heard the fanfares. He knew exactly how many there would be before the parade ended, and he quickly tucked his shirt into his trousers. Then he opened the bunk seat, and looked over the rifles.

✦   ✦   ✦

The baron and Helen asked one of the parking lot attendants which one was the Grimaldi trailer. He was taken aback when the man asked: "Where's your pass?"

"I don't have one, I am Baron . . ."

"Without a pass you can't be in the artists' section."

"I wish to speak with Mr. Grimaldi and his wife Ruda Kellerman. It's very important."

"No way. See the big tent—they'll be in there. I'm sorry, please leave. I can't let you wander around here. Go on through the barrier."

The baron was about to argue when Helen suggested that perhaps they should wait; it was obvious they would not be able to speak to either Grimaldi or Ruda Kellerman now.

"Sir! Mr. Grimaldi!"

Luis turned, quickly hiding the rifle beneath his rain cape.

The attendant ran to Grimaldi. They talked, then the boy pointed back to the baron and Helen.

"I told them to wait, sir. They have no pass, but they said it was important."

Grimaldi walked up to the baron. "What do you want?"

The baron asked if they could talk somewhere in private, but

Grimaldi shook his head. "Not before the show. What do you want?"

"It is very important. I need to speak to you about my wife."

"Your wife?" Grimaldi held his hand up to shield his face from the rain.

"Yes. This is Dr. Helen Masters, my wife's doctor. Have you seen Baroness Maréchal? We think there may be some connection between her and Ruda Kellerman."

Grimaldi hesitated.

Helen moved closer. "Please help us. She is very sick. We think she may have tried to see Ruda Kellerman."

"Is the woman called Rebecca?"

"Yes!" The baron stepped closer, but Grimaldi moved back sharply. "Is she here? Have you seen her?"

Grimaldi had to shout above the noise of the circus orchestra.

"She came here. She was with Ruda, but I don't know where she is now. Come to the trailer after the show."

"Did you speak to her?" asked Helen.

"Yes, yes I did. She's sick, you say?"

The baron gripped his hands tightly. "This is very important. Please, we must talk to her."

Grimaldi looked back to the tent. "I can't talk to you now, the show's starting. Your wife says she is Ruda's sister; they were together earlier. They said they're twins."

Helen grabbed hold of Grimaldi's rain cape. "Is Ruda Kellerman here?"

"She is about to go into the ring. Look, I don't know what you can do now. I'll try and find her, tell her you're here. Wait at the trailer, the big silver one over there—but after the show. I have to go!"

"Please, please wait—your wife, Ruda—"

Grimaldi backed away, pointed again to his trailer. "Meet me here, after the show."

The baron and Helen watched him hurry away, then stop and turn. He shouted for them to mention his name at the box office, if they wanted to go into the big tent.

Helen and the baron crossed to the box office.

"Louis, we'll do as he said, just wait until the end of the show. We'll buy two standing room tickets, please."

"You will have a very good view, it'll be worth it," said the cashier, and pointed toward the tent. "I'd hurry, the parade's already started."

The artists were lined up, waiting for their cues by the entrance to the ring: red for standby, green for go. The music blared from massive speakers as the orchestra gave each act an introduction. The ringmaster, with his red frock coat, his black silk top hat and whip, was in the spotlight.

Ruda Kellerman waited for her turn to enter. The hectic events both frightened and exhilarated Rebecca; her whole body trembled. Ruda kept tight hold of her twin's hand, describing some of the acts. Anyone close was proudly introduced. "This is my sister!"

Ruda was dressed in a tailored black evening suit, a white silk shirt with heavy ruffles at her neck, and a flowing black cloak lined in white satin. The trousers were skintight, and she wore black polished Russian riding boots. She carried a pair of white gloves and a top hat and smiled broadly, joking with friends as they passed her to enter the ring. Her red warning light flickered. The loud-speaker warned: "Stand by, Ruda Kellerman."

Ruda whispered to Rebecca that any moment it would be her cue. But Rebecca continued to cling to her. Ruda cupped Rebecca's face in her strong hands.

"Just for a moment . . . watch me!"

"*Ladies and gentlemen, the most daring, the most famous, the most audacious, fearless female wild animal trainer in the world . . . please welcome to Berlin the star of our show. Welcome to Berlin, Ruda Kellerman! . . . Ruda Kellerman, ladies and gentlemen!*"

Ruda stood with arms raised above her head, her cloak swirling around her. She stood motionless, held in the brilliant spotlight, then strode to the center of the ring. She turned to the right, to the left, bowing low, taking her applause. The cheers had never felt so sweet.

Torsen stared at the confident figure. Having met Ruda, he found it fascinating to see her now. Rieckert turned to Torsen. "She's something else isn't she? I can't wait to see her with the big cats."

Helen and the baron were five rows behind, in the standing room section. Helen could not even see the ring. Louis looked at her.

"I told you. This is a waste of time, we can't see."

Helen beckoned to Louis to follow as she pushed and shoved her way through the crowd.

"Look, Louis, there's four vacant seats in the second row. Why don't we just take a seat—if the ticket holders arrive, then we'll move. Come on."

"From Florida, America's Arabian Nights—the finest Arab horses in the world . . . the finest horsemen . . . the Franklynn Brothers!!"

No one stopped them. Louis and Helen now had a perfect view of the center ring. They took their seats. Helen leaned across to the couple sitting next to them and asked if she could borrow their program. Helen looked at it and passed it to Louis.

"Ruda Kellerman is on last, just before the intermission."

Louis held the program at a slight angle so he could read it in the semidarkness. The half-light accentuated his high cheekbones.

"The Bellinis! Please welcome—from Italy—Didi and Barbara Bellini . . . and their team of dogs!"

Ruda was hurrying around the back of the tent when she saw Luis. She called out to him with a broad smile. "What a house, can you hear them?"

He nodded. As they drew close, he could see her eyes were shining. "I can't wait . . . *I can't wait, Luis! Tonight . . . I will be the most magnificent, the best . . ."*

She was walking so fast he almost had to jog to keep up with her. She pulled off her white gloves and flicked them at him.

"You know what it means for me to have her here? For her to see me? You know, Luis, we used to make up stories and always, always, Luis, I would say: I am the lion tamer!"

She hurried back to the artists' enclosure, talking nonstop, unbuttoning her cuffs and the buttons on her shirt. Then she stopped and turned to him.

"You made my dreams come true, Luis. Did you know that?"

He had never seen her so happy. She seemed to dance as she hurried on, tossing the cloak to him. "You made my dream come true. *I am here, Luis,* and my sister is here. My heart, Luis, my heart is bursting!"

"I love you, Ruda."

But she had moved on. With his arms weighed down by her heavy cloak, hat, and gloves, he couldn't keep up with her. He trailed behind like a lackey, tripping, stumbling, and then he watched as Rebecca ran to Ruda. They embraced, Rebecca giving Ruda frantic childlike kisses.

"Rebecca! Wait! Your husband was here looking for you with a woman, a doctor!"

Rebecca stared wide-eyed at Grimaldi. She seemed terrified, but Ruda, impatient to change for the act, drew Rebecca toward the exit.

"Did you hear what I said? I told them to meet us at the trailer. . . . Ruda?"

They ignored Grimaldi and ran out. He saw the attendant stop Ruda and point at Rebecca. No one was allowed to bring guests to the back of the arena unless they had a special pass. Ruda flung a protective arm around Rebecca's shoulders and pushed the attendant out of her way. "She is not anybody, she is my sister!" she said.

✦   ✦   ✦

Torsen flicked through the program and turned to Rieckert, pointing out when Ruda Kellerman was on. He then put his arm around Freda's shoulders. She was laughing at the clowns who rushed around with a bucket filled with soap suds. The small clown, with his short legs and funny bowler hat, reminded Torsen of Kellerman. It could have been Kellerman—except he was dead and buried. As Torsen watched the diminutive figure tumble around the ring, all the facts he had been gathering began to gnaw at him. He was sure it was Ruda who had walked away from Kellerman's hotel, Ruda who had worn his hat as a disguise. She had lied to him, not once, but many times. She was strong enough to have killed Kellerman. The question was, how in God's name could he prove it?

Everything going on in the ring became blurred as Torsen started to piece together the evidence he had accumulated to date against Ruda.

"The wonders of the animal kingdom . . . Rahji the Elephant Man!"

Grimaldi had provided Ruda with an alibi, but the young boy, Vernon, had said Grimaldi had been on one of his binges. What if he had been drunk on the evening of the murder? Would he have known what time she came or went? Had Grimaldi lied? And where were the boots?"

"It's the elephants next!" Rieckert shouted, his tie loose, his face flushed.

Torsen grimaced to himself. They did not sleep in the same room. How could Grimaldi give his wife an alibi if he was drunk? Torsen remembered Ruda saying Grimaldi was snoring, that he had kept her awake! So obviously he had been sleeping. Could she—did she—leave the trailer, return . . . while Grimaldi slept?

Freda clutched his arm as the elephants started to enter the ring. They were within touching distance. Rieckert shouted excitedly to Torsen: "I hope they don't let the lions this close, eh?"

An elephant's trunk swung dangerously close to Torsen, and he pressed back in his seat—much to the delight of Rieckert, who shrieked with laughter. The animal gently placed his front feet on the ring rim: then swirled his massive trunk above their heads. They screeched and cowered as the elephant slowly turned back, and all eight elephants began to waltz.

Freda suddenly sighed.

"You okay? You weren't afraid, were you?" Torsen asked.

"It's sad in a way, isn't it? They are so wonderfully huge, and I don't like to see them looking foolish, dancing. It's not right."

At that moment a baby elephant began to perform what could possibly have been termed a pirouette. The crowd roared its delight. But Freda did not approve. Torsen liked her more and more. He leaned closer.

"If I get rid of Rieckert, would you have dinner with me? Tonight, after the show?"

She nodded, and his grip tightened. She rested her head on his shoulder and he didn't think of Ruda anymore.

◆ ◆ ◆

Helen was laughing, amused by the antics of the baby elephant. Louis turned to watch her. Her face was lovely, it was as if he had never really noticed it before this evening. He reached over and held her hand.

"You know, I don't think I have ever really said how much I appreciate your kindness, the way you have cared for Vebekka. You must think me a very . . ."

Helen withdrew her hand. "I think you have been under tremendous stress. I understand, and I hope . . ."

"I love her, Helen, I always have . . . I always will."

"Yes, I know." Helen knew no one could take Vebekka's place. He was a weak, delightful man. A charming man who had always found solace in women. Louis had turned to other women to survive. All Louis's infidelities were really substitutions. His weakness was his inability to face reality; instead of seriously trying to help Vebekka, he had others assume that responsibility for him.

"The fearless daredevil Dupres—from Paris, France . . . no safety net, ladies and gentlemen! The Flying Dupres defy death!"

The main ring darkened as slim, white-clad figures climbed the ropes to the roof of the big tent. Louis watched a young beautiful boy expertly swing the trapeze backward and forward, his eyes on the catcher who dropped down, his arms free, his legs hooked over the bar of the swing. The swing picked up momentum. The boy sprang forward, flying through the air. The swings passed each other, high above the audience's heads, and the crowd gasped as the boy performed a perfect triple somersault, the catcher reaching out with split-second timing to clasp his hands.

Louis looked at Helen. "You know . . . that is how she makes me feel—that it's up to me to catch her. I almost touch her hands, almost save her, but she slips away, she falls, each time. Helen . . . ?"

Helen put her hand on his. "We'll find her. You'll hold her, and maybe next time she won't fall, if she feels you are strong enough."

"Do you think this Ruda Kellerman is really her sister? It would be an extraordinary coincidence, wouldn't it? That she should be here in Berlin?"

Helen edged closer, whispering: "You know, Rebecca kept on saying, 'It's close, it's very close.' What if 'it' meant her sister was close? I mean if they are twins, then maybe it is likely there is some kind of telepathy between them. She sensed her sister was nearby, but because of what had been done to her, she couldn't bring to the conscious level the fact that she had a sister, and that she might be alive."

Louis gasped along with the crowd as a trapeze artist slipped. But it was a very carefully rehearsed mistake. The tent was silent as the artists prepared for a dangerous jump: springing from the swing onto a high wire in the darkness, a wire not visible to the audience. The man seemed to fly downward and then swung his body around the taut high wire, twelve feet below.

While watching the high-wire act, Helen tried to remember something Rebecca had said. Suddenly she felt her palms begin to sweat. She recalled the incident at the circus in Monaco. Rebecca had attempted to get into the ring—could she have done this because of a telepathic connection to her sister? Helen leaned against Louis.

"Louis, the time Rebecca attacked the circus clown . . . maybe Ruda Kellerman was with the circus then. Louis?"

But Louis was lost in his own thoughts.

"I wasn't there for her, Helen. I should have found out more about her past, cared more. Now I feel as if I have a second chance. I hope I am not too late."

✦ ✦ ✦

Rebecca helped Ruda into her costume, and then changed into trousers and boots herself, and put on one of the boys' red jackets.

"Now you don't have to stay by the entrance, you can come right into the ring! Stand outside the cages. Luis will look after you, won't you?"

Luis was not happy about it. He said that Rebecca would be in the way and besides it was dangerous; she might distract Ruda. Ruda dismissed his fears with a wave of her hand. "Nonsense. You take her in, she'll stand by you and then you take care of her."

He shrugged reluctantly.

"But you must go now. I'll take care of Rebecca. Please, you haven't been near the cages."

Ruda nodded, then took Rebecca's hand. "We're ready!"

Grimaldi stood beside Rebecca as Ruda went over to the boys. At last she seemed to be concentrating as she checked the props and cages. She gave a signal for the boys to start stacking the tunnel sections to the entrance. Two more acts and they were on.

Ruda moved from cage to cage. She had changed into tight white trousers, black shiny boots, and a white frilled Russian-style shirt. The simplicity of her costume made her look smaller and more vulnerable. She carried only a short stick. Rebecca stepped forward to follow Ruda, but Grimaldi held her back firmly. "No, no, you must leave her alone now. This is very important, she must get ready."

"Yes, of course!"

Ruda started pacing. Twice she stopped and looked over at Rebecca. She smiled, then asked the boys if the fire hoop was set up, the pedestals stacked. Back to her old self, she went over every detail. Grimaldi felt relieved.

Mike stood by the mass of stacked railings; four circus hands waited for the signal to spring into action. There would be two sets of clowns and jugglers covering the mounting of the cages in the central ring. The main ring would be in darkness as the safety barrier was erected.

Red light on. Mike looked to Vernon. "Stand by. . . . Okay boys, stand by, we got the red light. Red light, Mr. Grimaldi."

"*Two minutes for Kellerman's act. Stand by, you have red light . . . GO GREEN, MISS KELLERMAN, PLEASE STAND BY.*"

Luis looked at Rebecca. She was shaking; he patted her shoulder.

"When the red light comes on over there, that is our cue to go into the ring. We go in first, then Ruda will get her own red and green light."

In the darkened ring the cages were brought into position, the tunnel erected. The first cage was placed by the trapdoor of the tunnel.

Mike checked the trapdoor and used his walkie-talkie. "Cages in position for tunnel, over. . . ."

"Ladies and gentlemen! Schmidt's is proud to announce for your entertainment tonight, the most famous, the most daring wild animal act in the world. Please remain in your seats. Do not attempt to move from the ringside anywhere near the barriers. Please do not move down the aisles during this act. Any one of these wild animals can kill, please remain seated. . . . Any movement outside the barriers can distract the animals, can endanger their trainer."

The crowd murmured. The excitement became palpable as the orchestra began a slow drumbeat.

Grimaldi got the green light to enter the ring. He picked up his rifle and beckoned for Rebecca to follow. She kept close as he entered the darkened arena, making his way carefully to the far edge of the barrier to take up his "watching" position.

Vernon was already in place opposite Grimaldi, and he lifted his radio set piece. "In position, Grimaldi on the far side with the woman. Eh! Looks like he's got a bloody rifle!"

Mike kept his eyes on Ruda as she paced up and down. He lifted the radio. "He's just showing off, Vern. Okay, we got the red! Stand by for green!"

Ruda pulled on her leather gloves.

"Ladies and gentlemen . . . Ruda Kellerman!"

"GREEN GO! GREEN GO!"

Vernon withdrew the bolts from the trapdoor leading from the tunnel into the darkened ring. Ruda made her way in the dark toward the open trap from ring to tunnel. She backed into the tunnel, exactly ten paces.

"She's in position, over!"

Vernon heard Mike tell him the cats were released. *Bang!* Up came the central spotlight, pinpointing Ruda Kellerman running from the tunnel into the center of the ring, while close on her heels came Roja, followed by fifteen more tigers. The crowd murmured. It looked as if the tigers were chasing Ruda into the ring.

The act began. Rieckert gasped: "Holy shit!"

Helen gripped Louis' arm. "My God . . . look at her, look at her face!"

Louis half rose out of his seat: Ruda could have been Rebecca. Stunned, he couldn't catch his breath.

"My God, they're almost identical!"

Torsen released his arm from around Freda, and stared in astonishment. There she was, surrounded by a mass of cats, so close they seemed to brush against her legs.

Ruda was in full control as she issued commands. In perfect coordination the cats kept up the tight, circular movement.

"Good Roja . . . Roja good . . . ROJA BREAK!"

The massive tiger broke to his right. Now the sixteen animals formed two circles as Ruda backed to the barrier and picked up the reinforced ladder. The spotlight spilled over to the barrier, momentarily shining on Grimaldi and Rebecca. Helen stood up. "She's at the side of the ring, Louis. I saw her!"

The man behind Helen pulled on her jacket and told her to sit down. But Louis had seen too. White-faced, he turned to Helen.

"I saw her, too. She's with Grimaldi."

✦ ✦ ✦

Torsen was on the edge of his seat. He leaned across to Rieckert. "Did you see her? The woman across the ring, on the opposite side?"

Freda turned to Torsen. "What did you say?"

Torsen stared into the ring, and then gasped. "My God! Look what she's doing!"

✦ ✦ ✦

Ruda was backing up the ladder now. Roja turned inward, the circle getting closer, tighter around the ladder. From her perch, Ruda rocked the ladder dangerously.

"Roja! . . . move move . . . RIGHT . . . RIGHT! SASHA! . . . SASHA DOWN!"

This was the most dangerous part of the sequence. Ruda readied herself for her famous flying leap, the cats forming a tight group in front of her. Grimaldi and Rebecca moved closer to the bars.

"Sasha DOWN."

Grimaldi looked at Rebecca. She was repeating Ruda's commands word for word: "Sasha . . . Sasha . . . Sasha!"

Grimaldi looked back to the ring. Sasha was acting up. "DOWN! Sasha. Down, down!" Rebecca said.

Grimaldi grabbed her arm. "Shut up . . . shut up!" he hissed.

Rebecca turned to him, seemingly unaware of who he was.

"DOWN . . . DOWN!"

Grimaldi sighed with relief as Ruda sprang forward and lay across the cats' backs. After the cartwheel turn, Ruda jumped back onto her feet. She gave the command to spread out. The applause was deafening. Now the cats were running like a wild pack. Ruda bowed, and commanded the animals to form the chorus dance line.

Sasha was acting up again. This time she refused to back up onto her hind legs. She swiped at Ruda, snarling and growling. Then she began to fight with the tiger next to her. Ruda crossed over to them.

"SASHA, NO . . . Up, up, UP!"

Rebecca was shaking, repeating over and over: "Sasha . . . Sasha . . ."

Vernon became very tense. The cats refused several commands. Instigated by Sasha, fights were breaking out. Sophia, the female at the end, joined in. Sweat streamed off Ruda's face.

Ruda pushed, cajoled, shouted, and ordered. At one point she cuffed Sasha's nose—hard. Sasha lashed out, but at last they were in line, behaving. They began to form the pyramid, then the roll-over, as Ruda moved one of the pedestals into the center of the arena. It was a bright red pedestal with a gold fringe. As rehearsed, Roja broke from the row and nudged Ruda from behind. She turned round to face him, shaking her finger, then returned to setting up the next pedestal.

Vernon's eyes were glued on the waiting tigers. At Ruda's command, they all sat back on their haunches, paws waving in the air. Ruda looked as if she were gesturing to each one to keep in the sitting-up position. She moved in and out of their territory, giving small hand signals for one or another to try to get off their pedestal. They swiped at the air with their paws, as if refusing. Ruda put her hands on her hips in mock frustration.

Vernon got the radio message from Mike. "Mamon's on his way down."

With her back to the tunnel, still pretending to admonish the tigers, Ruda got a large bottle of milk and fed Roja, then looked back as if pleading for him to sit on the pedestal. The children in the audience shrieked with laughter.

A small spotlight moved to the entrance of the tunnel. Now Mamon crept out slowly, as if sneaking up behind Ruda. When she turned, she pretended not to see him, but actually gave him the command to move behind her, while still encouraging Roja to sit on the pedestal.

Roja refused. Ruda pretended to get angry; the children, as expected, began to shout: "He's behind you!"

As trained, Mamon kept moving stealthily behind Ruda. Every time she turned she gave the command for a tiger to head back down the tunnel. Each time she turned back to her row of tigers, one was missing. Ruda made an elaborate show of counting tigers and looking puzzled. Roja feigned an attack and Ruda sidestepped him. The audience hushed as Roja made another run at Ruda. This time she crouched down and he jumped over her head and ran into the tunnel. Ruda took out a bright red handkerchief and wiped her forehead. When she turned back, she stared in astonishment—all the pedestals were empty! All the tigers had gone down the tunnel!

Vernon whispered into his microphone. "All clear . . . all clear. Bolt on, wait for Roja, over. Okay, he's clear, he's out."

The children screamed once more. "He's behind you!"

Mamon roared and the children fell silent. Ruda turned in mock fear to face the big lion. Vernon got the radio message. "All back. Trapdoor down."

Ruda was now left with Mamon, and it was as if that had been his intention all the time, to clear all the other cats away and be the star.

Ruda issued Mamon the command. "Red!" and continued to look forward to the empty tunnel, pretending to be puzzled that the others had disappeared.

Grimaldi tensed up, Vernon moved closer. Mamon was behind Ruda, but he was nowhere near where he should be, nowhere near the pedestal. His head hung low and he was moving stealthily forward.

"Red . . . Ma'angel . . . Ma'angel . . . !"

Grimaldi heard Rebecca gasp. She broke free of him and clung to the bars. Her face was rigid. "RED . . . RED . . . RED!!"

The sawdust churned up behind Mamon as he made a fast U-turn, and at a terrifying gallop careened across the ring, flinging himself at the railings, toward Rebecca. He seemed crazed, swiping at the bars and snarling.

The audience became silent. Ruda moved to the center of the ring. Only the ring was lit, not the barrier, so the audience could hardly see Grimaldi or Rebecca. But Rebecca fell back, terrified.

Ruda kept the pedestal between herself and Mamon.

"YUPPPPPPPPPPPMAMON . . . UP UP . . . RED RED . . . MA'AANGELLLLLLLL!" He was too far across the ring to be forced back to the tunnel again. He began a crazed run around the barrier, teeth bared, his eyes crazy.

"Red, GOOD BOY . . . Ma'angel . . . Red!"

Rebecca was tugging at Grimaldi, saying over and over: "Red, red, red . . ."

Vernon snapped an order for someone to get ready to let Ruda out of the trapdoor on that side. Mamon was going crazy.

Torsen bit his knuckles, his face white. "He's out of control. Look at him, he's going for her!"

Rieckert sat back in his seat. "Bloody hell . . . she must be mad! He's going to attack her."

Mike sent one of the boys to stand by the trapdoor. Grimaldi signaled for him to get to his side. He pushed Rebecca forward.

"Take her out, just get her out of the way. I'll handle it, I'll see to the trapdoor."

Rebecca called out to Ruda, but the orchestra was playing at full volume. Only the few rows close to Grimaldi could sense something was very wrong.

Rebecca was dragged out, unable to tear her eyes from the ring. Grimaldi cocked the rifle. There was a gasp from the banks of seats close by.

Helen gripped the baron's hand. "Can you see him? He's got a rifle, but I can't see Rebecca. I think something is wrong . . . Do you think this could be part of the act?"

Mike listened as Vernon repeated into the radio that Mamon was going crazy, and that Ruda couldn't control him.

"He's acting up! No . . . no—hold the panic."

They faced each other. After Rebecca left, Mamon seemed to calm down. He still wavered, but Ruda moved in closer. Her whole body was covered in sweat. Adrenaline was pumping through each vein.

"Come on . . . come on Ma'angel. Up red . . . red UP! MAMON!"

She moved closer. His massive jaws were open and drool hung from his mouth as he tossed his head from side to side. There was silence now. The orchestra had just finished playing a segment of Wagner's *The Ring,* the moment when Siegfried discovers his beloved.

Ruda knelt on one knee and bowed her head. There was a gasp as Mamon sprang as if to attack her. Instead, he leaped over her head and landed perfectly on the pedestal. Slowly he lifted his front paws in the air. Ruda crossed to the pedestal and stood in front of him. Directly beneath him, she opened her arms to accept the applause, facing him.

"Mamon . . . good, good. Gently now, good boy." Ruda turned her back to Mamon, and he slowly lowered his front paws onto her shoulders. The spotlight shrank until it shone on Mamon's head. She turned to look at him. She could smell his breath, she could hear his heart pumping. She was at his mercy.

"Good boy . . . good, KISS!"

Ruda stepped quickly away. On command he was off the pedestal and running for the tunnel. She was left alone to bow, and take the thundering applause. The audience gave her a standing ovation.

"Ladies and gentlemen we now have an intermission . . . but hurry back to see the second half of the fearless, the extraordinarily daring Ruda Kellerman's act. Meet Wanton, the panther. Meet more of Ruda Kellerman's amazing family of wild beasts."

The lights came on as the ice cream girls streamed down the aisles. Many members of the audience remained in their seats dazed, unsure of what they had just seen.

Ruda was panting and patting her face dry with a towel as she ran across toward her trailer to change for the second half of the act. Grimaldi was waiting. "Don't take him into the second half, he's crazy. He refused to obey you time and time again."

She turned on Grimaldi. "I can control him, *I did*. Now back off. I know what I'm doing."

Only then did she stop, look around. "Where is she? *Luis, where is she?*"

Grimaldi snapped back that she was by the cages with Mike and Vernon. He continued to follow her: "She becomes as crazy as the bloody animals . . . Ruda—*Ruda, will you listen to me!*"

Ruda was splashing through the mud toward the trailer. "I hear you, Luis. But please don't ask me to *listen to you*! I saw the rifle, Luis! I don't want you in or near the ring for the second half, hear me? You are pitiful, *pitiful*! So desperate to be part of the act you have to stand there like something out of a Wild West show!"

She ran on. The sweat she had worked up in the ring now mingled with the cold rain, making her shiver. She entered the trailer, leaving the door open for Luis. "I'm cold. *I'm cold!* Run the shower."

✦ ✦ ✦

Rebecca was not with Mike, as Grimaldi had believed, but on her way back to the trailer. She was about to open the door when she heard Ruda's angry voice. She stood motionless as Grimaldi shouted. "Don't order me about as though I were a dog!"

"Then what are you? What possessed you to stand like a prick with that bloody rifle!"

"Maybe I was worried about you—you hadn't rehearsed, you were distracted because of this Rebecca business."

"She is my sister, *my sister, Luis!* You know what that means to me? Can you even contemplate what it means to have found her? She came to me, *she came to me, Luis!*"

Grimaldi sat heavily on the bunk bed, wiping his hair with the towel Ruda had tossed aside. She was pulling off her boots as she talked. Outside, Rebecca was frozen, unable to move from the trailer steps, huddled in Vernon's rain cape.

"Help me with my boots."

He held the toe and heel and jerked hard.

"She took a long time finding you. Why didn't she turn up earlier?"

The boot came away in his hand and Ruda fell back. She pushed her other foot out to him, and he began to pull off the boot. "She didn't know I was alive."

"She tell you she looked for you?" he asked.

Ruda pushed against him. "I looked for her, she looked for me. *Yes, yes, yes!* Oh come on, pull, Luis, I've got to change."

"There's something wrong with her, Ruda. I tried to tell you earlier. There was a man, said he was her husband. He was with a woman, a doctor. They said she was sick. I think they meant crazy sick!" He pulled hard at the boot heel. The boot came away and Ruda fell backward again.

"What did they tell you?"

"Nothing much. I just felt it from the way they were so desperate to find her. They knew about you. They were looking for you. I said they'd best come to the trailer after the show."

"Why did you do that?"

"What else was I supposed to say? I knew she'd been here— Christ! They wanted to try and find you there and then. If it wasn't for me they'd have been wandering around . . ."

"You should have just minded your own business."

"You are my business."

"Since when?"

Luis hesitated. "Since you killed Kellerman."

She stared at him and he sighed. "I know Ruda, so don't deny it. I know you killed him."

Ruda unbuttoned her shirt. "Ah, I see. You are going to blackmail me, is that it?" She pulled her sweat-soaked shirt off. "Try it and I'll get your bloody rifle and I'll shoot your fucking head off . . ."

Luis grabbed hold of her. "You know what I was prepared to do for you? That inspector—when I saw him arrive, you know what I wanted to do? Say it was me, say *I* killed Kellerman! I was going to do that for you Ruda, because—"

Ruda let the shirt drop. "Oh God, what did you tell him, you fool!"

"I told him nothing. They were just coming to see the show, they had free tickets. I said nothing."

She seemed almost amused. "You were really going to do that for me?"

He pointed to the clock. "You got ten minutes. I'll get the boys ready."

She unzipped her pants slowly, never taking her eyes off his face. "He took a long time to die. I never meant to kill him—but he threatened me and . . . there was this big green ashtray, very heavy. I kept on hitting him and his teeth fell out. I remember seeing his teeth on the carpet. He was always so proud of his white teeth, but they were as false, as fake, as he was."

She took a deep breath. "Oh God, Luis. He took such a long time to die."

Ruda kicked her pants off. The terrible jagged scars were shining with sweat. She looked up to him and held out her arms. He hugged her tightly.

"Nobody will hurt you. I won't let them."

She stroked his face. "So if they come for me, you'll say you did it? You'd really do that for me?"

Luis kissed her forehead. "Yes, yes, I'll say it was me. Nobody will ever hurt you again, I promise."

She cupped his face in her hands and kissed his lips. Her eyes searched his eyes. She traced his lips with her fingers. "Be nice to her, Luis, she was always the weak one."

"Yes, I can tell."

She gave a strange smile. "Can you now? I underestimated you."

Luis tapped his wrist to indicate the time, and brought her the costume. He heard the shower being turned on, and eased the plastic cover from the white jacket, glad to be needed.

Outside, Rebecca sat hunched on the steps. When she heard Ruda call out for her costume, she moved away, afraid to be seen. She lost her footing, falling in the thick mud. She tried to stand, but she had slid halfway beneath the trailer.

The trailer door opened. She could see the polished boots, and hear Ruda telling Grimaldi to bring her to the ring.

"And Luis . . . no gun! Promise me?"

As Ruda hurried away, Rebecca could see Grimaldi's feet. She crawled a few inches, calling out to him. The mud oozed beneath her. She could smell the wet earth, and she was lost. The dank stinking tunnel, the stench of the sewers, the scurrying rats. Two tiny girls forced to stay silent. They clung to each other. Above them they could hear the clank of steel-edged boot heels against the rim of the manhole cover. They were waist deep in filthy water. Rats swam around them. They heard the echoes of boots and screaming voices.

The darkness began to swallow her. Rebecca's heart beat rapidly as she tried to force the memories away. She tried to concentrate on getting herself out from beneath the trailer, but the fragmented memories overpowered her.

◆ ◆ ◆

Ruda snapped at Vernon that she could handle Mamon, all they had to do was their job, and she would do hers. Vernon backed off and looked at Mike. They were radioed up to the main soundboard, ready to start the second half of the show. Ruda asked Mike, "Where is she?"

Mike's thoughts were on Mamon and for a moment he looked blank.

"My sister. She was with you, wasn't she?"

Mike shook his head. "She went back to the trailer."

"Go and get someone to find her, she might have gotten lost. Tell her to stand by Grimaldi."

Ruda was pacing up and down as the orchestra started the second-half intro. "Mike! I don't want him with that bloody rifle. If he comes in with it, get it away from him. Don't let him go in the ring with that goddamned thing."

Mike nodded. He didn't even know where Grimaldi was, and he would not risk looking for him now. He signaled to one of the helpers to go and look for Grimaldi and Rebecca.

Ruda edged closer to the entrance. She stamped her feet. She was wearing her second costume, a white jacket, black trousers, and black boots, with black leather gloves. The white shoulders of the jacket were padded since she would be working with Wanton. He was very unpredictable and could give a nasty scratch. She was in fact always more worried about Wanton, though he was only a quarter of the weight of Mamon. Panthers were more difficult to train by far.

The release cages were lined up. Three male lions paced up and down, as eager to get into the ring as Ruda. Behind the lions came the lioness, behind them the tigers. The last two cages held Wanton and Mamon.

"Ladies and gentlemen—Please take your seats for the second part of the show. Take your seats, please. . . ."

Ruda turned to the standby board. The red and green lights were not on. She looked back to the ring, and tilted her head from side to side. Her neck was tensing badly. "Come on, come on," she murmured, her hands clenched at her sides.

Mike received the radio signal that Grimaldi was in position on the far side of the ring. Alone.

Vernon came to Ruda. He pressed his earpiece. "Bit of a delay with a big party on the left bank of seats."

"Shit! Any money it'll be the bastards that haven't paid to get in anyway."

Ruda shifted her weight from one foot to the other and sighed impatiently, then gave a fleeting look around for Rebecca and asked again if Mike had located her. Mike smiled, gave the thumbs up. Ruda nodded. "Make sure she's okay, will you?" Again he nodded, and Ruda breathed in deeply.

Ruda closed her eyes trying to concentrate on the act, but she couldn't stop thinking of Rebecca. When she'd helped Rebecca change, she'd noticed her clothes, even her underwear, were of the finest quality. She had worn a big diamond ring. Ruda tapped her stick against her leg. Rebecca had four children, a rich husband. Her life must have been very different from her own. She wondered if Rebecca *had* tried to find her, tried as hard as she had. . . . Ruda opened her eyes, forcing herself to concentrate. "Are the pedestals set up?" Ruda asked no one in particular. Vernon replied that they were. Ruda looked again to the lights. "What the hell's going on! Come on, light up. Red, come on red . . . green, red, green!"

Rebecca curled her body into a tight ball beneath the trailer. The colors came in rapid succession. She had to remember each color, she had to give them to Ruda. If she didn't give them to her sister, Ruda would be given no food, they would hurt her. She heard Papa's voice, saw the cards being laid out, red, green, blue. . . .

The red light flickered. "Stand by, Miss Kellerman."

Ruda stood rigid. She didn't see the draped entrance to the main ring, but instead the dark green curtain. The hand that drew the curtain open was clean, with red painted nails; the woman had beautiful blond hair swept in a perfect coil. Her eyelids were painted, her cheeks rouged and powdered like an actress's. The dark red lips were often parted in a half smile. Ruda could see him behind the glass, just a fraction to the right of Red Lips, one of his gloved hands resting against the high dentist's chair. He had oiled, slicked-back ebony hair, chiseled features, and wore an immaculate uniform. They made a handsome couple. When he smiled his teeth were even and white.

Rebecca wore a frilly dress, white socks, and black patent leather shoes. Once, when the curtain was drawn back Ruda saw that she had been holding a doll, and she had held it up for Ruda to see. A doll with orange hair and a porcelain face, pink-cheeked, pink-lipped, with delicate china hands. Ruda had pretended that when they drew the curtain back she was looking into a mirror, seeing herself. It had calmed her and made the pain go away.

Papa made the unwrapping of a toffee into an art, holding each end of the wrapper delicately between finger and thumb, as if afraid to get so much as a trace of toffee on his white gloves. Ruda's mouth was always dry, tasting of metal. She longed for the sweet, watched the elaborate unwrapping of the treat with desperate eyes. When he smiled and touched Rebecca's chin to indicate she should open her mouth, when he looked through the glass to Ruda and smiled as he popped the sweet into Rebecca's mouth, Ruda could taste the sweet, soft caramel. The green film over her baby teeth became sweet and delicious.

Days or weeks later when Red Lips drew back the curtain, Ruda could see Rebecca had changed. The frilly white dress was dirty. Her mouth gaped open. She could see the tears, could see her fighting and scratching and sobbing, but she couldn't hear because the curtain draped a soundproofed cage. She was desperate to get to her sister, desperate to know what frightened her so much, what terrible things they were doing to her. She too would scream and scream, but Rebecca couldn't hear her either.

What Ruda could not have guessed was that Rebecca was screaming because they were showing her what they had done to Ruda.

Vernon shook Ruda's shoulder, once, twice. She turned, startled. "My God! Hurry, you've had the green light twice . . . are you okay?"

Ruda collected herself, then nodded. They were repeating her intro music. She waited a beat, then walked into the ring. Cheers and loud applause greeted her entrance. *"Ladies and gentlemen—Ruda Kellerman!"*

20

REBECCA REMAINED HUNCHED under the trailer. Her head started to pound and she prayed for it not to happen, not here. Someone was squeezing her brain. Then through the throbbing pain she heard his voice. He was saying over and over that she was a bad girl, she had not tried hard enough, now she would see what she had done. They tied her in the chair. She was paralyzed with fear, screaming for them not to draw back the curtain. But they did, slowly, inch by inch. And there was Ruda.

Ruda's body was covered in open sores. They had cut off her hair. Rebecca could see lacerations on her scalp, see the wires attached to her head. She could see them propping Ruda up, too weak to walk, too weak even to stand.

Ruda, unable even to hold up her head, smiled through the glass. She gave a tiny, pitiful wave as if to say: "I am still here. I'm still here, Rebecca."

The pain was excruciating. Rebecca sobbed, buried her face in the mud. All she could see was Ruda's tiny wretched face. Was this the memory she had blotted out of her mind? She wanted the pain to stop, wanted the memories to go away—but they kept on coming.

"Please help me, somebody help me."

Papa kissed her, unwrapping a sweet. "Good girl. Now if Ruda can repeat that exact formation of cards, when I open the curtains the next time, she will be beautiful again. . . ."

"Please help me, somebody help me."

But no one could hear her, everyone was at the big top. She couldn't stop them from coming. Rebecca could see herself in the frilly white dress, feel the urine trickle down her legs. She was afraid they would open the curtain, she was afraid to see what she

had done to Ruda, and she tried desperately to remember what Papa
wanted. What was it he wanted . . . what was it?

Red-red-green-blue-red-red . . . roses are red, violets are blue,
pass the colors from me to you. . . .

◆   ◆   ◆

Sixteen tigers, three lions, and the black panther. The ring seemed
to seethe with cats. Ruda attempted twice to give the command for
Roja to move to the red pedestal, but couldn't. Instead in rapid
succession she repeated four colors. It was as if her mind were
locked. Command after command became confused and the cats
started to veer away from the pedestals and meander around the
ring.

Vernon moved close to the bars and whispered urgently into
his walkie-talkie. "Hold back Mamon. Is he in the tunnel yet? Shit!
Don't open the trapdoor yet, keep him in the tunnel. Repeat. Don't
release Mamon, don't let him through. Get Grimaldi."

Mamon moved stealthily down the tunnel and reached the midway gate just as it clanged shut in his face. He backed up and ran
at it angrily. Vernon prodded him backward with one of the long
sticks. Mamon growled and swiped at the stick, but moved back
down the tunnel to the safety of his cage.

Ruda remained motionless. The pain across her eyes blinded
her. The spotlights began to blur. Her voice was hardly audible as
she repeated in a monotone: "Red-red-green-blue-red-red-green."

Gradually the cats became seriously disoriented. In their confusion, led by Roja, the tigers reverted to the first part of the act.
They formed a circle around Ruda's motionless body. The audience
was mesmerized. No one knew anything was wrong. The orchestra
played on; the conductor, who took cues from the act as it pro-
gressed, saw the cats forming a circle and cut the music to a low
drumbeat.

Grimaldi opened the side trapdoor leading into the arena. He
carried a long whip and the cats immediately turned toward him.

"Roja UP . . . RED UP . . . SONIA, green, SOPHIA,
blue . . . UP!"

Ruda stared ahead, still mumbling colors, unaware of Grimaldi.

He came quietly, authoritatively, to her side and took her left hand, smiling—but his eyes were focused on the cats.

"Jason . . . Green. Good boy . . . UP UP!"

The cats seemed relieved that order had been restored. They returned to the pyramid formation, Grimaldi all the while drawing Ruda gently back from the center of the ring. He felt her hand tighten in his, but he kept his attention on the cats.

"You okay?"

Ruda gasped. She had completely blanked out and the realization of what was happening made her panic momentarily. Then she was back in control. Grimaldi and Ruda worked together, and the audience applauded as the cats sat poised on their pedestals. Slowly Grimaldi handed more and more of the commands back to Ruda, standing a few feet behind her just in case he was needed.

Wanton began to leap from one high pedestal to the next, and the audience cheered. Grimaldi saw Ruda turn toward the trapdoor, expecting Mamon.

From behind her he said softly: "No Mamon, Ruda. Finish the act on Wanton!"

Ruda was confused again. The she looked to Luis and gave a brief nod. As Wanton made his final leap to the top rung, Vernon passed the hoop of fire between the bars. Ruda took the flame torch and showed the audience the hoop. The orchestra picked up again. Ruda fixed the hoop to its stand, then stood back as she touched the cloth to set it alight. It blazed, while spotlights pinpointed the cats. The trapdoor to the tunnel was slid back.

Back at the cages the helpers cajoled and pushed Mamon back into his small cage. They had to move fast to push the cage out of the way of the cats coming back down the tunnel from the ring. The men were sweating from exertion. Mamon was frantic, lunging at them, trying to swipe at them through the bars.

"Don't even try to put him back in his main cage. Let him calm down. Get him out of the way. Come on, move it!"

The tractor was hooked up to Mamon's cage and wheeled out of the clearing. In the ring, Roja jumped through the hoop and ran straight to the tunnel. One by one the cats followed, leaping gracefully through the flames as the lights flickered and spun, herding them back down the tunnel to their cages.

Wanton was the last to leap. From forty feet in the air the cat sprang and for a moment the spotlight caught him in midair. He sprang from the lowest pedestal and upward through the hoop in one fluid movement, his sleek black body bursting through the blazing hoop.

The ring went black and the lights came up with Wanton draped over Ruda's shoulders. He rested across her, impervious to the wild cheers. Ruda slowly bent on one knee, dropped her head, and Wanton sprang off and returned down the tunnel.

Ruda took Grimaldi's hand and they bowed together. As she leaned forward she felt the ground give way beneath her feet. Grimaldi swept her into his arms and, smiling, he carried Ruda from the ring, acknowledging the rapturous applause.

The safety barriers were dismantled quickly and as the helpers took out the gates, they saw Ruda assisted to a chair by Grimaldi. They brought her water and she drank thirstily, leaning against her husband. She covered her face with her hands. "Oh God. Oh God . . ."

She rocked backward and forward on the chair. Grimaldi angrily waved Vernon away as he approached. "No. Leave us alone. Leave us alone, she's okay."

He didn't want anyone to see her in this condition. He knew how gossip spread and he didn't want it said that Ruda Kellerman was sick. They had six more weeks, and a chance to go back to the States. Grimaldi lifted her to her feet. "We'll go and change for the final parade, okay, Ruda? All right guys, everything's under control. All the cats back in their cages?"

The tractor was pulling all the cages into their covered tent to be put back into their regular, heavier cages. Mamon growled and hissed, swiping and butting the bars. Grimaldi helped Ruda from the arena, then gestured for Mike.

"Be careful with the bastard, he looks mean," he whispered. "Don't move him if you're worried, we'll deal with him when he's calmed down."

Mike nodded and murmured that he'd get the feeds ready, then looked back as Mamon roared his fury. Mamon's cage rocked dangerously as it moved out of sight. Grimaldi didn't have to repeat his order: No one would go near him.

The cold air made Ruda gasp. Grimaldi put a protective arm around her shoulders. Her chest was heaving. "You were right, Luis. I should have listened to you. Seeing Rebecca again made my mind go, but I'll be okay . . . maybe I need to lie down for a while."

As Grimaldi walked her to the trailer he stepped on Vernon's yellow rain cape, left by the side of the steps. He chucked it aside and helped Ruda inside. She sat down on the bunk, her head between her knees. Grimaldi poured a brandy and held it out for her. Ruda took the glass, cupping it in both hands. "You did okay out there, you old bastard."

He grinned and got himself a drink. "Well you know me, I always did like a challenge."

He caught his reflection in the mirror and chuckled. "I felt good. It's been too long. Maybe if we did the first half we could work something up together. But I won't work with Mamon, he's your baby. Look back at tonight's show—you don't need him. Maybe we could try and get another panther. Wanton's a great crowd-pleaser, they loved him. Did you hear that applause?"

Ruda pulled off her leather gloves. Grimaldi was staring at himself in the mirror.

"I'll start working out, get this fat off me." Grimaldi slapped his belly.

Ruda sipped her brandy, turned her face away. "Where's Rebecca?"

He sat opposite her, the way they used to in the old days, his long legs propped up beside her.

"Vernon's taking care of her, you just relax."

Grimaldi cocked his head. "You want to tell me what happened? I mean, you blanked out, Ruda. In the middle of a big act! It made the old ticker jump."

He smiled, but Ruda was worried about Rebecca. "You sure she's with Vernon?"

"Yes, just relax. Eh! Did you see how fast I shot through that trapdoor? They were going into the first part of the act again, Ruda. Ruda?"

"You sure she's with Vernon? I feel her. God, it's hot, I'm so hot."

✦ ✦ ✦

Rebecca was cold. Her head ached and she didn't know how long she had been there. Had she fainted? This had happened before so many times—hours blanked out, even days. She was about to crawl out from beneath the trailer when she heard Ruda's voice and the darker, heavier tones of Grimaldi directly above her.

Ruda pushed open the trailer window. "She has no memory of what happened. Strange, she remembers nothing. But she is to blame for what happened tonight, I know it."

"Oh, come on. I don't think you realized the emotional impact on you at seeing her. I warned you."

"You don't understand."

"Why don't you help me understand, Ruda? I want to."

She laughed, some of her old anger returned. "Oh aren't you suddenly Mister Wonderful! You think I don't know why? Got your balls back tonight, did you? I may have fouled up, but you'll never replace me. It's my act, Luis, it's mine."

"How the hell do you think you'd have got out of there tonight without me? Maybe I did get my balls back, but it's good I still had them! I admit I've been scared, Ruda, but tonight I faced it, didn't even think about it. The fear went, I had no fear, Ruda!"

"*What the fuck do you want me to say?* You did great, you did good. Now leave me alone. I need to think about something. Just leave me alone."

"One of these days, Ruda, I might do just that."

He patted his pockets for a cigar. He struck a match, puffed the cigar alight, then turned back to her, prepared for a fight. He was surprised by the soft tone of her voice.

"I kept on seeing colors. I couldn't give the right commands."

Luis drew the ashtray closer and was about to interrupt when she continued.

"We were so young, they could only do the tests with color cards . . ."

"You told me!"

"No, you don't understand. We could transmit coded colors. Don't you realize how our minds are linked? That's what was wrong tonight, it was me, Rebecca . . ."

She suddenly stood up. "Oh my God, where is she?"

"Look, just forget her for a second, okay? Sit down." He poured another brandy, but Ruda couldn't sit still. She knew Rebecca needed her.

Grimaldi handed her the brandy and stood over her. She stared into the glass. "What was any of it for, Luis? We were just another one of his insane experiments. He tried with other twins, too. He was able to identify which of the twins could receive—it was always the stronger of the two, the weaker one was the transmitter."

She gave him her glass. "I don't want it." She breathed in heavily. Her body trembled as she rubbed the scars at her temples. "They clamped these wires to my head, which would burn. I didn't understand what they wanted. When I finally did, it was easy. I always knew what she was thinking. If she bruised a knee I felt it. I always knew, Luis, as if she were inside my head, you know?"

He said nothing, simply watched her.

"After—years after, I sometimes felt she was close. It was strange. You ever had the feeling? Like you know you are about to meet someone, see someone, and you do. Well, I would often have the feeling she was close by. It would just be a feeling, and I would concentrate on her, as I had at the camp, I'd picture her face. But then the feeling would go away and we'd travel on. But so many times I was sure she was there. I remember once I was in New York, I was so sure she was close, and then here—remember me saying I had this feeling? Well, she's staying at the Grand Hotel."

He saw her hand tighten into a fist. "I knew, always knew she was alive."

"Why didn't you tell me about her? If you knew she was alive, we could have searched for her together, put ads in the papers, there's even organizations that—"

She interrupted him. "I searched, I never gave up hope, that's why I started all my astrology letters, remember them? I was always thinking about her. You know, hoping maybe one letter would be from her. Everywhere I went I'd put ads in the papers, things that only she would understand, and I thought about her, concentrated on her."

He sipped his brandy and waited.

"I would think about what she owed me, what I had done for her. Then I would become angry, because I knew she had to feel me too, had to know I was alive, and I would curse her, hate her for not coming to me. I wanted her to come to me, I wanted to put my hands around her throat and choke her to death."

"What?"

"She left me . . . she left me, Luis, she left me." Her voice was hardly audible. He poured himself another brandy, uncertain if what he was hearing made any sense. Ruda was silent, staring from the window. When she continued her voice was stronger.

"I kept her alive. But when the Russians liberated the camp, I saw her from the hospital window walking hand in hand with a soldier. The soldier lifted her up onto his shoulders. I saw him give her chocolate. And she never turned back, never came back for me."

She bit her fingernails. "She never tried to find me. Luis, I could have forgiven everything, if she'd just tried to find me. With her rich husband, her children, she had money, she could have found me. I know that now."

"It was a long time ago, she was a child. Maybe you . . ."

"Maybe I nothing, Luis. Everything with you is always maybe this or maybe that. I know she knew what they were doing to me, she knew because she could *see*. They starved me and fed her like a pig. They put these things on my brain, and they gave her dolls. She knew what they were doing to me. I hate her."

He tried to put his arm around her, but she shrugged him away.

"Ruda, what difference does it make now? She's here, you're reunited. You can't really hate her, she's part of you. Now you can make up for all the—"

She screamed at him: "You don't understand!"

Luis put his hands up. "Jesus Christ—I am trying, Ruda! I wasn't there, Ruda. All I know is what I hear, what you tell me. You're angry because you blame what went on in the ring tonight on her."

Ruda kicked at the table. *"Shut up! You don't know! You weren't there!"*

"I know that, sweetheart, of course I don't know."

"No you don't know. How could you? Nobody can even imagine what happened there. Nobody did, it's forgotten. They kept on telling me to forget. It was over, I should forget. I couldn't speak. I couldn't tell them. The longing, Luis, I longed for her so much, it was like a well inside me, that filled up and drowned me. I drowned with longing for her to come to me, to . . . make what had happened real."

"Who told you? I can't follow what you're saying. Who are *they?"*

She sighed. "The doctors, the nurses, the stupid fat-faced nurses in the asylum. They put me in with crazy people because there was no place else. Just forget, just forget, they said. Take this, swallow this, this'll make you sleep. Nothing happened, it's all over. Forget? How could I forget when every white coat made me remember, every needle terrified me, until I learned to keep silent, until I learned never to speak to anyone. There was no point."

Her lips trembled. "Forget? Tell me how! There were all these babies, newborn babies. But not one was alive, they were blue from cold. Some were bloody, some still had their cords dangling out of their bellies. And they were stacked on a concrete block. Rebecca thought they were dolls. She asked if she could have one. But I knew they were dead babies. I knew, because from my window, where they kept me, I would see them being born, outside on the slabs in the snow. Don't touch them, Bekki, they're not to play with. Don't touch them. But she had one, Luis, she had one in her arms."

Her face twisted into a silent scream. She covered her mouth as the wounds that had been locked up inside her for so many years began to open. "You remember. You can't forget. Every time you see a baby you remember. Papa told me it was all right, he used to stand with me and watch the babies coming. He held my hand, and I didn't think anything was wrong because he whistled. He was always whistling. The next time I saw Rebecca she had a doll, he had given her a real doll so she could play at being a mama."

Luis felt sick. The image of the dead infants haunted him. Ruda's hands plucked at her jacket. "He liked me to call him Papa."

Her voice became no more than a whisper. She tried to say the name of the man whose face was buried inside her mind, the man who had tortured her and caused her indescribable anguish. For deep beneath her scarred body lay a consuming, confused, and heartbreaking guilt. Slowly it began to surface: She was once again the little girl sitting on his knee, hands clasped around the sweet he had given her. The little girl who said, "It's mine!" He had kissed her cheek and pinched her chin, teasing her. She could hear his voice.

"Open it, you can open it!"

"No."

"Don't you want it?"

"My sister, I want it for my sister."

He had laughed then and jerked his knee hard so that she fell to the floor. "What is your sister's name?"

"Rebecca."

"Ah yes. Is she well?"

Ruda nodded, and he crouched low, resting on the heels of his polished boots. He traced her cheek with his white-gloved hand. "Tell me, do you feel pain when your sister is hurt?"

"Yes."

He seemed delighted. He brought out a box of sugar almonds with a pink ribbon, and gave a small bow, clicking his heels. "These are for you and your sister."

She reached out, but he withdrew the box. "I want a kiss." She stood on tiptoes, slipped her arms around his neck, and kissed first his right, then his left cheek. He smelled of limes. With the box of almonds tucked under one arm, her hand in his, they walked into the hospital wing.

"Bring her sister, I want her sister! These are going to be my special twins. . . ."

Grimaldi said nothing, simply sat watching her. When Ruda lifted her face up to him, her eyes had a faraway expression. She stared unseeing as the face of the monster emerged. The face of the man who had embraced the child with love, and yet tortured her tiny body. The being who had twisted her mind for experiments that had benefited no one. Why had he never stood trial? Why had he never been punished? The Dark Angel's wing had overshadowed her life. She could never pretend that it had not happened. It had . . . and slowly her rage against him began to unfold.

◆ ◆ ◆

Rebecca pressed her body against the side of the trailer. She could feel the rage growing inside her. For the first time she could separate herself from the rage and watch it manifest itself. She could see her hands clench and unclench. Before when it started happening, she had always lost control and would have no memory of what had occurred. But now she knew the rage was not hers, but Ruda's. Now their minds entwined, like an electric circuit fusing, ready to ignite. . . .

Rebecca fought against its taking over. She tried to reach the trailer door, to call out that she was there, that she had not tried to find Ruda because she had been forced to forget. But now the memories came back in a blinding, red-hot blaze.

◆ ◆ ◆

Luis saw it happen and couldn't stop it. The rage exploded inside Ruda: Her body tensed, the veins in her neck throbbed, her hands beat the air, and her mouth opened in a terrible silent scream. But above all, it was the madness in her eyes that made him freeze.

The fury she had held in check for so long blinded her, and she attacked Luis—she believed him to be Papa, and she had to destroy him. . . .

◆ ◆ ◆

Mamon lay with his head resting on his paws. Mike, easing open the trapdoor, pushed the feed tray inside. Vernon was carrying bales of clean straw. He called to Mike. "Eh! I wouldn't try that, Mike.

Leave it for her. They'll be going to join the parade any minute.''

Mike half turned, his hand still on the bolt of the trapdoor. At that moment Mamon lunged forward, his full weight hitting the side of the cage: The trapdoor flew open, knocking Mike off his feet. Mamon was out.

Vernon dropped the bale of straw and threw himself out of the way, but Mamon wasn't interested in either of them; he was loping toward the open tent flap, churning up the sawdust. His roar was terrifying in its volume and intensity.

"Oh *shit!* Oh my God . . . Get the nets! Fucking get the nets!"

Word spread fast; within minutes the area was cordoned off and gatekeepers and parking attendants warned that no one was to be allowed beyond the barriers. The helpers ran toward the trailer park, their flashlights flickering as they questioned anyone who might have seen where Mamon had run.

As panic spread the security men were alerted.

The grand parade was just drawing to a close, the audience cheering, flowers and balloons tumbling from the top of the tent.

Thousands of chattering, laughing people streamed from the exits. They gathered alongside buses, or made their way on foot back down the road. Some walked to their parked cars. Children were carried in parents' arms, fast asleep, while others ran whooping and screaming, carrying circus maps, toys, and balloons.

The sky opened again with a heavy roll of thunder. Rain came lashing down.

Mike ran hysterically to the Grimaldi trailer, while Torsen and his group headed back to their car, via the trailer park.

Helen and the baron were pushed and buffeted along by the crowd as they headed for the trailer park barriers.

Inside the trailer Grimaldi tried desperately to control Ruda. It was difficult to move out of her reach. Twice he had caught her arms, but she had struggled free. She scratched, kicked, and tore at him. She had overturned the table, ripped the sofa cushions. She couldn't hear him, the rage consumed her. Her jaws snapped like an animal's.

Grimaldi gripped her by the hair. Ruda twisted and punched

her elbow into his stomach. As he released his hold and buckled over, she pulled his head up, forcing him back. Her hands clenched his throat.

Rebecca banged and pushed at the door, hit it with the flat of her hand and then ran to a window, screaming to be let in. Ruda turned. For an instant she froze, then she picked up a chair and hurled it at Rebecca's face. It shattered the window. Grimaldi got on his feet, but Ruda went for him again. Rebecca tried to crawl through the broken window. A jagged sliver of glass cut her cheek. Her hand flew up to her face.

Ruda backed away, her hand pressed to her cheek as if she were the one who had cut herself. Then she reached out and hauled Rebecca inside, crushing her in her arms. It was a killing embrace, a furious protection. They were locked together as one.

Grimaldi grabbed hold of Ruda from behind, wrenched her away and Rebecca screamed. She felt as if she were being plucked out of her own body.

Grimaldi slapped Ruda's face hard, jerking her head from side to side.

"You're killing her! . . . Ruda! Ruda!"

She seemed to calm down. He gripped her face in his hands. "Ruda, it's me, *it's me!*" Rebecca clawed Grimaldi, desperate for Ruda's embrace.

Running toward the trailer, Mike screamed out: *"Ruda! Ruda!"*

Mike was at the shattered window. "He's loose, Mamon's loose. Nobody can find him, we've got the nets standing by."

Ruda's push sent Grimaldi crashing into the wall, banging against Rebecca. They fell in a tangled heap as Ruda threw herself out of the window. Grimaldi staggered to his feet, but he was too late. He could see Ruda running after Mike.

Rebecca started to scream and he crouched down beside her. "Listen to me, stay here. Do you understand? Don't leave the trailer, stay inside."

"Ruda, I want Ruda. Ruda, *Ruda!*"

Grimaldi lifted her off her feet, sat her down. "Just do as I say. Don't leave the trailer. We'll sort everything out."

Rebecca shook with terror as Grimaldi threw the bench cushions aside, searching for his gun. In her confusion she believed he was going to shoot Ruda. She lurched toward him, clinging to his arm. "No! Please . . . please don't hurt her!"

Grimaldi pushed her roughly away. "The hurting's been done. Just stay inside, *stay inside!*"

"She needs me. I have to go to her."

He turned on her in a fury. *"You are too late. Stay in the goddamned trailer!"*

Grimaldi slammed the door shut and ran toward the torchlights and shouting voices. Every available man had formed a human wall cordoning off the trailer area from the crowds. A voice shouted that Mamon had been spotted. He was behind the animal tents. Hand-in-hand the men walked forward, step by step, drawing the chain of arms tighter as the helpers with the nets ran to the clearing by the tents.

Ruda was running ahead of Mike, repeating: "Don't hurt him . . . don't let them hurt him."

✦ ✦ ✦

Helen and the baron were confronted by two parking attendants. "Stay outside the barrier. No one is allowed inside."

The baron demanded to be let through.

"I'm sorry. No one can come into this area until we have clearance. Please wait!"

Helen explained that they were to meet Grimaldi at his trailer. She was informed that no one was allowed beyond the barrier.

"This is ridiculous, Louis, we've been told we can meet him."

"Look over there, can you see?" Louis pointed to the lights. Helen looked, she could see the chain of men, some still in costume, moving closer and closer.

"What's going on?"

Suddenly they saw Torsen and his group.

"It's the inspector. Maybe he can help us."

They hurried to Torsen, but he was unable to do anything. He too had been asked to leave. They all stared across to the lights.

Two men ran into view carrying a large net. They were shouting. "They got him cornered on the open ground over by the garbage cans. We're getting the nets around the back, too. Just in case!"

Torsen stepped forward. "I am a police officer. What's happened?"

The gatekeeper waved his hand to indicate they should all stay behind the barriers. "Everything's under control now, sir. Just keep moving, please leave this area."

Torsen looked to Rieckert, then to the baron. "What do you think's wrong?"

Again the baron approached the gatekeeper. "My wife is with the Grimaldis. Has something happened?"

"Please. Just stay out until I've got clearance. It'll soon be all over . . ."

"What will, for God's sake?" Louis was furious. He looked back to the lights, and caught sight of Rebecca. He shouted to her but she disappeared. "That was my wife. Please, please let me through!"

"*No, sir* . . . I'm sorry, this is for your own safety."

"*Would the public please leave the premises as quickly as possible. No one is allowed near the artists' trailer enclosure. For your own safety, please remain outside the barriers. . . .*"

The baron and Helen did not budge, but Torsen and his group began to make their way back to the patrol car. The loudspeakers repeated the warnings. The barrier was now heavily guarded. A group of boys in jeans and T-shirts soaked from the rain tried to climb over. The gatekeepers ran to chase them out. Overexcited and unaware of the danger, the boys dodged the gatekeepers, as if it were all a game.

Helen and the baron pushed back the barrier and made a run for it, just as Torsen returned to help the gatekeepers catch the boys. They made their way toward where they had spotted Rebecca. They could now see clearly the human chain edging closer.

◆ ◆ ◆

Torsen and Rieckert found themselves in an ugly scuffle with the boys. One of them knocked Torsen to the ground. He shot back on his feet and gave the boy a good belting. "I am a police officer.

Now, do as you're told or I'll arrest you for disturbing the peace. Go on—*out, get out!*"

The boys trudged away. The gatekeeper thanked Torsen. "A big cat is loose, sir. That's what the panic is about. Obviously I can't tell the kids, they'll think they're tough and try and get back in. But it's under control now, the animal is over on the open ground by the trash cans, that's what the nets were for."

Torsen wiped his bloody nose. "You sure they don't need a couple of extra hands?"

"Thank you, sir, but for your own safety just stay back there. It's all under control now."

One of the clowns ran past shouting that more men were needed over on the far side. Torsen called Rieckert. "Come on, let's go."

Rieckert and his girlfriend clung to the barrier. "Maybe I should stay with the girls. No need for both of us to go!"

"Fine. You do that. Get them into the car, I'll see if I can help."

✦ ✦ ✦

Mamon was weaving in and out underneath the big trailers, his body low to the ground. The burning torches stuck at regular intervals provided some light. As long as they could see him, there was no reason to panic. They preferred to wait until all the crowds had gone before closing in on him. Meanwhile the nets were being linked up, cornering Mamon.

Ruda put on a pair of heavy gloves and picked up a long pole. Mike followed with a bucket of meat as she pushed her way through.

"Thank you. Please stay back, please back! And keep quiet. Thank you."

"He's under the big trailer with the red shutters, been there a good five minutes!" a trapeze artist informed. Ruda moved on. She entered the circle, two men parted hands to let her in.

Ruda looked around at the fearful faces. "Okay, everybody. I want to entice him back out into the open. Those with loose nets move in closer, everybody else stay back until I give word. He's probably panicky, but I can control him. Stay back . . . and keep silent."

They did not need to be told twice: No one wanted to get close. The boys began lining up the barriers used in the act, to make an open-air caged arena. A tractor towed Mamon's main cage in close. When everything was quiet, Ruda moved further into the clearing.

The back wall of the tent cut off one route and now the barriers hemmed Mamon in on all sides. He slid between the trailer wheels, his fur flattened, his paws muddy. Then he darted under another trailer, but the lights were on him, and the trailer was low. He struggled, began to toss his head, and eased himself out backward.

"Ruda, he's between the two trailers," Mike called out, then turned as Grimaldi came up behind him. Mike saw the gun, looked at Ruda, but said nothing. "They've got him trapped."

The cage was drawn closer, the trapdoor was open. Mamon could see it directly ahead of him. He was fifty to sixty feet away from the clearing, standing in an alley, trailers on either side. Behind him were the nets. The only clear route was ahead. He began moving slowly toward the arena. He paused, sniffing the air. He picked up Ruda's scent.

"Good boy! Come on, come on, Ma'angel . . . good boy. Come to Mama, come on. . . ."

Mamon's eyes glittered like amber lights, his teeth gleamed as he approached her. Panic made his chest heave, saliva dribbled from his open jaw. Ruda bent down slightly, whispering encouragement. He kept on coming.

"Come on, good boy . . . come to Mama! He's coming, please keep silent. Don't unnerve him."

Rebecca slipped under the linked arms of two men. For a brief moment they were confused, thinking she was Ruda. By the time they realized their mistake, it was too late to stop her—she was already running between the trailers.

Rebecca saw the flares and the nets, but they meant nothing to her. She wanted to get to Ruda.

By now, Helen and Louis had been told what was going on and remained waiting outside the ring of men. They couldn't see Mamon, but they could feel the electrifying tension in the crowd.

Torsen joined them. Helen explained that they were still trying to capture the lion. Louis tried to make out Rebecca in the flickering lights, but he couldn't see her, and looked toward Ruda. He was struck by the eerie likeness, her long shadow directly behind her, making her look like a giant.

Mamon continued his slow journey down the aisle between the trailers, while Rebecca ran the last few yards between the ones adjacent to him, and suddenly she burst into the clearing.

"Ruda . . . *Ruda!*"

There she was between Ruda and Mamon, unaware that the big cat was no more than twenty feet behind her. Mamon froze. Head up, he sniffed the air, then lowered his head and growled, darting back. Crazed, he ran toward the nets, then made an about-face, snarled with anger, and charged back into the clearing.

The men were ready with the nets. If Mamon came within range they would release the poles to drop the mesh over him. But he was wily, and kept his distance, moving further into the clearing. Now there was nothing between him and Rebecca.

Rebecca turned, saw Mamon, and looked back to Ruda in terror. Ruda's voice was soft, persuasive, cajoling, and calm. "Don't move. Stay perfectly still. Don't move, keep your hands at your sides."

Ruda inched forward, moving a fraction to her right, keeping Mamon directly in her line of vision. Mamon tilted his head to the right, to the left. He stepped forward, stopped. Crouched. He was ready to spring.

"Move toward me, one step at a time."

Grimaldi knew the cat was enraged enough to attack. He cursed the stupid bitch, his heart pounding, but he knew that if he were to make a move now it could be fatal for both women—like everyone else he remained motionless, his hand clenching the rifle.

Rebecca took one step forward, her back still to Mamon. He was watching her. She moved forward again, and he followed, low on his haunches.

Grimaldi raised the rifle, trying to release the safety catch silently, but the click made Mamon lift his head.

Ruda heard the slight sound, but did not take her eyes off Mamon. Her voice remained calm.

"Don't touch me, just move very slowly behind me. You can do it, nobody will hurt you, Bekka. Come on, I'm here. Ruda's here."

Rebecca edged behind Ruda, into her shadow. "Good, Bekka, good. Now, when I step forward, you step back. But slowly, very slowly. Wait!"

Mamon hurtled from the aisle, his outline clear to everyone. He seemed to begin a lunge and then stop, his chest heaving as he glared around. The sisters remained together.

"Back! Mamon, back . . . MA'ANGELLLL!"

The baron tried to break through the chain of men, but he was pushed back, forced to watch with everyone else as Ruda moved closer to Mamon, placing herself in danger as, step for step, Rebecca moved away to safety.

Louis pushed forward and grabbed hold of Rebecca. If she knew it was he, she gave no indication. She was rigid, her eyes riveted on Ruda.

"Is she safe?" Ruda kept her voice calm, never taking her eyes off Mamon. "Is she safe?" she repeated.

Grimaldi took a step into the arena. "I've got her. Now back up to me, I'm about four feet behind you, just start backing toward me, sweetheart, I'm here . . . Ruda?"

Slowly Ruda lifted her right arm, and let the whip drop. Then she lifted her left arm. Both her arms were now open wide, and there was a moment of total silence. No one moved, no one spoke. Luis, expecting Ruda to step back, shifted a fraction to his right, aiming the rifle. It happened in a split second.

Ruda did not move back, she stepped forward. Mamon and Ruda seemed to move simultaneously toward each other; then he reared up onto his hind legs, and sat back on his haunches. His massive paws enveloped her head and shoulders in a terrifying embrace.

Perhaps he was simply obeying a command, a command he was used to being given in the ring: KISS. Nobody heard the command, but she had said something. Those nearest her clearly heard her say "Ma'angel." Then the shots rang out.

The first bullet hit him in his right shoulder. His jaws sprang open as the second bullet hit him just above his right ear. The third bullet entered his right side. It struck his heart, but he was already dead. The big animal fell forward still holding her, his weight crushed her and snapped her neck. Ruda made no sound, no cry.

Four men had to roll him off her body. Her hands were clenched tightly to his fur, his blood covered her shirt. At first they thought one of the bullets had hit Ruda. Only when Grimaldi took her in his arms did they realize her neck had been broken. The big man held his wife, rocking her gently, sobbing. The helpers moved in closer, as if protecting him, shielding him. They formed a circle around him, and bowed their heads.

Mamon's carcass was dragged away in the nets. In death he seemed pitiful. All power gone. His limp body was sodden from the rain, his claws and feet caked in mud. The three bullet wounds were hidden beneath his thick fur, but the dark blood matted his coat.

Helen and Louis took Rebecca to the first aid room. She was dazed, robotlike. By the time the doctor came to see her, she was catatonic. She did not know where she was, she did not recognize Louis or Helen. When Dr. Franks arrived an hour later, they arranged for her to be taken to his clinic.

Torsen sat in the patrol car, his face so pale it seemed almost blue. "She's dead. The lion attacked her, she's dead . . ."

Rieckert swore. "Shit! What a thing to miss. Wish I'd been there."

Torsen shook his head. "No. No, I don't think so. It was one of the saddest, most horrifying things I have ever seen. I don't think I can drive home. Will you drive us back?"

Torsen moved to the backseat, and Freda held his hand. She knew he was crying, but that made her feel even closer to him.

"She seemed to give herself to the animal. She had no fear. From where I was standing I could see her face . . . and she smiled, I am sure of it. . . . She smiled, as if she knew she was going to die."

Freda stroked his arm. "I see it every day, those who are afraid to let go, and those who welcome the end. It's strange, when it's over all the pain in their faces is gone."

He was quiet for a moment. "I know she killed once, maybe twice. No one will ever know exactly what happened and I doubt if I would ever have been able to prove it!"

✦ ✦ ✦

Luis Grimaldi, wearing a big overcoat, stood by the stonecutter, whose face and overalls were covered with a fine film of dust. The man's large, gnarled hands held the sheet of paper tightly, because of the wind. The rain that had not stopped for days made the ink drawing run.

"Can you do it?"

"Yes. It'll take a while, and I'll need a very large block. Black marble is the most expensive. I have to have it shipped in from Italy."

"I'll pay whatever it costs. I've brought you photographs. If there's anything else you need, you know where to contact me!"

The stonecutter watched the big broad-shouldered man walk out of his yard. He carefully folded the damp sheet of paper. He had received some strange requests for headstones in the past, but never one like this.

When the marble arrived he set to work. In truth, he relished the challenge. As the massive head began to take shape, it seemed to take on a life of its own. He buffed and polished, then stood back to gaze in admiration. He felt an enormous sense of achievement. This work surpassed any of the other angels he'd carved to guard over the dead.

✦ ✦ ✦

At first he had considered taking over the act, but every animal reminded him of Ruda, and he sold all the cats to the Russian trainer. He then sold the trailer to the circus management. Now there was nothing left to keep him in Berlin. He made no attempt to find Rebecca, but wrote her a brief note care of the Grand Hotel giving details of Ruda's burial. He also sent her the small black tin box, feeling that perhaps the contents would mean something to Rebecca. But he did not want to see her. He blamed her for Ruda's death.

Luis had no thought of what he would do next, he was at a loss. Without Ruda he didn't seem able to function in the world to which he had introduced her.

He knew just one thing. He had to wait until the headstone was ready.

The sky was clear and cloudless the day he went to say his last good-bye. Grimaldi could see it immediately, towering above the other tombstones, and his breath caught in his throat. He had done something right. Immediately after Ruda's death, when he had been inconsolable, blaming himself, the tears he had shed had broken from him in gasping sobs. Now he wept gently, tears welling up and spilling down his cheeks.

He towered above her, his wonderful head resting on his paws, his black mane, his wide black eyes. His jaw was open in warning not to touch or trespass upon the grave. Carved in gold was his name. MAMON.

RUDA GRIMALDI.
Died February 1992.
A Wild Animal Trainer.
May she rest in fearless peace.

21

AFTER THE TRAGEDY Rebecca was in a catatonic state for quite some time. She had no memory of Ruda's death. She was kept heavily sedated until Dr. Franks felt she was mentally and physically strong enough to continue the sessions under hypnosis.

Helen Masters had returned to France. The baron wrote her about Rebecca's treatment, as if the letters were in some way therapeutic for him. The sessions took place every other day, to give Rebecca time to absorb and accept each new insight. Under deep hypnosis she began to recall the incidents that her adopted mother had sought to cover up. Her breakdowns were linked directly to Ruda's proximity. Whenever Ruda had tried to contact her, be it out of hatred or love, Rebecca's rages began. Louis Maréchal checked the date of each incident against circus schedules. In each case, unbeknownst to Rebecca, Ruda had been physically near.

Rebecca's more recent mental breakdowns had coincided with the arrival of Mamon in Ruda's life. Mamon's strong will and expressiveness had forced Ruda to use all her determination to train him. In teaching him to learn the colors of the pedestals, she had tapped into Rebecca's subconscious. When Ruda was in close proximity, these color drills created havoc in Rebecca's head.

Gradually the jigsaw puzzle became clear: Rebecca was taken back to Birkenau. She described horrifying events, as she saw them when she was a child. At times she was quite cheerful. She spoke about the babies, how she had wanted one as a doll. She chattered on, about the funny thin people, the wires, the other children. At one session she actually stunned Dr. Franks by laughing.

"What is so funny?"

She recalled a young guard who used to play with the children.

He would rip up little bits of paper, put them on the end of his nose and blow them away like snowflakes. "We called him the Snowman!"

"Was this man kind to you?"

She fell silent, and Franks repeated the question. She whispered that he was not very nice, not all the time. Franks tried to find out why, but she was unsure . . . she said he would take children across the wire fences to the gray hot place where they baked bread. Whoever he took away never returned.

She talked at length about what her Papa had given her: the white frilly dress, the white socks, and patent leather shoes.

She giggled and she said she loved him. "I got a dolly with yellow hair. He said it was as yellow as the dirty Jews' stars."

The sessions disturbed Louis. He felt a hopelessness, a fear that Rebecca would never be returned to him. Often he had to walk out of the viewing room, but always he came back.

✦ ✦ ✦

Six months after Ruda's death, Franks decided Rebecca was strong enough to delve more deeply into the past, sometimes without hypnosis. She talked of the woman whom Ruda had nicknamed "Red Lips." Franks surmised that the woman was the notorious Irma Griese, known for her beauty—and remembered for her cruelty to the inmates at Auschwitz and Birkenau. Rebecca recalled that Griese always smelled of flowers.

"Ruda said she wanted to be like her when she grew up. Red Lips used to have a whip tucked into her boots, like a lion tamer, and when she was near, because of her perfume, we didn't smell the bread. They made bread, day and night. Papa told us that was why the flames were red, the ovens had to be hot for the sweet bread."

At the next session, Franks noticed a physical change in his patient. The child in Rebecca was beginning to recede, she was subdued. When he asked if she was feeling unwell her voice took on a strange dullness.

"My frock is dirty."

Franks waited but she said nothing more. He hypnotized her again and she sat throughout the session with her head deeply bowed. She no longer smiled.

"Where are you, Rebecca?"

She slowly lifted her head. Her eyes were dead, her mouth open. "Ruda's gone with the Snowman!"

"Where are you?"

She spoke in an almost drugged monotone as she described sitting in the dentist's chair in the glass booth with the dark green curtain. Rebecca seemed old now and wizened, yet she could have been no more than four.

She spoke of seeing what they had done to Ruda, how they had forced her to look at her sister through the glass window.

"Papa took out Ruda's insides. He said it was because I was naughty. He cut off Ruda's hair, and put something in her belly, he said it was a baby like me. Papa said I was a bad girl because I couldn't remember . . . I tried, I tried hard to remember! Tried to feed her . . ."

◆   ◆   ◆

That night, after that session, Rebecca refused to take her sleeping pill. She rang the bell by her bedside with insistence. She didn't want Maja, she didn't want Louis, she wanted to see Franks. By the time he came over from his house she was hysterical. As he walked in, she attacked him.

"Why are you doing this to me? Why? Why are you making me remember these things. *Why? You are killing me!*"

"No, no I'm not. I am helping you. These things happened to you. You have to face them, go through them."

"Why?"

"So that you may heal, leave with your husband, and be with your children. These events are real. You have been denied the remembrance, and all I am doing now is allowing you to recall the past. If you wish, I can stop. It is up to you."

She became quiet and sat on the edge of the bed. "I want to tell you something . . . about Ruda."

Franks rested his chin on his hands, waiting. Rebecca tugged at her blanket as she explained how she had seen Ruda through the glass. Then she looked up. "It was a mirror. I didn't see Ruda, it was a mirror."

"I don't understand, what mirror?"

"He cheated me, *he lied to me.*" She twisted the blanket around and around in her hands in a wringing motion. Franks quietly asked who had lied to her and she let it out.

"Papa lied! Don't you understand? It could not have been Ruda I saw."

Rebecca became visibly more and more distraught, and Franks suggested that she rest. She dismissed the idea with her hands. "No, no, listen to me. I understand now. I mean it wasn't logical, how could her hair have grown overnight? He didn't show me Ruda. It was me, in a mirror."

She went to the window and gripped the white painted bars. "I saw myself in the mirror. Not Ruda, but me. They gave me cakes, sweets, milk—and I ate everything, I saved nothing for her."

Franks put his arms around her shoulders. "You were a baby then. You cannot blame yourself, there is no guilt."

"There is. She hates me. I ate and ate, and she went hungry."

"Nobody hates you, and you should rest. Try to get some sleep. Rebecca?"

She sighed and flopped down onto the bed. "Rest? You open my mind and expect me to sleep at night?"

She closed her eyes. "The memories plague me, even when I'm alone. It's as if I cannot stop the past . . ."

"No matter how painful, that's good. What are you remembering?"

"A soldier, the one who took me away from the camp. He took my hand and asked if I wanted some chocolate. I demanded a piece for Ruda also because she was inside me. She needed a piece of chocolate, but . . . please, please don't leave me alone."

Franks assured her he would stay. He watched as she stared at her reflection in a small mirror, repeating over and over, "It was a mirror. . . ."

Throughout the session, which lasted the entire night, Franks was able to piece together what it was she was desperately trying to release.

Gradually, as the telepathy succeeded beyond his first expectations, Mengele did not want Rebecca to see that her twin had not been rewarded or fed as he had promised, so he tricked her by placing a mirror across the booth's window. Thus, Rebecca did not see Ruda in the white dress, but she saw herself. Only now did Rebecca recognize the deception. She became consumed by guilt because she had not understood the horror of it.

Franks watched Rebecca wrestle with her own conscience.

"How could I know? And Papa was very pleased with me, he kissed and cuddled me and one of the *Schutzhaftlings* took me over to the warehouse to choose a new dress. I wanted to show off my new dress. We passed a group of inmates designated to clean latrines and they spat at me! One woman hurled mud at me . . . I remember the way they shouted after me. The children hit and kicked me and I cried and cried. I shouted back that when Ruda came back she would make them cry, too. They told me she'd gone with the Snowman; that she would never come back for me."

Two days after Rebecca had been given the new dress, the camp was liberated. In the mayhem that followed Rebecca and a number of other children from her ward ran into the main hospital wing. She ran from bed to bed looking for Ruda.

Ruda was skin and bone. Lice crawled like black ants over her shaven head. Her skin was paper thin, a deathly bluish white, and tubes full of congealed blood protruded from her stomach. A filthy bandage partially covered a jagged wound in her distended belly. Rebecca saw the pitiful bundle of rags, and perhaps had even known it was her sister, but she was so horrified that she ran away screaming, right into the arms of the young soldier. He held her tightly, he too was crying. He carried her from the ward, not wanting her to see the corpses, the dying.

They went past the glass partition, and, unwittingly, past the mirror . . . and Rebecca saw Ruda again—this time she was with her, in the soldier's arms. It was at this moment that Rebecca began to believe totally and utterly that she and Ruda were one.

Aware that the adult Rebecca had emerged at last, Franks talked with her about the events that took place at the time of the liberation. When Mengele realized that the Russians were advancing he hastened to destroy all the evidence of his experiments. With manic energy he cleared the camp of the dying; only days before the liberation, thousands lost their lives in the gas chambers. Mengele himself escaped after burning all the documents along with the corpses.

Never brought to justice, never paying for his crimes against humanity, the "Dark Angel" haunted the survivors. The young, whose minds he had twisted, whose bodies he had tormented and crippled, were taken to hospitals and institutions. Many siblings were separated in a desperate bid to give them the medical care they needed so badly. Ruda and Rebecca were just two of these tragic children.

Rebecca was given many carefully chosen books from Franks's personal library to help her understand fully those nightmare years. She had become calm, and often discussed her reading with the doctor. Then late one afternoon, Maja called to Franks at home saying that he was needed urgently at the clinic. Rebecca had become destructive, abusive, and violent. In a rage she had systematically wrecked her room, though she hadn't hurt herself or any of the nurses. As Franks hurried along the corridor, he heard her hoarse screams, and a terrible banging and thudding of furniture being hurled against the walls. He looked through the peephole and asked Maja to bring him a chair. He sat outside the room until the banging and the shouting stopped. Then he entered the room.

Rebecca stood by the window, exhausted. She was utterly drained, her eyes red from weeping. He knew instantly that this was no longer Ruda's rage. At last this was Rebecca's own blazing fury at what had been done to her. Finally, she had embraced her anger, and she was cleansed.

✦　✦　✦

After almost a year of treatment, Franks thought that Rebecca was ready to be told the truth about Ruda. Louis was not allowed to be present, but he was nearby, as he had been throughout the entire year.

Sasha had stayed with him at the hotel during her school holidays; no nanny, just father and daughter. In the time together, he had tried to explain her mother's illness in terms she could understand. When Sasha asked if her mother was well now, Louis had hesitated, knowing Rebecca was at a critical point. Franks had cautioned him that learning of Ruda's death might cause a major setback. Considering her delicate state, the impact of hearing that Ruda had been alive and had now died could send her over the edge—an edge on which she had balanced precariously for years. Louis told Sasha that they would know very soon.

✦ ✦ ✦

Franks began in a soft gentle voice, asking her if she did recall going to the circus. Rebecca surprised him, looking at him with a tranquil, gentle expression.

"I was wondering when you would speak to me about it, but I know. And I know that her last words were about my safety. . . . It all came back to me days ago, but I didn't want to tell you, I wanted to face it by myself. I needed time alone. She was, you see, always the stronger . . ."

"Do you blame yourself in any way?"

"Yes, of course. I endangered her, I ran into the clearing, I was stupid, but . . . I think she could have gotten him back in his cage. She was very calm."

She gave Franks a strange, direct stare. "She was also very disturbed, confused. I wish, I wish we had found you together, but . . ."

Franks leaned forward, "But?"

"But we didn't. . . . Throughout my life I have been searching for a mother. I have expected too much, loved too much—and caused a lot of pain to those I have loved. Now at last I have found her. She lies within me. Having mothered my sons, my daughters—

albeit distressed them, terribly—I think I have found my first mothering experience—with you."

She smiled at him. "You have given me the unconditional, loving acceptance I have always sought, the support I have always needed, the understanding I have craved. You have given me back my childhood, but most important, through my relationship with you, I have learned to accept and love myself, to give myself the kind of caring that will heal me from the inside. I am going to get stronger. I know that, because I want to live—for my children, for my husband—most of all, I want to do something with my life. My experience must be used, you must use me, reach out for others like me, Dr. Franks, because I am strong now and I want to do this for me and for Ruda, who was the only mother I ever really knew. . . ."

Franks couldn't help himself, he leaped from his chair and wrapped his arms around Rebecca. "You're wonderful! You know what you are? A fighter . . . God bless you!"

✦ ✦ ✦

Dr. Franks, with his hands stuffed into his pockets, waited for the baron to arrive at the clinic. He had remained in Berlin, and brought his younger daughter, Sasha, to stay at the hotel. Sasha waited with her father for news of Rebecca, of her mother's recovery.

Louis knew by the expression on Franks's face that they had at last broken through.

Dr. Franks held Sasha's hand, smiling warmly. "You stay with me a few moments, Sasha." And to Louis: "Go and see Rebecca."

She was leaning against the chair. Louis was unable to contain himself; he sobbed as he lifted his arms to her. He clasped her to him, as if afraid to let go of her. They kissed and clung to each other.

"I'm coming home, Louis. I want to come home."

✦ ✦ ✦

Dr. Franks tapped on the door and asked if another visitor could be made welcome. He ushered in Sasha. The child hung back a moment, then ran into her mother's open arms, and Rebecca swung her around and around, then bent down on her knees and cupped the girl's face in her hands.

"Sasha! My beautiful Sasha . . . I am coming home!"

✦ ✦ ✦

The Mercedes made slow progress through the snowbound streets. Rebecca sat between Louis and Sasha. On her knees lay Ruda's black box. She opened it, and Sasha looked inquisitively inside.

"Do you know what this is?" Rebecca held up a small hard object. "It's a potato!"

"But it looks like a stone, Mama!"

"When we were in the camp they were prizes worth keeping, and my sister Ruda kept this potato, oh, for so long, and then when we came to eat it . . . it was hard, like a small rock. It became her talisman, this funny little hard potato!"

The car drew to a halt outside the clinic, and Dr. Franks hurried from the doorway in a woolly hat and a big scarf and squeezed himself into the backseat. Franks let Sasha sit on his knee as the chauffeur drove away.

"This is for your mama." Franks gave Sasha a small square leather box to hand over to Rebecca.

Sasha watched as Rebecca lifted the lid. It was a gold Star of David. She kissed it, then rested her head against Franks's shoulder.

"Thank you," she whispered, then gave a soft laugh. "You know, I think you have telepathic powers! This morning, before these two were even awake, I went to a synagogue to pray for Ruda. I have never been in one before. It felt . . ."

Dr. Franks had to look away, out of the window to the snow-laden streets. He was moved.

"Go again, go for the faith denied you, denied Ruda!"

They fell silent, a comfortable warmth between them. Only when they were within half a mile of the cemetery did Rebecca stiffen. She raised her head, sensing a presence. She knew Ruda was close by.

The car stopped and Franks opened his door. Sasha bounded out, but he caught her hand. "Just wait a moment, Sasha!"

The baron was about to offer his arm to Rebecca, but Franks gave him a small signal, an indication to let her walk alone.

Rebecca walked ahead of them, at first unhurried, then she quickened her pace. Dr. Franks, Sasha, and Louis looked on as Rebecca suddenly began to run. Threading her way among the dark tombstones, across the narrow, snow-filled lanes, she knew intuitively where to find her.

Grimaldi had chosen not just the headstone, but the plot where Ruda lay. It was separated from the other graves by a semicircle of high trees. The sun broke through the gray sky, streaking brilliant shafts of light that glanced off the trees above her tomb, making a delicate white crystal cradle over the wondrous black marble head of Mamon. He roared in icy silence, protecting his beloved beneath him.

Rebecca stood gazing at Mamon, then knelt down and placed the treasured stone between his paws. She let her hand rest a moment, and closed her eyes. She didn't weep.

"Good-bye, Ruda, I'll come back," she whispered.

✦ ✦ ✦

Dr. Franks followed, watching Rebecca, now hand in hand with her husband and daughter.

The snow was melting in the wintry sun, it trickled in tears from Mamon's sightless eyes. Franks knew there were tears still to be shed, lost souls to be reunited. Memories that must not be forgotten, or hidden, but kept alive so that the living will never forget. Must never forget.